Amy Andrews is a multi-award-winning *USA TODAY* bestselling Australian author who has written over fifty contemporary romances in both the traditional and digital markets. She loves good books, fab food, great wine and frequent travel—preferably all four together. To keep up with her latest releases, news, competitions and giveaways sign up for her newsletter—amyandrews.com.au.

Award-winning author **Louisa George** has been an avid reader her whole life. In between chapters she's managed to train as a nurse, marry her doctor hero and have two sons. Now she writes chapters of her own in the medical romance, contemporary romance and women's fiction genres. Louisa's books have variously been nominated for the coveted RITA® Award and the New Zealand Koru Award, and have been translated into twelve languages. She lives in Auckland, New Zealand.

HARPER AND THE SINGLE DAD

AMY ANDREWS

IVY'S FLING WITH THE SURGEON

LOUISA GEORGE

MILLS & BOON

First published in Great Britain 2023
by Mills & Boon, an imprint of HarperCollins*Publishers* Ltd,
1 London Bridge Street, London, SE1 9GF

www.harpercollins.co.uk

HarperCollins*Publishers* Macken House, 39/40 Mayor Street Upper, Dublin 1, D01 C9W8, Ireland

Harper and the Single Dad © 2023 Harlequin Enterprises ULC

Special thanks and acknowledgement are given to Amy Andrews for her contribution to the A Sydney Central Reunion miniseries.

Ivy's Fling with the Surgeon © 2023 Harlequin Enterprises ULC

Special thanks and acknowledgement are given to Louisa George for her contribution to the A Sydney Central Reunion miniseries.

ISBN: 978-0-263-30608-8

06/23

HARPER AND THE SINGLE DAD

AMY ANDREWS

MILLS & BOON

I dedicate this book to my three co-conspirators in this quartet—Emily, JC and Louisa.

Thanks for the laughs, ladies. xxx

CHAPTER ONE

HARPER JONES COULDN'T decide if it was a good thing or a bad thing to be thrown straight into a cardiac arrest on her first day as head of the emergency department at Sydney Central hospital. It would have been nice to get through all the introductions, at least. Meet the nurses and doctors, figure out who was who and who knew what and give a little spiel on her background and expectations.

But that wasn't how it worked in the ER.

When a walk-in collapsed at the front desk that was what you focused on instead of shaking hands and exchanging small talk. That was how it worked. And, an hour later, as the CCU team whisked the gravely ill patient away, Harper had come to know this group of people better than she could have at any polite meet and greet session.

She knew they were efficient and dedicated. She knew they were well-oiled and worked perfectly as a team. She knew their strengths and weaknesses.

Most importantly, she knew she'd fit in here. She'd made the right decision to leave London and finally come home.

'Dr Jones?'

Harper glanced up from the computer screen where she was completing paperwork for the cardiac arrest patient. 'Harper, please,' she corrected the nurse with a smile.

'Ambulance Control has just notified us of an incoming.'

She glanced down at the paper in her hand. 'Emma Wilson, twenty six years old. Twenty-four weeks pregnant with twins. Burns from a house fire. Paramedics estimate twenty per cent with a mix of full and partial thickness.'

Something deep and dark twisted inside Harper at the word *fire* and her thoughts automatically went to the one man she'd been trying not to think about since arriving back in the country five days ago.

Yarran.

He still lived in Sydney. He was still a fireman. She hadn't deliberately kept tabs on him, but it was difficult not to know stuff in the age of social media and when Yarran was so entwined with her old friendship group. His twin sister, Alinta— older than him by five minutes—had been one of her closest friends, after all.

Before Harper had broken his heart twelve years ago, anyway…

But she couldn't think about that now. She couldn't think about how badly she'd screwed everything up and the bridges she had to repair. Because there was a pregnant woman suffering from significant burns who must be scared out of her wits. Harper's brain raced as she thought about how much more complicated the fluid resuscitation would be with two babies on board.

'She was trapped under some fallen debris and sustained legs burns,' the nurse—Taylor, according to her name tag— continued, oblivious to Harper's internal disquiet. 'She also has singeing around her nostrils and a soft stridor although she's sat'ting at one hundred per cent on a rebreather mask. ETA five minutes.'

Harper nodded, chewing on her bottom lip. *Stridor.* There were probably some inhalation burns with resultant airway swelling. Which meant they might need to tube her. Exactly *not* what was best for a pregnant woman.

'She's Aaron Wilson's wife,' Taylor added, and it was obvious from the nurse's tone the name should mean something. But it didn't.

'And he's someone I should know?'

'He's a TV celebrity. Front man for *If You Build It*—one of the most popular reality shows on television for people who fancy themselves as handy.'

'Ah, okay. Thanks.'

The premise sounded vaguely familiar given how much Australian TV content took up UK airwaves, but Harper had been a little too busy building her career to keep up with television. One thing she did know was that Aaron Wilson's celebrity could potentially complicate things for the hospital, as intense media interest often did.

'Is he accompanying her, did they say?'

There was no doubt a security protocol for this type of thing. At least Harper hoped so because the last thing she wanted was paparazzi in her ER, getting in the way.

'Apparently he's out of town but making his way back now.'

'Okay.' Hopefully Emma would be out of the ER before Aaron Wilson made an appearance and it would be the intensive care unit's problem. 'Where are we putting her?'

'Resus cube five.'

'Cool.' Harper nodded. 'I'll be there in one.'

Harper was putting on a plastic gown over her forest-green scrubs—the colour denoting medical staff—when she heard the first wails of the ambulance siren. Both the burns and obstetric team had been notified and were heading to the ER and she was mentally preparing herself to come face to face with

Alinta. Her ex-friend was, after all, head of the obs and gynae department so it was natural she would attend such a case.

A man in his thirties wearing smart trousers and a business shirt sans tie strode across the ER towards Harper. 'Hi,' he said as he approached. 'I'm Felix Rothbury, senior reg O & G.' He held out a hand. 'You must be Harper. Nothing like being thrown in at the deep end on the first day.'

Harper shook his hand automatically. 'Oh…hi. Sorry, I was expecting Ali.'

'Boss is filling in for a colleague who had to pull out of their presentation last moment at a maternal morbidity symposium in Canberra today. She'll be back tomorrow.'

A rush of relief flooded Harper's chest, which probably made her a terrible person and an even worse friend, but there it was. She *was* going to have to face Ali sometime as Ivy, another friend from Harper's past and Head of General Surgery, had pointed out this morning as they'd left Ivy's apartment, where Harper was staying temporarily.

Just not today. Not her *first* day.

'Fluid resus is going to be tricky,' he said, launching straight into logistics as the siren, which had grown louder and louder, suddenly stopped. The ambulance had obviously turned into the emergency vehicles entrance.

'Yeah.' Harper nodded. 'If you could assess what the babies are doing—' she tipped her chin at the ultrasound unit just outside the cubicle '—we can work with the burns team to figure out how to go forward.'

Because of the massive fluid shifts within the body in significant burns, it was imperative that fluids were replaced and intensely monitored. But this wasn't an ordinary burns case—they wouldn't be treating just one person, they'd be treating three. And if, as the nurse had suggested, the patient had inhalation burns requiring ventilation, then that was a whole other ball game.

If the pregnancy had been more advanced a caesarean would have been the first course of action, but no one was going to deliver twenty-four-week twins unless the mother's life was in immediate peril.

Hello, rock, meet hard place.

The ambulance-bay doors opened and two paramedics rushed their cargo inside. Harper's gaze flew to the woman on the stretcher. Emma's distressed cries could be heard easily from behind the plastic mask covering her nose and mouth even over the loud hiss of high-flow oxygen keeping the attached bag inflated. Her rounded belly was also obvious even below the shiny silver of the space blanket the paramedics had tucked around her to keep her warm.

The patient was wheeled into the cube, and the brakes applied. As the paramedics gave their handover, the team descended, seamlessly transferring the patient from the stretcher to the specially equipped resus bed before moving on to their assigned roles. The tank oxygen was switched over to the wall supply, Emma was hooked up to the cubicle monitor, the fluids currently running into two IVs placed in the crook of each elbow were switched to the hospital pumps, and baseline observations were recorded.

Harper concentrated on the information coming from the paramedic as the nurse in charge of the resus took position at the head of the stretcher and talked soothingly to the distressed patient, who was fretting about the babies. The professional, rapid-fire handover helped Harper mentally triage her priorities. The airway trumped everything. Then a full burns assessment was required and the fluid protocols for acute burns would be enacted. The condition of the babies needed to be ascertained.

And that was just for starters.

The crinkle of the space blanket being removed barely registered as the patient's legs were exposed. Whatever Emma had been wearing was now a mess of shredded fabric rucked up to her groin. Harper's gaze moved south inspecting the wet gauze dressings applied from mid thighs to toes, noting there didn't seem to be any circumferential involvement of the legs.

'I'm sorry but I need to get in there—'

Harper's gaze flicked to Felix and then to the fireman he was addressing. Engrossed as she'd been in her mental assessment and the paramedics' handover, Harper hadn't taken much notice of him there holding the patient's hand. Until now. Until he lifted his gaze to meet Harper's and for a few mad seconds everything stopped. A wild rushing filled her ears.

She knew that head with its thick, dark, wavy hair. And even with soot settling in the fine lines, she knew that face—the taut stretch of skin over that square jaw and those killer cheekbones. She knew that mouth with its two perfectly formed full lips. She knew those black-on-brown eyes, a little bloodshot though, as though it'd been a while since he'd slept. And full of compassion.

Yarran.

The years fell away and it was as if they'd never been apart. As if the last twelve years had never happened. Looking into those two deep, still pools now felt as it always had. There was such wisdom there. Wisdom not born of this time. And an incredible sense of self as well as a...*connection* to something much bigger.

A completely foreign concept to a girl who had grown up in the foster system.

If he was taken aback by seeing her, Harper couldn't tell. Unlike her own internal tumult, those eyes remained as calm and knowing as always and for those brief seconds she was twenty again and wanted nothing more than to drown in them.

But she wasn't twenty. And neither was he.

They were both forty and he had been married *and* widowed *and* had an almost-four-year-old since last she'd seen him. And she hadn't come home to rekindle anything. She hadn't come home for him, full stop. This was just the next step in her career.

And right now she had a patient who deserved her entire attention.

Dragging her eyes off him, Harper planted a trembling hand at the foot of the mattress as she mentally quashed the wash of emotion flooding every cell with a yawning kind of ache. She tamped it right down where everything else she'd ever dared feel had been hidden away, and tuned back into the handover.

'Sorry,' he said to Felix, his voice piercing her concentration more effectively than a bullet. 'I'll get out of your way.'

Given there were now seven medical personnel in the cubicle along with the bulky machine that was a no-brainer. Sure, everyone was gliding around each other in some bizarre medical ballet bringing a strange kind of fluidity to the chaos, but less, right now, was more.

The paramedics were still speaking but Harper found her eye drawn to Yarran as he leaned over and smiled at the woman on the stretcher, dwarfed in people and plastic and clearly scared out of her brain. 'I'm going to move out of the way now, Emma, so they can do their job.'

'No!' Emma's knuckles whitened as she gripped Yarran's hand tighter.

'Hey, it's okay,' he soothed. 'You're in good hands.'

'But you said—' Her voice broke on a sob as she pulled the mask away from her face. 'You said you wouldn't leave me.'

'I'm not leaving.' He patted her hand with a gentle patience so familiar to Harper it caused an almost violent gut clench. 'I'm just going to step outside so they can work but I'm not leaving. I'll come back in as soon as they tell me I can, and I won't leave until Aaron gets here.'

'You promise?' she demanded through more tears.

'I promise.'

Harper knew better than anyone that Emma could take that promise to the bank.

He left then, but not without a brief yet cataclysmic glance at Harper. One that seemed to say, *I've done my bit...now it's up to you.*

So...no pressure.

Harper mentally regrouped, pushing Yarran *freaking* Edwards from her mind. She had to, because Emma Wilson deserved a doctor on top of her game, not one dwelling on the past.

'How are the babies, Felix?' she asked, squeezing past to the head of the stretcher.

'Neither appear to be in distress,' he murmured, not lifting his gaze from the screen as he manipulated the probe with one hand and fiddled with buttons on the machine with the other. 'Both membranes are intact. Twin one's heart rate is slightly less than twin two's, but both are in healthy range. Good foetal movements.'

Okay. *Good.* For now, anyway. But Emma's stridor was a worry. 'Hi, Emma, I'm Harper Jones, the doctor in charge here today.'

Harper smiled confidently at her patient, who was looking flushed and wild-eyed. The paramedics had reported she'd refused anything for pain because she was worried about the effect on the babies, something that Emma reiterated as she pulled her mask aside again. 'Promise me you'll do everything you can to keep my babies safe?' she demanded in a husky voice.

Nodding, Harper gently returned the mask to Emma's face. 'Of course.'

But Harper knew the next couple of hours would be a tricky tightrope between doing what was best for Emma while trying to be as protective of her pregnancy as possible.

'You in pain?'

Emma shook her head. 'It's bearable,' she dismissed.

But Harper could see from the rigidity of her frame and the elevation of her blood pressure, she clearly *was* in pain. Which was, in a lot of ways, encouraging. Full thickness burns often weren't painful due to the depth of the injury, which hopefully meant that the majority of the burns were partial thickness. Emma would still need grafting, but they might be able to get away with doing less, which, given the pregnancy, would be preferable.

Just then a tall, lean guy with dark brown hair greying at the temples entered the cubicle followed by two women with stethoscopes slung around their necks. 'Hi,' he said. 'I'm Lucas Matthews. Head of Reconstructive Surgery.'

He appeared to be about forty and quite the looker, Harper supposed. The kind who naturally drew the female gaze and yet, she felt nothing. Not with the visceral pull of Yarran Edwards so fresh in her brain. But it was good to meet the surgeon who would be tasked with Emma's grafting.

'Harper Jones,' she replied. 'Are you happy to assess the thermal injuries while I keep on here?'

He plucked a pair of gloves out of the wall-mounted box. 'Sure thing.'

Harper returned her attention to her patient. 'Emma, I'm very worried about how noisy your breathing is. Sometimes when you're really close to a fire like you were, just breathing in the heat from it—as well as the smoke and sometimes the chemicals from whatever's burning around you—can cause damage to the mucous membranes lining the lungs and respiratory tract, which can cause them to swell. I think that noise I can hear when you breathe may be an indication of some swelling so I'm going to have a look and assess it.'

'Okay.' Emma nodded, her voice sounding husky now. 'What happens if there's swelling?'

Then they'd probably have to tube her before it got worse. Between the thermal injury and the significant amount of fluid she was about to receive, the tissues of her respiratory tract were going to take a hammering.

'It depends on the degree.' Harper wasn't trying to be evasive but there was no point distressing Emma or getting too far ahead of themselves. 'Let me just have a look down your throat and we'll go from there.'

Two hours later they had stabilised Emma enough to get her transferred to the intensive care unit. There had been only slight redness of the upper airway so Harper hadn't needed to intubate but she suspected it would probably be required in the coming hours. Lucas had assessed the burns at twenty-five per cent—fifteen per cent of which were full thickness. Which meant extensive grafting.

Emma Wilson was here for the long haul.

Harper sent a swift prayer into the universe as the ICU team whisked a lightly sedated Emma away. After assurances from

Felix that the babies were doing well and a small amount of pain relief would be fine, Emma had acquiesced. With it, her distress had settled, which had, in turn, settled her breathing and improved her stridor.

For now.

The Sydney Central was a top-notch hospital and Emma was in the best place possible but her pregnant body had also suffered a severe insult, which had the potential to get worse, jeopardising both her life and the babies' lives. Babies who were far too premature to be delivered and expected to survive. So, she was by no means out of the woods just yet. But she was at least settled for now, sleeping a little, giving her stress levels a much-needed break.

Stripping off her gloves, Harper tore the ties of her plastic gown and removed it, tossing it in a bin and heading for her office. She stopped dead in her tracks when she spotted Yarran sitting by himself in a row of four chairs in the corridor just outside the resus area, his head lolling back at an awkward angle against the wall.

Asleep.

A fascinating section of whiskery throat was exposed to her view and Harper felt a repeat of that moment back in the cubicle. That visceral gut clench. How was it possible he could affect her like this after twelve years apart?

Sighing, she approached—he'd get a crick in his neck if he stayed like that. Plus, she'd promised Emma she'd let Yarran know she was being transferred to ICU. Apparently, he'd been the one to pull her out from under the collapsed section of roof.

She'd called him her hero and looking at him now, oozing sheer masculinity even in his sleep, Harper agreed. Everything about him screamed big and capable. The guy who strode in when everything was burning down.

The guy who got it done.

From the tips of his soot-blackened, heavy work boots to the way his navy polo shirt stretched across his shoulders and abs, to the bands of reflective material encircling thighs and calves encased in thick navy trousers. Everything about him screamed 'hero'.

'Yarran.'

He didn't stir and Harper's heart did a little flip-flop behind her ribcage. Half of her wanted to let him sleep and the other half wanted to stroke her finger along the darkened shadow on his jawline and whisper his name as she used to.

As if they'd never been apart.

She wanted it so bad, her finger tingled in anticipation. But that wasn't going to happen. It could never happen.

They were so last decade.

Taking the safer route, Harper shook his arm, watching him as he stirred. He winced as he righted his head and cracked open an eye, looking at her in confusion for a moment or two before clarity returned. He stood abruptly, suddenly alert despite the overwhelming exhaustion stamped across his features.

'Emma?'

He was now significantly closer, looming in front of her and she could smell smoke but also something familiar, something that struck a chord deep in her reptilian brain. 'Just gone to ICU.'

He checked his watch. 'Has Aaron arrived?'

'He's apparently a few hours away.' It was then Harper noticed the congealed blood on the inner side of Yarran's forearm. She frowned. 'You're hurt.'

'Hmm? Oh—' He glanced at the injury, clearly annoyed it had the audacity to exist. 'It's nothing.'

'Why don't you let me be the judge of that?'

'It's fine,' he repeated, his tone testy. 'I need to get to ICU.'

Harper shook her head. 'Emma's sleeping at the moment and they won't let you in until they've got her settled anyway.'

'Is she going to be okay? Are the babies okay?'

Folding her arms, Harper raised an eyebrow. 'Let me look at that and I can fill you in on where she's at.'

He regarded her for a few moments. 'Fine.'

Yarran followed Harper into a treatment room still not quite able to believe she was here. He'd known she was back in the country. Known she'd taken the job at the Central. But he hadn't expected to run into her *ever* really, or not so soon, anyway. And certainly not on what was, according to the recent conversation he'd had with his twin, Ali, her first day.

He had given seeing Harper a brief thought sitting beside Emma in the ambulance but had dismissed it as fanciful. Surely her first day as department chief would involve a lot of meetings and HR stuff. Not being in the thick of an emergency right off the bat.

And certainly not attending to a lowly superficial scratch on his arm.

She flicked the lights on as she entered what was a typical hospital treatment room—cold, the bright white light making it seem even more so. The clinical aroma of antiseptic was pervasive yet comforting. Without a word, Harper pointed at the high, narrow bed pushed against the far wall and Yarran mentally apologised to the pristine white sheet as he levered his soot-covered ass onto the middle, his legs dangling over the edge.

They didn't speak. He just watched her gather the things she needed, in that quiet, efficient way of hers, as if they didn't have a whole truck full of baggage dominating the space between them. Her economy of movement hadn't changed in a decade. Nor had the shape of her body. Beneath those scrubs—she *still* looked good in scrubs—he could make out the leanness of her legs, the trimness of her frame, the high, tight thrust of her breasts.

His palms tingled as he remembered the feel of her under him and he pressed them to the bed. God…he must be tired to be thinking like this.

And he *was* tired. Actually, exhausted was probably a better word. Fatigue invaded every muscle cell he owned. His team had taken over at a factory fire when they'd come on shift last night and had spent seven hours getting it under control. Fighting a fire over a prolonged period was hot, sweaty work and manning a hose required extraordinary strength. Doing so for hours, even more so.

Then, two hours before the shift was due to end, they'd been called to the Wilsons' house fire. It hadn't taken long to get under control but the adrenaline that came with a suburban fire took its own kind of toll. Unlike the abandoned warehouse, the potential for people being trapped and the fire spreading to neighbouring properties was ever present.

So yeah, he felt weary to his bones. He stunk of smoke and was streaked with soot. His eyes were gritty from ash and fumes and weariness. He wanted a shower and he wanted his bed. He did not want to be here with Harper Jones staring back into a past he suddenly wasn't sure now he was as over as he'd thought.

Turning, she pushed a metallic trolley laden with dressing equipment towards him. She halted close enough that the outside of her thigh brushed the outside of his knee as she snapped on a pair of gloves. A flare of heat flashed up his quad and the fatigued muscle protested the involuntary tightening. Harper didn't look similarly affected as she held out her hand, clearly expecting him to present his arm.

Yarran sighed. 'It really is fine.' But she just stood there, implacable as ever. Implacable as that night she'd turned his proposal down.

Sliding her hand onto his forearm, she flipped it over so she could examine the underside then lifted it slightly to examine it closer. Yarran didn't resist—he didn't have the energy. Although clearly his body wasn't *that* tired as a warm buzz flushed through his system at her touch.

'What happened?' she asked with such brisk efficiency Yarran was left in no doubt he was the only one feeling the buzz.

'I don't really remember. I think it might have been when my shirt caught on something as I pulled Emma out from the debris.'

She lifted her gaze and their eyes met and locked and Yarran was conscious of how close they were, of how easy it would be to slide a hand onto her hip, to tug her near and bury his face in her neck. She smelled so good and looked so fresh and so...*here*. After all this time. It had been over a decade and yet it felt like yesterday.

'You didn't feel anything? It must have hurt.'

Yarran shrugged. 'Nope.' It wasn't unusual in the midst of a fire or a rescue, with adrenaline surging, to sustain a minor injury or burn and not even know it.

Their gazes held for a beat or two, her hazel eyes familiar to him on such an intimate level. How many times had he stared into those eyes as they'd chatted about their days, their plans, their future?

How many times had he stared into them as they'd made love?

She quirked an eyebrow at his brief response. 'People

come into emergency departments demanding morphine for papercuts.'

He shrugged again. 'I didn't feel it.'

Shaking her head, she dropped her gaze back to his wound and set about thoroughly cleaning the area. As promised, she filled him in on Emma's injuries and condition with a brisk, businesslike demeanour that helped keep this moment in perspective.

Once all the soot and dried blood had been removed it was, as he suspected, a superficial cut *not* requiring any medical intervention. Still, he had to grit his teeth a little as she scrubbed directly at the ten-centimetre laceration with an anti-bacterial solution. He grunted as she swabbed it again.

'Sorry.' She glanced at him quickly. 'Don't want it to get infected.'

'Not much danger of that,' Yarran grouched. 'My arm's never been cleaner.'

Ignoring his grumpiness, she returned her attention to his arm, inspecting it carefully. 'Okay, it's just a superficial cut.'

Yarran rolled his eyes as he stared at the curve of her cheekbone and the half-moon shadow created by her eyelashes. 'Yeah.'

She released his arm, reaching for a wound dressing. 'I'll just pop a dressing over it.'

Yarran sat passively as she applied it, taking her time adhering the sticky edges to his skin, working out a wrinkle from a section daring to not sit perfectly. It was torturous, cool her fingertips trailing against the flesh of his inner arm, light and cool, sensation curling upwards his arm, light as smoke.

A slice of her hair fell forward. It was still the same vibrant red as always, no sign of any greys to dull its glory. She wore it shorter, though, the tips brushing her shoulders rather than her waist, but it looked as lush and soft as always and he was shocked by the sudden urge to sink his hands into it, to feel the glide of it as it sifted through his fingers, to bury his face in it.

To see it fanned over the pillow beside his.

Something deep and hard kicked him in the chest and he started. Fifteen minutes ago, all he'd wanted was a shower and his bed and now he wanted…what? To…rekindle something with the woman who had smashed his heart into a thousand tiny pieces?

He hadn't wanted anybody for a long time. And now this? With *Harper*?

'There now,' she said, oblivious to his inner turmoil, her eyes meeting his. 'You want a lollipop?'

A smile played on her mouth and lit those hazel eyes. The same hazel eyes that had clouded over when he'd dropped to his knee and proposed all those years ago.

What are you doing, Yarran? Get up, please, just get up.

He still remembered that moment. The look of horror on her face, the icy cold fingers wrapping around his heart and squeezing. He'd been so sure. *So sure* of her and how she felt. That she wanted the same thing he did—a life together. He remembered the heavy pain in his chest as his heart had cleaved right down the centre.

And then she'd bolted—to the other side of the planet— leaving Yarran dead inside. So dead he'd never thought he'd feel anything again. And he hadn't—for a long time. Then Marnie had come along six years ago and breathed life back into him. He'd loved again and when they'd had their son— Jarrah—Yarran had felt complete.

But then Marnie had been so cruelly taken from him in a car accident just after Jarrah's first birthday and his world had turned bleak. *So bleak*. Thank goodness for Jarrah. His son had given him reason to keep going.

Reason to laugh and feel joy again and he'd clung to that.

It had been a long process, but he was finally in a good place. He had a kid he adored, a job he loved and a supportive family. He didn't *need* anything else.

Hell, he didn't *want* anything else.

He certainly didn't want to go backwards. And Harper was the very definition of backwards. Yarran was a different person today. Not the same guy who fell so quickly and trusted so easily. And he had responsibilities now. He had Jarrah. And Jarrah came first.

'Yarran?'

Her husky voice brought him back to this moment. This woman so familiar yet so *not*. So close. *Too close*. Frowning at him, her brow crinkled, those eyes searching his, everything around them coming to a stop. The busy emergency ward noises in the corridor fading. The breath in his lungs stuttering to a halt. The trip of his heart pausing.

He was conscious only of her—of her breathing and the aroma of her hair. Of the hot lick of desire throbbing to life inside him. His gaze dropped to Harper's mouth and the urge to kiss the hell out of her rode him like the devil.

She swallowed. *'Yarran.'*

Her voice was low and rough, husky with warning. One he would do well to heed but now he was caught up by the fascinating bob of her throat, the flutter of her pulse at the base, the memory of kissing her there so many times. How good it had been.

Until it wasn't.

Panic flooded in then, riding shotgun with his desire. Hell. What was he thinking? This was Harper. *Harper*. He wasn't thinking. At all. He was tired—so tired—and seeing her again after all this time was a shock.

Yarran stood abruptly, forcing Harper to take a step back. 'I've got to go,' he said gruffly, manoeuvring around her stationary body. 'I promised Emma I wouldn't leave her.'

He wasn't asking for her permission and he didn't wait for it, he just walked out of the room, not looking back, refusing to think about how close he'd come to doing something so incredibly stupid. His body might be caught up in a time warp, but his head was not.

There could be no do-overs with Harper Jones.

CHAPTER TWO

A FEW HOURS LATER, Harper was standing in line at Perc Up, the café bar over the road from the hospital. It was obviously popular given the size of the queue and she could see why. Big windows looked out on the busy road while, overhead, myriad bare light bulbs clung to the ceiling Hollywood-mirror style. Multiple comfy-looking faux chesterfield lounges in buttery leather faced each other over worn Turkish-style rugs.

The view through the glass was partially obscured by creeping vines that spilled from pots sitting on shelves affixed above the windows and real potted palms—not plastic—sat on multiple surfaces throughout. They were large and lush, their leaves showy and tropical, and Harper had no doubt she'd have admired the décor a hell of a lot more on a different day.

Just not this day. Several hours after the shock of seeing Yarran again so soon and that *almost kiss*. Because she had no doubt that was where it had been heading...

It was all just too much to process today on top of two emergency cases in quick succession. How could there still be such an intense *thing* between them? Because he'd obviously felt it, too. It had been *twelve* years, for Pete's sake. They'd both moved on. They weren't the twenty-year-olds they'd been when they'd first got together. She'd had several liaisons since—although none serious—and he'd *married*, for God's sake.

He had a kid.

'Hey, you.'

Harper started at the sound of Ivy's voice but was inordinately grateful she was here dragging Harper out of circuitous thoughts. 'Hey.'

'I hear your first day got off to a real bang.'

Dr Ivy Hurst had formed part of Harper's tight friendship circle back in the day, along with Ali and Phoebe Mason. They'd all met in med school and, much to Harper's surprise, had all clicked. She wasn't sure what they saw in her—Harper Jones, the outsider—but she was exceedingly grateful these women had been patient with her reticence and drawn her in, holding her close when her instincts had always been set to flee.

'You could say that.'

'How's the burns patient?'

Harper filled Ivy in on the case as the queue moved closer to the counter. 'I rang ICU just before I came over and her airway swelling had started to get markedly worse so they've tubed her.' Harper shook her head. 'The pregnancy complicates everything drastically.'

Ivy nodded, her caramel hair swishing. She was shorter and curvier to Harper's taller, sportier figure. 'True. But she has the best damn multi-disciplinary team in the country working around the clock to give her and the babies the best care. And, it could have been worse. A ceiling collapse in a house fire?' Ivy shuddered. 'She was lucky to get out alive.'

Which brought Yarran squarely back into Harper's thoughts. Looking all big and broad and sooty. And tired. So tired. Yet, so damn *good*.

'Yeah.'

'Hey.' Ivy snapped her fingers in front of Harper's face. 'Where'd you go?'

'Sorry.' Harper grimaced. 'I—'

She shook her head, contemplating whether to tell Ivy about Yarran. Harper's early years had taught her to be self-reliant, even secretive, so it had never felt natural to blurt out personal stuff. Then she'd become friends with Ivy, Ali and Phoebe and learned it was okay to share things with your besties.

They listened, they commiserated, they advised. And they never ever judged.

It had been over a decade since they'd shared that dynamic, but Harper had been hoping, with her return, it could be re-kindled. So maybe this was a good place to start.

'I...ran into Yarran.'

The expression on Ivy's face was almost comical '*What? Shut up!*'

Harper laughed; she couldn't help it. 'Nope. He came in holding Emma's hand.'

Ivy fluttered her hand over her chest in a hubba-hubba way. 'Of course he did. That man, honourable as the day is long and, Lordy...forty looks *good* on him.'

Harper couldn't have agreed more as Ivy's gaze turned speculative. 'How was it?'

Intense. Cataclysmic. Unsettling. 'Weird.'

'Bad weird, or—' she waggled her eyebrows '—good weird.'

'There's a good weird?'

'With old boyfriends? Sure.' She waved at the air as if the question was a no-brainer. 'Was there some residual...*somethin'-somethin'*?'

Oh, yeah, there'd been that—with bells on. But Harper wasn't ready to share that just yet. She was barely processing it herself. 'Are you forgetting I rejected his marriage proposal and broke his heart twelve years ago? *And* he'd been married and widowed in the interim?'

'Sure.' Another air-wave. 'But…if there was a little *weakening* below the belly button, then what?'

The question hung in the air, tantalising in ways Harper didn't want to either acknowledge or understand. 'Ali would have my guts for garters.' She'd been furious at Harper's rejection of Yarran.

That whole 'twins feeling each other's pain' thing was *real*.

'Right. Which is why we need to get the gang back together.' Ivy held up a hand to still Harper as she opened her mouth to object. 'I know you wanted to get settled into your own apartment before reconnecting with Ali beyond any hospital interactions but, hon, that's just not going to work now. Yarran is for damn sure going to tell Ali you guys met because they tell each other everything.'

Ivy was right. And Harper did want to reconnect with her old friends. She'd love to be able to get back to what they had been. She'd *missed* her friends. She'd missed *Ali*.

Smart, passionate, protective, loyal Ali.

Ivy, obviously sensing Harper wavering, moved in for the kill. 'There's a lot to be said for ripping the plaster off, hon.'

She sighed. 'Yep…okay, sure.'

'Yes—reunion dinner!' Ivy did a little body shimmy. 'Friday night. Phoebe's back from her conference by then and we can strike while the iron is hot.' She happy sighed. 'It'll be like old times, just you wait and see.'

Harper nodded and smiled, not wanting to dampen Ivy's enthusiasm, but she figured it'd probably be a while before it felt like old times. Except of course for Yarran. Her body was firmly in old times territory where he was concerned. Remembering every kiss and touch, every magical minute.

Great. Just great…

* * *

It was six in the evening before Harper got away. As first days went, it was one for the books and she was looking forward to a shower and kicking back with Ivy when she was through with her rounds. Walking across the spacious lobby, she admired the towering glass atrium showcasing the last streaks of sunlight gilding the clouds vibrant oranges and reds.

The architecturally designed hospital had won awards for its use of glass to amplify the space and light and Harper made a mental note to go up to the renowned rooftop gardens and watch the sunset some time soon. But right now, a shower was calling.

She slowed as she approached the bank of lifts, suddenly noticing a clutch of what she assumed were media cordoned off beyond the front entrance, if the presence of zoom lenses and a hovering security guard was anything to go by.

Anybody would think they were harbouring a new royal baby inside.

The hospital had issued a standard *no comment* in a media release several hours ago—as had Aaron's management—but that hadn't stopped a pack of hungry reporters descending.

She'd heard a very harried Aaron Wilson had run the gauntlet of them as he'd swept into the hospital half an hour ago and it seemed as though they were now camping out for the duration.

Absently she registered the lift dinging and, as she drew level, the doors opened and Yarran strode out almost directly in her path. They didn't crash but they were both forced to stop abruptly and then they just stared at each other for what felt like a lot longer than the probable few seconds it actually was.

He'd washed up a little, his face now free of sooty streaks, but she could still smell smoke and that vaguely familiar aroma she couldn't put her finger on. His wavy hair looked as though it had been finger-combed for hours. The curls were in total disarray and, for a crazy second, Harper wanted to push her hands into the dark silky mass and brush it back into place.

Except she couldn't move. Not when his eyes roved, holding her firmly in place. They travelled from her hair to her face then down over the fit of her scrubs, his gaze hungry and heated as if he were seeing her for the first time again after her long absence from his life.

Harper felt the rawness of it—the urgency—in every cell. In the catch of her breath, the clench of her stomach and the wild flutter of her pulse at the base of her throat. A pulse he noticed, his gaze zeroing in, her nipples hardening at the intense sexuality of his scrutiny.

'You're still here?' Harper said, finally finding her voice as she tore herself back from the frighteningly intense draw of him.

'Yeah.' He cleared his throat as though the effort to pull himself back had been difficult too. 'Aaron's with Emma now so…'

'You're not on shift tonight?'

'No. I have a couple of days off now.'

The front entrance sliding doors opened, admitting some hospital staff along with the calls from the press, who clearly thought anyone in uniform was fair game to share insider information on the Wilsons. The click of the cameras echoed around the atrium like gunfire.

'Ugh,' Harper muttered. 'That looks like fun. *Not.*'

The last thing she wanted was to have to brave that lot. She glanced at Yarran, who was obviously going to be a prime target with the fire service emblem embroidered on the pocket of his T-shirt and the high-vis piping around his legs.

'You ready to gird your loins?' she asked and then immediately wished the floor would open up and swallow her.

Do not mention the man's loins, idiot.

Thankfully Yarran left it alone as his expression turned grim. 'No way.' He shook his head. 'Come on. I know another way out of here.'

She supposed he did—his sister worked here and, apart from the fact he'd probably been to the ER frequently over the years, she knew part of the fire service's job was knowing the layout of city hospitals in case of evacuation. But she hadn't been prepared for him to grab her hand as he did as he turned on his heel and tugged.

Harper followed without comment, too aware of him and their intimate hold to risk conversation. She just lengthened her stride to keep pace and, before she knew it, he was dragging her through the bottom of the fire escape. Ignoring the stairs, he strode across the well to the door on the other side and pushed it open.

They stepped out into a wide, clean alley that appeared to be some kind of service corridor, if the nearby forklift was any indication. But, more importantly, it was blissfully free of media. It was only then that he let go of her hand.

'Thank you,' she said, her voice ridiculously husky, her palm tingling as she became aware she was alone with him—again.

Which was dumb—they were in an *alley*, for God's sake. There was heavy machinery six feet away. It was hardly intimate. And yet the gentle kiss of twilight seemed to bathe the area in a romantic deep lavender glow.

'Are you in the car park?'

'Yes.' She nodded. 'What about you?'

'I'll get an Uber.'

Of course. He'd have come to the hospital in the back of an ambulance. 'I can drop you back to your station to pick up your car?'

She had no idea where his fire station was these days and probably being alone with him in a car wasn't wise, but it seemed churlish not to offer—they *had* been friends once, for crying out loud. And if she and Ali were ever going to get close again, Harper needed to accept Yarran was going to be back in her life, too.

Which meant they had to find some kind of way to get beyond their past. A way to be friends. Like giving him a lift back to the station. Friends gave each other lifts, right?

'Nah, it's fine.' He shook his head. 'I got the bus into work last night. It's easy to grab an Uber.'

If Sydney Ubers were anything like London's during peak hour there'd be some ridiculous surcharging going on. She had no doubt he could afford an Uber, but it didn't seem right letting him do it when she could easily drop him home. 'Or...' she smiled '...I could just drop you home.'

'I live in Sunrise Bay.'

'I know.'

His eyes widened a little. 'You been keeping tabs on me, Harper?'

There was a gravelly undertone to the enquiry that sent Harper's pulse fluttering again, which made her irritable.

Enough already!

'Well, I don't know your *exact* address or anything, but I am Facebook friends with your sister,' she said waspishly, 'and while I've been too busy building my career to endlessly scroll social media like most people on the planet, I've seen enough here and there to gather you live near your parents.'

'Right.' He conceded with a small smile. 'Which is the opposite direction to Ivy's.'

So, he knew she was staying with Ivy... Harper quirked an eyebrow. '*You* been keeping tabs on *me*?' The only social media she was on was Facebook, and Harper never posted anything. She barely ever looked at her feed.

He shrugged. 'I overhead Ali mentioning it to Mum.'

'Ah.' Harper nodded absently, undecided whether she was okay that Yarran *hadn't* been keeping tabs on her. 'Well... anyway...' She shook herself out of her contemplation. 'I'm perfectly fine to drive you twenty minutes to Sunrise Bay.'

He regarded her solemnly for a beat or two, his lips pursed as if he was weighing up all the pros and cons, and she had to stop herself from rolling her eyes. Once upon a time, Yarran had been spontaneous. That was one of the many things she'd loved about him. So different from her and her cautious approach to life. But, she supposed, not a lot had gone according to plan for Yarran so she could hardly blame him.

'Okay.' He nodded slowly. 'Thank you.'

They sat in silence as Harper manoeuvred her rental out of the hospital car park. The radio was came on once they were out of the parking garage and Yarran seemed content to listen as he stared out of the window. He didn't even give directions. Not that she needed them—not yet anyway. It might have been over a decade since she'd lived in Sydney but she still remembered how to get to Sunrise Bay.

Once upon a time the Edwards house had felt like hers as she, Ali, Phoebs and Ivy spent many a night cramming for uni exams there, being kept in carbs and caffeine by Ali's mother. And then, as she and Yarran became a thing, spending nights and staying weekends.

Feeling loved and included. Almost feeling like one of them.

As though she almost belonged. But not ever really trusting that she could have it all.

Constantly on tenterhooks as the years passed and chatter about weddings and *babies* grew louder. Wanting Yarran but too scarred from her past to trust—not in him, but in herself. Living with the constant slick undercurrent of panic. Waiting for the moment it would all come crashing down. When it would all end and she'd have to leave.

Because that was better than being left.

So when the opportunity came up to go to London, it had been perfect. Harper had jumped at it. How was she to know Yarran had picked the very night she was going to tell him about moving to the other side of the world to propose?

'Who looks after your son?' she asked into the growing silence. Anything to take her mind off that night. 'When you're at work.'

'Jarrah.' He turned his head to look at her. 'His name is Jarrah.'

Harper nodded, her hands gripping the steering wheel a little tighter. Jarrah. Yarran's *son*. Harper hadn't ever wanted kids—apart from a couple of blissful years with a great-aunt, she'd had no motherly role models to speak of—but as her relationship with Yarran had continued his parents had started mentioning grandkids.

Yarran's children. With Yarran's dark eyes and his dark curly hair and his beautiful brown skin. And that had added to the panic.

'Does he have a nanny or childcare or...?'

'A little bit of everything, really. Like most single parents it's a bit of a juggle and between kindy and after-school care, as well as Ali and Mum and Dad, I have a village helping me.

He's been at Mum and Dad's the last few days. They take him when I work nights or weekends.'

'You're lucky to have them.'

He gave a half-laugh. 'Don't I know it. I wouldn't have managed without them after…'

Yarran looked back out of the window without finishing his sentence. He didn't need to. Harper knew what he'd been about to say—*after my wife died*. And it gave her a perfect opportunity to do what she should have done three years ago. 'I'm so sorry about your wife…about Marnie. I sent a condolence card.'

And she'd felt crappy about it. She should have picked up the phone, talked to him, but so many years had passed and there'd been no contact and she hadn't known what to say. Sorry had seemed so inadequate. So, she'd chickened out.

'I got it. Thank you.'

Harper wanted to say more. Wanted to ask more. About her. About Marnie. The woman Yarran had loved after he'd stopped loving her. She hadn't been jealous or upset he'd moved on; in fact, she'd felt a strange kind of kinship with this other woman. Yarran was one of the best people she'd ever known—one of the good guys—and Harper had been grateful to her. And relieved and happy Yarran had been able to move on.

Unlike her.

But she didn't speak. She didn't ask the questions pushing at the back of her throat. There'd been a bleak kind of finality to his voice and his body language was saying *don't*.

Maybe just seeing each other again was enough for one day.

So they remained silent until she turned into Sunrise Bay and Yarran directed her to his place. Harper inspected it as she pulled up outside—neat, two storeys, brick, with beautifully landscaped gardens bordering a manicured lawn. She'd bet there was a big backyard and probably a pool.

'How long have you lived here?' she asked as he made no move to get out and the silence weighed hot and heavy against her.

'A few years. It was easier to be closer to Mum and Dad with Jarrah.'

She nodded. 'It looks lovely.'

'Yeah.' Yarran glanced up at the building. 'We like it. Poor Wally didn't know what to do with himself though, when we moved in. All that space in the backyard after a tiny square of grass at the old place.'

Harper blinked. *'Wally?'* Her gaze landed on his profile. 'Wally's still alive?'

Yarran turned his head and their gazes met. 'Yep. Fourteen years and still kicking.'

They'd plucked Wally, a four-month-old chocolate Labrador, out of the shelter a couple of years before Harper had left. It had been love at first sight for all three of them and leaving the doggo behind had been just one of the many wrenches of her move.

'He has some arthritis now, which makes him a little slower, but he can still open the fridge when you're not looking and he's very protective of Jarrah.'

Another stupid lump lodged in Harper's throat. 'I assumed… I didn't know… Wow.'

'Yeah.' Then he smiled and Harper wasn't prepared for it. Cheekbones and dimples, she thought absently. It wasn't fair the man should be blessed with both. 'You want to come up and see him?'

This was one of those times when Harper knew she should definitely say no. Those dimples alone were a blaring foghorn and there'd already been a *lot* today. That near-kiss moment in the treatment room a warning shot across the bow.

But… *Wally*!

She smiled back and switched off the engine. 'I'd love to.'

Harper walked through the front door as Yarran pushed it open and indicated she should precede him. She caught a waft of something familiar again as she brushed past tempting her to linger but she didn't, walking straight into an open-plan living, dining and kitchen area.

Warm downlights glowed from the ceiling, bathing wooden floorboards in soft yellow light. At the far side was a bank of floor-to-ceiling sliding doors, which led out onto a deck lit by a string of fairy lights entwined around the railings.

It was homely, with comfy patchwork couches, and a corner piled high with transparent plastic tubs of toys. A big-screen TV hung from the wall opposite the three-seater couch, where several stuffed toys were discarded. A large wooden coffee table sat just in front of the couch with several toy trains sitting on top. A train track, complete with stations and signals, looped around the base.

'This is nice,' she said as the door clicked shut and Yarran moved past her, heading for the kitchen.

'Thanks. We like it.'

Harper followed him slowly inside as he placed his keys and mobile phone on the bench top before turning to open the fridge door. 'You want something to drink? Tea? Coffee? A glass of wine?'

She halted on the other side of the central island bench. *Wine?* The last thing she needed right now, with his back view looking just as fine as his front, was to have her inhibitions lowered. Being in his home, getting an insight into what his life had been without her, felt confronting enough without alcohol.

The sweet ache of nostalgia mixed with a heavier feeling of regret to form an unholy alliance, needling at her skin.

'No. Thanks.'

He reached for the carton of juice and turned back to her, lifting it to his mouth and drinking it straight from the carton, his Adam's apple bobbing, his eyelids sweeping shut. He'd always done that and, instead of finding it annoying like his mother, Harper had found it utterly freaking masculine. And strangely erotic.

As if his thirsts weren't easily contained by manners and propriety.

His eyes fluttered open and Harper's breath stuttered to a halt as their gazes met. It was only for a couple of beats but long enough for her heart to bump against her ribs and for her thighs to tremble and her nipples to tighten.

Hell, Harper couldn't believe her scrubs weren't smouldering.

A dog barked then and Harper dragged herself back from the pit of quicksand she'd been circling. Back to the present. To their baggage. To the stick-figure crayon drawing behind Yarran's head that was fixed to the fridge with a *best daddy ever* magnet.

Yarran was not the same person he'd been twelve years ago. And neither was she.

Her pulse loud in her ears, Harper turned to the sliding doors to find another piece of her past squirming his body towards her. 'Wally!'

Tossing her car keys on the island top, she strode towards the dog and had the door open within seconds, much to Wally's delight. She dropped to her knees and hugged him tight, a wall of emotion lodging in her throat and pricking at the backs of her eyes.

'I can't believe it's you, Wally.' She sighed contently then laughed as he shimmied his entire body in her arms, making it impossible to hold him properly.

Harper sensed Yarran coming closer and Wally barked happily at his master as he madly wagged his tail and wriggled on the spot. Yarran laughed. 'I know, boy.' He scratched behind Wally's ears and the dog's eyes rolled back in ecstasy. 'She's back.'

She's back.

Two little words stabbing into her soul. Had he known she would be? Had he wanted it? Had he lain in bed at night, yearning for her the way she'd yearned for him?

Giving herself a mental shake, Harper glanced up from the greyed muzzle of Wally the wonder dog, as they used to call him. 'You think he recognises me?'

'Yeah.' Yarran's steady look pierced through her as he continued to show Wally some love. 'I do.'

Harper never had a pet growing up so she wasn't familiar with dog stuff. 'It's been so long. I…figured he'd forget me.'

'You're a lot of things, Harper Jones, but forgettable is not one of them.'

She swallowed at the gravelly pitch to his voice. He hadn't forgotten her. Just as she hadn't forgotten him. No matter how much she'd told herself she had.

Told herself she *should*.

Breaking eye contact again, she sank down and Wally shimmied into another squirmy hug. Shutting her eyes, Harper held him tight, the press of his wriggly body bombarding her with a hundred memories. She was conscious of Yarran standing over her, conscious of an ache, of a restlessness that fizzed between them in a purely sexual way.

And she suddenly couldn't take any more. Her system was in nostalgia overload and she had to get out. 'I've gotta go.' She stood abruptly, heading for the kitchen.

'Harper.'

Ignoring him, she passed between the island and the bank of kitchen cupboards against the wall to fetch her keys, which had slid across the surface when she'd tossed them there. Taking a breath she said, 'Thank you,' then turned slightly to acknowledge him—it would be rude not to, after all.

Except she'd thought he'd still be over with Wally. But he wasn't. Wally was outside, looking in through the screen door, and Yarran was behind her. Right there. So close. And looking all big and broody and so... *God*...so good. And she wanted to walk into his arms and lay her cheek on his chest as she'd done so many times before, but she couldn't because she'd screwed it all up. The thought caught like a burr in her throat and Harper blinked back a well of stupid tears.

His expression softened as he took a step closer. 'Harper...'

Harper's pulse thrummed frantically at her temple. 'I'm fine.'

But she wasn't because he was so near and she'd missed him so much. *So much.* Why had she underestimated how hard it would be to see him again?

Slowly, he shook his head. 'I don't think you are.'

Then he took another step, his hand reaching for her, his palm sliding onto the side of her neck, his fingers gliding into the hair at her nape, his thumb drifting lazily across the angle of her jaw.

'Harper,' he murmured, his head lowering, his gaze scorching her mouth.

Her name rumbled from his lips and every pulse point keened to his touch. Her breathing constricted as a low throb—hot and slick—flared to life between her legs. But still, she *could* have pulled back, *could* have stepped away. She could have stopped this.

She just didn't want to.

When his mouth touched down it was soft and tentative and she sighed against his lips as if she'd been waiting for this moment from the second their eyes had met again in the ER. The lightest of brushes and yet every part of her melted as she swayed towards him and he swayed towards her, their bodies *just* skimming—thighs, hips, chests—while her heart just about thumped out of her chest.

He tasted tangy like orange juice as she breathed in the aroma of him—smoke and that familiar back note that had been bugging her all day except now she knew what it was. *Acqua di Gio.*

She'd bought him his first ever bottle.

'God,' he muttered, pulling back enough for Harper to see his eyes clouded with lust and confusion. 'It's like you never went away.'

Then he kissed her again and made a noise at the back of his throat so damn urgent and needy and...*feral* it exploded through her body in a flash of white-hot light and the kiss went from tentative to explosive.

From zero to nuclear in one beat of her heart.

His hand jerked her closer, their bodies locked tight now as she clung to him, drowning in lust and Acqua Di Gio. Yarran's mouth grew hotter and harder and more demanding and Harper met him at every turn and twist, inhaling noisily as she shifted restlessly against the hard planes of his body trying to get closer.

Trying to *get inside* him.

He moved slightly and suddenly she was trapped between the hardness of his body and the immovability of the bench-top, her nipples a hot ache as they rubbed against his chest. Then he slid a thick thigh between her legs, pressing against the scream of nerves at the apex, and she thrust her hands into his hair, twisting her fingers hard. He grunted at the bite but Harper was too far gone to care as she whispered, *'Yarran,'* urgently against his mouth.

The jangle of his phone sliced through the red-hot veil of Yarran's lust like a machete. It was his mother's ringtone and he jerked out of the kiss as if he'd been hit by a cattle prod, his pulse thudding through his neck, his chest, his groin. His breathing as erratic as Harper's.

Yarran stared at her for a beat. He'd done that. He'd made her noisily drag air in and out and her mouth all wet and puffy. He'd put that hazy sheen of lust in her eyes. He was respon-sible for her bewildered expression. The way she'd twisted her fingers in his hair when he'd pushed between her legs…

And, hell, if that hadn't rushed to his head at a dizzying speed.

'That's Mum,' he said as the ringing continued, his voice weirdly husky. 'I've got to get it.' Yarran had rung his mother earlier to explain where he was and ask her to pick up Jarrah from school and keep him at theirs for a while longer.

He hadn't mentioned seeing Harper again. No, he didn't know why.

Harper nodded as if she was unable to form coherent words and Yarran couldn't help but feel a stab of male satisfaction. Her breath caught as he eased his thigh from between hers and, hell, if he didn't want to ignore the damn phone and jam his leg right back in there.

Rub and grind against her. Hear her call out his name again as if she couldn't get enough of him, as if they'd never been apart.

He stepped away instead and reached for the phone.

'Hi, Mum,' he said as he answered it, leaning his butt against the counter and watching Harper as she moved away, sliding her hands onto the bench opposite, her back to him.

'Hi, darling. Just ringing to check if you're back from the hospital yet and want us to bring Jarrah around or should we keep him another night so you can crash?'

Harper turned then, lust still lingering in her eyes, and he had to grind his feet into the floor to stop from tossing the phone and putting his mouth back where it belonged. 'Just got home,' he said, fighting an internal battle against the temptation his mother was offering.

There wasn't one part of him that didn't know he and Harper could pick right back up where they'd left off. There wasn't one part of him that didn't want it, either.

'Bring him over whenever you're ready.'

It wasn't great parenting to put his kid between him and temptation but, right now, it was all he had. Because this thing between him and Harper today was madness. It was nostalgia and muscle memory—and he would do well to remember Harper had run from a commitment twelve years ago when there'd only been him.

And it wasn't just him any more.

Maybe she was different now but he couldn't risk his heart again, not when he had Jarrah to consider. Jarrah, who had already lost one important woman from his young life.

Yarran didn't have the luxury of being young and stupid

any more, pinning his hopes on someone he'd always known, on some deep visceral level, had one eye on the door.

He'd just been so certain she loved him more than her insecurities and he could love her enough to make her stay.

Hanging up from his mother, he glanced at Harper. 'Jarrah will be home soon.'

She nodded and cleared her throat and Yarran watched the last vestiges of their passion clear from her eyes. 'Of course.' She pushed off the bench. 'I'll be on my way.'

'Wait.' Yarran held up his hand and she stopped. 'Let's go out for a drink on Saturday night.'

A frown knitted her brows together. 'I don't think that's wise, do you?'

'Look.' Yarran shoved a hand through his hair. 'You're back. And we're going to run into each other. Between our jobs and Ali, it's inevitable. So...let's clear some air, talk about what happened twelve years ago, get it out in the open. I think half the problem today was that we've never talked. And maybe if we did, we could finally put it and any residual feelings behind us and get on with our lives. Hell, maybe we can become friends, Harper. We used to be friends...'

For about three seconds anyway. Before their attraction took over.

She nodded slowly. 'It would make things easier with Ali if we were friends.'

'Okay. Good. What's your number? I'll text you the details.'

Yarran tapped in the number as she reeled it off then she scooped up her keys and, without looking back, headed for the door. He wondered, as he watched her go, if seeing her walk away ever got easier?

CHAPTER THREE

'Nervous?'

Harper nodded as butterflies fluttered in her belly. 'A little,' she acknowledged as she and Ivy walked to Ali's apartment near the hospital Friday night. Seeing Yarran had been hard but unexpected so there'd been no time to work herself into a tizz.

As she was now.

The prospect of facing Ali again was *nerve-racking*. They'd been close once—as close as it was possible for Harper to be to anyone, anyway—and she'd messed it all up and she knew Ali blamed her for breaking Yarran's heart. She knew because hot-headed Ali had told her in a confrontation the day before Harper's plane had left.

It had been awful and Harper had felt utterly heartless.

But it had been the right thing to do because she and Yarran had been together so long—too long. They'd been living on borrowed time. Eventually the relationship was bound to fail and Yarran would leave.

Like everyone else.

Harper knew Ali felt *acutely* every single sling and arrow her twin brother felt. She understood Yarran's pain was Ali's pain. That Yarran's heartbreak was just as visceral for his sister. She didn't blame Ali for being on Team Yarran. She didn't blame her for the ugly words. As someone who'd never really had a family, Harper knew better than any of their group how vital that was.

But it sure made her nervous tonight.

Especially with that hot kiss from Monday still playing over and over in her head. She didn't think Ali would still hate her for her desertion—they were all older and wiser and a lot of water had flowed under the bridge—but it didn't take a genius to figure out Ali would be super protective of Yarran. She wouldn't welcome any rekindling of their relationship. And she certainly wouldn't be happy about them seeing each other tomorrow night, no matter how pragmatic the reason.

And she sure as hell would not be happy about their make-out session at Yarran's.

'She won't bite, you know.'

'I know. But she has every right to be angry.'

'What?' Ivy squeaked indignantly as she rolled her eyes at Harper. 'It was *twelve* years ago, Harper. Yarran got past it. He married and had a kid, for crying out loud. *He's* fine. Well… I mean…apart from the whole widower thing but you know what I mean. And if *he* is, she should be, too!'

Harper shrugged. 'It's the twin thing, I guess. She was bound to feel his every emotion it more acutely given how in tune they are.'

'Even so. Time to forgive, don't you think?'

'Maybe.'

Harper loved Ivy's loyalty and practicality. As a former army brat, Ivy was used to rubbing along with people and her sunny personality had helped her fit in wherever she went. But Harper was a kid of the system and understood family dynamics in a way people with families never had to explore.

She could certainly see Ali's side. Harper's guilt was still acute at times why wouldn't Ali's rage be just as intense?

'She might just need some time to get used to having me around again, Ivy. I know you want us all to go back to being besties but let's cut her some slack, okay?'

Ivy pursed her lips. 'I guess. I just want it to be like it was.'

Harper smiled and nodded. 'Of course.' But, unlike Ivy, she wasn't naïve enough to think that was possible. Harper had broken one of those unwritten rules—mess with a bestie's sibling at your own cost—and she knew it would take a while to win back Ali's trust.

Ivy paused outside a swish apartment block and Harper looked up. It was a groovy new low rise, lights shining from the apartments showcasing row upon row of balconies.

'C'mon.' She steered Harper in the direction of the doors. 'Let's get the hard part over and done with.'

Harper swallowed as her butterflies took flight.

The door opened abruptly to reveal a grinning Phoebe, her dark blonde hair as straight as always. Dr Phoebe Mason was Head of Neonatal Surgery and, like Ivy, was on the shorter, curvier side. 'Harper!' she exclaimed, practically vibrating with excitement.

'Phoebs!' she said as Phoebe yanked her close and hugged her.

Harper squeezed her eyes shut to stop the sudden spring of tears. She'd made a conscious decision to ease out of regular contact with Phoebe and Ivy over the years. They were all busy building careers that demanded insane hours so there hadn't been much time for more than a Happy Birthday/Merry Christmas message, anyway.

And setting the boundaries gave *her* the control.

'I missed you,' Phoebe whispered, emotion husking her voice. 'I'm so glad you're home.'

Home. The word had always felt foreign to Harper and yet being unconditionally accepted by these women had given her a sense of belonging her younger self had never imagined possible. She'd been a stranger, but they'd embraced her anyway—despite her inbuilt wariness—and held on tight.

Phoebe's hard hug went on and on and Harper, uncomfortable as ever with easy affection, laughed as she opened her eyes, about to protest being squeezed to death. Until her gaze met a dark brown one, eerily similar to Yarran's.

Alinta.

As fraternal twins Yarran and his sister didn't look particularly alike but their eyes? They were freakily identical.

The other woman's expression was cool and Harper's laughter faded as she and Ali shared a long, loaded look over Phoebe's shoulder. It had been a long time and yet it felt like no time at all as Harper stared at the woman who had dragged her into her circle at uni and then into her family home, involving her in the Edwardses' family life.

Introducing her to Yarran.

Ali had been thrilled at the developing relationship, encouraging it with outrageous enthusiasm and all the while hinting at her desire to be sisters one day.

Sisters. The magic word.

Harper had always longed for the unconditional love of a sibling. A real one, not another kid who just tolerated her presence in their house. And, in the end, she'd convinced herself that being with Yarran had been about that—finding a family—not *love.* And that wasn't fair to him. He'd deserved more than an ex-foster kid who didn't know *how* to be in a functioning, healthy relationship.

It had been one of the ways she'd justified walking away.

'Hi, Ali,' Harper murmured as she eased out of Phoebe's embrace.

Ali's nod was a little stiff but she managed a, 'Hi,' in return.

She wore a slim-fitting white vest top that practically glowed against her brown skin and showed off her toned arms. Like her mother, who had been an athletic champion in her day, Ali was long and lean, her brunette curls brushing the tops of her shoulders.

'It's nice to see you again,' Harper offered tentatively.

Harper didn't expect Ali to offer some kind of rote, polite reply—that wasn't Ali's way and she hadn't been seeking a compliment. It was just…the truth. It *was* nice to see her old friend again. Still, Harper was surprised to hear Ali say, 'Yeah. It's nice to see you, too.'

Their gazes held and while Harper saw an entire storm-tossed *ocean* of reserve in those freaky eyes, she also saw sincerity. The same kind of sincerity echoed in her voice.

And that would do for now.

'All righty, then,' Ivy said, grinning at both of them as she slid an arm around each one. 'Enough of the awkward stuff, I could murder a glass of wine.'

An hour later, Harper was feeling much more relaxed. They'd eaten amazing succulent Greek food, delivered from the local restaurant, out on the balcony then moved inside to sit on the floor around the coffee table eating freshly popped popcorn as they'd done when they'd been cramming for exams all those years ago. With no one on call, they'd even shared two bottles of red wine.

And they'd laughed. God, how they had *laughed*. So much and so hard as they'd caught up on years and years of stories

Harper hadn't heard. Then it was her turn to share her own funny anecdotes for some laughter.

Sure, Ali's reserve was still in place, but she didn't make it awkward. In fact, Harper doubted Phoebe and Ivy were even aware of it. It was just that, like most ex-foster kids, Harper was intrinsically attuned to tension, her Spidey senses constantly alert to any frisson.

Which was fine. As Harper had told Ivy earlier, it was going to take some time.

But, she realised, sitting here with these women who had once meant so much to her, she *did* want to get the gang back together. Barring any unforeseen eventualities, Harper planned on being back in Sydney indefinitely and she'd missed female friendships, preferring to stay on the peripheries when she was in the UK.

But if she was truly coming home to finally put down some roots then that involved more than bricks and mortar and a regular pay cheque. It involved relationships. With *people*. And these three women were the best ones she knew.

She had to be *all in*.

'Any updates on Emma Wilson's condition, Phoebs?' Ali asked, switching the conversation back to present day.

As Head of Neonatal Surgery, Phoebe was part of the multidisciplinary team consulting on the case. 'She's generally stable but quite oedematous and overloaded as all that fluid from her resus makes its way back into her system, which is putting a lot of extra work on her heart and lungs. The ICU team are having a tricky time trying to manage it all as well as juggle her sedation needs for her ventilation without potentially harming the babies.'

Ali nodded. 'Are they doing okay?'

'Surprisingly, yes. We're closely monitoring them and all

seems to be in order but the fact is, while Emma is reasonably stable, she's still in a critical condition, so any number of things could suddenly happen necessitating the delivery of the twins and they're just far too little to be born right now.'

'How's her husband coping?' Ivy asked.

'He's trying to hold it all together,' Phoebe said. 'But it's hard, obviously. He's so focused on getting Emma through this and making sure we know *her* life is paramount, I think he's kind of disassociated from the babies. Which then makes him feel guilty because he knows Emma would want the opposite. He's seeing the ICU psychologist, but I think he feels stuck between a rock and a hard place.'

'God...' Harper was used to seeing difficult medical decisions play out in the ER so she knew how wrenching it could be for those grappling with them. 'The poor guy.'

Phoebe nodded. 'Yeah.'

'It must be hard for you, too, Phoebes,' Harper mused. 'Being the one having to prioritise the babies. Has that caused any issues?'

'Not issues, just trying to balance a lot of competing priorities. Like several calls a day from Lucas Matthews reminding me about the need for speed in the grafting process.'

Harper squinted as she thought back to Monday, trying to place the name. 'Lucas Matthews... He's Head of Reconstructive Surgery, right?'

'Yep,' Ivy confirmed, a flat edge to her voice and a curl to her lip. 'Couldn't have got a more perfect speciality for that pretty boy.'

Three sets of eyes flicked to Ivy, regarding her for a beat. 'What?' she demanded, scowling at each of them in equal measure.

Phoebe glanced at Ali then at Harper before looking back at Ivy. 'You have a problem with Lucas?'

'You mean apart from the fact he's arrogant and cocky, walking around the hospital in his Gucci suits with the most entitled swagger to ever swag?'

Phoebe did another glance around the circle. Ali lifted an eyebrow at Phoebe and pressed her lips together to suppress a smile. Phoebe followed suit. Harper's lips also twitched. It appeared Ivy might be protesting just a little too much.

'Well… I mean, he is very good-looking,' Ali murmured.

Ivy snorted. 'He *thinks* he's good-looking.'

Harper propped her chin on her hand. 'Yeah, I mean because hot, tall, super-competent guys in bespoke suits who probably drive a sports car and have that sexy greying-at-the-temples thing going on are generally considered unattractive.'

Phoebe and Ali both laughed out loud and Ali winked at Harper, causing her to catch her breath. It was such an inclusive gesture in this moment and warmth suffused her chest. She was home and although things hadn't got off to a great start with Yarran, she took heart that rekindling her friendship with these women had.

Even Ali.

Phoebe pressed her lips together once more. 'Ivy, do you have a little crush?'

'What?' Ivy bugged her eyes at them. 'On that egotistical…? No way. I've learned my lesson with flashy, smooth-talking men.'

Ivy had filled Harper in on how badly burned she'd been by her cheating ex, Grant.

'Maybe,' Ali mused. 'But I think you're protesting a bit too much and you know the best way to get over one man, right?'

Phoebe's eyes sparkled as she waggled her eyebrows. 'Get under another one.'

'Ew.' Ivy's nose wrinkled. 'I'd rather perform an appendicectomy on myself without a general anaesthetic.'

More laughter as Ivy's cheeks grew pinker. 'Oh, honey,' Phoebe said, 'he's about as far from *ew* as possible. I mean, you don't like him? Sure. But, objectively, he is a very fine specimen of manhood.'

'You like him so much, *you* get under him.'

Casually, Phoebe plucked a kernel of popcorn out of the bowl and brought it to her mouth. 'Maybe I will,' she half whispered as she pushed the popcorn past her lips, watching Ivy as the other woman's mouth tightened.

Phoebe's grin grew at Ivy's obvious discombobulation. 'Ivy and Lucas sitting in a tree,' she sing-songed. 'K-I-S-S-I-N-G.'

Rolling her eyes, Ivy threw a piece of popcorn at Phoebe's forehead, which bounced right off. 'Oh, shut up,' she said, resigned to the teasing as they all dissolved into laughter.

'And what about you and love, Harper?' Phoebe asked.

Harper glanced at Ali as the question sat between them with the potential of an unexploded bomb. 'It's okay,' Ali assured her with a shrug. 'I assumed you'd moved on too.'

Ali couldn't have chosen her words better. The underlying message was that *Yarran* had moved on. That no matter how hurt he'd been he *had* moved on. And whether it was a deliberate message or not—Harper heard it loud and clear.

'So?' Ivy asked. *'Is* there anyone special waiting for you back in the UK?'

Harper shook her head. 'There's no one. I've been concentrating on my career.'

Ivy frowned. 'No one recently?'

Harper's gaze met Ali's. 'No one at all.'

'For *twelve* years?' Phoebe bugged her eyes. 'Are you telling me you haven't seen anyone in *twelve* years?'

Harper's eyes cut to Phoebe and she gave a half-laugh at her horrified expression. 'I've had a few brief, mutually beneficial, mutually pleasurable encounters. That's it.'

'Oh, thank God,' Ivy said, pressing a hand to her chest. 'You can't let that stuff build up. I don't believe in blocked chakras but hell…everyone needs to blow off a bit of steam.'

Harper had never been comfortable indulging in sexual gossip and she squirmed a little, very conscious of Ali sitting across the table. 'I hope you're taking your own advice, Ivy,' she deflected with a smile. 'I hear there's this guy who drives a sports car and wears Gucci who knows how to unblock a chakra or two.'

'Hmph.' Ivy went from relieved to irritated in a second, her brow wrinkling. 'I'm not letting *him* anywhere near my chakras.'

Ali, Phoebe and Harper laughed at the endearingly cranky expression on Ivy's face and the stubborn little set to her chin. Ivy picked up more popcorn and threw a kernel at each forehead, causing more laughter. And it was amidst all this friendly frivolity that Harper came to a decision. When the laughter started to die, she dropped her gaze to the popcorn and reached for a handful.

'I ran into Yarran.'

The words cut through any residual laughter like a lightsabre through a sponge cake. She hadn't been going to mention it, but it felt as if she and Ali were starting to build a rapport again and Harper knew that brother and sister talked all the time. If Yarran mentioned it and Harper didn't? It felt…deceptive.

As though she had something to hide.

And yes, okay, there was no need to reveal all the intimate

details of their encounter, but not saying anything felt dishonest and Harper didn't want to start off on the wrong foot.

Phoebe and Ivy exchanged a look as Ali asked, 'When?'

'On Monday. At the hospital. With Emma.'

'Ah…' Ali nodded slowly. 'He didn't mention.'

Harper swallowed, dismay smothering her optimism as she watched the retreat in Ali's eyes as irrevocable as the outgoing tide. But the damage was done now so she might as well get it all out there. The PG bits, anyway. 'And later on, too.'

'Hey.' Ivy raised an eyebrow. 'You never mentioned you saw him twice?'

Ali's gaze cut to Ivy. 'You knew?'

Ivy opened her mouth to say something but Harper didn't give her a chance. 'We were leaving the hospital at the same time. He didn't have his car so I gave him a lift home.'

Ali blinked. 'I see.'

Nobody said anything for long silent moments. Harper could tell the other two women were dying to know the details but she also knew they wouldn't ask. Not right now.

'He's good now, Harper.'

Hot prickles stabbed at Harper's nape and she swallowed. 'I know.'

'He's *really* good now.'

'Nothing…' Harper let the word *happened* slip away unsaid. Now she'd decided to fess up there was no point compounding it with a lie. 'There's nothing between us.'

Which *wasn't* a lie. Sexual tension was inconvenient but it wasn't *feelings*.

'He wasn't for a long time,' Ali continued as if Harper hadn't spoken. 'And then there was Marnie and…' She drew in a shaky breath. 'He's been through a lot but he's finally *good*.'

Harper would have to have been deaf *not* to hear the message. Which was fine by her—she had no plans to rekindle their relationship. 'I *know*.'

Ali regarded her for long moments before giving a nod. 'Okay.'

'Okay.'

Ivy and Phoebe traded another look as the silence built again. 'Okay,' Ivy said, breaking the silence with a smile and a chirpy, 'Who wants coffee?'

Harper broke eye contact. 'Yes, please. I'll help.'

The tension eased as Harper stood and followed Ivy into the kitchen on very wobbly legs. Despite the loaded moments as she and Ali had faced each other across the coffee table, Harper was glad she'd spoken up. She wanted to re-enter this friendship circle, and this new part of her life, the way she meant to go on—openly and honestly.

Which would be a new concept given she'd never been fully open and honest with these women. Sure, her friends knew she'd had a rough childhood, that she'd been in the foster system, but she'd never gone into details. She knew that it was almost impossible for people who had grown up in *normal*—safe, functional, loving—families to truly understand the damage caused by the anxiety of impermanence.

But going forward, she'd like to be more open about the challenges of her upbringing.

So, that was the plan—a new kind of honesty. She just wasn't going to start with her and Yarran's passionate clinch. Because it had just been some weird slip of chemistry and nostalgia that had been bound to happen.

But *would not* happen again.

Sitting at the Opera Bar, with the iconic white sails of the Sydney Opera House rising majestically before him and the lit-up façade of the Harbour Bridge behind, Yarran checked his watch for the third time. Harper was fifteen minutes late.

Now there was something he *hadn't* missed.

Being involved with a doctor meant a lot of running late for dates—not that this was a date—and sometimes even last-minute cancellations. Because something had come up at the hospital or her pager had gone off a few minutes before she was due to finish or a resus case had just come through the doors.

And he was fine with all that. He got it. He was an emergency worker too. You couldn't put down a hose or stop in the middle of CPR because your shift had officially ended. It was just that, tonight, her lateness was giving him a lot of time to think.

Too much time to think.

About that kiss. About how much he *shouldn't* be thinking about that kiss. About the attraction sizzling between them more electric than ever. About how twelve years could pass and yet his pulse still skittered when he saw her that first time as if they'd never been apart.

He'd convinced himself it had been like muscle memory for him. He'd once loved Harper deeply and their chemistry had been insane. You couldn't just switch that kind of thing off—it needed to burn out. And it had still been blazing when she'd run away, so their heated making out had been inevitable in a lot of ways.

But that was *done* now. Out of the system. And after their talk tonight, hopefully a few other demons would be put to rest so they could get on with being friends. Something they perhaps should have stayed all those years ago—for everyone's sake.

'Oh, God, Yarran... I'm so sorry.'

Yarran dragged his gaze off the city skyline and the reflection of the lights on the black surface of the harbour to find Harper hurrying towards him looking harried, her loose red hair flying around her head. A sheer, silky wrap slipped down her arms as the satiny skirt of her shamrock-green dress streamed behind her, the fabric outlining the shape of her thighs.

He half stood but she waved him down as she pulled out her chair and sat opposite.

'Traffic has got so much worse, hasn't it? The Uber driver got me as close as he could.'

'Yeah, a lot has changed in twelve years.'

Maybe if he said it out loud, he'd remember because, looking at her all fresh and lovely and so damn close he could reach out and touch, nothing felt *done* about them.

'This hasn't though,' she said as she took a moment to look around. *'Wow.'* She shook her head. 'It's a pretty spectacular sight.'

It *was* spectacular, sitting here at a waterside table on the lower concourse of Bennelong Point, the harbour lapping below the solid fluted cement railings. It was still warm out for a May evening and people were taking full advantage of the weather while it lasted.

Light glimmered all around them from the neon of the skyline to the warm glow of streetlights on the upper concourse, to the way the Opera House was lit both inside and out. White lights on the sails emphasised their curves and made them appear almost luminescent while the internal yellow glow shone out through the glass curtain walls.

Everything sparkled and he was glad he'd thought to book here just to see the lights shimmering in her clear lip gloss.

'It is,' he said. And so was she.

A waiter approached and asked Harper if she wanted a

drink. She cast a quick eye at Yarran's frosty beer glass before ordering. 'A Prosecco, please.'

'You want something to eat?' Yarran asked as the waiter departed. He handed over a menu, which she declined.

'No, thanks. I'm fine for now.'

She folded her arms on the table in front of her and looked around her again, checking out the people this time. 'Gosh, it's busy,' she murmured.

Yarran nodded, non-committal, too busy looking at her to pay heed to anyone else. He couldn't drag his eyes off her. Off the way her hair brushed her shoulders, the way the fabric of her dress sat against the slope of her breasts.

The shine of that lip gloss.

And he couldn't think of a single thing to say because all he could think about was the kiss. *He couldn't stop thinking about the kiss.* He was supposed to be here clearing the air and yet he couldn't get the smell or the taste of her out of his head. He couldn't *not* remember the way she had shifted in his arms, the way she'd moaned.

He hadn't looked at or thought about another woman since Marnie's death and here he was—sitting opposite his first love, with every brain cell he owned on the fritz.

But then she looked at him and said, 'Who's looking after Jarrah tonight?' and it was like a defib to the electrical dysfunction storming his body.

Jarrah. His son, his heart, his life. His reason to get up in the morning.

Finding and losing love twice had been a painful way for Yarran to learn he couldn't count on romantic love. But the love for his child? *That* was everything. And he thanked the universe Harper had given him something else to think about.

'He's at Mum and Dad's.'

'And did you…' she hesitated '…tell your mum where you were going or who you were meeting?'

'No.'

'She didn't ask?'

Yarran chuckled. 'Are you kidding? Mum was so pleased I was actually going out somewhere socially she didn't dare question it in case I changed my mind.'

Harper laughed. 'Not much of a carouser these days?'

'Ah…no.'

He had been for sure, back in the day. *Before she'd walked out of his life.* But he wasn't going to point that out. Not when her voice was light and her hazel eyes were sparkling. He didn't want to spoil the moment.

'I guess having a four-year-old is not conducive to carousing?'

'No.' He laughed. 'Definitely not.'

'Tell me about him,' she requested. 'Jarrah. If you don't mind?'

Yarran regarded her, ignoring the warmth in his belly. She was curious—it was only natural. And it was what people did, when you had kids—they asked after them. It was polite conversation. 'I don't mind.'

'Do you have pictures?'

'Duh.' He rolled his eyes as he pulled out his phone.

For the next half an hour he talked about his son—a topic on which Yarran could chat for *hours*. He talked about how he'd been a colicky baby and how he'd walked early and the trials and tribulations of getting him to eat vegetables when he'd happily survive on bananas and fairy bread. He talked about how he suddenly needed a night light because he was going through an afraid-of-the-dark phase and how he loved mucking around in the garden with Yarran and adored flowers and how he called his aunt Alinta *Li-Li*, and how he was looking forward to his fourth birthday party in a few weeks.

Four years old. God...where had that time gone?

He didn't mention Marnie. Or that Jarrah had no memory of his mother. Or that for months after the car accident, Yarran had *let* Jarrah eat nothing but bananas and fairy bread because at least it was calories and just surviving the day had been hard enough without throwing in a tantrum or two.

Whether that was because it felt strange mentioning one woman he'd loved to the woman he'd loved *first*, or whether he just didn't want to go down that emotional rabbit hole on a night they were supposed to be talking about *them*, he wasn't sure. And maybe she sensed that because she didn't ask either.

She shook her head as she gazed down at a picture of Jarrah raking a garden bed with his grandfather. 'Man...he looks like your dad.'

Yarran laughed. 'Yep.' It was odd because he and Ali, despite their non-identical appearance, both looked more like their mother, and like their mother's aunties and uncles, who still lived on Gundungurra and Darug country near the Blue Mountains just outside Sydney.

'How are they?' she asked, handing back his phone. 'Your parents? All those siblings of yours?'

'They're great.'

Yarran smiled, conscious, as always, of that note of envy in her voice. Harper had adored his big, loud, messy family but he'd known, without her having to say it, they were a double-edged sword. The Edwards mob made Harper acutely aware of her *lack* of family.

'Mum's now an indigenous liaison for Olympic athletes and Dad's resisting retiring from the ambulance service but he does some lecturing for the intensive care paramedic course at the uni a couple of days a week, so he has taken a step back from active service.'

Yarran was pretty sure they'd have to push Coen Edwards out on one of those flashy stretchers.

'Kirra, Lucca and Marli all have kids. In fact, Marli is pregnant with number three. There're ten cousins altogether and I'm their favourite uncle.'

Harper laughed as she reached for her Prosecco. 'You were always king of the kids.'

Something thunked hard deep inside Yarran's chest. It was true—kids had always gravitated towards him. It was the firetruck thing mostly, but he'd always been up for pushing a swing or a piggyback ride.

He wanted to ask her about children but she'd been adamantly opposed to having any during their time together. And, knowing a bit about her background, Yarran had never really pushed. Nor was he going to, tonight. She was forty years old; he figured if she was going to change her mind, she probably would have by now.

The rosemary fries and second beer he ordered arrived and they paused their conversation momentarily. Yarran watched Harper as she turned her head to take in the harbour view, a light breeze ruffling her hair, those familiar flyaway wisps at her temples as fascinating as always.

The waiter departed and Yarran pushed the bowl of chips into the middle of the table. 'Tell me about your time in the UK,' he said as he took one.

'What?' She grinned. '*All* of it?'

Yarran's breath stilled in his lungs. When she smiled like that, so candid and unguarded, it lit up her whole face and he'd loved this side of Harper. It had taken him so long to work through her defences, to be trusted enough. But breaking through had been utterly rewarding—despite her frequent relapses.

Being with Harper had sometimes felt as if he were constantly reinventing the wheel but she'd been worth it. And that was what people did for those they loved.

It was what he did, anyway.

'Fine,' he said, recovering his senses and his breath. 'Give me the CliffsNotes.'

By the time she'd given him the rundown, they'd laughed a lot more and they'd been at the bar for an hour. Two drinks each had been consumed and Harper was relaxed and happy and maybe it wasn't the best time but the question he'd been swallowing down came to the fore and he couldn't stop it any longer.

'Why'd you come back, Harper?'

Slowly her smiled faded, her gaze holding his for what felt like an eternity. She tucked her hair over an ear, exposing one of her gold hoop earrings, which had been playing peek-a-boo all night. Her fingers absently toyed with the hoop as she parted her lips to speak.

Nothing came out as she continued to maintain their eye-lock and Yarran's ribcage rocked with the hard thud of his heart as he waited. For one crazy beat he thought she was going to say *because of you*. I came back *because of you*. But then she closed her mouth and her gaze shifted over his shoulder and he castigated himself for such fanciful thinking.

As if he were in a position—or stupid enough—to risk love again with Harper.

Her eyes flicked back to his face and Yarran knew, whatever she'd been going to say—that moment had passed. 'I was... headhunted. And...' she shrugged '...the job was great, just what I was looking for—the next step in my career. The perfect step, actually.'

He nodded slowly. Harper's career focus had always been laser-like. And he'd loved that about her. She'd grown up with *nothing*, and yet she'd made it into med school and she'd been determined not to squander the opportunity. 'It's a prestigious role. Ali said there were several high-level candidates.'

'There were. I'm very fortunate.'

'No.' If there was one thing he knew about Harper Jones, it was how hard she worked. And she was a brilliant doctor. They didn't give out prestigious head of department jobs to people who weren't the top in their field. '*You're* good.'

She shrugged and said, 'That too,' then laughed.

Yarran joined her. He'd always found her unshakable confidence in her medical skill a turn-on. It had been such a stark contrast to her ingrained insecurities. So when it flashed out like this, like a beacon from a lighthouse, it hit him with a hot jab to his groin.

'And you,' she said, a smile still hovering on her mouth. 'Ivy tells me you're a captain now. You must be close to making chief. That's what you wanted, right?'

'Mmm.' Yarran leaned forward, propping his elbow on the table and his chin on his palm. 'Not any more. Or at least not now, anyway. It's a lot of extra work and while Jarrah's so young... I mean, Mum and Dad are great, but they have a life too and... I don't know. I guess my priorities changed after...'

His words drifted away and she just nodded, clearly not requiring him to clarify. 'And besides,' he said with a smile, shaking himself out of the drag of old memories, 'who wants to be chained to a desk when I can be facing down a roaring fire?'

A half-laugh slipped between her parted lips as she shook her head. 'As long as I live, I will never get the attraction to something so dangerous and, well...*hot*.'

Yarran grinned. 'We're a special breed.'

She laughed again. 'You are.'

The waiter approached and asked if they'd like another drink and Harper shook her head. 'No, thank you.' She glanced at him. 'I should go. I told Ivy I'd only be a couple hours.'

'Of course.' Given the easy mood between them and the low buzz of attraction fizzing thorough his veins, it was probably wise to quit while they were ahead. They hadn't really talked about their issues, but they had proven they could be in each other's company and not argue or jump each other.

'Can I give you a lift?'

For a moment she looked startled at his offer before she shook her head. 'Oh, no, you're in the opposite direction, it's fine.' Grabbing her bag, she hauled out her phone. 'I'll just order an Uber.'

Yarran's eyes roved over her profile, the warm hue from the candle picking out gold highlights in her hair. 'I have my car, Harper. And it'll give us the chance to talk a bit more. Please, let me return the favour.'

She glanced up from her phone, indecision writ large across her features as she caught her bottom lip between her teeth. Maybe she was trying to duck the conversation they'd avoided so succinctly or maybe she was remembering what had happened last time they'd shared a car. He gave a self-deprecating smile. 'I won't come up.'

Harper gave a rueful smile in return. 'Okay.' She put her phone in the bag and pulled her gauzy wrap up over her shoulders. 'Thanks.'

CHAPTER FOUR

WITHIN FIFTEEN MINUTES of leaving the restaurant, Yarran was pulling out into traffic. They hadn't talked very much on the short walk to the car park. There'd been so much going on around them with the city sights and the throngs of people out enjoying the delights of Darling Harbour, conversation hadn't been necessary. But, as he drove and she sat quietly in the passenger seat looking out of the window, the silence grew more and more loaded.

Yarran was trying to parse which words to use to break it, when Harper got in first.

'I didn't just come back for the job,' Harper said, her eyes still trained on the view outside her window. 'I've missed waking up to kookaburras in the morning and Christmases on the beach and looking up and seeing the southern cross. Seeing stars full stop.' She shook her head slowly as she stared outward. 'Not a lot of stars in London.'

'No.' Yarran had been to London twice. Once for a high-school trip when he was fifteen. The other with Marnie for the first wedding anniversary. It had been weird knowing Harper was in the same city.

'I missed my friends,' she continued. 'I missed...'

His throat grew thick as he pulled up at a red light, his fingers tightening around the wheel. Was she going to say she'd missed *him*?

Did he want her to?

'I missed home. I didn't know—with all the crap in my childhood—that I was capable of that. Which made it easy and almost…freeing when I left here but…despite everything, I realise I did.' She rolled her head along the backrest until she was facing him. 'You know?'

'Uh-huh.'

He did know. The blood of his indigenous ancestors, his mother's stories, the presence of mob in his life, had imbued him with a keen connection to country and that ancient pull of home had always grounded him. But for someone who'd only known dislocation, who had felt rootless all her life? He supposed that *would* make leaving easy.

'Twelve years is a long time to be away from home,' he murmured.

She gave a small smile. 'Yeah.' Then turned back to the view.

The light turned green and Yarran accelerated away, wondering if maybe their past was better left in the past. Tonight had proven they could be around each other and get on in polite company—maybe that was enough.

'I'm sorry about the way it ended.'

Yarran's fingers tightened around the steering wheel. 'It's fine, don't worry about it.'

'No, it's not.' She half turned in her seat to face him. 'It's why we're here, tonight, isn't it? So let's talk about it.'

He flicked a glance at her before returning his attention to the road. Her brow was furrowed and her mouth was set in a stubborn little line he knew too well, the green of her dress in the darkened confines of the cab turned up the glitter in her hazel eyes. At the start of the night, *this* had been his agenda but, surprisingly now, he was willing to let it go.

What would be the point in dissecting everything from over a decade ago? Would hearing her say she'd missed him, that she'd come back for him, make a difference? When they were ancient history? When they were nothing more—could be nothing more—than two missed connections.

'My life was going so well and…that never worked out for me in the past. Something was always around the corner, ready to take it all away. So… I learned to mistrust that feeling and to try and get out ahead of whatever was around the corner.'

Yarran had always suspected this about her, he just wished she could have spoken to him about it when they were together. Wished he'd prodded more. 'Did you think I'd stop loving you?'

'Like everybody else in my life?' She turned back to the window but not before he saw the shimmer of tears. 'Yes.'

'I wouldn't have.' He knew that as sure as he knew up was up and down was down.

'Life taught me to never get comfortable staying in one place too long and I'd well and truly pushed the boundaries with you because I loved you and I wanted normal so bad, but normal never lasted very long for me and people around us were talking marriage and kids and I started to feel…hemmed in. It made me nervous and…itchy. Like ants marching under my skin. And the job was there and it seemed like a lifeline but… I didn't know you were going to propose that night, Yarran.'

'I know.'

'And when you did, all I could see was *disaster*, a slow-moving car crash from which I might never recover. So, I panicked.'

'Yeah.'

She looked over at him. 'I truly never meant to hurt you, but I know I did and I am really, really sorry.'

Yarran nodded. She hadn't apologised that night. Hell, she hadn't even apologised when she'd visited before she left in her attempt to *set things right*. She'd been brash and confrontational, talking about it being *her* life, and how *she* got to decide what she did with it. Obviously, she hadn't ever had anyone apologise unequivocally to her in her life and just hadn't known *how*.

But she clearly needed to now and do it properly so she'd obviously come a long way during her years overseas. 'Thank you,' he said, smiling at her as he decelerated to turn into the street where Ivy's apartment was situated.

He was surprised at how much hearing her finally say the *s* word had actually helped and wondered, as he navigated the right turn, if saying it had also helped her. Wondered, too—not for the first time—if maybe she would benefit from another kind of help. Like talking to a professional about her childhood traumas.

Yarran had skirted the issue when they'd been together, but Harper had always clammed up at the merest suggestion and, well...basically he'd been too much of a coward to persist. He'd been too scared, or maybe just too selfish, to jeopardise what they had.

Maybe that was forgivable in his early twenties but at forty? With the benefit of hindsight and carrying the weight of his own trauma on his shoulders?

'Do you think it might be possible to be friends?' she asked. 'I'm loving being back with Ivy and Phoebe and Ali but...your sister is obviously wary and I'm not blaming her,' she hastened to add. 'She's pissed at me for hurting you and I get that. But maybe if you and I were friends she'd see that if *we're* happy to move on from the past then maybe she could, too? I know it's a lot to ask and maybe you need some more time to—'

'No,' Yarran interrupted. 'I don't. I would very much like to be your friend, Harper Jones.' It'd have to be easier than this strange kind of limbo they were in now.

But maybe he should start as he meant to go on? That was what *friends* were for, right?

Pulling into the loading zone in front of Ivy's apartment, he switched the engine off and turned in his seat slightly to face her. The street outside was deserted and not well lit, the dashboard glow the only light inside the car.

'Please don't take this the wrong way,' he said, his voice low but resonant in the fat bubble of silence between them. 'But… have you ever thought about seeing a therapist?'

She didn't say anything for a long time, her gaze drifting to the windscreen. Twenty-year-old Yarran would have backpedalled about now but silences weren't as scary at forty.

'Just…you know.' He smiled at her profile. 'One friend to another.'

She laughed then, her gaze cutting back to him. 'Yes.' She sighed. 'Then I usually do something to distract myself until the thought goes away.'

Yarran grinned. 'Very mature.'

She arched an eyebrow. 'Right?'

They grinned at each other but it was brief as they both sobered. 'Honestly, Harper, isn't it exhausting carrying around all your stuff? Feeling *hemmed in*, feeling like something's always just around the corner waiting to turn your life upside down?'

'Yeah.' She nodded slowly. 'Very.'

His words weren't said with any kind of pity, but her response sounded so forlorn something broke a little inside Yarran and he desperately wanted to pull her in for a hug. Instead he said, 'I saw a therapist for a while. After...' He swallowed. It wasn't easy to talk to Harper about Marnie. 'After my wife died. It helped.'

'I know.' Her glance returned to the windscreen. 'I do know and it's on my to-do list.' She gave a half-laugh. 'See shrink is right after rekindle old friendships, move into new apartment and become the best damn director of ER to have ever existed.'

She glanced back at him and smiled, which Yarran returned. He knew she was joking, maybe seeking some levity in a heavy moment, but he sincerely hoped she did follow through. He didn't know half the stuff she'd been through, and he had no medical training, but he knew enough about grief and loss to know sometimes it was just too heavy to deal with alone.

'Thank you,' she said, her voice soft as she slid her hand onto his forearm and gave it a squeeze. 'I'm glad we did this.'

There was nothing sexual about the touch. It was impersonal. One of those gestures between *friends* but while Yarran's head was on board with the *friend* thing, his body was clearly not. He was so conscious of her in this moment—aware of her nearness, of their aloneness, of the dark enclosed confines—every hair on his body prickled with awareness.

He could smell her perfume—something fresh and zesty—and wondered if she still dabbed it behind her knees. His pulse surged in his belly and through his groin, his breath suddenly hot as lava in his lungs.

Yarran cleared his throat. 'Me too.' And he *was*. Or he would be. Once she was out of his car and the temptation had passed.

She smiled and leaned in, her hand still on his forearm, for what he assumed was a friendly peck and he shut his eyes as her lips touched down on a point midway between his cheekbone and his mouth. It was nothing more than a brush of her lips but it might as well have been a full-on pash as sensation rushed *everywhere*.

Hell, he could barely breathe for the calamity of it.

And that was when he became aware she wasn't shifting away. Her lips had stayed well past what could be considered chaste and had moved to lingering. It was certainly no peck. In fact, he was damn sure it had turned into a *nuzzle* as her fingers curled into the flesh of his forearm and a warm sigh brushed his skin.

'Harper,' he whispered, angling his head a little to facilitate her nuzzling even as the backbeat in his brain was blaring, *Friends, friends, friends.*

But then a small, almost *feral* kind of noise slipped from the back of her throat blaring *want* and *lust* and *need*, spiking Yarran's pulse and clutching at his groin, and whatever tenuous hold he had over his libido snapped clean in two.

'God… *Harper*…' He turned his face, to nuzzle her. Her cheek, her temple, her ear. His senses filled with the aroma of her shampoo and something far…earthier. Her eyes were fever bright as his hands cupped her face. 'Why can't I stop wanting you?' he whispered as he took her mouth with his.

Her answer, if there was one, was lost to a rush of heat obliterating sense and noise and freaking *time*. Yarran was aware of nothing outside the press of their lips, the hammer of his heart, the harsh suck of his breath competing with the harsh suck of hers. Not until her hand moved, anyway, sliding up his chest, her fingers hooking into the fabric of his shirt as she leaned fully into the kiss.

He leaned in too, the centre console the only thing stopping them from full upper-body contact, but that didn't stop his hand from travelling down her arm and onto her hip because he *had* to touch her—he *needed* to touch her. She tasted of Prosecco and smelled like a shot of Limoncello, and Yarran wanted to gulp her down more than he wanted his next breath as his fingers dug in, urging her closer. His tongue tangled with hers and she whimpered in a way so *unholy* it was like a punch of hot lead to his groin.

Christ, he *wanted* her. Right here, right now. In his car. In the front of her apartment.

A sudden bang from outside eviscerated that thought as Harper tore away from him, sucking in air, blinking dazedly, as if she hadn't quite been in her body.

He knew how she felt.

It took Yarran several seconds to compute the scene before him. One guy thumping on the bonnet of the car like a drum, two of his friends laughing and hollering behind as they pointed at the car. None of them appeared to be able to stand very steadily.

'*Oi!* You two,' drummer boy said. 'Get a room!' He gave one last thump and they all weaved away, laughing too loud, clearly thinking themselves hilarious.

Yarran glanced at Harper, who was looking at him with equal discombobulation. Silence filled the space between them as Yarran tried to pull something coherent together in his muddled brain. To make sense of what had just happened— the act, not the interruption.

Because it sure as hell didn't make any sense to him. The first time maybe, at his house, he could understand. But this time? How had they gone from 'let's be friends' to necking like teenagers in a matter of minutes?

'Harper... I—'

'No.' She shook her head. 'It's okay.' She patted his chest

absently before withdrawing her hand. 'We'll get better at the friends thing.'

He huffed out a husky laugh. 'Really?'

She stared at him, her gaze brushing over his mouth and for a moment Yarran thought she might actually come back in for more, but then she gave her head a shake. 'I've got to go.'

'Okay.'

'We *will* get better,' she said before opening her door and slipping away.

Yarran sincerely hoped so. They could hardly get worse.

'Okay, ready?' Harper asked the three nurses standing around the stretcher bed where an unwell, grizzly toddler—Remi—was looking up at them, eyes bright with fever and round with terror. His tearful mother was up near the head of the bed, stroking his hair and dropping tiny kisses on his forehead as she whispered soothing words. She'd been up for three nights in a row with her sick child and was exhausted both physically and emotionally.

It wasn't often the head of the department was called on to put in an IV, but children were often tricky to cannulate—dehydrated ones even more so. Two attempts had already been made by more junior doctors leading to an overwrought child and an even more stressed mama. But Remi needed fluids so the big boss—who'd been on her way out of the door—had been put on the job.

Harper had done a year at Great Ormond Street in London, during which time she'd inserted hundreds of cannulas into children in varying places—hands, arms, feet and even scalps. And she knew she could get this one into a vein in Remi's foot, as long as he was still.

Sure, the area had been numbed and Remi wouldn't feel the

needle going in but it was psychological now. The child was already deeply mistrustful of them, breathing choppily as he looked at the faces above him, clearly contemplating leaping up and running away.

Hence the *muscle*.

'Okay, little dude.' She smiled at Remi, whose chin started to wobble as she tightened the tourniquet sitting just above his ankle. 'Mummy's going to count to twenty and then we'll be done, okay?'

She crossed her fingers behind her back, hoping like hell it was so. She didn't, necessarily, have a problem stretching the truth a little if it helped allay a child's—and their parent's—fear. But it suddenly struck her that Remi was the same age as Jarrah and somehow it just seemed more...personal.

He started to cry as soon as the nurses took their positions. The one closest to Harper—Darren, an Englishman who'd been in Australia for ten years—held the foot around the ankle and at the toes, angling it to best expose the vein. The second leaned in over Remi's knees and legs while the third did the same for his torso. They weren't lying across him as of yet but they were primed to do so should Remi start to buck and squirm.

With the area already cleaned, Harper picked up the cannula off the trolley by her side and lined it up where it looked like the best insertion point a few millimetres from the skin. 'Okay, Mummy, let's do it.'

The mother started to count haltingly, her voice thick with emotion, which was Remi's cue to cry then wriggle. The nurses at his legs and torso used their weight to gently restrict his movement and Darren held the ankle a little firmer as the needle tip touched down.

'Good boy, Remi,' Darren said in his booming Geordie accent. 'You're doing well, mate. As soon as we're done here, I'm going to make you a glove animal.'

Far from placated, Remi cried louder—more from the restraint, Harper suspected, than the prick—and wriggled harder in their grasp. Thankfully he was sufficiently confined for Harper to do her job. Blocking out the frantic little boy's cries and the choked sobs of his mother, Harper was able, after minimal manoeuvring, to slide the cannula into the vein.

'Done,' she announced triumphantly, raising her voice to be heard over the crying as she unclipped the tourniquet. 'Just gotta tape it now and it's all over.'

One-handed, she grabbed the short extension tubing already primed with a saline syringe attached, then she removed the inner needle to leave the plastic cannula straw in situ. A bleb of blood swelled at the cannula hub but didn't spill due to the pressure she was applying over the cannula tip on the outside. Quickly, she twisted the extension tube in place and flushed the line.

The saline flowed in smoothly and she nodded with satisfaction. Bridie, the nurse across Remi's torso, eased off to help Harper tape the cannula in place and within two minutes they had it secured, the foot had been boarded and wrapped in a bandage and Remi was sitting cuddled up in his mother's arms.

A rush of something utterly foreign flushed through Harper's chest at the sight. She'd never known the mother-child bond but, watching Remi and his mum, she was struck by how much it resonated.

What the hell?

Confused, she turned to Darren, who was currently blowing air into a glove as if it were a balloon, puffing up the fingers like udders.

'I'll write up some fluid orders,' she said, and then she fled the cubicle.

* * *

In fact, after she'd written the orders, she fled all the way to the rooftop garden. Her shift was over—although she was on call tonight—and she was waiting to hear from Ivy about whether she wanted a lift home. And up here was as good as any place to wait—quiet and peaceful, the gardens beautiful, the view amazing and the evening lovely. The sky was a palate of pinks and mauves with the evening star now shining bright.

She could breathe up here. She could think. It was Wednesday and she hadn't had time to think much about Saturday night. The ER had been exceptionally busy, which had given her no time to mull over the *friendship* between her and Yarran.

Not coherently, anyway. With all that analytical thinking she supposedly possessed.

The night-time thinking didn't count. It wasn't analytical. It was hot and hazy and restless, those kisses playing on repeat as she tried to wrangle her body from arousal to practicality. They'd agreed to be friends so fantasising about his kisses was pointless. And now a mother and child making her feel restless but in a different way—what was that about?

Coming home, it seemed, was rousing a whole bunch of feelings both familiar and foreign and, although she didn't regret it, she hadn't expected to feel so whammed. It had been *twelve* years and yet, when Yarran had asked her on Saturday night why she'd come back, for one crazy moment she almost said *because of you.*

Which was madness.

Yarran hadn't entered the equation at all. She'd known she'd be in his sphere, of course, but she'd figured they'd moved on and were both adults. Yet it had been right there, on the tip of her tongue. She'd almost said it.

Because of you. For no earthly reason…

The door opened and Harper glanced over her shoulder to see Aaron Wilson stepping into the garden. Their eyes met and she saw the moment he recognised who she was. 'Hey,' he said as he ambled in her direction, crossing to where she stood at the railing.

'Hey,' she replied politely.

'You're the doctor, from the ER, right?'

'Yeah.' Harper smiled sympathetically. He was a good-looking guy—she was sure the TV cameras ate him up—his indigenous heritage affording him the noble bone structure and poise of his ancestors. And yet, right now he looked a worrying combination of haggard and wired. As if he was surviving on very little sleep and a lot of bad hospital coffee.

'Harper,' she said and held out her hand.

They shook then Aaron leaned his elbows on the railing and stared out over the city lights, a slow steady breath leaving his lungs, as if he'd been holding it in for a while.

'You hiding from them?' she asked, tipping her chin at the reporters down below still hanging around the entrance. Their number had decreased over the last week but there were still a few die-hards hanging on.

He stared down at them and muttered, 'Bloody vultures.'

Neither of them said anything for long silent moments before Harper broke the peace. 'How are they going? Emma and the babies?'

'Stable, they say. But…' He didn't turn from the view, just stared straight ahead.

Harper nodded. She knew *stable* still looked pretty dire to the lay person. 'Yeah.'

'Plastics wants to start Emma's grafting so they're just trying to work out the best approach for her and the twins.'

'There's a lot to consider.' It *wasn't* a straightforward burns case after all.

'Too much. When I think of everything that's ahead of us...'

'It's a lot,' Harper agreed. 'Just gotta take it one day at a time.'

'So they keep saying.' He gave a harsh humourless laugh.

'Please know you couldn't have a better team looking after them. Lucas and Ivy and Alinta and Phoebe—they're the best.'

He nodded. 'Yeah, I do know, I'm very happy with what they're doing for Emma and the babies, it's just...' He stared out at the light again. 'You know, you're going along and you think life is good, and you have it all, and then *bam*! It can just be gone in a flash. And you realise none of it means anything if the people you love are hurting or in trouble.'

Harper had always felt pretty much alone but she knew what it felt like to be blindsided by the unexpected. She'd spent a lifetime in flight mode trying to keep one step ahead of the unexpected, after all. 'Yeah, things like that make you reassess your priorities.'

Her phone rang and she pulled it out of her scrub pocket. 'Sorry, I have to take this.'

He nodded. 'Of course.'

'I'll see you around.'

'Yeah.'

Harper answered as she crossed the roof to the door. 'Hey, Ivy.'

'Sorry, I just got a ward call to a hot appendix. I'm taking it straight to Theatre. I'll see you in a couple of hours.'

'No worries.' That was the doctor life, after all.

Ivy hung up as Harper opened the door and stepped inside. Forgoing the lift, she crossed to the fire escape and took the stairs. Her phone vibrated in her hand and she almost stumbled at the name on the screen. A text from Yarran.

I have something of yours. Ring me when you're free.

If he only knew he had more of her than was good for her sanity. But she smiled at the screen and before she could second-guess herself, she tapped on the message and called him as she made her way down the fire escape.

'That was quick.'

His voice was warm as honey in her ear and she almost stumbled again. She gave up trying to multitask and stopped, leaning her butt against the cold wall of the stairwell.

'Phone was in my hand.' Harper stared at her shoes. 'You have something of mine?'

'I do. It's green and silky.'

Harper could hear the amusement in his voice and her belly clenched as she thought back to Saturday night. The wrap. She must have left it in his car. 'Oh, I didn't even know it was missing.' She *had* been kind of bamboozled when she'd exited his car.

'I think it must have slipped off your arms when...'

Her breath caught as his voice trailed off. *When they'd been necking like teenagers?* And sprung like teenagers, too.

'Anyway,' he continued, 'I was looking for a toy car of Jarrah's under the seat when I came across it. It must have slid down between the seat and the centre console.'

Very probably. Considering how her hands had been all over him. Harper cleared her throat. 'Okay, thanks. Where is it now?'

'It's still in the car. I can drop it in to the hospital or to Ivy's? Or did you want to come and pick it up?'

No. God, *no*. The last thing she needed was for Ali to see him dropping off her wrap. Or for Ivy to be home when he called. And going to his place? Yeah, not after last time. She was all for getting their friendship on track but it was probably best in the company of others.

Maybe they could meet out somewhere? With lots of people. Then go their separate ways. She pulled her bottom lip between her teeth. 'Where are you now?'

'I'm at work. Second of three nights.'

'Excellent.' Perfect, actually. Dropping by the firehouse would be public and, given he was at work, she wouldn't be able to linger. 'Can I drop by now and pick it up?'

'Works for me.'

'All right. See you soon.'

Harper pulled up outside Yarran's fire house forty minutes later after driving through a KFC window and grabbing two buckets of fried chicken and a dozen boxes of chips. She knew, both from her prior association with Yarran and through her work in the ER, how hard firefighters worked, the risks they took with their lives.

And how much they liked to eat.

She wasn't a baker or a Michelin-starred chef but she did have a credit card and she wasn't afraid to use it to show her appreciation for these guys and what they did. Plus, as a fellow shift worker she knew how much the night shift sucked.

Also, she was starving. One serving of chips had already made its way into her stomach.

Hiding the bag of food behind her back, Harper rang the night bell at the front door. The engine-bay doors were all shut but light shone through the narrow windows situated above the doors and through the windows of the adjoining building, which was where the bell was located and where, she assumed, the fire crews did their thing when not on truck.

Harper was surprised when a blond Adonis in his mid-twenties answered and not Yarran. 'Hey…' he said, laying a *How you doin'?* smile on her as he leaned into the door frame.

'Oh. Hi… I'm looking for Yarran Edwards?'

He clutched his chest in a dramatic fashion and grinned. 'That old guy? Could I interest you in someone a little younger? Better moves. More stamina?'

Harper laughed at the flirting—it was impossible not to. 'It's nothing like that,' she assured him. 'We're just friends. I'm just here to pick up something. And also, I bought this.'

She produced the bag of fast food, which had the desired effect. 'Where can I get a friend like you?' He grabbed the bag. 'Brock,' he said, holding out his hand.

She shook. 'Harper.'

Brock gestured her in with a flurry of his hand. 'Entray vooze.'

She laughed at his butchery of the French language as she stepped into a foyer area with several offices and a staircase rising in front of her. 'He's up there talking on the phone to the big boss. C'mon, I'll show you.'

Harper followed him up the stairs, which was no hardship—Brock had a fine-looking butt. 'Heads up,' he announced, raising his voice a little, as he climbed. 'We got female company so everyone put their clothes on.' Brock reached the top and turned left. 'Also.' He lifted the bag in the air. 'We got chicken.'

There was whooping and hollering as Harper reached the top and also turned left to find a large open room with a huge-screen TV on one wall and a fully kitted-out kitchen on the opposite one with a long dining table off to one side. Several couches were scattered around and, in the middle, six guys sat around a coffee table playing cards.

Far from undressed, they were all in their fire-issue cargo pants and navy T-shirts. Okay, they weren't all as cockily good-looking or young as Brock—there was a range of ages and sizes—but they were all big and solid and there was just something about a blue-collar guy that did it for Harper.

'This is Harper,' Brock introduced. 'She's here for Yarran.'

Six sets of eyes cut to her. The laughter and camaraderie falling silent. An older guy with a solid gut and bushy beard streaked with silver regarded her speculatively. 'Really?' It wasn't hostile but she was left in no doubt they were forming ranks around their captain.

She supposed, as Yarran's colleagues, they knew his history. And a woman turning up out of the blue *would* make them wary. 'Oh, no.' She shook her head. 'We're just friends.'

Trying to be anyway.

And maybe she should practise saying it out loud because it didn't sound very convincing even to her own ears.

'Well,' silver beard said, nodding slightly, 'any woman who brings chicken is welcome here.'

'Amen,' a redhead guy said as he snatched the bag out of Brock's hands and headed for the table and everyone seemed to relax. 'Grub's up,' he announced as he pulled the food out of the bag and plonked it in the middle of the table.

'You want to join us?' the redhead asked, glancing at her.

She was saved from answering by a door opening behind her. 'Oh, hey,' Yarran said as she turned. 'Sorry, I was on the phone.'

Harper was hyper aware they had an audience who were watching the interplay between her and Yarran but she was *more* aware of Yarran and the way her body lurched. Seeing him in uniform had always turned her on and apparently nothing had changed.

It seemed the universe just wasn't going to cut her a break.

'It's fine,' she dismissed.

'I see you met the guys,' he murmured, tipping his chin in their direction.

'She came bearing chicken,' Brock said, brandishing a leg.

Yarran looked at her then, cocking an eyebrow. 'You are such a suck-up, Jones.'

It surprised a laugh out of her. She'd forgotten he used to call her that, back in the day. She turned back to the table where the food was currently being devoured. 'Gotta support my fellow shift workers, right, guys?'

'Solidarity, sister,' agreed a guy with a beanie on his head.

'Hey, Harper,' Brock said, licking his fingers. 'You any good at trivia?'

She shoved her hands on her hips. 'Played on the winning hospital trivia team five years in a row.'

'Hospital?' Bearded guy looked at her scrubs. 'Nurse?'

She shook her head. 'Doctor.'

Everyone appeared suitably impressed and the bearded guy said, 'You're in, then. Sunday arvo.'

'I am?'

'We're one short for trivia at the Slippery Eel.'

'Ignore Riggs,' Yarran said, with a glare at the other man. 'He doesn't know how to ask because he sucks at talking to women.'

'I heard he was still a virgin,' Brock quipped.

There were hoots of laughter as Riggs, who sported a gold wedding band, said, 'Bite me,' and bit into some chicken.

'It's fine.' Harper shook her head. 'It'll be fun. I'd love to.'

Why not? Before leaving London, she'd played regularly at

the pub over the road from the hospital. Plus, that was what friends did—accepted invitations. They'd be in company and it could be a good way to establish their friendship—for them *and* for others.

So everybody could see they'd moved on and were perfectly fine spending time together and absolutely did not want to jump each other any more.

Riggs and Brock high-fived. 'We're going to kick *ass*.'

Yarran sighed and shook his head as he looked at her. 'You don't have to.'

'All good. I love trivia.'

'Okay, great…thanks.'

His smile seemed a little fixed though and Harper wasn't sure *he* wanted her there. 'So…' she prompted. 'My wrap?'

'It's in the car, out the back. C'mon—' He gestured to the stairs. 'I'll show you.'

Harper nodded. 'Thanks.'

'Leave me some chicken, you douche bags,' he threw over his shoulder.

'We're making no promises,' Brock said.

Harper waved at the guys. 'Bye. Nice meeting you all.'

'See you Sunday,' Riggs said.

CHAPTER FIVE

THEY HEADED DOWN the stairs as the ruckus of smack talk resumed. When she got to the bottom he directed her around behind the stairs to where the door to the engine bay was located, opening it for her.

It was a voluminous space, dominated by three bright red engines gleaming under the downlights as if they'd just rolled off the factory lot. The chrome dazzled and the deep red of the body looked lush and glossy as cherries. It had been a long time since she'd been in a fire house, but the strong stench of petrol, grease, smoke and *nostalgia* was almost overwhelming.

Yarran pointed left. 'Back door down there.'

Harper spotted it but she didn't move. 'Which is your engine?' she asked. She knew firefighters rode on all vehicles but they were usually assigned to one engine.

He tipped his chin at the nearest. 'Number 352.'

Nodding slowly, Harper wandered over, conscious he was watching her intently. Absently, she stroked the duco of the front driver door. It looked as if it had been spit-polished, it gleamed so damn hard, and her hand glided with ease across the surface.

Yarran had explained to her once a shiny engine was a source of pride for a firefighter. Just like the shiny buttons and polished shoes of the formal uniform worn on ceremonial occasions. Firefighters needed to be in tip-top shape and so did their equipment—truck included. A dirty engine didn't inspire public confidence.

'Shiny as ever,' she said, more to herself than Yarran.

'Yes, ma'am.'

She turned to face him, her shoulder blades sliding against the duco. He was standing against the wall, his arms folded, one knee bent, the foot placed flat against the wall behind. It was a thoroughly casual yet utterly masculine pose. Emphasising the breadth of his chest, the meatiness of his quad.

He looked every inch the fireman.

'You still love it?'

He smiled and dimples softened the angles. 'What's not to love about spending your work hours with that bunch of clowns?' He tipped his head to indicate the guys upstairs. 'What about you? You still love being a doctor?'

'I do.'

'You're good. That day with Emma…it was your first day and it looked like you'd been in charge there for years.'

'Thank you.'

She took his compliment and yet, standing here in front of him, Harper couldn't deny the hollow kind of feeling that had taken up residence in her chest seeing him with his team. She felt…envious, she realised. Envious of the easy relationship Yarran had with his colleagues. Sure, she was well respected at the Central and people deferred to her, but it wasn't the kind of camaraderie that developed when you spent every shift at the coal face with your colleagues.

People didn't divulge anything to the boss.

Which was why she really wanted to make it work with her old friends. And maybe saying yes to trivia was part of that?

'About trivia…' Maybe she'd been wrong about that hesitancy she'd seen but she'd rather talk about it now than let it go—they'd done too much of that in the past. 'I don't have to come if you don't want me to. I just thought it might feel less… weird between us if we started seeing each other socially, you know, in a group sort of setting. Maybe the quickest way for us to become friends is to start acting like it?'

'It's fine.' He shook his head. 'It's a good idea.'

'You seemed hesitant…'

'No, I just… You were put on the spot. I wasn't sure if you were being polite.'

'I wasn't,' she assured him.

He didn't say anything for a beat. 'I do want you to come.'

There was an intensity in his voice and his gaze that caused a tiny little skip in Harper's pulse and emphasised the brooding masculinity of his foot-against-the-wall stance.

'Okay, good, well…that's settled.' She pushed away from the truck. 'I better let you get back to the guys.'

Dropping his foot to the ground, Yarran headed for the back door. Ever the gentleman, he opened it for her, pushing down on the bar, the loud clunk echoing around the engine bay. Harper was careful not to brush against him as she exited the building, which was no easy feat when the aroma of Acqua di Gio stirred heady memories.

Spying his car, Harper crossed the parking space. They didn't say anything, their footfalls on the gravel the only sound in the whole car park although the more distant sound of traffic could also be heard.

Removing his keys from his pocket, Yarran activated the door unlock and they thunked open as the parking lights flashed twice. Harper reached the car, leaning her butt against the back door as he opened the front passenger door. Leaning inside, he opened and shut the glove box before straightening and turning to face her.

'I don't think it got too crumpled,' he said as he passed it over.

Harper took it, one end of the narrow silky sheath escaping to trail on the ground. 'It's fine,' she dismissed as she hauled in the errant tail, winding the fabric around her hand. 'Thank you for finding it. I don't really wear that dress often so it probably would have been ages before I realised it was missing.'

'You should wear it more often. You looked amazing.'

She glanced up to find his gaze fixed on her and she was glad for the solid weight of the car behind her. They were close, she realised. A bolt of heat struck her deep and low as another waft of his cologne made her a little dizzy and just like that, she was back in his car Saturday night, the air in her lungs hot and heavy.

'A well-designed dress can make anyone look amazing,' she dismissed.

He chuckled and it was all low and warm. 'You never could take a compliment.'

Harper opened her mouth to object but shut it again. It was true, there was no point in denying it. Praise had been in short supply where she'd grown up and she'd learned to regard it with mistrust. It had taken some time getting used to Yarran's easy compliments.

His eyes roved over her hair and she wished she could look away but their dark interest was as compelling now as always and she wished it were falling around her shoulders, soft and shiny like his fire engine, instead of hanging limply in some end-of-shift bedraggled ponytail nightmare.

'Green always suited you.' Yarran's gaze returned to hers.

Yarran had said that many a time. And standing here in this car park it was as if all the years between them evaporated and they were the way they'd always been after a night out together, revelling in the low buzz between them, the tug in her belly as strong as ever.

'God, Harper...'

He shook his head slowly and she was too afraid to press him for more or ask what he meant because she knew.

'One of these days I'm going to see you and not want to kiss you,' he muttered, his gaze dropping to her mouth. 'But this is not one of those days.'

He took a step in and Harper's breath hitched, her pulse a living, breathing thud inside her head. Wanting it. Not wanting it. Knowing they *couldn't* keep doing this. Knowing they had to ignore this insane chemistry if they were ever going to be friends.

She shut her eyes as his hands slid either side of her face, trying to block out the temptation of his face, of his mouth.

'You looked so damn good against my truck,' he muttered, the warmth of his breath caressing her face. But he didn't kiss her, he just pressed his forehead to hers, their noses brushing, their lips close. Oh, so close.

The raggedness of his breath mixed with the raggedness of hers.

'Yarran,' she whispered, her hand sliding over top of his, sensing he was hanging on by the same thread she was. 'We can't.'

It took a beat but he heaved in a deep, shuddery sigh. 'Yeah,' he said, his voice like gravel as his hands slid away and he took two steps back. 'C'mon.' He shoved his hands in his pockets. 'I'll walk you out.'

Harper followed him on very wobbly legs, wondering how many near misses would it take before the dam broke and the *can'ts* became *why-nots?*

Harper hurried into the busy beer garden of the Slippery Eel on Sunday afternoon. She hated running late but traffic had been a nightmare with everyone, it seemed, heading for the popular beachside suburb of Manly to enjoy the last of the warm weather before winter really made itself known.

Of course, she'd also changed three times...

Scanning the bench tables, at the end of one she spotted Riggs, who waved her over. Because half of the table was hidden behind a central bar area, she couldn't see the other end, but as she made her way through and around the crowded area more of the table came into view and she recognised quite a few of the guys from the station on Wednesday night.

It wasn't until she was almost at Riggs's side she could see all ten occupants, including Yarran, who was sitting at the opposite end.

With Jarrah on his lap.

She'd seen the pictures of him, of course, and even if Harper hadn't known either of them from a bar of soap, she'd still know they were father and son. Jarrah was a mini-me version of his father. Gorgeous brown skin, dark curls, dark eyes and, as he smiled at something his father said, two wicked dimples.

A rush of something she couldn't identify flooded her chest as Yarran looked up and their gazes locked. Knowing, logically, Yarran was a father was one thing—seeing it in action was entirely another. It looked *good* on him.

'Glad you're here,' Riggs said. 'It's starting in fifteen.'

Harper turned her attention to Riggs but was excruciatingly conscious of Yarran's gaze on her profile. 'There's table service and a menu down there.' Riggs tipped his chin towards the other end of the table. 'We saved you a seat.'

'Down here, Harper.' Brock gestured, sliding down the bench seat a little to make room for her at the end. Which put her immediately to Yarran's right.

Yarran smiled at her tentatively as she made her way down. It seemed half welcoming, half apologetic and maybe because she was already feeling a little blindsided at the unexpected tumble of her emotions, it made her kind of angry.

He didn't have to apologise for bringing his kid to a social outing, for crying out loud.

Plastering on a smile, she said, 'Hey,' to Brock then turned to Yarran. 'Hey.'

'Hi,' he said, causing Jarrah to look up from his colouring to regard her with those eerily familiar brown eyes. So like his father's. So like his aunty! He smiled then and, *holy crap*, those dimples.

'And you must be Jarrah,' she said.

He looked puzzled in that comically inquisitive way only small children could pull off. 'How you know my name?'

'Because I'm a friend of your daddy's.'

It felt awkward saying it. *It felt like a lie.* But right there in front of her was the reason why they had to stay friends. Yarran had a son. He'd moved on, and he had other responsibilities. A child to think about. To put first. 'That's right,' Yarran agreed. 'This is my…friend. Harper. She's Aunty Li-Li's friend as well.'

His eyes went large, as if knowing Ali were magic. 'You know Aunty Li-Li?'

'Yes, I've known her for a long time. We're old friends.' She crossed her fingers under the table.

'Did you know my mummy?'

Yarran's swiftly indrawn breath covered for Harper's surprise. But she recovered quicker as Yarran gaped at his son. 'No, I didn't. But Aunty Li-Li tells me she was *great*. And I know she loved you and your daddy very much.'

In truth, Harper didn't know any of those things. But she knew *Yarran*. And, on another level, she knew how it felt to be motherless. She knew the ache of that absence and how she'd held onto her mother's whispered *I love yous* through all the back and forth of her childhood because they'd trumped *everything*.

Her terrible choices. Her poor coping. Her inability to manage at life.

As a child, knowing she was loved by her mother had been more important than the actual mothering. Every kid should *know* that.

Harper met Yarran's gaze and for a moment they just stared at each other. 'Thank you,' he mouthed over Jarrah's head.

She gave a small shrug. She might not be the most maternal woman on the planet but she wasn't a complete novice with kids either. The gaze held for a beat too long before she broke it to return her attention to Jarrah.

'Now, let me guess,' she said. 'You're…nine years old, right?'

He laughed. 'I not nine. I three.' He held up two fingers. 'Almost four.' He put up another finger.

'And do you want to be a fireman when you grow up, like your dad?'

'No.' He shook his head. 'I want to be a policewoman like my mummy.'

Harper nodded, ignoring Yarran's flinch. 'Fantastic. I bet she'd be super proud of you.' A quick glance at Yarran told Harper he wasn't quite ready to enter the conversation. 'Whatcha colouring in, there?'

'It's all the things I gonna has at my party,' Jarrah continued, switching out a yellow pencil for a blue pencil, not noticing his father's stillness.

'You're going to have a pony?'

His eyes widened again as he looked at Harper. In a *very loud* whisper, he said, 'We gonna have an entire *zoo*.'

'Wow.' Harper glanced at Yarran with a raised eyebrow.

'A petting zoo,' he confirmed, his voice thick.

'But you can't tell no one,' he said, his eyebrows beetling as he stared at Harper with seriousness. ''Cos it's a surprise.'

'Okay,' Harper agreed solemnly and mimed zipping her lips.

Jarrah giggled, his dimples flashing. 'And there's gonna be lots and lotsa nanas.'

'You like bananas?'

'Nanas are my favourite.'

'The lolly ones?' Yarran clarified and their gazes held for a beat at the significance.

'Really?' Harper dragged her eyes off Yarran. 'They're my favourite, too,' she said, trying to keep her voice even. Yarran had always kept her in a steady supply. She held her hand up for a high-five, which Jarrah dutifully offered. 'And are all your friends coming?'

'Uh-huh.' He nodded as he concentrated on colouring between the lines.

'I'm coming, aren't I, bud?' Brock said.

Harper had been so busy conversing with Jarrah and worrying about Yarran's discomfort, she'd forgotten Brock was even there. 'Unca Brock gonna dress as a fireman for the mummies.'

Yarran, who had been taking a sip of his drink, almost spat it out as Harper turned her head and raised an eyebrow at Brock. 'Oh, really?'

Completely unabashed, he shrugged. 'Why should the kids have all the fun?'

'Daddy?' Jarrah turned a little to look at his father. 'Can Harper come to the party?'

Yarran did his best not to look alarmed, but Harper knew

him well enough to see the signs. Frankly, she was feeling a little alarmed herself.

'Yeah, Daddy,' Brock added. 'Can Harper come?'

Harper vaguely noticed the narrowing of Yarran's eyes in Brock's direction but she was too busy scrambling for a way out of the invitation to kick Brock under the table.

'Oh, I don't think—'

Yarran started at the same time Harper said, 'I'm not sure...'

'Oh, *please*, Daddy, please!' Jarrah's gaze turned impassioned and his expression endearingly earnest as he gazed at Yarran. 'I gots friends and you gots friends so Aunty Li-Li should have a friend too.'

Harper would have laughed at the irony had she not been in the middle of a near panic attack. She was possibly the last person *Aunty Li-Li* would want to see at Yarran's house. And, on that, they agreed. It was one thing to be friends but another entirely to get involved in Yarran's family life again. To see his parents. His brother and sisters. People who had once upon a time been a big part of her life.

She was hoping that would come with time, not be thrust on her all at once.

'Aunty Li-Li will know everyone at the party.'

'But she wants to come, don't you, Harper?' Jarrah switched his attention to her.

Harper blinked. How did she say no to such sweet earnestness? It was as if the happiness of his entire life hinged on what Harper said next. 'Umm—'

'*Please?*' Harper swore the kid actually batted his eyelashes at her. Long, sooty eyelashes women the world over would kill for. 'I'll even share my nanas with you.'

'Jarrah,' Yarran said, warning in his voice, an apologetic expression on his face.

It would have been easy, she knew, to just say, *I'm working* and be done with it. But…she *couldn't*. She didn't want to see him crestfallen. As a kid who had been disappointed a lot in her life, she didn't want to dish that out to this kid.

To Yarran's kid.

She smiled at Jarrah. 'I would love to come to your party.'

'Yes!' Jarrah threw his hands up in the air triumphantly.

And then he did something completely unexpected. He threw himself at Harper. Given they were sitting at right angles and the corner of the table was in the way, it was mostly unsuccessful, but he did latch onto her arm and hug it tight, pressing his little cheek against her biceps.

She vaguely noticed that his hair smelled like apples and his skin like cookies and cream and there was something sticky on his hand before everything around Harper faded to black. The chatter from all around, the clink of glassware, their table companions—everything disappeared. It was just her and this little boy, hugging her arm as if she'd given him a year's supply of nanas.

And his father, looking on with an anguish that tore at her very soul.

Yarran's phone ringing thankfully dragged her back to the moment as he answered it with a gruff, 'Hi.' He nodded a couple of times. 'Yep…great…thanks…be right out.' Hanging up, he said, 'C'mon, mate, Granny's here to pick you up.'

Jarrah gave her one last squeeze before letting Harper go, his attention already shifted as he scooped up his paper and slid off his father's lap. 'Say goodbye,' Yarran said, collecting the pencils and shoving them in a small backpack.

'Byee-byee,' he sing-songed.

Everyone waved and Brock high-fived him then Yarran

ushered him out. Harper watched them go, wondering what the hell had just happened.

'Cute kid, huh?'

Harper blinked as she glanced at Brock. 'Very.'

Too. Damn. Cute.

Yarran took a minute to gather himself as he waved Jarrah and his mother off. What the hell had just happened? He'd figured Harper and Jarrah meeting today had been inevitable when his mum had messaged to say she was running late and, in truth, he had been nervous about it.

But he hadn't expected the wild churn in his gut seeing Harper with Jarrah. Joking and laughing and chatting with him as if she was an old hand with kids. Not talking at him as if he were a baby as so many people did, just treating him as if he had something interesting to offer.

For a woman who proclaimed she didn't want kids, she'd built a quick rapport.

Still, Jarrah had thrown her—and him—some curve balls which was…not cool. Mentioning Marnie a couple of times when he didn't really speak much about her at all. And then inviting Harper to his birthday party. What on earth had possessed him to invite someone he'd known for five minutes?

Clearly, almost-four-year-olds weren't known for their executive thinking, but Yarran had not been expecting *that*. Not least because he wasn't entirely sure how he felt about having Harper at the party.

But the most shocking thing today had been that hug. Just out of the blue. Jarrah was usually more guarded around people he didn't know well so it had been a surprise to say the least— for them both, if the look on her face was anything to go by.

More than that though, it had hit Yarran in a deeply personal place. Seeing Jarrah hugging Harper had made him acutely aware of the gaping hole in his life, in his *son's* life, and, probably most shocking of all, for the first time since Marnie's death, Yarran's mind hadn't automatically gone to the woman who'd left that hole.

It didn't go to Marnie. Because it had been full of Harper, of how good she looked holding his son, of how he could get used to it, of how she'd make a great mother.

And, *Christ*, he didn't even know what to do with that...

Striding inside five minutes later, he resumed his seat near Harper. She was wearing a strappy sundress in a swirly pattern of green and blue, her auburn hair all loose and he had to fight the urge to brush it aside and drop a kiss on her bare shoulder. As he once would have done without thinking twice.

Trivia had started but his gut was still all churned up and the need to apologise for what had transpired rode him hard. She'd barely acknowledged him arriving back at the table but she hadn't looked comfortable being put on the spot by a kid—*his* kid—so it was the right thing to do. She was participating in a whispered discussion over whatever question had been asked just prior to him entering the garden but it wouldn't take long.

'I'm sorry,' he murmured as he leaned towards her. 'About Jarrah putting you on the—'

Turning to face him abruptly, she scrunched her brow. 'What's a funambulist do?' she asked, cutting him off. 'I think it's a tightrope walker, but Riggs thinks it's someone who collects matchbooks.'

Her gaze locked with his and he got the message loud and clear. She did *not* want to talk about this now. Or maybe ever, given Harper's tendency towards avoidance.

'I'm not sure,' he said, trying to clear his head of the jumble of thoughts and emotions. 'But I don't think it's matchbooks.'

'It's gotta be the tightrope thing,' Brock whispered. 'Fun and ambulist—right?'

Riggs's eyebrows beetled together. 'It's too obvious.'

Harper, who had turned her attention back to the table, shook her head a little. 'I can't be certain, but my gut tells me I'm right.'

'Hmph.' Riggs regarded her with his unflinching stare. 'How often is it right?'

She stared right back, also unflinching. 'Almost always.'

He pursed his lips for a second. 'Okay, then.' He wrote the answer down. 'Just so you know, you get this one wrong, you won't be asked back.'

Yarran could tell Riggs was just yanking her chain but only because he'd known the man for over a decade. 'Ignore him,' he said, addressing Harper as he bugged his eyes at the guy down the other end of the table. 'Riggs takes this a little too seriously.'

'Like I said,' Brock said, whispering conspiratorially, 'Riggs is a virgin.'

Which cracked everybody up, but Harper just shook her head. 'No, no. I like it. I get it.' She nodded at Riggs. 'I *respect* it.'

'Oh, God,' Brock said, looking from Harper to Riggs then back to Harper again, feigning horror. 'There are two of them.'

More laughter ensued but the next question was asked and the team dug in for the remainder and it was *so* nice watching Harper laughing and smack-talking with his friends. It was nice seeing her unguarded and then miffed when the team—the Fireman Sams—was just pipped at the post.

'Jesus, you two.' Brock shook his head at Riggs and Harper,

who were triple-checking their score against the other teams on the score board. 'We're not playing for sheep stations.'

'We were robbed,' Harper muttered.

'Yep.' Riggs nodded. 'We'll get them next time.'

She cocked an eyebrow and Yarran watched the small smile tugging at her mouth wishing he were on the receiving end. 'So I passed muster, huh?'

He pointed the pencil at her. 'You're one of us, now.'

'That's right,' Brock agreed. 'You can check out but you can never leave.'

She laughed and Yarran's heart went *thunk*. Harper was really something when she let down her defences. Something she hadn't done often, except with him. And he knew that had scared her the most about them.

A large box of fun-sized chocolates was delivered to the table as their second prize and they all feasted on their reward. Harper grabbed a purple-wrapped chocolate and stood. 'My round, who's up for another drink?'

Several light beers were ordered. 'Not me,' Riggs said, also standing. 'Gotta get back. See you next week?'

Harper nodded. 'I'll be here.'

Brock offered to help her carry the drinks and they both departed. Riggs made his way down to Yarran and sat in the seats Harper and Brock had just vacated. The muscles in Yarran's neck shortened as the other man regarded him for long silent moments.

'That one,' he said finally, pointing to Harper, who was standing at the bar, laughing at Brock.

Yarran's jaw tightened. 'It's not like that.'

'Uh-huh.' It dripped with disbelief.

'We're just friends. We go a long way back.'

Riggs grunted. 'Has she got a partner?'

'No.'

'So?'

'It's too soon.'

'It's been three years, man.'

Yarran shook his head. 'I've got Jarrah. He keeps me busy enough.'

Riggs snorted. 'Yeah… I don't think you're going to have a problem with the little fella. He seemed quite taken.'

Yarran wished he could deny it, but Riggs was right—his son had taken to Harper. And she, it seemed, had taken to him. But… 'She never wanted a kid.'

'Yeah, but having your own is different from mothering one already in existence.'

Yarran didn't know. He was forty years old and she'd been back in his life for two weeks and everything was upside down. 'She's a *friend*, Andy.'

'Hmm.' Riggs obviously knew from the use of his Christian name that he'd pushed enough for one day. 'Okay.' He rose again, placing his hand on Yarran's shoulder as he passed by. 'Just so you know, you lose me this trivia partner and I'm going to leave your sorry butt stuck halfway up a ladder one day and you won't know where or when it's going to happen.'

Yarran laughed at the comically empty threat. 'Noted.'

CHAPTER SIX

HALF AN HOUR LATER, Harper had finished her lime and soda. Apart from some awkwardness there at the beginning with Jarrah, it had been a thoroughly enjoyable afternoon and it was still only just after three. The sun was shining and she had the urge to go to the beach. She hadn't been since her return and she knew within a matter of weeks it'd be too cold and she'd be completely disinclined to go.

And Manly Beach was only a five-minute walk from here. 'I'm going to go and dip my toes in the ocean,' she announced. 'Who's in?'

'Yeah, I'll go,' Yarran said.

She nodded at him, unperturbed by his eagerness. They were supposed to be old friends, after all, and there were eight others at the table. Except no one else, it appeared, wanted to go, declining one after the other. And it would be hard to back-track in front of everybody because why wouldn't she want to go to the beach with her *old friend*?

So, as everybody departed for their vehicles, she and Yarran walked out of the back gate of the beer garden. She could have changed her mind after everyone had left, begged off with some forgotten chore, but she supposed they should talk about the whole party invite thing.

Plus, now the urge had struck, she really *did* want to wriggle her toes in the sand.

They didn't talk much as they made their way to the esplanade navigating around family groups and other clumps of people on the main street. In his white T-shirt, floral boardies and flip-flops, Yarran looked casually sexy and way more appropriately dressed for the beach than she was, but Harper was liking the sun on her shoulders.

An ice-cream truck was parked on the grassy foreshore in the shade of a towering Norfolk pine, just one of the many dotting the sea frontage. Yarran brought two chocolate-dipped soft serves.

'Thanks,' Harper said as he passed hers over. She bit into it and sighed as the chocolate made a cracking noise and sweetness burst like rainbows across her taste buds.

They headed for the esplanade where one railing and a drop of several feet were the only things separating them from the sand. The beach wasn't as crowded as it would have been earlier and most people were concentrated in the area around the yellow and red flags.

The turquoise ocean was relatively calm, waves breaking close to the shore giving swimmers something to play in, while a line of surfers rode the swell out further. Two jet skis traversed the bay further out again, their jets of water spraying in an arc out the back. Laughter floated on the light breeze along with the cry of seagulls squabbling over old chips.

'Looks cold,' she mused as she pulled up at the railing and leaned on it.

'Nah.' He shook his head. 'This is perfect swimming weather.'

Harper glanced at him sideways just in time to see him take a swipe of his ice cream—a long slow lick with the flat of his tongue, which brought back a hell of a lot of very *non-*

friendly images. She glanced quickly away. 'You always did have the pelt of a seal.'

'You're just a cold frog, Jones.'

She opened her mouth to object to the name but licked her ice cream instead. Yes, it was a nickname, but it was a friendly one. It wasn't an endearment. Not something lovers called each other.

'If by that you mean I prefer not to turn blue when I get in the water, then guilty as charged.' She smiled at him sweetly. 'C'mon, I want to get some sand between my toes.'

Kicking her flats off, she carried them in one hand and the ice cream in the other. Yarran followed suit and they took the nearby concrete stairs down to the beach, heading in the opposite direction to the clump of beach-goers. The sand still held some of the warmth of the day beneath her feet as Harper licked at her ice cream.

'So…what does one get a four-year-old for a birthday present? I'm guessing a teddy bear is too young and a scientific calculator is a little too old?'

'I really am sorry about him springing it on you like that.'

'It seems like he sprung it on you as well.'

'Yeah.' He chuckled. 'He did.'

'I don't have to go if you really don't want me to. I just… didn't have it in me, to say no, not when he was pleading with those big brown eyes of his that look…'

She didn't finish the sentence but Harper felt his long, assessing glance almost as a physical caress and had no doubt he knew exactly what she'd been going to say. 'Yeah,' he said eventually, 'he uses them to good effect.' And then after a beat, 'I don't mind you coming to his party. The more the merrier.'

Harper was down to the cone now and she bit into it and

crunched while she gathered the courage to voice the next question. 'And your folks,' she asked. 'Will they mind?'

'Of course not.' He shook his head. 'They'd love to see you again.'

'So, they're not angry with me?' Strands of hair blew across her face and she shook her head to remove them. 'Like Ali?' Harper had adored Lyn and Coen, which had only made her decision to leave harder.

'My parents were disappointed. *For me.* No parent wants their child hurting.'

Harper tried not to flinch. Yarran was talking generally, she knew, but it spoke volumes about their vastly different childhood experiences. Her mother's actions had caused a lot of hurt in Harper's life—intentional or not. Harper truly believed if it had been within her mother's powers to stop her self-destructive behaviour then she would have.

But some people, as her great-aunt had said, weren't equipped to deal with life.

'They were just old enough and wise enough,' he continued, 'to know that sometimes in love you win and sometimes you lose and that's life. Ali is just…' His eyes strayed ahead as he bit into his cone. 'She feels what I feel, you know?'

'Yeah…' Harper pulled herself away from old, *old* memories. 'I know.' In truth, it had always freaked Harper out a little. Never having had a sibling, she found the synergy Yarran and his sister shared wholly unrelatable.

'They know you're back and Mum asked if it was okay by me if they invited you over in the next couple of months, so I'm pretty sure seeing you at the party will be a treat.'

'Oh.' A little flutter of relief flared to life in Harper's chest as she nibbled around the edges of her cone. She knew she'd burned bridges when she'd left—some almost irreparably—

but maybe some had only been a little singed. 'And is it okay by you?'

'Of course.' He smiled. 'We're friends, right?'

She nodded and smiled back, a little flutter of hope in her chest. 'Right.' If anyone had cause to despise her it was him. And yet, he didn't.

He finished the rest of his cone in two bites while Harper continued to savour hers in small nibbles as they walked with nothing but the sound of the waves between them.

'Thanks again for what you said to Jarrah. When he asked if you knew Marnie.'

Harper shrugged. 'Of course.'

'He doesn't mention her much any more so it kind of surprised me.'

'Is it hard?' she asked, feeding the last bit of the cone into her mouth before continuing. 'To hear him talking about her?'

'Not at all.' He shook his head. 'We all try and talk about her as much as possible. He has a photo of her by his bed and we have a couple more scattered throughout the house. I know he doesn't remember her so I want to be able to keep her alive any way I can. I just—' he sighed '—want him to know how much Marnie loved him.'

Harper slowed and turned to face him. His voice was clouded with doubt, as if he wasn't sure what the hell he was doing. But, from where she stood, he was putting his kid first and prioritising love and that was all Jarrah needed. 'You're a good father, Yarran.'

He stopped too, shoving a hand through hair made even more unruly by the wind, the fabric of his shorts blowing against the muscular definition of his quads. He gave a half-laugh. 'It doesn't feel like it a lot of days.'

'Oh, yeah?' She smiled to lighten the moment as she also brushed hair back from her face. 'What *does* it feel like?'

'Like I'm one of those rats running on a wheel while simultaneously trying to juggle a dozen pieces of cheese and having them constantly fall on my head.'

Harper laughed. 'You never were much of a multitasker.'

He laughed too. 'I can face a fiery inferno without thinking twice and then I walk through my door and Jarrah smiles at me like I'm his whole world and he depends on me for *everything* and—' He blew out a breath. 'I wasn't supposed to do this alone.'

'He just needs you to love him, Yarran. To put him first. Take it from someone who knows.'

Their gazes locked. He regarded her for a beat then gave a slow nod. 'Yeah.'

Harper broke eye contact at the sudden rash of goose bumps prickling at her arms. Absently, she rubbed her hand up and down her forearm to quell their march. 'Ugh.' She glanced at her hands. 'Sticky.'

Tossing her shoes on the sand, she headed for the ocean, aware Yarran was following her at a slower pace. She stopped as the water lapped at her feet and almost yelped at how cold it was. The weather might be going through an unseasonably warm patch but, as she had predicted, the ocean hadn't got the memo.

Gathering up the skirt of her cotton dress as she crouched, Harper dipped her hand in the incoming wash, shocked anew by the frigid sea water.

Yarran crouched beside her. 'See, I told you,' he said. 'Positively balmy.'

Harper had no idea what devil made her do what she did next. Maybe it had been the heaviness of their conversation.

Maybe it had been the remnant of that earlier lightness she desperately wanted back. 'Oh, really?' she said sweetly, then scooped up a handful of positively balmy ocean and splashed his face.

He shut his eyes on impact, his face frozen for a second before they blinked open, staring at her. *Yeah, not so balmy now, buddy.* But then his expression changed and a frisson of something that was both primal and sexual flared at the base of Harper's spine.

His dark eyes widened. 'I'm going to get you for that, Jones,' he growled.

Harper didn't know whether she should be amused or turned on, but she knew she should *run*. But not before she splashed him again. 'You gotta catch me first.'

He roared as he lurched after her and Harper squealed as she sprinted up the beach, away from the water, her hair and her skirt flying behind her.

'I'm going to dump you in the ocean when I catch you.'

'Oh, yeah?' she threw over her shoulder. 'Talk's cheap.' Harper knew she had no chance of outrunning him, particularly in the softer sand, but, *God*, it was fun trying.

It was…exhilarating and she felt *giddy*.

He was soon on her, as she knew he would be, and she dodged and weaved, laughing so hard she almost fell over, but within the next few seconds he'd snagged a handful of her hem to slow her, then reel her in.

'Gotcha,' he crowed.

She laughed and panted and twisted to try and get away— she wasn't going to make it easy for him—but eventually he had her, their bodies colliding. Their feet got tangled as she squirmed though and she started to topple, grabbing for him as she went. But all she succeeded in doing was bringing him down with her and they both landed in the sand in a tangle of limbs, laughing and out of breath.

It took probably longer than it should have for it to sink in that Yarran was half on top of her, although her body was intimately aware. One thick thigh was thrust between her legs, high and hard. His chest was half across hers, his forehead pressed to her cheekbone, his silky hair caressing her temple, his nose brushing the angle of her jaw, his lips dangerously close to that sensitive point just behind her ear.

Hot puffs of his breath fanned goose bumps down her neck as a low buzz in her pelvis made itself known and Harper's senses filled with the essence of Yarran and the freshness of Acqua Di Gio. It was heady and dizzying and Harper felt like her most primal self as she turned her head slightly to inhale.

'You still wear the same cologne,' she said, her pants more ragged than when she'd been running full tilt.

What she should have said was, *Get off me, you great big lump.* That would have been wise. It would have been sensible. But everything pulsed and hummed and buzzed and he felt so good like this, chest to chest, and she was almost out of her skin with wanting him.

She was far, *far* beyond wise and sensible.

He lifted his head, his eyes roving over her face as if he was cataloguing all the changes twelve years had wrought and liked what he saw. He was also distractingly out of breath.

'Why ruin a good thing?' he murmured huskily as he fingered a strand of her hair, lifting it to his face, rubbing it against his cheek before letting it fall.

His gaze drifted to her mouth then and Harper's belly squeezed and her lips parted involuntarily, and she was pretty sure she made some kind of noise at the back of her throat because his eyes widened and he muttered, 'God help me,' under his breath then lowered his head and kissed her.

And it felt like coming home.

His lips glided over hers, slowly at first, thoroughly, as if he was relearning the contours, then became more demanding as desire sparked like an inferno between them, raging under her skin, scorching her from the inside out. That resolve she'd had at the fire station the other night to resist this *burn* between them also going up in flames.

He groaned and it reverberated straight into her bones as his hand swept down her body, landing on her hip, pulling her closer, their bodies perfectly in line now. Their ragged breathing in sync. The pound of his heart pounding in time with hers. And it didn't matter that they were *very publicly* making out because all that mattered was this man, big and hard and so much a part of the fabric of her life, kissing her as if they'd never been apart.

The facts there was going to be sand in places that shouldn't have sand or anyone on the beach could walk by and see them weren't a concern either. Hell, they could have an entire audience *grading* their performance and Harper couldn't have cared less.

She just needed to be closer.

Draping her leg over his hip, she moaned as the hot, slick centre of her came into intimate contact with the hot, hard thrust of him.

Closer. She needed to get closer.

Sensing her need or perhaps just responding to his own, Yarran slid his hand to her ass, holding her tight, his erection pressing at just the right angle over sensitive flesh. Even with several layers of fabric between them it felt so damn good she moaned again, her fingers fisting in his shirt.

'Yarran,' she muttered against his mouth, her voice not much more than a rasp. 'I need…' She rocked against him, desperate to be *closer*. 'I need…'

'I know,' he panted, 'I know.'

He rocked then, too, and Harper realised he *did* know. He knew exactly what she needed because he needed it too.

Closer.

And God alone knew how much *closer* they might have got but for the sudden urgent wail of a siren slicing through their cocoon of intimacy.

They startled apart, Harper's ragged pants and the loud wash of her pulse through her ears almost obliterating the god-awful noise. 'What the hell is that?' she asked, looking around, confused as to why an old-fashioned air-raid siren was echoing around the beach.

Yarran fell back against the sand, a hand on his abdomen, his breathing as ragged as hers. 'Shark sighting.'

Even though her body was still in an absolute uproar, Harper somehow managed to glance over at the flagged area. Lifesavers in their iconic yellow and red ran into the shallows urging people in with loud speakers. Not that anyone needed it as everyone hurried for the safety of the beach.

'There's a shark?' she asked absently, a strange kind of disconnectedness descending.

One second, she was dry-humping Yarran in full public view and the next there was a…shark? Could there be *anything* more Australian?

'Maybe,' he muttered, his eyes firmly fixed on the sky overhead.

Harper also fell back against the sand, still too discombobulated by how they'd ended up making out *again* to be able to compute that there might be some large predator stalking swimmers. Had she been that way inclined, she might be tempted to believe there was some kind of divine intervention going on to keep them apart.

She wasn't but perhaps she'd do well to heed it, anyway. It seemed stupid to look a gift shark in the mouth.

'Saved by the shark,' Yarran muttered, still staring at the sky.

The urge to laugh hysterically pressed against her vocal cords but she quelled it. 'I think it's a sign.' One that reinforced what they'd already agreed on—staying *friends*.

He sighed. 'Yep.'

'I should go.' It was a statement that didn't come out with a whole lot of conviction because there was a stubborn part of Harper that didn't want to move a single inch.

'Think I'm just going to…lie here for a bit.'

'Okay.' Rousing herself, she sat, putting her skirt to rights and dusting the sand off the backs of her arms and out of her hair. Then she pushed to her feet, walking to where they'd discarded their shoes and scooping them all up.

He hadn't moved when she returned to his position and tossed his shoes down. Given the vastness of the beach surrounding them, she'd have expected Yarran to look dwarfed but his presence was as virile as ever, lying there, his eyes hot on hers. How was it even possible for him to look just as potent horizontal looking *up* at her as he had looming *over* her?

Maybe it was the way his gaze ate her up or the very definite bulge in the front of his shorts. Either way, if she didn't leave now she might be tempted to do something about that bulge that could well get them arrested for indecent exposure.

Harper swallowed. 'See you later.' And she departed without waiting for a reply.

* * *

The sound of children's laughter greeted Harper the following Saturday afternoon at four-thirty as she followed the instructions on the hand-painted sign festooned with balloons and made her way around the side path of Yarran's house. It had been almost a week since she'd seen him and her pulse kicked up in anticipation.

She'd made up her mind on Wednesday morning to ring him that night and make an excuse for not being able to go to Jarrah's party, but then Ali had attended the department for an emergency placental abruption on Wednesday afternoon and commented on how Jarrah hadn't been able to stop talking about Harper attending.

And she hadn't been able to do it.

She did, however, decide to set some mental boundaries, going forward. *After the party.* Like restricting their time together to Sunday trivia, only. This way they got to progress their *friendship* but in a very controlled environment. A public place. Plenty of people around. And also, no more sexy dalliances on Manly Beach!

No more sexy dalliances, full stop.

The party was in full swing when Harper stepped into the backyard. She was late because she hadn't known what one wore to a four-year-old's birthday party. Even settling on the casual midi-dress with a square neckline and a tight shirred bodice, she still wasn't sure she'd got it right.

Streamers hung from every branch of every tree occupying the neat garden beds and fairy lights criss-crossed the yard from the balcony railings to the railings of the pool fence. They were on but the full effect wouldn't be able to be appreciated for a couple of hours yet.

Individual helium balloons on plastic sticks had been poked

into the top of the hedge at the back fence to spell happy birthday and, just in front of the hedge, a table groaning with food
had been set up. In the far left back corner was the petting zoo
and several children wearing party hats were sitting on hay
bales tending to an assortment of animals. One held a rabbit,
another a fluffy yellow chicken, the other was patting a tiny
goat. Several more were stroking a Shetland pony as a han-
dler hovered nearby.

Other children chased each other around the yard, flitting
between groups of chatting adults, while others bounced mer-
rily on a large round trampoline, fully enclosed in a mesh
safety net. Wally watched the proceedings from the deck, his
ears pricked.

Harper spotted several of the guys from trivia as well as
Ali and Phoebe chatting near the table of food. Ivy had been
called in to the Central and hadn't been able to attend. Yarran, looking far sexier than a man wearing a pointy party hat
should, was talking to his parents.

Harper's stomach flopped over. It had been twelve years
since she'd seen Lyn and Coen, but they hadn't changed a bit.
Yarran's father was still tall and broad, with a calmness honed
from decades as a paramedic. And Lyn, ex-Olympic sprinting
champion, still boasted a mix of grace and athleticism from
years of physical training and her indigenous heritage.

Coen said something and Yarran and Lyn laughed, her hand
sliding around her husband's waist in obvious affection. Harper
had always laughed at the combined groans of the family over
their parents' public displays of affection, but she had person-
ally *adored* Lyn and Coen's closeness and a familiar rush of
envy lanced her right through the middle.

There was so much *love* in this backyard. Yarran and Ali had
been lucky to grow up in such a loving family. So was Jarrah.

Harper glanced away, spying Brock in the middle of a group of women. One was laughing as she placed her hand on a bulging biceps, testing out its firmness. Brock's youthful charm clearly didn't have an off button.

'Harper!'

She started at the sudden excited exclamation as Jarrah burst forth from a clutch of kids and barrelled towards her. She was conscious of curious looks as he threw his arms around her legs. 'Oh.' Harper froze for a second, momentarily at a loss as to how she should act, especially with what felt like the entire party population waiting for her next move.

'Hey…bud.' She patted him awkwardly on his back as the hug continued. Did he greet everyone with such enthusiasm? Or was he just tripping on a nana high?

He pulled away and looked up at her, his hat sitting atop his wild mop of curls. 'You gotsa come and see my pony.'

'Ahh…' She looked around, unsure as to the right protocol for a children's party. Should she give him his present first? 'Okay.'

'Jarrah, let poor Harper get in the door first.'

Lyn. Harper looked up as she approached, smiling that genuine smile of hers, and the tension that had worked its way into every muscle in her neck eased. Lyn Edwards didn't look as though she was holding any grudges.

'Hey, you.' She grinned and it was big and clearly sincere. 'It's *so* lovely to see you again.' And then she pulled Harper into a big hug.

Harper shut her eyes on a wave of emotion. Lyn had always been free in her affection with Harper and tears pricked the backs of her eyelids as she relaxed into the familiar hold. It had taken her a long time to get used to such open fondness but she'd sure as hell missed it.

When her eyes blinked opened again, she could see Coen approaching with a similar look of welcome. But it was Yarran bringing up the rear she was most aware of. He wasn't frowning like Ali, but he wasn't smiling either, and she wished she could read his mind.

Was he also feeling a weird sense of déjà vu?

'Long time no see,' Coen said as he joined them, also reaching for a hug.

'It's been a while,' Harper admitted, her voice muffled in his shoulder.

He patted her on the back a couple of times. 'It feels like yesterday.'

'Ha!' Lyn snorted as Harper eased out of Coen's embrace. 'Apart from these ruts in my forehead and the grey hair.' She poked at the fine lines, clearly annoyed at their presence.

'I adore your ruts,' Coen said with a smile, earning him an affectionate eye squint from his wife before turning his attention back to Harper. 'How are you settling in? I bet it's like you never left.'

Harper couldn't look at Yarran lest everyone see that, where he was concerned, it definitely felt as if she'd never left. 'Settling in well,' she confirmed. 'My apartment will be ready next week so that will help.'

'Is that my present?'

Harper glanced at Jarrah, who was shifting from foot to foot. He'd been very patient letting the adults get reacquainted. 'Yes.' She handed it over and hoped like hell he liked it.

Unprompted, Jarrah said, 'Thank you,' and ripped off the paper in three seconds flat.

It was a small terrarium with an African violet sporting one lone purple flower. He looked at it quizzically and Harper

chewed nervously at her bottom lip. It wasn't exactly a toy—
you couldn't *play* with it.

'Wow!' Coen said to his grandson. 'A terrarium. That's
awesome.'

Jarrah studied the glass bowl as if he wasn't entirely sure.
'Daddy...' She stumbled over the word. It was still strange
thinking of Yarran as *daddy*. 'He said you liked to help him
in the garden so I thought it might be nice to have an inside
plant?'

'That's a great idea,' Yarran concurred.

Jarrah, however, didn't look convinced. *Good one, Harper.*
Buy the kid a dud present, why don't you? She suddenly wished
she were anywhere but here under the scrutiny of a bunch of
people who probably *didn't* suck at kids' birthday presents
while being judged by a newly minted four-year-old.

Yarran's newly minted four-year-old.

A sudden desperate urge to be liked by him spurred her on.
'And...see those pebbles? They glow in the dark.' She'd remembered Yarran saying he was afraid of the dark and thought
it would be a super-cool alternative to a night light.

Or maybe some horrible triffid nightmare... *Crap.*

But suddenly, Jarrah's eyes lit up as he gazed at her. *'Really?'*

God...those eyes. 'Cross my heart.'

'Daddy!' He turned those excited eyes on his father, his
expression bordering on wonder. 'Glow-in-the-dark rocks!'

Yarran laughed. 'That is *super* cool.'

'Thank you, Harper,' he said, his voice hushed with awe.
'I gots to show Sammy.'

He took off then as if he were holding the Holy Grail and
everyone laughed, but Harper felt utterly unsure of herself.
Which was ridiculous. She was the head of ER. She could

crack open a chest and perform open heart massage if needed but a four-year-old's birthday present had her totally bamboozled.

She shot an apologetic smile at Yarran. 'I'm sorry, I didn't know what to get him.'

Yarran frowned but it was his mother who spoke first. 'What? No.' She shook her head. 'It's a *great* gift. Really thoughtful. It'll last longer than half of the plastic crap he'll be getting today.'

'It's perfect,' Yarran assured her, his eyes warm. 'Really.'

She met the sincerity of his gaze with appreciation and opened her mouth to thank him but before she got anything out, a *'Daddy!'* rang out from the opposite side of the yard and Yarran gave a low chuckle.

'Sorry, Daddy duties. Gotta go.'

Daddy duties. He hadn't rolled his eyes or grimaced—he'd just laughed indulgently and gone eagerly to his son. It did funny things to her equilibrium to see Yarran *the father*. Also stirred the murky pit of guilt she carried where he was concerned. She'd have denied him this—fatherhood—had she stayed.

And *that* would have been a tragedy.

'Come on,' Lyn said, squeezing her arm gently, and Harper dragged her attention back to the other woman, whose gaze was kind, as if she knew Harper's thoughts weighed heavily. 'Let's introduce you to some people.'

CHAPTER SEVEN

HALF AN HOUR LATER, Harper had met every single person at the party and been reacquainted with Yarran's other sisters—Kirra and Marli—and she was now chatting with Ali and Phoebe, who hadn't moved from near the snacks table. Wally occasionally barked up on the balcony as kids dashed hither and thither, some even splashing around in the nearby pool under close adult supervision. Jarrah had brought her a hat and insisted she wear it, with which Harper had dutifully complied, and maybe it was the hat, or maybe it was that most people didn't know her here, but she started to relax and enjoy the atmosphere.

Even more so when conversation turned to work and, inevitably, Emma Wilson. Given the complexity of the case and the public interest due to her husband's celebrity, there was quite a buzz around her and the babies at the Central.

'She's what?' Harper asked as she bit into a lolly banana. 'Twenty-seven weeks now?'

'Twenty-six plus six days,' Ali confirmed.

'Tough enough for a single pregnancy to survive, let alone a twin birth,' Phoebe added.

'Yep.' Harper nodded.

'The babies appear to be doing well though, despite the continuing fluid and ventilation challenges for Emma.' Ali also grabbed a few bananas from the bowl and chomped one in half.

'I saw yesterday's ultrasound report,' Phoebe agreed. 'Twin two is slightly smaller than expected but still just within parameters and neither are showing signs of distress.'

'I would think with all that sedation it'd be pretty chill in there,' Harper said.

Phoebe laughed. 'True.'

'Seriously though.' Harper's gaze was absently following Yarran as they talked. Between attending to Jarrah and the other kids and mingling with their parents, he was working the party like a pro. 'Are either of you worried about the long-term effects on the twins of any of the drugs being given in ICU?'

'Not really.' Ali shook her head. 'Emma was well into her second trimester when the thermal injury occurred so the babies were essentially fully developed. And they're avoiding benzos and opiates for sedation. But who knows? It's not like we see these cases every day. Not a lot of precedent to study in literature.'

'I guess not.' Harper nodded as a woman and her partner approached Yarran. She smiled and rubbed his arm briefly before her face scrunched in something akin to concern.

'Doesn't he get sick of that?'

Harper glanced sharply at a plainly irritated Phoebe, who was also watching Yarran, her eyebrows beetled. 'Sick of what?'

'Having all those bloody sympathy arm rubs. He's not a... pet.'

Ali shrugged. 'People feel extra bad for him today. But they don't want to mention the elephant in the room.'

Harper blinked. The elephant in the room?

'Right,' Phoebe muttered with a shake of her head. 'Like this is the first time he's woken up and *not* thought, great, another day I have to be teeth-achingly happy for my son on his birthday while being excruciatingly aware the woman who gave birth to him on this day will never be around to celebrate it.'

It dawned on Harper then. The *elephant in the room* was Marnie.

And she felt terrible. She'd been concerned about herself and how she was going to face him after their beach make-out and worried about seeing his family again and fretting over the birthday present without any thought to how difficult this day must be for Yarran.

How bittersweet.

Celebrating the joy and miracle of Jarrah's birth while knowing the person who'd grown, nurtured, birthed and loved their son *first* was gone for ever. It must take an enormous amount of fortitude to *bear* a day like this, let alone throw a party and *entertain*.

Harper watched as the woman chatted away but Yarran's gaze drifted, landing on Jarrah, who was laughing as a mother belonging to the little boy standing next to him, guided his arm back and forth to show him how to make a bubble come out of an enormous wand.

A wonky bubble finally squeezed out and Jarrah grinned in excitement, looking at the other woman as if she were some kind of bubble whisperer, and the flash of raw anguish Harper saw in Yarran's gaze in that unguarded moment whammed her in the chest. It only lasted a nanosecond before he covered it up with a broad grin, but she felt its impact all the way across the yard. The expression—*his pain*—squeezed at her windpipe.

Was he thinking that the random mother should have been Marnie? That Jarrah had been ripped off? Short-changed? That'd *he'd* been short-changed? Had he just been faking his smile today to cover the great yawning hole in his life?

Harper wished she had a magic wand she could wave and bring Marnie back. For Jarrah so he could *know* the love of his mother. And for Yarran. Even though her own feelings for him were complicated, Harper had only ever wanted him to be happy.

And that, she realised now, had played a huge role in her leaving twelve years ago. Because he'd deserved someone who loved him unreservedly. He'd deserved Marnie. And if she could have filled that hole for him—and for Jarrah—right now, she would have.

'They mean well,' Ali said, her quiet musing breaking into Harper's thoughts.

Phoebe sighed. 'I guess. But I bet he's going to shut the door on them tonight, turn some music up real loud and scream at the top of his lungs.'

Ali laughed. 'Probably.'

Harper laughed too because the images of the friendly polite host working the party just now and a grown man screaming into a void of loud music were so at odds, and yet Yarran had always sworn by the virtues of loud music.

'He always said metal was good for railing against the fates,' she agreed.

Ali frowned a little and Harper got the distinct impression she wasn't ready for any affectionate forays into the past. She might have been able to get past the hurt Harper had inflicted, but she hadn't forgotten.

Thankfully, the mood was interrupted by the ball of energy that was Jarrah. 'Aunty Li-Li.' He grabbed his aunt's hand. 'Come and watch me ride the pony.' He reached for Harper's hand. 'You, too.' His little hand slid into hers and he tugged.

A tug Harper felt on the inside as well. Hell, she felt it all the way down to her toes.

'Yeah, yeah.' Ali rolled her eyes adoringly at her nephew but held her ground. 'Where's my kiss from the birthday boy first?'

Jarrah mimicked his aunt's eye roll. 'I kisst'ed you already.'

'You're four now, you gotta kiss me four times. It's the rules.'

The boy regarded her through suspicious eyes. He clearly smelled a rat. 'I heard it was the birthday boy who was supposed to get four kisses?' Harper said, her heart full at the obvious love between Ali and her nephew.

Jarrah's eyes widened. 'Yeah!'

'Hey.' Ali frowned playfully at Harper, which made her feel even lighter. 'Whose side are you on?'

'The birthday boy's, of course,' she said with a grin.

'Oh, well, then…' Another exaggerated eye roll from Ali. 'If you insist.' She hauled him in, wrapping her arms around him. 'Better pucker up, birthday boy,' she said with a faux growl. 'I'ma coming in.'

Jarrah squealed and squirmed as Ali planted tiny kisses all over his face. 'Stop, stop,' he protested as he laughed and wiggled and giggled.

Ali relented only when she'd considered him thoroughly kissed and Jarrah tugged on both their hands again. 'C'mon,' he urged, 'it's my turn on the pony.'

And, conscious of Yarran's gaze on her from across the yard, Harper could no more have resisted that tug on her hand than she could the tug around her heart.

The fairy lights in the yard started to glow around six as the party broke up. Hyperactive children with party bags in hand were protesting as they were led away by their parents, while the petting zoo people packed up. Harper had tried to leave half an hour prior when Ali and Phoebe had departed to go on to other engagements, but Jarrah had pleaded with her to stay and watch him do tricks on the trampoline, so she'd stayed.

And then, as she'd supervised several of the kids all bouncing around, Lyn had approached and asked a favour.

'Can you stay for a while after the party tonight?' she'd asked. 'It's a bit of a birthday tradition that Jarrah has a sleepover at our place and he gets to stay up and watch his favourite movie with us on his pa's big-screen TV, then we do morning-after birthday pancakes the next day. But… I worry about Yarran being alone.'

Harper's gut clenched. *Oh, no. Please, Lyn, no.* Why her? He had plenty of friends who could keep him company, surely?

As if the other woman had read her mind, she said, 'He refuses all company no matter who I try to set up, but when we bring Jarrah back the next morning, he always looks…*dreadful*. Very hungover. And I can't help but think if he had something other than a bottle of whatever around, it might give him something else to think about.'

'Lyn…' Harper understood what she was saying but she didn't think her hanging around would have the desired effect. 'I'm not sure my company helps.'

'I disagree. Having someone who *wasn't* around when it all happened might just be the ticket. Besides—' she gave a wry smile '—he's much too polite to kick *you* out.'

Lyn might be right on both accounts, but she didn't know what had been going down between the two of them these past few weeks. So Harper had opened her mouth to politely decline. But then Lyn had touched her arm and said, 'Please, Harper. Just for a bit?'

And she was sunk. Harper always had found it hard saying no to Lyn and tonight had been no exception. It seemed as though the whole darn Edwards family had her wrapped around their little fingers!

So here she was out under the fairy lights picking up the toys scattered around the pool deck and placing them back in the basket. Lyn and Coen and a few others had stayed behind to help clean up the yard and kitchen but they'd left with Jarrah—clutching his terrarium—twenty minutes ago and everyone else had departed soon after. Yarran was outside somewhere seeing off the petting zoo people so Harper had the backyard to herself.

With the party all cleared away, it was still and quiet now, just the trill of evening insects. She leaned on the top rail of the pool fence, draining her beer as she watched the lights winking on in the houses beyond the back fence. She'd never pictured Yarran in suburbia, and yet he was clearly thriving. The house was welcoming, the yard was immaculate and, given how many neighbours had been at the party, he was clearly well liked.

If she'd stuck around, would this have been their life? Harper couldn't imagine it, but strangely, it wasn't a panic-inducing thought.

A car door shutting out on the street roused her from her reverie and her gaze fell on the trampoline. Some kind of toy was lying discarded on the mat and she wondered if it belonged to Jarrah or one of the other kids.

Letting herself out of the pool gate, she placed the beer bottle on the nearby garden edge before making her way to the trampoline. The teddy bear looked old and well loved, which meant there'd no doubt be a parent looking for it soon enough. Unzipping the safety netting, Harper tried to bounce the toy closer but only succeeded in bouncing it further away.

Resigned to fetching it out, she climbed the ladder, pulling her dress out from under her knees so she could crawl to the middle, the trampoline giving easily under her weight. Harper couldn't remember the last time she'd been on a trampoline so instead of backing out once she'd scooped it up, she flipped over and took a moment to breathe in the evening air.

It was surprisingly nice just lying here in the lazy hush of a suburban Saturday evening, purples fading to black. Stars winked to life although the fairy lights and the glow from the house prevented her from getting the full celestial display. As if the universe had heard her thoughts the house and fairy lights went out one after the other.

'Hey up there,' she said as her eyes adjusted, hundreds of stars popping overhead.

'Harper? Where are you?' The house lights flicked back on.

She could hear the frown in Yarran's voice as she rolled her head to look up at him. Wally was by his side, lapping up an ear scratch. 'On the trampoline.'

There was a pause for a beat or two. 'Did my mother harangue you to stay?'

Harper laughed. 'Yes.'

She could hear his sigh drift all the way down from the balcony. 'Sorry 'bout that.'

'It's fine,' she assured him. Even though it wasn't. But she'd agreed so there was no point complaining. 'Turn the lights out again, will you? I can see the stars so much better.'

The lights flicked out and Harper's eyes adjusted again, finding even more stars as he clomped down the stairs then padded towards her across the grass.

'Mind if I join you?' he asked as he reached the ladder.

She knew she should say yes. Should get off the trampoline and go inside where she would be in his house, surrounded by a life she hadn't been a part of and where she wouldn't be so damn *horizontal*. She could make coffee and they could eat left-over birthday cake and talk about the weather and then she could get the hell out of Dodge.

But his mother's concerns, her *'Please, Harper'* ricocheted around her brain, so she simply said, 'Sure.'

Harper rocked a little as Yarran climbed onto the mat and made his way to the centre. She shifted to give them each some space but with their combined weight forming a dip in the middle of the trampoline the sides of their bodies touched whether she liked it or not.

Unfortunately, Harper's body liked it—a lot.

She didn't know if he was as acutely aware of it as she, but he at least seemed inclined to ignore it as he pointed. 'Southern cross.'

Harper nodded. 'Uh-huh.' And then neither of them said anything for a while, they just lay there, staring up as the sky went from indigo to black and more stars appeared.

She wondered what he was thinking. Was it about Marnie and Jarrah and the emotional gut-wrench of this day? Or was he thinking about the many birthdays to come and the other milestones to come in Jarrah's life where his loss would be constantly compounded?

'Don't be mad at your mum.'

'I'm not.'

'She means well.'

'I know. I just…it's nice to be alone after having to be so *on*. It's exhausting having to assure everyone I'm fine.'

'And are you?' she asked, her voice quiet and tentative in the night.

He paused. 'Mostly.'

Harper fell silent. She supposed, given it had only been

three years, *mostly* was pretty damn good. 'It must be hard for you,' she said eventually, probing some more. 'This day.'

She wasn't sure this was a Lyn-approved topic of conversation. Yarran's mother had hoped she'd be a distraction from his past—not hold a mirror up to it—but Harper knew enough psychology to know sometimes people wanted to talk, they just needed an opening.

He shrugged. 'It is what it is.'

Harper felt that shrug down the whole side of her body making her excruciatingly aware of his heat and hardness. Forcing herself to concentrate on their conversation, she conceded Yarran wasn't really giving her any openings so she decided not to push.

'How did you find seeing my mum and dad again?'

'Oh, it was…lovely.' Harper happily picked up what he'd put down as she rolled her head to look at his profile.

He chuckled but didn't look at her. 'I told you it would be okay.'

'Yeah, yeah.' Harper returned her attention to the sky. 'They haven't changed a bit.'

'Apart from the ruts in the forehead.'

Harper laughed. 'I should be so lucky at your mum's age to look that young.'

Shaking his head, he said, 'She hates them.'

'I can't believe Kirra has *four* kids.'

'Neither can I. But I love that Jarrah has so many little cousins all living nearby.'

He didn't say *in lieu of siblings*, but Harper knew intuitively it was what he meant. 'Yeah, he's lucky.'

As soon as the words were out, she could have bitten off her tongue. She shut her eyes briefly, mentally castigating herself. On today of all days, she had to go and say something so asinine. 'I mean—' Her eyes flashed to his profile again. 'I meant—'

'It's okay...' He rolled his head to the side, too, his gaze meetings hers. 'I know what you meant. He *is* lucky in lots of ways. His mother died...' Yarran's voice turned husky '...but he has so much family and love around him in this little village of ours. Sure, they're big and loud and over-compensating...' He gave a rueful smile. 'But that's not nothing.'

This little village of ours.

She'd been part of that village once upon time. And now here she was again, on the outside looking in—her nose pressed to the windowpane. The next words slipped out of her mouth without much thought. 'I wish I'd had a family as loving as yours.'

'Yeah.' He nodded slowly. 'I wish you had too.'

A slight smile touched his mouth before he turned back to the stars and they returned to contemplative silence as the heavens winked above them. Harper wasn't sure how long they lay like that, but it didn't feel stretched or awkward. And maybe that was the lasting legacy of their long-term relationship—they didn't need to fill the silences.

'Can I ask you something?' Yarran said eventually.

'Sure.'

'You don't...' He hesitated. 'Don't have to answer if you don't want to.'

A prickle shot down Harper's spine. 'Okay.'

'How did it feel...to grow up without a mother?'

Okay, well...she hadn't expected him to go there. It said a lot about them that they were together for eight years and he didn't know the answer to that question nor feel okay even broaching the topic over a decade later. He *had* tried to get her to talk about it in the beginning, but she'd been close-lipped and he'd eventually stopped asking.

'I know you grew up in the foster system so it's not the same thing. But loss is loss and…the *mother* is such a profound figure in a child's life. And I look at you and you're this amazing, articulate, intelligent go-getter and yet I know there's a little girl in there somewhere that suffered.' He rolled his head to the side, his gaze meshing with hers. 'That still suffers, I think. And I can't…bear the thought of it.'

Harper knew he wasn't probing for himself. He was asking *for Jarrah*. He couldn't bear the thought of his son suffering. And it clawed at her gut to know he was willing to push against a wall he knew only too well was gnarly with vines and practically immovable, to get answers. To be best prepared for his kid.

Like a true parent.

So perhaps it was time to be moved. Maybe that was something she *could* do for Yarran after all these years. Give him answers. For Jarrah's sake. And hadn't she been thinking that sometimes people just needed an opening?

Yarran waited, unsure if Harper would answer. Would finally go there. The fact she hadn't got up and left was encouraging, but that didn't mean she wouldn't, which was cranking up his anxiety.

She was right, today *was* a hard day—how could it not be?

But Harper's presence had, for the first time since Marnie's death, managed to take his mind off the fact she was no longer here to celebrate the special day. Being excruciatingly aware of Harper's every move from the moment she'd stepped into the backyard instead of the weariness of grief and the hovering scrutiny of the people who loved him had made the day so much more bearable.

Even more so, watching her go from clearly anxious standing there in that knockout dress, clutching that present looking as if she wanted to flee, to supervising kids on the trampoline—laughing and joking and rubbing banged heads and soothing bruised egos—had been marvellous.

And the way she'd been with Jarrah? Wearing the party hat he'd bequeathed her as if it were a tiara and letting him drag her all over. Not to mention the absolute genius of her present—one she'd obviously put a lot of thought into. She'd remembered Jarrah liked to garden and that he slept with a night light.

She'd always been thoughtful and watching her morph into the old Harper—the Harper he'd loved—had been just what he'd needed, today. And now here she was, breathing huskily into the night, seriously contemplating—he thought—talking about a subject she'd *never, ever* wanted to talk about.

'My mother...'

Her voice was halting and Yarran swore he could actually hear her swallow. Out of some instinct he couldn't put a finger on, he reached for her hand. With their arms jammed together, it wasn't hard to find. When her cool fingers curled against his, he gave a light squeeze and she continued.

'She died when I was nine.'

Yarran blinked, turning his head to look at her. 'Oh...' That he hadn't expected. 'I'd assumed she'd died when you were much younger.' He'd assumed that was the reason she'd been fostered.

'Nope.' She didn't look at him, just kept her gaze fixed overhead. 'She was an addict. Functional for a long time. Until a few years after I was born when things really started to go off the rails. That was the first time they took me away from her.'

The first time? Yarran closed his eyes.

'I bounced back and forth for the next six years. She'd get clean and… I'd go back.'

'Sounds very…disruptive.'

'It was. But I *wanted* to go back. She was my mum. I loved her. She loved me. I *know* she loved me. She might not have been very good at managing life but those times we were together, when she was first clean again, they were *happy*. We weren't rich and I didn't have a lot of stuff but she had the sweetest laugh. And she always cut my school sandwiches into different shapes. I never knew what I was going to get when I opened my lunchbox.'

She laughed and, despite how sad it sounded in the night, Yarran could feel how much Harper had loved her mother.

'I know that if it had been within her power to change, she would have. But…some people just aren't equipped to pull themselves up by their bootstraps.' She shook her head. 'God, I hate that phrase. She was a victim of gross multi-generational family dysfunction. Not many people come back from that.'

'No,' he agreed, 'they don't.'

'I was in a temporary foster home when she overdosed. The social worker came and told me and I remember just being… numb. I remember them telling me it was okay to cry but I *couldn't*. I think I always knew it was the way it was going to end and I was just…' she gave a harsh half-laugh '…pissed off to be right.'

Yarran squeezed her hand harder. He hated that Harper had been through such hardship but, more than that, he hated that she'd borne it all alone. He hated that he hadn't pushed her more about this when they were together—maybe he couldn't know her pain or take it away, but he could have listened. He could have wrapped her up and hugged her as he wanted to now.

'I'm sorry,' he said.

'Thank you.'

'And I'm sorry I didn't ask these questions all those years ago.'

She turned her head and their eyes met. 'You tried.'

Yarran nodded. He had. But… 'We were together for eight years. I should have tried harder.'

'No.' She shook her head. 'I was too used to burying it by then. Too frightened to show anyone my scars in case it was too much and they left.'

'I wouldn't have left.'

'Of course. But…everybody left so…' She looked back up at the stars. 'I know it doesn't make any sense. It doesn't make much sense to me either. It's not about logic though, it's about a very deep, very old wound and the mental lengths a child goes to for emotional protection.'

God. No wonder he hadn't been able to unpick that narrative.

She squeezed his hand. 'It's okay, I don't blame you for not pushing me. I was pretty good at shutting you down.'

Oh, yeah, she'd been an expert at that. And as much as he'd wanted to know her story, he'd known then and he knew now, he wasn't *entitled* to it so he'd always let it drop when she'd made it clear she didn't want to talk.

'I debated pushing for more all the time.' Hoping that one day he'd ask and she'd *want* to tell him. 'But I didn't want to lose you either.'

'And you would have.' She rolled her head to look at him.

'If you'd pushed too much, I would have walked away earlier. My flight instinct was always well honed.'

Yarran nodded. 'Yeah.' So he'd dropped it—every time.

As they both returned their attention to the stars, he thought about their eight years together and which moments he would have been prepared to give up to go into the fray with Harper.

None of them. Not a single one.

'Did you go to her funeral?' he asked after they'd been silent for a long time.

'Yes. Me and my case worker and some of my mother's friends from NA.'

The bleakness in Harper's voice painted a picture more vivid than any words as he examined her profile. He didn't say anything, just waited for her to continue.

'I don't know how many foster homes I went to over the next few years.'

'You weren't given a permanent foster placement?'

'Ah, no…' She shook her head. 'I was angry and…well… suffice to say, I wasn't exactly a treat of a child. But when I was in grade nine, a great-aunt of mine—Jacqueline—turned up out of the blue and I was with her for two years.'

Yarran frowned. 'She just turned up?'

'Yep. I know it sounds incredible but she was estranged from her family for many years, which is unsurprising given what I know about my mother's family. I'm pretty sure Mum never knew she existed. She lived in the UK for twenty of those years and it was only when she got back that she found out about Mum dying and me and…' Harper shook her head. 'She just kind of swooped in and it was—' she sighed '—wonderful. Like… nirvana. She had this quirky apartment and all these pictures of London on her walls and for the first time in my life I actually felt like it was all going to be okay.'

Oh, God. He didn't like the sound of that. 'What happened?'

She didn't answer for the longest time and Yarran watched Harper's profile as it ran the gamut of emotions. Her throat bobbed and he swore he heard her swallow. 'She died of a massive heart attack playing golf when I was at school one day.'

'Oh, God... *Harper.*'

Yarran's lungs felt too tight for his chest. How much was one person expected to bear? Turning on his side, he drew her hand up, kissing the knuckles absently before tucking it against his chest.

'It's fine,' she said eventually but she still didn't look at him and if she'd registered the brush of his lips, she didn't acknowledge it. 'I had two amazing years.'

Fine? It was *awful.* Even worse was Harper's low expectations, as if she'd never thought her good fortune was going to last, anyway.

'She used to say to me, "Listen, girlie, life's dealt you a crappy hand and I wish I could go back and change that but I can't. I *can* tell you the only way you don't end up like your mama and my sister and our mama before us is to get the best damn education you can. I wish I could tell you I had the money to help but I can't tell you that either. You are, however, whip smart and that's what scholarships are for."'

Harper laughed then, as if she was caught up in a memory. 'She'd shake her finger at me and say, "You got that, girlie?" and I'd nod and she'd tell me she was proud of me and even though I ended up back in the system again afterwards, I worked my arse off to get a full scholarship for her. For me, too, of course, but mainly for her.'

Yarran had known she'd gone to uni on a full scholarship, but this extra information had given him new insight into why she'd busted her ass at uni. God knew she'd cancelled numerous dates with him in deference to studying.

'So…yeah.' Harper blew out a breath, the rush ruffling some strands of flyaway hair at her temples. 'Growing up without a mother sucks. In an ideal world every child would have two loving parents, but you and I both know that's not the way it goes.'

She turned her head finally to look at him and their gazes meshed.

'Whenever I think about my mum, despite her being what was quite a disruptive influence in my life—unintended or not—it feels like a piece of me is missing. Like something vital. An organ or a limb. It's not as acute as it used to be but it's still there. And yeah, Jarrah will probably always feel like that too, even though he won't necessarily understand it because he won't have any tangible memories of her. But he has an amazing support system around him—big and loud and overcompensating as they may be.'

She smiled then and Yarran smiled back.

'And kids need that more than one parental figure that's been held up over centuries as the *ideal*. They need unconditional love and absolute protection from someone they trust and there doesn't have to be a *mum* for that.'

She looked away, her eyes turning back to the sky as she drew in a long shuddery breath. 'Sometimes,' she said, her voice husky, 'there can be a Great-Aunt Jacqueline.'

Yarran watched as a tear slid out of the corner of her eye, slowly trekking to her temple. Her voice was utterly desolate and even though they were so close they were touching, she looked so damn alone. And he couldn't *bear* it.

Levering himself up onto his elbow, Yarran stared down into her face. Her gaze shifted from the sky to his meet his, blinking up at him through twin puddles reflecting sorrow and starlight. Yarran's heart tore in his chest as another tear spilled.

'Oh, love,' he whispered, his hand slipping from hers to cradle her face, his fingertips funnelling into her hair. 'I'm sorry.' His breathing was rough, as he kissed the tear from her cheek. 'I'm so, *so* sorry.'

He kissed the other side, sipping up another, his pulse a slow, thick thud at his neck. Then he kissed all over her face—nuzzling her eyes, her nose, her forehead, her ears, the corners of her mouth, murmuring, 'I'm sorry,' each time his lips touched down.

Cool fingers slid around his wrist, encircling it. 'It's fine,' she replied, her voice rough and low. 'I'm fine.'

'I know,' he said as he pulled back slightly to stare into her eyes again. He'd never met a woman who held herself together more. Which was why her tears *eviscerated* him. 'But don't you ever want to feel more than just fine?'

Her eyes roved over his face as if she was mapping it in the dark. Or maybe re-familiarising herself. Her hand slid from his wrist to his jaw, up his cheekbone, to his forehead, ploughing into his hair and pushing it back. 'Yes.'

CHAPTER EIGHT

YARRAN KISSED HER THEN. Properly. On her mouth. Gently, not seeking or probing, just holding, his pulse a water hammer through his head. Then she moaned, her hand gliding to his shoulder as her mouth opened, allowing him in.

Past her lips. Past her walls. Past a dozen years of absence.

And he took it, tentatively though, the slow side of his mouth on hers soft and seeking rather than hard and conquering and it was familiar in all those good ways. But it was new, too. Breathy and tremulous, straining at the leash, caught somewhere between enjoying the moment and the brink of possibility.

Her moans whispered their delight through his head, they stroked against his body and fizzed like pop rocks on his tongue. She tasted like birthday cake and beer—who knew that was such an intoxicating mix? She filled up his senses until he was dizzy.

A little too dizzy for his own good.

But, even caught up in the slow turn of her mouth and the low burn of arousal heating his muscles to jelly, he knew he was far too melancholic tonight to just *make out*.

'God...' he muttered, breaking their lip lock. He pulled back slightly, his heart thumping behind his ribcage, the warm, husky rush of her breath calling to him. 'I wish—' He dropped his forehead against hers, not sure what he wished at all now, just too *overcome* with her. With *Harper*.

Harper back in the country. Harper back home. Harper back in his life.

'What?' she whispered. 'What do you wish?'

He gave a half-laugh. 'I don't know exactly.' That they'd never been apart. But then he wouldn't have had those amazing years with Marnie. He wouldn't have Jarrah.

Maybe that they'd parted differently? Without so much left unsaid.

Lifting his forehead, Yarran took her in again, his thumb stroking against her temple. 'I wish I could kiss you without wanting more. I just…don't think I can. Not tonight.'

'Maybe that's our problem,' she murmured. 'We've been trying to ignore this chemistry between us, telling ourselves *no*, hoping it'll go away.'

'Yeah.' Yarran nodded slowly. 'That hasn't really worked, has it?'

She shook her head. 'So maybe we should let it burn out in one flash of heat?'

Yarran's breath hitched at the suggestion. A very sensible suggestion. One that sank into his bones in all its profound glory. *One flash of heat.* Blood surged anew through his veins and arteries, heat suffusing every cell, his body going hard—everywhere.

'Maybe the better question to ask is, what do you *want*, Yarran?'

'I want you,' he muttered, his gaze holding hers, his voice low and rough. Three little words yet the relief at letting them out flushed hot and heady through his system.

'Because you don't want to be alone tonight?'

'No.' He shook his head vehemently. Being alone didn't

bother him. 'Because I can't stand another second without being inside you.'

There it was. Right there. Plain and simple. And he *throbbed* with it.

Yarran swallowed. 'What do you want?'

The hand at his shoulder clutched now. 'I want you inside me more than I want my next breath. I want tonight.'

Heat and blood and sex and triumph roared through his veins. He could give her tonight. 'Good answer.' Then he rolled up on top of her.

Every pulse point in Harper's body leapt as the weight of him pressed her deeper into the trampoline mat. She parted her legs, the hard jut of his erection finding the screamingly sensitive place at the apex of her thighs. He was big and hot and heavy and she revelled in it. Revelled in the weight of him, in the way he looked at her. Lust and desire and something darker sparking in his gaze.

She wanted him, this man she'd never really shaken from her system. Except she wanted him more than ever. More than she'd thought it possible to want a man.

They'd tried denial. Surrender was the only thing left.

Harper didn't wait for him to kiss her, she lifted to him, their mouths meeting on a rush of air and a groan that sounded as if it had escaped from the recesses of Yarran's soul.

Yes. This.

This man. This mouth. The hot probe of his tongue and the slow grind of his erection hitting just the right spot. Her hands slid from his shoulders down his back to his ass, holding him hard against her as she wrapped her legs around his waist.

The movement adjusted the angle slightly and she gasped. *'Yarran.'*

He groaned. 'Need you *now*.'

And she knew exactly how he felt. Groping between their bodies, she found his fly, yanking down the zip as he rucked up the material of her skirt. It was a hasty choreography of grasping, grabbing, fumbling fingers, the thud of her pulse and their heavy breathing was the soundtrack.

He found her panties, his fingers slipping inside finding her wet and needy, at the same time she reached inside his underwear finding him hard and just as needy and they both gasped, their lips parting, staring into each other's eyes as they familiarised themselves with long-forgotten contours, fingering and fondling, their breathing rough in the night.

'I don't have a condom,' he muttered, his forehead once again pressed to hers.

'I have an implant and haven't had sex in over a year.'

He groaned as she slid her hand up and down his shaft. 'Three for me.'

Harper knew at some point that information would need to be parsed but, right now, all she saw was a giant green light. Dragging his head down, she kissed him, her tongue sliding against his as she guided the delicious hardness in her hand to her centre. She moaned at the thick nudge of him—*God*… had it always felt this good?

He thrust then, sliding in on a long groan until he was high and deep and she remembered—*yeah, it had*. It had *always* felt this good. He withdrew and thrust again, in case she needed another reminder.

Oh. God. Yes.

'Yes,' she whispered, her fingers ploughing into the hair at his nape, her heels pressing hard into his ass. '*Yes*. Don't stop.'

He didn't stop. He withdrew and entered again. And again. And again. A guttural kind of grunt spilled from his lips with each thrust, the give and bounce of the trampoline seating him deeper each time. Harper pressed her face into the side of his neck as the pressure and the stretch undid her, shooting darts of pleasure through her pelvis like fireworks in the night.

Placing the flats of his forearms either side of her head, Yarran surged over her again and again, seeming to know just the right pace and angle to rub just the right spot with his steely length. She was a moaning, mindless mess in his arms, trembling as much beneath him as he seemed to be trembling over the top of her.

'God,' she panted, a bright flare of sensation deep behind her belly button starting to ripple. 'Close, so close.' And it felt *right*. As if the old rhythm they'd had wasn't lost, merely suppressed. And was now fibrillating wildly to life.

Without missing a beat, his mouth left hers, his hand yanking at the shirring of her bodice, pulling it down, exposing a naked breast and its rapidly burgeoning nipple to the cooling night air before he took it in his hot, hot mouth and sucked.

Hard.

It was like a bolt of lightning, a flaming arrow straight to her core, the bright flare blowing out, her orgasm rushing forward, swamping her in a blink. She gasped, every part of her pulsing, from the flutter of the tiniest arterioles to the thick pound of her abdominal aorta to the rhythmic squeeze of her centre clenching around the rigid thrust of him.

Harper twisted her fingers in the hair at his nape as she came apart. *'Yarran...'*

His mouth left her nipple to claim hers, licking up her pants and her gasps and her cries, intoxicating her with his taste and weaving magic with his tongue. His pelvic thrusts slowed inexorably, teasing and prolonging, dragging in and out, stoking her to new heights.

She opened her eyes as the pleasure rained down anew, the stars overhead a blur as she shuddered and trembled in his arms. But now he was shuddering too, his biceps quaking, his breath coming in short, sharp puffs.

'Harper.' Yarran grunted, the piston of his hips discordant now. 'I can't... I need...' He breathed hot and heavy into her neck as he hunched over her, gathering her close.

'Yes,' she murmured, her orgasm shifting in intensity as he switched up the angle and pace of his stroke once again. *'Yes.'*

He cried out then, his mouth pressed into her temple as he came, his breath hot and harsh, his thrusts turning wild, shuddering against her as he found his bliss until there was nothing left and he collapsed on top of her, the trampoline bouncing beneath them.

'I don't think this is what your mother intended when she asked me to stay,' Harper said, trying to drag in some oxygen beneath his boneless, sated weight.

'I wouldn't be so sure,' he panted then laughed into her hair.

When Yarran's eyes blinked open the next morning it took him a few seconds to get orientated. He was in his bedroom—yep, Jarrah's dyed-pasta mobile he'd made at kindergarten was hanging from the hook in his ceiling. But something felt different.

Internally.

The usual heavy feeling inside his chest, that dark cloud in his heart, wasn't there. Sure, it had lifted over the last year or so but every morning, upon waking, he still felt the weight of it. He still woke thinking about what he had lost.

But not today.

He squinted against the harsh morning light blasting in through the open curtains he usually drew before getting into bed and that was when he became aware of a warm body beside him and everything came rushing back.

Harper.

He turned his head to find her facing him, his sheet pulled up to her chin, her red hair spilling over the pillow next to his, her face relaxed in slumber. Snatches of their night together came back to him as the long sweep of her lashes cast shadows on her cheekbones. Watching the stars together on the trampoline, her finally opening up to him about her past—her frankness, her tears.

Making love to her.

Moving upstairs for a repeat performance. Rousing her in the night at some point with his lips trailing down her body, feeling her hand sink into his hair as he reached her slick, sweet core, encouraging him to stay and feast until she came so hard he was sure he'd have a bruise from her heels in the centre of his back. Then her returning the favour...

So much for one flash of heat.

He waited for the guilt to flood in. But it didn't. And not just because he knew Marnie wouldn't have wanted him to feel any shame or remorse but because Harper was no Marnie substitute. She wasn't some woman he'd picked up to help him expunge three years of grief and pain. A hook-up to help him forget. A random warm body.

Despite what had happened between them, Harper Jones was woven into the fabric of his heart. And he wasn't going to feel guilty about reaching for a little comfort with her.

As if she knew he was watching, her eyes blinked sleepily open, the slumberous blast of green zapping all the way down to his toes. Like him, it seemed to take her a second or two to orientate herself before her body went very still and her eyes widened.

He could practically see her synapses firing behind those eyes, assessing the situation.

Would she be annoyed? Anxious? Would she regret it? Would she freak out?

She didn't do any of those things. After a beat or two she seemed to relax and she offered him a tentative smile. 'Guess we kinda screwed up, huh?'

It wasn't accusatory or panicked and Yarran gave a half-laugh. Well…they'd definitely *screwed*. 'Maybe. It doesn't really feel that way though.'

'No.' She shook her head slowly, contemplatively. 'It doesn't.'

She'd said one blast of heat, right? And that was what they'd done. But, hell, if he didn't want to reach for her again and pick up where they'd left off. Hell, if she didn't look as if she wanted it too as her gaze dropped to his mouth and lingered, fanning the coals of desire he suddenly realised hadn't been fully banked.

They were saved from the moment by a very loud rumble. Yarran blinked. 'Was that your stomach or mine?'

She laughed. 'Mine. I'm starving.'

'Well…' He grinned. 'We did burn a lot of calories last night.' Yarran glanced at his watch—quarter to eight. His parents were bringing Jarrah back at nine. Which meant they had time to eat. And talk.

With their clothes on and far away from proximity to a bed.

'There's a little suburban café about a ten-minute walk from here with great coffee and pastries. You want to stretch your legs?'

She chewed on her lip for a second or two. 'I should probably just go.'

'If you want. But…maybe we should talk about last night?'

More lip-chewing then another tummy rumble. 'Yeah.' She nodded. 'You're right.'

* * *

Ten minutes later, Yarran directed her to the walking path that cut a swathe through an area of bushland before skirting a large local park and onwards to the local shopping precinct. Birdsong accompanied them as people passed by also enjoying the sun's attempts at breaking through the cooler morning temps. A woman jogging with a pram. A young family with two little kids wobbling along on tiny bikes with training wheels.

Neither said anything as they walked for a minute or two. She was in yesterday's dress and he wondered how warped it was to get so much satisfaction seeing her in it *today*. Knowing it was because she'd spent the night with *him*.

'So…' she said eventually. 'I'm your first…since Marnie.'

He nodded. 'Yes.'

'And you feel…guilty?'

'No.' He glanced at her sharply. 'I always thought I might the first time, but I don't.'

'Oh. Well…good.'

She sounded surprised and he searched for clarification. 'I think if it had happened straight away or if it had been with anyone else…'

He let that drift off, shying away from where it might take him but that was the truth of it and she just nodded, as if she didn't want to dig too deeply into it, either.

'I guess I was just…ready. Marnie and I used to talk about what would happen if either of us died. We were both in high-risk professions and, as parents, you have to talk about the what ifs—to be prepared for all eventualities.'

'Yeah.'

'We both agreed there wasn't only one person out there for everyone and I know,' he hastened to assure her, 'last night wasn't about that. But we each wanted the other to be happy. For ourselves but also for Jarrah.'

'Neither of you were worried the other would end up with someone who wasn't keen on having a child in the picture?'

Yarran shook his head. 'No.' He supposed from what Harper had seen in her life, it was a reasonable question, but he knew in his bones that that was a no-brainer. 'She trusted I would put Jarrah's welfare before everything and I trusted she'd do the same.'

'As someone whose welfare often *wasn't* put first by my mother, I gotta say she sounds pretty great.'

'She was the best.' He gave a laugh. 'She was fun and funny. And I think it was the cop in her, but she just radiated a kind of calm that put anybody at ease in any situation.'

Yarran smiled thinking about Marnie now, marvelling at how easy it was to discuss her with Harper. He'd have thought it would be awkward but it felt as though the three of them were somehow inextricably linked. Without Harper, he would never have known Marnie.

'You would have liked her, I think,' he added. 'She would have liked *you*.'

'Did she…know about me?'

'Oh, yes.' He glanced at her and their eyes met. 'I told her everything about you.' Yarran returned his attention to the path. 'She'd been through a similar break-up with a long-term partner, and we spent a lot of time talking about you and him.' He gave a half-laugh. 'Kinda like therapy, I guess.'

'I'm pleased you found her. And *really* sorry you lost her. You deserve to be happy.'

'And what about you? Don't you deserve to be happy?'

'Hey, I had several orgasms last night.' She bugged her eyes at him. 'I'm happy.'

He laughed. Yeah, they'd made him pretty damn happy too. And gave him an opening. 'So, about that.'

Sobering, she said, 'Yeah.'

'It was…nice.' Which was about the understatement of the year.

She huffed out a breath. 'Yeah.'

'I was thinking…it could be extra nice to share some more orgasms. You appear to be in a pretty big deficit too so maybe we could do it again sometime?'

Yarran hadn't kissed her last night with this as an end goal. Nor had he woken this morning with the possibility on his mind. But, as they'd walked side by side like this, heading to breakfast as they'd done hundreds of times in the past, he'd thought—why not? They'd have to go slow because there was Jarrah to think of but maybe with time they could find their way back to each other.

The thought shimmered and twisted like a sunbeam in front of him.

'I don't know, Yarran. I'm only just back and I'm trying to make a new start—new job, new place. Find someone to talk to about all my…stuff. It's very, *very* tempting—' She grinned at him. 'But I think friends is probably the best option for us now.'

Yarran nodded, unsurprised Harper was, once again, the hesitant party. 'Of course.'

The fact she was actively talking about getting some therapy and recognising it wasn't good to muddy those waters with a new/old emotional entanglement was a good thing. A sensible thing.

'I guess we could do—' she shrugged a bare shoulder '—occasional…benefits.'

He cocked an eyebrow. 'Oh, I see. You just want to use me for sex, Jones?'

'Maybe? Occasionally.' She gave him a small smile. 'And vice versa. I just think we have a lot going on, you and I and... maybe we shouldn't make too many plans.'

Yarran wasn't sure he was comfortable with a proposal that didn't make any firm commitments, but Harper *was* right, he did have a lot going on. *And* he wasn't twenty any more. He'd learned the hard way that relationships didn't come in one-size-fits-all packages so maybe friendship with an occasional side of naked times was perfect for this stage of his life?

'Yeah.' He nodded. 'Okay. I can live with that.' He smiled then, ignoring the niggling little voice whispering *for how long* and reached for her hand. 'Come on, I can smell the croissants from here.'

She stared at his hand and, for a moment, Yarran thought she might snub it, but then she slid hers into his hold and he tugged.

Harper was feeling pretty good half an hour later as they made their way back to Yarran's house along the wide pathway. The night had been spectacular, their talk about their relationship going forward had been fruitful and the croissants were to die for—things were looking up. She had wrangled with the decision to return to Australia far more than she had with the decision to leave, but, so far, it had worked out better than she'd hoped.

The elation lasted another ten seconds, the bubble pierced by a loud, high-pitched scream followed by, '*Help!* Please somebody help me!'

Harper glanced around her in alarm, her pulse spiking at

the fear and urgency in the voice. Yarran, already taking off, threw, 'It's this way,' over his shoulder.

As they rounded the bend in the pathway just ahead, Harper could see the problem. A woman was crying loudly over the inert body of a man who was lying half on the grass, half on the path. She was shaking him and yelling at him to wake up.

Yarran reached them seconds before Harper. 'It's okay, we're here now, ma'am,' he said, crouching beside her, gently trying to pry her away from the prostate form. 'What happened?'

The woman—Harper thought she was maybe in her late sixties—looked at Yarran wildly, as if she couldn't even see him. She was clearly in shock as she wailed, 'Help my husband, please just help my husband.'

Harper's attention was already on the man on the ground as she pressed two fingers to the carotid pulse in his neck. His lips were dusky and sweat drenched his thinning hair, running down in rivulets from his forehead. Adrenaline shot into her bloodstream, spiking her pulse and honing her focus.

Her provisional diagnosis? Myocardial infarction.

But whatever it was, he didn't have a pulse and there was no evidence of chest movement, so he needed CPR—stat.

'We were just walking along,' the woman sobbed. 'He's been having terrible indigestion the last few days and thought a walk might help. And then he just clutched his chest, cried out and fell down.'

Yep—definitely an MI.

'Heart attack?' Yarran asked.

Harper nodded, tapping triple zero into her phone then jamming it between her ear and shoulder as she positioned herself and leaned in to deliver two rescue breaths. What she'd give to have an Ambu bag, a defibrillator, a cardiac monitor, an intubation kit… Hell, she'd kill for access to a cath lab right now. But all she had was herself. And Yarran.

And she was never more grateful for his presence.

'Ambulance,' she said into the phone as the person on the other end enquired which emergency service she required.

The other woman cried harder. 'Is he going to be okay?'

Harper moved on to the chest compressions. She'd shut everything down, her adrenaline pumping as she concentrated on what she needed to do, leaving Yarran to deal with the distraught wife.

'We think your husband has had a heart attack,' Yarran explained, which caused more sobbing as the ambulance service asked Harper what had happened in her ear.

'I have a man, possibly late sixties, collapsed from suspected MI. Not breathing. No pulse.' She rattled off the details as her hands pushed down on the centre of the stranger's chest. 'I'm an emergency doctor at the Central. I've commenced CPR.'

'There's a defib at the chemist back there,' Yarran murmured, his voice low but serious, clearly aware of the gravity of the situation.

Harper allowed herself a tiny morsel of relief as the person on the other end rattled off a series of questions. 'Get it,' she said, her gaze drilling into his hoping to convey her urgency. A defib was probably this man's only chance given the terrible stats on out-of-hospital cardiac arrest. 'Run.'

Yarran didn't need to be asked twice. He sprang to his feet and ran off and Harper thanked the universe Yarran had Lyn's natural athleticism and that they weren't far from the shopping precinct.

'Ma'am. I need you to talk to the ambulance, please, they're asking about his history.' She paused temporarily to hand the phone over but the older woman just shook her head helplessly, clearly finding it hard to function. 'Ma'am…' Harper used her ER doctor voice. 'An intensive care paramedic is on the way, but they need information I can't give them. You want to help your husband? Talk to them.'

Responding to the absolute authority in Harper's voice, the older woman took the phone with shaking hands as Harper delivered a couple more breaths before starting on the compressions again. She barely heard the discussion, concentrating as she was on the actions of her hands, pushing fast and deep on the sternum, mentally counting, ignoring the ache already niggling away in her triceps.

Another elderly woman stopped to help, comforting the other woman as they both watched on. Yarran was back within five minutes and Harper could have kissed him. 'You all right to set it up?' she asked as he threw himself down beside her.

She knew that Yarran, as a fireman, was trained in first aid and that these defibs units were designed for lay people, but it was one thing in theory and something else in actuality.

'Yep,' he said briefly, his fingers moving efficiently, unzipping the case then lifting the man's shirt and affixing the sticky pads to his sweaty chest in the spots indicated on the packaging of the pads. 'ETA on the ambulance?'

'They said eight minutes so hopefully not much longer.'

He nodded as he pushed the power button and awaited instructions from the machine. Harper stopped compressions so it could get a reading. Three young guys passed by gawking and Yarran pointed back towards the chemist. 'Go wait near the road so the ambulance knows where to come.'

They took off just as the electronic voice on the machine said, 'Shock recommended. Stand clear.'

Harper and Yarran moved back, making sure no part of

them was in contact with the patient. The machine delivered a shock, the man's back bowing a little, his shoulders shrugging as the charge arced from one pad to the other.

'Analysing,' the machine said. And then, 'Recommence CPR.'

Damn it—the shock hadn't been successful.

'Can you do the compressions?' Harper asked Yarran. The most experienced person always took the airway and now she had Yarran to help, she could manage it properly.

He nodded and she shuffled around to the head as Yarran took her place, planting his big hands on the centre of the man's chest and pushing, counting under his breath.

That was when they heard the first wail of the siren.

It was nine-thirty by the time they turned back into Yarran's street, as Harper and Yarran had stayed and helped the intensive care paramedic on the scene. They'd got a pulse on their third zap just as the paramedic arrived but lost it again quickly after and she'd intubated the patient—Gary—right there on the grass.

'You did good back there,' Yarran said.

Harper, feeling wrung out now from the after-effects of adrenaline, smiled absently as she came back to their surroundings. She'd been mentally walking through every step back at the scene and calculating Gary's chances. 'I couldn't have done it without you.'

Yarran had been an efficient and effective third hand, keeping up the compression as required while she and the paramedic had worked together to stabilise the critically ill patient.

A snort blew Yarran's hair off his forehead. 'Of course you could have. Hell, Gary couldn't have picked a better place or time to collapse what with the chief of the ER at a major city hospital less than twenty metres away.'

Harper flapped her hand dismissively. 'Yes, that was fortunate.'

He grabbed for her hand then and squeezed it, halting them in the process. Harper half turned to face him, his dark eyes serious as they sought hers. 'You were amazing, Harper. Really amazing.'

Ridiculously, Harper's cheeks flushed. She was good at what she did and she didn't need praise or compliments but it felt special anyway. 'Thank you,' she said, and they just stared at each other, holding hands in the street.

After what felt like an age, he grinned. 'Turned me on a little, if I'm being honest.'

Surprised, Harper blinked, but his grin was infectious and it felt just like the old days, only better because she'd finally shone a light for him to see into all her dark places and that felt so bloody...freeing. She laughed. 'Weirdo.'

'What? Competence porn, it's a thing, you know?'

He tugged on her hand and they continued along until they rounded the curve towards his house and Harper spotted his parents' car parked outside. Ali's was parked beside Harper's, which was still sitting conspicuously in his driveway, exactly where she'd parked it yesterday.

'Oh, Jesus.' Her hand loosened from his, dropping to her side, and her pace slowed. What the hell were they all going to think?

'It's okay,' he whispered. 'It's not any of their business.'

But as they neared, they could hear the stricken, wrenching cries of a child getting louder and louder. *Jarrah.* Yarran swore under his breath and, for the second time this morning, he ran.

Gripping the strap of her handbag, Harper picked up her

pace too, her adrenaline blipping again, a surge of nausea roiling through her gut. She contemplated jumping in her car and careening away but she couldn't do that to Yarran. Briefly, she wondered if she could get away with a story about her joining him this morning for a platonic breakfast together but—how did she explain being in the same dress as yesterday?

By the time she opened the front door and stepped into the fray, Jarrah was wrapped up in his father's embrace but still apparently inconsolable. His skinny arms were clinging around Yarran's neck and Yarran was hugging his son tight, his eyes closed as he rocked Jarrah back and forth.

'Hey, Harper,' Lyn greeted, her face scrunched into an expression of concern as she stroked Jarrah's back.

Coen nodded and said, 'Morning, love,' shooting her a sympathetic smile as he hovered nearby.

Yarran's eyes flicked open then, meeting hers, and she saw maybe more than he'd intended. He might not have felt guilty earlier, but he definitely did now. His eyes were awash with anguish and self-recrimination.

He closed them again. Closing her out.

Harper's gaze met Ali's next. It was stony as her eyes swept up and down Harper's dress, her lips thinning as she looked away.

'I thought…you were…' Jarrah breathed jerkily, hiccoughing his anguish '…d-d-dead too, Daddy… Like Mum… Mum… Mummy.'

Harper sucked in a breath at Jarrah's heartfelt confession. He'd seemed like such a happy-go-lucky kid the two times she'd seen him. That was the thing though, with emotional trauma—conscious or not—it lay in wait and came at you at the most unexpected times.

'It's okay. I'm right here. I'm not going anywhere.' Yarran's voice was muffled in Jarrah's neck. 'I'm right here. I'll always be here for you.'

Harper blinked at the bold statement. *What?* Nobody could make that kind of guarantee—what was Yarran thinking?

'How about we go into your bedroom?' Lyn suggested. 'Daddy can read your favourite book. Grandpa and I can come too, if you like?'

Jarrah nodded. 'Yes, p-please.'

Harper watched as the four of them headed for the hallway, leaving her alone with Ali. Her hands trembled a little as she absently noticed Wally, sitting outside the back door, whining slightly in sympathy.

'Is he...? Does that happen often?' Harper asked quietly, her gut still churning.

She had felt completely out of her depth in the face of Jarrah's anguish. She'd dealt with many a crying kid in her job, but sick kids were different. Kids in her ER she knew what to do with. She could order a test or set a broken bone or give some medication. An emotionally overwrought kid hyperanxious about parental death?

Not so much.

'Not usually, no,' Ali replied, stiffly. 'He told Mum last night someone at kindy the other day had apparently asked about Marnie and what would happen to Jarrah if his daddy died too. So when we got home and Yarran wasn't here...'

The accusation in her voice was clear. 'We were delayed by—'

'No.' Ali cut her off with a head shake and a glare. 'I told you he was good now.'

Harper swallowed, a dark pit splitting open inside. 'Ali... no...'

'You said, okay. I thought we had an understanding. I all

but *begged* you,' she said, lowering her voice, 'to leave him alone, Harper.'

'It's not like that.'

'Oh?' Ali folded her arms. 'So you didn't spend the night with my brother?'

Harper shut her eyes briefly before facing the anger in Ali's eyes head-on. She might not have to answer to Ali in any real sense but deep down, Harper knew she had to—morally. And for the sake of their friendship. 'We're not getting back together.'

'Good,' she snapped, keeping her voice low. 'Because look what happens when he's with you. You left the country and ripped his heart out and now you're back and in less than a month you've turned his life upside again. It's not just him any more, Harper. You don't just get to pick up where you left off. You don't just get to think about yourself this time.'

If Ali had slapped her, Harper couldn't have felt more rocked back on her feet. Her pulse throbbed at her temples and her jaw ached from clenching it so tight. Ali was right— what the hell was she doing? Jarrah was inconsolable, Yarran looked as though he'd been gut-punched and her fragile truce with Ali was in tatters.

Harper swallowed. 'You're right.' God…what had she been thinking? That she and Yarran could be friends with maybe some sex on the side and everything would be fine? Nothing had ever been that simple between them.

'I'm sorry.' *Damn.* 'What can I do to make this right?'

Ali dropped her arms by her sides on a loud sigh. 'Just *go*, Harper. Leave him be.'

The message dropped like a lead sinker in her stomach, but there was a simplicity to its devastation nonetheless. She could walk away. She'd done it before. And there was a certain comfort in the familiar.

Except… *Ugh*. It *hurt*.

Wally whined then and Harper glanced in his direction. He wagged his tail a little, looking utterly forlorn. God, she'd even caused the dog distress. Clearing her throat, she dug in her handbag for her keys. 'Please apologise to your parents for me. Tell them I was called in to work, would you?' She might be walking away but she didn't want Lyn and Coen to think she'd caused this ruckus and callously fled the scene. Even if she had.

'Of course,' came the stilted reply.

She left then, not looking back at the dog or Ali. Not looking back at the house or the street or the suburb sign as she drove away, leaving them all behind in her rear-view mirror, tears falling unchecked down her cheeks.

CHAPTER NINE

YARRAN EASED AWAY from Jarrah, who, after several reads through of his favourite book, had fallen asleep. He crossed the room to the window, placing his hands wide on the sill as he stared out over the pool, pressing his forehead to the warm glass. What the hell had just happened?

How long had Jarrah been worrying about him dying?

The sobbed confession had been like a hammer strike to his solar plexus and Yarran still felt as if he couldn't breathe properly. Guilt that his absence had triggered such tumult for his son weighed like a block of granite on his shoulders. He should have been there when Jarrah got home, not…galivanting around with Harper. Sure, the medical emergency had been an unforeseen delay in their return, but the fact was, if he hadn't been out—making eyes at Harper—he'd have been home when Jarrah arrived.

As a good, responsible father would have been.

Harper had said it herself—*'He needs you…to put him first.'* Well…not being home when Jarrah needed him *wasn't* putting his kid first. Jarrah was the most precious thing in his world and then Harper had come back and apparently everything in his brain had fritzed.

They shouldn't have gone out this morning. Hell, who was he kidding? He should have kept it zipped last night. He clearly couldn't multitask when it came to Harper and he had a four-year-old boy who needed his absolute attention. He shut his eyes, dropping his head between his shoulders as he silently castigated himself.

What would Marnie think of this lapse in his parenting?

'I'm sorry,' his mother said quietly as she came to stand at one side. 'We rang several times.'

Yarran's phone had been on vibrate but he hadn't felt it during the resus or even thought to check it as they'd walked back to his place. He'd known they were late getting home but he'd also known Jarrah would be safe with his parents. He filled her in on the reason for their delay and she told him about what the kid at kindy had said, which made Yarran feel worse.

Why hadn't Jarrah felt he could share that with him? Had he sensed Yarran's head was elsewhere?

'It was just the perfect storm, love,' Coen said from the other side of the bed.

Yarran shook his head. 'I *should* have been here.'

'You would have been had it not been for your good Samaritan act,' Lyn soothed.

'No.' Yarran shook his head vigorously. 'I shouldn't have gone out at all. I shouldn't have…' He blew out a breath and tried not to think about how much last night had meant. 'I should have sent Harper home last night.'

'Yarran…' His mother slipped her arm around his waist. 'You deserve a life too. We've been so worried about you for so long and you've been so…different since she's been back. Like the old Yarran.'

'She's right, son,' Coen agreed.

Yeah. She was. *He'd* felt differently, too. But… 'He's too young, Mum. He needs me to be focused on him. I'll get a life later.'

'But what if you could have both?' Lyn pressed.

Coen nodded. 'It doesn't have to be either or, Yarran.'

Yarran turned to face the bed, leaning back against the sill. Jarrah's face was relaxed now but the strands of his anguish still wrapped around Yarran's heart as if it were a bug wrapped up tight in a spider's web. 'Yeah, it does,' he murmured. 'For now.'

'Sweetie…' Lyn also turned. 'You are my son and I know you like I know my own heartbeat.'

Yarran met his mother's gaze, her eyes so like his. He swore sometimes when she looked at him intently like this he could see generations of Gundungurra and Darug women staring back at him with their wisdom and compassion.

'You have a heart as big as a lion—trust me, it can love again. I know that because after Harper it made room for Marnie. And then for Jarrah. Love doesn't divide, Yarran, it multiplies.' She squeezed his arm. 'And it's okay to want to have a life partner. It's human to want to be loved. And not just by your family but by that one special person.'

Yarran knew if he had a friend in this situation he'd be saying exactly the same thing. But this was *him* and there was too much at stake. 'She doesn't want to be a mother.'

And he had Jarrah.

'Honey…that was twelve years ago. Maybe she feels differently now? Have you asked her?'

'No.'

'Maybe you should?' Coen raised an eyebrow. 'I watched Harper with him yesterday—she was great. Hell, he didn't stop yakking about her and that terrarium all night.'

Yarran glanced at his father, surprised. And…pleased. Which only ramped up his inner conflict. Was it wrong he wanted Jarrah to like her?

'Sweetie.' Lyn squeezed his arm again. 'It's been three years and you and I both know Marnie would want you to love again. And I think you *are* in love with Harper, right?'

No. Yes. He looked at his mother helplessly. Maybe...

'I don't think you ever fell *out* of love with her,' she added.

'I...don't know how I feel.' And what did it matter? He wasn't about to take some wild punt—he wasn't twenty any more.

'Fair enough.' His father nodded. 'You don't have to. You don't have to rush into anything. But, son, she looked kinda devastated out there too and you *did* spend the night with her so I'm guessing this isn't the way she pictured it was going to end. Jarrah hysterical, you walking away barely acknowledging her. Maybe she doesn't know how she feels either, but she probably needs some assurance none of this was her fault.'

Yarran blinked. *What?* 'I don't blame her for this.'

'Good.' He nodded. 'Now go and tell *her.*' He tipped his head at his grandson. 'Jarrah's out for the count. Your mother and I will sit with him, you go talk to her.'

His father was right, of course. Whatever mess was here today, he didn't blame her for it. It was nobody's fault a man collapsed, making them late. Nor was Jarrah's current emotional fragility her fault, either. His feelings might be muddied and complicated, but he couldn't abide the thought that she might blame herself.

Suitably chastised, Yarran nodded. 'Okay, thanks.'

But when he returned to the lounge area, she was nowhere to be found. There was just Ali making herself a coffee in the kitchen.

'Where's Harper?'

His sister's shoulders tensed as a visceral blast of her simmering anger hit him in that place they'd shared from as early as he could remember. She turned to face him, cradling a mug, their eyes meeting. 'She left.'

Yarran's brow furrowed. 'Why did she leave?'

Ali's gaze dropped to her coffee. 'Something about being called into work.'

Prickles spiked at Yarran's scalp. She was lying. In all their years they'd never been able to lie to each other. They were too finely attuned to get away with it. But why would she lie? Unless… 'Ali? What did you say to her?'

'Nothing.'

'Ali!'

Her eyes flicked to his and if he hadn't already sensed it, he'd have known it from the guilt stamped across her features. It was quickly replaced by a mutinous expression. 'She tore your heart out and she stomped all over it, Yarran. You were *gutted.* I know because I felt every single second of your pain like an axe blow to *my* heart.'

Yarran gaped as his sister blinked back tears. He knew she felt his pain because he felt hers too and he knew how wrenching it was to have this kind of emotional ESP. But what was happening between Harper and him was none of her business.

'It was a long time ago.'

'Except now she's back, leaving just as much turmoil in her wake and I can't bear you being hurt again. I don't think you'll survive another broken heart at her hands. And I'm damn sure I won't. So… I told her to go. To leave you alone.'

Yarran's heart thundered like a storm in his chest, a hot gush of rage rising in him, and he really hoped his sister felt all its sharp, jagged edges because he was *furious.* Ali had always taken her *older* sister duties seriously, but he was all grown up now.

'Goddamn it, Alinta,' he snapped, stalking towards her,

wanting to yell it at her with the weight of all his fury but conscious that Jarrah was asleep and his parents were probably also listening. 'You had *no right*.'

'Somebody's got to save you from yourself,' she hissed back.

God…was she kidding him now? 'Stay out of it.' He spread his hands on the island countertop and leaned over it as she glared at him from the other side. 'When I want your help, I'll ask.'

'Save your breath,' she muttered. 'I won't help you break your heart.'

A well of frustration rose in Yarran's chest as he pushed off the bench and stalked to the back door. He fumbled for his phone in his back pocket. He had to talk to Harper. To apologise. For his sister. And for the way he'd handled Jarrah being so upset.

Wally whined as he slid the door open and stepped out onto the balcony and Yarran absently petted him. 'It's okay, Wal, everything's okay.'

He stabbed at Harper's number and shoved the phone to his ear. It didn't surprise him when it rang out. It also didn't surprise him when it rang out a second time, his frustration burgeoning with each ring. It *did* surprise him when she answered on his third attempt. He'd fully expected Harper to not answer at all, which meant he'd have to leave message after message begging for her to pick up or call back.

'Hello, Yarran.'

Despite her greeting lacking any emotion, it took all of the puff out of his sails as a wave of gratitude swamped him. He really hadn't been looking forward to talking to her voicemail for the next however long. 'Harper…*thank God*…you picked up.'

'I figured you'd just keep ringing so we might as well get it over and done with.'

Yarran swallowed at the flatness to her tone. 'I'm so sorry about Ali…she had no right to tell you to go.'

'It's fine. I understand. She's your sister. She's looking out for you.'

Her voice had turned cool and Yarran could feel her slipping away, and desperation seized him, bashing away like a tiny hammer at his temple. He didn't know what he wanted where they were concerned, but now she was back he'd never *not* want her in his life.

'It's not fine, it was—'

'It was a mistake, Yarran,' she cut in, icicles hanging from her words. 'Last night.'

'Harper. No…'

'Yes. But that's okay. It was always bound to happen. We agreed it was one flash of heat so let's just leave it at that.'

Had they agreed, though? Or had there just been a tacit acknowledgment of what was happening? And their discussion on their walk had surely changed things? 'But this morning we talked about being friends, sometimes even being the kind of friends who enjoyed benefits.'

He wasn't sure why he was making such a case for what they'd said this morning given he didn't know how to feel about any of it. All he knew was this entire conversation made his skin feel too tight, as if it were about to split wide open.

Because it felt like goodbye. *Again.*

'Yeah, I think we both know now that can't happen.'

She didn't mention Jarrah's meltdown but it was obvious she was alluding to it. 'What happened with Jarrah wasn't your fault, Harper. What happened between us last night had nothing to do with this morning.'

She didn't say anything for several interminable beats of time. And then, 'I think it's best we just let it be.'

The coldness in her voice almost sucked Yarran's breath away. It was chillingly convincing and he wished he could hit rewind on the whole damn day. He sure as hell needed to speak to her face to face. Not over a damn phone line. He wanted to see her face when she told him they were one and done.

'Look… Harper. I'd like to talk to you. Not on the phone. But I can't leave Jarrah now. Can I come over sometime in the next few days?'

'No. I'm sorry, I don't want to see you again.'

And then she hung up the phone and all he was left with was the dial tone ringing in his ear.

Three days later, her words were still echoing in Harper's head. It had killed her to say it and slain her to admit it. But, even utterly miserable as she was now, she firmly believed she'd done the right thing.

Why she'd thought she could even *flirt* with the idea of having something with Yarran again was ridiculous. She'd come to start a new life, not fall back on the old, and Yarran had other responsibilities.

Thankfully it had been a busy week. Her apartment was ready on Monday and her stuff from the UK had been delivered so she'd moved out of Ivy's. That hadn't been a bad thing because Ivy knew something was up and wasn't the kind of friend who sat silently by waiting for an opening. But Harper hadn't been up to analysing it and nor had she wanted to put Ivy in the middle of something between her and Ali.

On top of that, the flu season has started with a vengeance, making the ER even busier than usual. Harper had worked late the last couple of nights and then spent several hours unpacking boxes when she got home. Which meant she was exhausted.

Yet, she couldn't sleep.

Every time she shut her eyes she saw a kaleidoscope of images from last Saturday night and Sunday morning. Yarran, his face screwed up in pleasure. Jarrah, his face crumpled in aguish. Ali, her face twisted in anger.

By five o'clock Wednesday afternoon, Harper was running on empty. Fatigue sapped every cell in her body, her eyes were bleary and she was being exceptionally irritable with her team. She was about to knock off and she was pretty sure they were all going to high-five each other as soon as she left the building.

But first—another case had just come through the ambulance bay doors. A woman who'd not long given birth to a baby girl during an assisted midwife delivery in her home, with a suspected post-partum haemorrhage. The Obs and Gynae registrar had been paged as Harper listened to the paramedic handover and the team buzzed around the cubicle getting the woman hooked up to monitors and IVs.

'Hey.'

Harper blinked, surprised to see Ali standing beside her, nodding politely and smiling at the paramedic to continue. Her registrar must be held up and they'd sent in the big guns.

The paramedics left after the handover was complete and Harper made an executive decision not to overcrowd the room. Emergency situations were fraught enough without any weird juju between the people supposed to be in charge. And they had an ace team—the head of Obs and Gynae, an ER registrar and resident as well as three nurses.

Everyone was efficient and capable. They didn't need her as well.

'I'm pretty sure you can handle this,' she murmured to Ali and turned to leave.

Ali frowned at her, flicking a quick look over Harper's appearance, her hand sliding onto Harper's forearm. 'Are you okay?'

Harper fixed a smile on her dial. 'Just peachy.'

She walked out of the cubicle and didn't stop until the greenery of the rooftop garden surrounded her. She didn't plan to leave until she knew the patient had been stabilised. Seeing Ali again had brought all the emotion of last Sunday back and she couldn't breathe.

The air was fresh and crisp up here and the garden deserted. It was a good place to clear her head. To remind herself of all the things she did have, how fortunate she was, how *lucky*. To breathe deep and give thanks for those blessings.

The rooftop garden had rapidly become her favourite place in the hospital and she'd never been more grateful for it than she was right now.

Leaning on the rail, Harper looked out over the changing mood of the city as the sun set and the lights winked on. She was truly blessed to be here, in this stage of her life—she'd outlived her mother by over a decade—and if the re-entry to Australia had been a little bumpy, then that was hardly unexpected.

And tomorrow was a new day.

Harper wasn't sure how long she stood there just breathing and letting her mind go blank but, at some point, the door behind opened. She looked over her shoulder to find Ali heading her way with an expression of grim determination.

'Everything okay with the patient?' Harper asked as Ali's elbows slid onto the railing next to hers.

'Yes. Haemorrhage has resolved and she's stable. I've arranged for her transfer to HDU overnight. They're getting a cot from maternity for the baby to room in.'

Harper nodded. 'Excellent.'

They stood for a while looking at the rapidly fading light over the city, not talking until Ali broke the silence. 'Look... I'm sorry about Sunday, I was out of line.'

Harper blinked. She hadn't expected Ali to apologise. She knew how fiercely she loved her brother. How seriously she took her role as his *older* sister. She knew they had a connection people who weren't twins could never really understand.

'It's fine.' It had been the jolt she'd needed.

'No.' Ali half turned to face Harper. 'It's not. Yarran was furious with me and hasn't returned any of my calls. It was a terrible sister thing to do. And a...terrible friend thing.'

Harper glanced at her, surprised. So, they were still going to be friends?

'Jarrah's hysterics put us all on edge and I was speaking from an emotional place. That's not an excuse, it was just where I was at. What I didn't say but *should* have was that it's been a long time since I've seen Yarran look as happy as he did on Saturday. He's been in a good place this last little while but I could still feel the *weight* in his heart. And then you rocked up to the party and he looked at you across the yard and I could feel it lift. I could feel his...*joy*. And he hasn't felt joyful in a long time.'

Ack. Joy. Why did Ali have to use that word? She'd accepted her reunion with Yarran had been short-lived but at least their brief flirtation had left no time for *feelings*. Except, apparently, she'd given him joy. Which now she was stealing away again.

'Well...it doesn't matter anyway.' Harper returned her attention to the last golden hue gilding the building tops. 'I told him I'm not seeing him any more. It's for the best.'

Harper could *feel* the intensity of Ali's glare on her profile. 'Yeah… I can see that's working out well for you.'

Irritated, Harper turned to Ali. 'What the hell does that mean?'

'You look terrible.'

'Gee, *thanks*,' Harper muttered, wishing she could refute it. 'Are you sick?'

Harper bit back a laugh lest it come across as slightly hysterical. 'I'm just tired. Work's crazy, I've moved into the new apartment. I'm not sleeping very well.'

Ali opened her mouth to say something, but her phone rang and she dug in her pocket for it. She glanced at the screen, her brow furrowing a little. 'It's Mum.'

Harper turned back to the view as Ali took the call. 'Hey, Mum…okay… Wait… Mum…*slow down*. What happened?'

The note in Ali's voice shot an itch right up Harper's spine and she turned to hear her say, 'What do you mean, he's missing?'

Missing? A sense of dread descended. Jarrah? *Yarran.* 'What?' she demanded. 'Who?'

Ali shook her head. 'It's Harper. She's here with me now… Why was he all the way out there fighting a fire?'

Fire… Harper's breath left in a rush and she grabbed the railing for support as her legs went weak. *Yarran.* Missing. In a fire zone. The faces of every fire victim that had ever come into her ER played in full Technicolor on a loop through her head.

Harper pressed her hand to her chest, trying to try stop the pain there. Her pulse beat like a drum through her head. She couldn't breathe. Why couldn't she breathe? *God…*was she having a heart attack?

'Yes…' A nod. 'Yes…' Another nod. 'Yes. We're coming now.'

Ali glanced at Harper for confirmation and Harper nodded her head vigorously. She wasn't sure where they were going but wild horses wouldn't have stopped her going.

'What happened?' Harper asked as soon as Ali ended the call.

'He volunteered to go out to the Blue Mountains this morning to help them cover some sick leave. There was a bit of a blaze up there that took a few hours to bring under control. He's currently…unaccounted for.'

It was delivered dispassionately but Harper felt every word like a bullet and she knew Ali did too.

'Oh, God…' A sudden rush of blood to her head made her feel dizzy and *nauseous*. 'Oh, God,' she whispered, holding her side as she bent at the waist to ease the dizziness. Once it passed she levered herself upright. 'Well?' she demanded. 'Are they looking for him?'

Ali nodded, because she was blinking back tears and obviously couldn't *word* right now. Without thinking, Harper reached for her and they hugged—*hard.* 'Can you…?' Harper's voice was thick with emotion as she released Ali and looked earnestly into her face. 'Can you feel him? Is he lost or in pain or—?'

Harper cut off, covering her mouth. God…she couldn't even say the words.

'No.' Ali shook her head vehemently. 'He's not dead. He's *not.*'

A wave of relief swept through Harper—cool and full of hope. It might not be particularly scientific but she would back Ali's gut regarding her brother any day.

'You love him, don't you?'

The question was quiet but also rang with certainty and she

felt the answering ring deep inside her gut. Harper nodded. She did. 'I never stopped.'

And it felt so freaking good and awful all at once saying it out loud, finally giving voice to something she'd been suppressing for ever. She loved Yarran Edwards with her whole heart.

That was just the way it was.

'Really?' Ali's eyes probed hers. 'Cos you can't just say that and walk away if things get hard again or a little too emotionally close for you. I don't know what's happened to him but if it's something serious...' her voice wobbled a little '...he's going to need you and so is Jarrah. That's what being in love with my brother looks like twelve years down the track. He's a package deal. And even if he's perfectly fine, that equation doesn't change. So if you're in, you better be all the way in or I swear I will leave you behind on this roof.'

Harper swallowed the lump of emotion rising in her throat. Ali was absolutely right—there could be no equivocation going forward. Nor did she want there to be. She hadn't been equipped to trust what Yarran had offered her all those years ago. But there came a point in a person's life where they had to decide to be happy, to reach for that chance and trust it would be okay.

And she wanted that with Yarran. With Jarrah.

Meeting Ali's eye, she nodded and said, 'I'm all the way in.'

Half an hour later, Harper and Ali walked into Yarran's house where things had gone so wrong only a few days ago. It had been such a *low* moment but utterly insignificant now.

'Any word?' Ali asked as her parents stood and Jarrah ran to her, launching himself at her body. The television was on a news channel with the sound turned low and a radio was also on somewhere tuned to a different news station.

Lyn was clearly worried but trying to hold it together. Coen, quietly stoic, absently rubbed his wife's back. 'Nothing yet,' he said.

Smiling at Harper, Lyn wrapped her up in a huge hug. 'It's so good to see you.'

It was good to see *her*. Lyn had always given the best hugs. Coen hugged her too and tears sprang to Harper's eyes. Why had she let childhood fears deny her vital emotional support?

The next hour passed in a blur. Lyn bustled around making tea and coffee and trying to interest everyone in food. Coen flicked between news channels. Ali and Harper sat on the three-seater couch, Jarrah between them. Aunty Li-Li read to him, trying to keep him occupied. He'd been told that his father had got himself a bit lost out in the bush when he was fighting a fire, but people were looking for him and he'd be home soon.

A half-truth to be sure, but an age-appropriate one. Jarrah obviously internalised a lot more than his family realised so they hadn't wanted to keep him out of the loop but they hadn't wanted to worry him either. There were enough people in the house doing that, including Wally, who had taken up position on the floor in front of Jarrah.

As time dragged, a hard lump of nerves knotted and looped in Harper's belly. Waves of nausea came and went as Harper entreated the universe.

Please let him be alive. Please let him be all right. Please don't let him die.

She didn't really believe in any kind of divine influence but, in this moment, it felt as if she was at least doing something.

Her only bright spot was that Ali was absolutely certain her brother was still alive and that gave her *hope*.

'Jarrah, why don't you get Vi and show Harper how big she is now?' Lyn suggested.

'Oh, yeah!' Jarrah leapt up and careened down the hallway, Wally close on his heels.

Harper raised an eyebrow at Ali. 'Vi?'

'The African violet.'

'Ah.'

Jarrah was back in seconds and, much to Harper's astonishment, he climbed right into her lap, settling there as he presented the terrarium. 'See, Harper? Vi's gots five flowers now.'

'Four,' Ali corrected with a laugh.

'Wow...' Harper said automatically but the truth was there could have been two dozen flowers and it probably wouldn't have registered. She was still getting over the emotional whammy of Yarran's son crawling into her lap. He'd been great with her at his party but there was an easy, familiar intimacy to this action that stole her breath.

As if she was one of the family.

Harper wanted that desperately, she realised as she gazed down at the curly hair, so like his father's. Twelve years ago, the mere thought had terrified her, now she wanted *more* for herself. She wanted to grab the chance.

Of course, given how cold she'd been during their last conversation, Yarran might not want to give her that chance. Hell, he might not make it home.

She scrubbed the thought from her brain but when Jarrah turned his face up, looked at her intently and asked, 'Is my daddy going to be okay?' it pushed the thought front and centre again.

Harper's breath caught in her throat. The enquiry was innocent enough but those dark eyes—Yarran's eyes—stared back at her with a heart-wrenching solemnity. Quite why he'd asked her, Harper wasn't sure. He'd have been better to ask Ali, whose twin ESP was keeping them all a little buoyed. But this was a little boy who'd already lost one parent and was obviously seeking reassurance.

And he'd chosen her.

'Absolutely.'

She remembered being shocked at Yarran's sweeping statement of assurance when Jarrah had been crying hysterically last Sunday. She'd never had anything sugar-coated in her life and it had felt wrong for Yarran to do that. But she *got* it now. There was time for brutal truths and time to give the gift of hope—false or not—because it was only human to want to hold onto the positive in any situation and, as a parent, sometimes, that was the job.

And in this moment, she would do anything, *say* anything, to allay the fears she could see lurking in Jarrah's dark expressive eyes.

'Your dad is smart and brave and *very* good at his job. He's going to be just fine.'

'Do you promise, Harper?'

She swallowed, the look of complete trust in his gaze more than she could bear. 'I promise.' And she hoped like hell it was true.

Come home, Yarran. Come home.

Coen's phone rang into the charged silence and Harper swore she could hear a collective intake of breath as he stood and answered. Lyn and Ali also both stood and hovered as Coen said, 'Yes, this is he…' And then, 'Yes…yes… Oh, *thank you*—' He huffed out a huge sigh and Ali and her mother embraced. 'That is good news. *Thank you.*'

Harper's breath released in a rush and she swallowed back against a surge of threatening bile as all the fears she hadn't dared give free rein suddenly flew away like dandelion puffs, leaving her light and airy and utterly elated.

'They found him. He's fine,' Coen confirmed as he placed the phone down, grinning from ear to ear. 'Concussed but otherwise uninjured. They're taking him to the Central.'

Jarrah's little face lit up in wonder as he turned his eyes on Harper. 'See,' she said with a huge smile. 'What did I tell you?'

Then he threw his little arms around her neck and hugged her and Harper knew, in that moment, she would do any-thing—*anything*—for this little boy.

Yarran slept heavily for he didn't know how long. Time was an unreliable narrator as he opened and closed his eyes, squinting against lights that were too bright and wincing at pain that was too damn much. His head thumped as flashes of memory chased each other in a foggy kind of never-ending dream.

A falling branch, the smell of burning and the aroma of eucalypts and a loamy forest floor. The scratch of dry leaves on his cheek. Then a siren and long corridors, things that beeped, the feel of crisp bedsheets and the smell of disinfectant and laundry detergent. Voices and faces, some he didn't know, others he did. His family—Jarrah and Ali and his parents. His other siblings.

And Harper. Who he loved. Harper, who didn't want to see him again.

More pain, grimacing at its intensity, wanting to tear his head from his shoulders, followed by periods of floating and the cool bliss of sleep.

Before it started all over again.

Then suddenly he broke through all the sluggishness weighing down his eyelids and he was awake. *Very* awake. Blinking at the bright lights and a *very* white ceiling. Not his bedroom. Way too white and…clinical. But the pain was much better, more like a dull backbeat than the symphony of pickaxes that had been chipping away at his skull.

Discombobulated, he just lay there for a moment, staring, trying to orientate himself and place the low *beep, beep, beep* he could hear somewhere off to the side. As he slowly turned his head to try and locate the noise, his eyes fell on a big chair beside his bed. Some kind of recliner, although the occupants were curled up on it rather than stretched out.

Harper. *And Jarrah.* Snuggled up together fast asleep. Jarrah hugging his…terrarium? Was he still dreaming? If he was, he didn't want to wake up.

A sudden prickle of moisture stabbed at his eyes and he had to shut them because it hurt too much. His eyes and his damn stupid heart. He opened them again, half expecting the apparition to be gone, but there they were. His two people. The little boy who'd become his whole world and the woman he'd loved for ever.

Yarran could hear the beeps getting faster, which instantly roused Harper, whose eyes flew in the direction of the beeping before cutting quickly to him, their gazes meshing. She was startled for a fraction of a second then almost fell out of the chair as she lurched quickly forward while trying to balance Jarrah.

'Yarran?'

'Hey,' he said, his voice croaky, his mouth dry as dirt and just as tasty.

Harper's moving had disturbed Jarrah. His eyelids fluttered a couple of times before opening then widening. *'Daddy?'* He glanced at Harper with huge eyes. 'Is Daddy awake now like you said he would be?'

She beamed down at him. 'Yes, buddy, he is.'

Then they were both off the chair, crossing to him, and his heart was so damn full he thought it might explode. He didn't know how they'd got here—everything was fuzzy and it hurt to think too hard—but Harper was here—here with Jarrah—and it was all he cared about.

Harper helped Jarrah up on the bed. 'Be careful,' she said. 'Daddy's going to be sore and sleepy for a while so you have to be very gentle with him.'

Weak as a kitten, Yarran lifted his arm, encumbered by a drip. Jarrah slipped in beside him and kissed him on the shoulder with such sweet tenderness, Yarran wanted nothing more than to wrap him up in a huge hug. But everywhere, it seemed, there were drips and wires and bandages and he felt utterly feeble.

'We were scared, Daddy,' Jarrah whispered suddenly. 'Weren't we, Harper?'

She smiled and stroked Jarrah's head as she looked at Yarran. 'Yes, we were.'

Yarran held her gaze for long moments, reaching for her hand and holding it against his cheek. 'How long have I been sleeping for?'

'Two days.'

Yarran blinked. 'Bloody hell.'

'Oops, Daddy did a swearsy,' Jarrah said, laughing in delight.

Harper laughed too, as did Yarran despite how much it hurt. Her hand stroked his head, her fingers pushing into his hair, and he shut his eyes, it felt so good.

'How's your headache?'

He grimaced. 'It's there. But not like it has been.'

Suddenly the door opened and a nurse entered, followed by his parents and Ali as well as Brock and Riggs, and it was all kinds of pandemonium as everyone talked at once and there were tears and laughter and hugs galore and a hundred questions were answered and gaps were filled in and a doctor came and chatted about how lucky he was to escape with some superficial burns to his forehead and a mild concussion.

Yarran had to wonder, if this was mild, what a major case of concussion felt like because his exhaustion was brutal. Less than an hour later he was yawning as if it were an Olympic sport and he were going for gold. His nurse—bless her cotton socks—called time.

'Okay, everyone. Yarran needs to rest now.'

Harper agreed and everyone was dutifully shooed out. 'C'mon, you,' Ali said to Jarrah. 'You too.'

'But I wants to stays with Harper and Daddy.'

'He's okay,' Yarran said.

Harper glanced between him and Ali then back to him briefly before turning to Jarrah. 'Did you know the hospital has a garden on the roof?'

Jarrah gasped. 'Really, Harper?'

Yarran laughed. He wasn't sure when in the last couple of days Jarrah had started deferring to Harper, but he liked it.

'Yep. Really. It's my favourite spot.'

'How about we check it out?' Ali suggested. 'Then I'll bring you back to Daddy.'

'Okay.' Jarrah slipped his hand into his aunty Li-Li's and they headed for the door.

'Mmm.' Yarran shut his eyes as they departed and peace descended, the thump of his head lessening several degrees. 'I never noticed how loud they all were before.'

Harper laughed. 'I did.' He flicked his eyes open in time to see her face getting closer and closer, her forehead coming to rest on his cheekbone, her lips near his ear. 'You scared the living daylights out of me, Yarran Edwards. Don't ever do that again.'

Yarran smiled. 'No, ma'am.'

She kissed his cheek then and whispered, 'I love you.' Then she kissed all over his face whispering those three little words.

I love you.

'You do, huh?' he murmured as she brushed her mouth against the corner of his mouth. His tired body wasn't so tired suddenly.

She pulled back a little and nodded. 'I do. I know I said I didn't want to see you again but I was terrified I'd screwed up after everything was such a mess with Jarrah that day. And I figured that was fine because I hadn't even been back a month and it was too early for feelings. But I was with Ali when she got the call about you going missing and I felt physically ill thinking about you out there…injured, alone or *worse*…' She shuddered. 'And I knew that I loved you. I knew I'd never stopped.'

'When I opened my eyes and saw you and Jarrah snuggled up asleep before…' Yarran ran a finger down the side of her face, pushing a strand of red hair that had fallen forward back behind her ear '… I thought I must be hallucinating.'

'Not hallucinating. We've been clinging to each other for two days. I think maybe deep down we hoped you'd feel our combined love pulling you through.'

'I think maybe I did.' He smiled and even that hurt. 'Thank you. Thank you for being there for him while I've been like this. It means the world to me.'

In fact, he loved her for it. *He loved Harper Jones.* For a lot of reasons, but for Jarrah in particular. Love multiplies, his mother had said, and she was right if the love trebling in his heart right now was any indication. It was so full it was fit to burst.

'*You* mean the world to me.'

She smiled tentatively. 'I do?'

'You do. I've just been guarding my heart for so long now, too frightened to risk it for me *and* for Jarrah. But the truth is I never fell out of love with you, either. Then I met Marnie and the love I felt for you became this thing in my past. But it didn't go. It was still there, it just…existed in a different time zone. And now here you are again and this love has bubbled back up whether I wanted it to or not because it's too strong to deny and it's made me feel whole again after feeling broken for the last three years.'

'Oh, *Yarran*.' She kissed him then, lightly, gently. 'You and Jarrah and coming back into your family has made *me* feel whole again. I used to feel what we had couldn't be real. Not for the likes of me. But I've never felt more whole than when I was with you and I want that again if you and Jarrah will have me.'

You and Jarrah. As far as three little words went—they were corkers.

'Except I'm going to trust it this time.' Her green eyes blazed sincerity. 'Trust you. Trust *us*.'

'Yes.' Yarran's fingers trembled as he pushed them into her hair. He'd never thought he'd have a second time around with his first love, but here she was, and he wanted nothing more than to spend the rest of his life with her and Jarrah as a family. 'Yes. We'll have you.'

He kissed her then, not gentle but with a hunger and desperation he could finally give free rein, his blood pressure spiking, heat flooding his groin. Until he hit her in the head with his IV tubing and a solar flare from the centre of his headache jabbed him straight through the eye.

He grunted as he broke off their lip lock. 'Okay...this might have to wait though,' he said on a half-laugh.

She laughed too and it sang in his blood. 'It's okay.' She smiled at him, stroking her cool fingers over the throb at his temple. 'I can wait.'

'Yeah.' Yarran smiled. He could too.

They had forever.

EPILOGUE

Two weeks later...

HARPER WAS NERVOUS. Her pulse fluttered madly at her temples. She couldn't believe she was about to *go there*. It had only been two weeks since Yarran had woken in his hospital bed and apart from the odd headache and still being on medical leave, he was back to normal.

But, if the incident had taught her anything, it was to make the most of every moment.

She knew intimately that no one was guaranteed happiness in life but falling for Yarran all over again had given her the courage to take it anyway. Realising that she *deserved* to be happy had come to her late in life—thanks to Yarran—and she didn't want to waste another moment.

'Hello? Earth to Harper?'

Harper tuned back into the conversation. They were at a table on the lower concourse of Bennelong Point again, the sails of the Opera House glowing white in the background.

'Sorry… I was…'

What? Thinking something so ridiculous he might reject her outright?

Yarran leaned forward, his hand sliding over hers. 'Okay, what's up? You're acting funny. What's going on?'

She shook her head. 'It's fine. I'm fine.'

'Harper...'

He clearly wasn't convinced, and Harper knew it was now or never. She'd spent a lifetime not thinking she was worthy of love or happiness but the last two weeks with Yarran and Jarrah had given her courage.

Taking a deep breath, she eyeballed him. 'Okay... I'm about to float something so crazy I wouldn't blame you if you wanted to run a million miles away but, please, just let me get it out because I don't know if I'll ever be this brave again.'

He smiled that gentle smile of his and squeezed her hand. 'Okay.'

Harper took a breath. And then another, trying to quell the beat of her heart. 'Twelve years ago, you asked me to marry you and I wasn't ready. But I am now. And I know it's only been two weeks and we have to take it slow because we have Jarrah to consider and I have *no* issues with that. But I need you to know that I'm totally, absolutely, *utterly* in love with you. More than the first time around if that's even possible. And I never want to be with anyone but you and Jarrah and, when you're both ready, I'd like to walk down an aisle and have you *both* waiting for me down the other end.'

He blinked and Harper suffered a moment of panic. She'd gone too hard, too fast. But then common sense took over. Yarran loved her. She knew that. He was just going to need a minute, considering she'd been Little Miss Commitment-phobe.

'I'm sorry.' She grasped his fingers. 'I know it's a lot. Maybe too much, too soon.'

'No.' He shook his head, smiling in a way that sent her heart into a flutter. 'I've wanted to marry you since the moment I met you. It's not too much or too soon.'

He couldn't have chosen more perfect words. And when he leaned in and kissed her, his lips hot and needy, she believed him. She felt the usual tug at their contact but she knew—despite the yumminess of his kisses—this wasn't the moment for heated passion.

It was the moment for cool heads.

Pulling away, she pressed her forehead against his. 'Let's not make this a thing right now. We won't make it official. Let's be guided by Jarrah and where he's at.'

Yarran nodded, his smile sweet. 'Thank you. That means a lot to me. And we will be guided by Jarrah absolutely. But if you think I'm not going to want you as my wife every single day between now and then, you are seriously underestimating how much I want you by my side.'

'Oh, I think I know,' Harper murmured, her heart alive with the passion of his commitment.

He grinned. 'Oh, yeah? How much do you know?'

She produced a hotel room key, sliding it across the table. 'Five minutes away.'

He smiled a smile that flared an inferno in her underwear. 'Are you trying to seduce me, Jones?'

'Yes. Is it working?'

He caught the eye of a waiter. 'Cheque?' he said, and Harper smiled.

* * * * *

IVY'S FLING WITH THE SURGEON

LOUISA GEORGE

MILLS & BOON

Writing is always better when you're part of a team.

So thank you to Amy Andrews, Emily Forbes
and JC Harroway for making this project such fun!

CHAPTER ONE

PAPERWORK WAS INVENTED by someone with a sick sense of humour. Probably a man.

Dr Ivy Hurst stared at the hundreds of messages, results and requests in her work inbox and sighed.

Once upon a time I had a life other than this.

But at least paperwork didn't cheat on you.

Her phone vibrated on her desk and the upbeat ringtone she used for her three best friends, Phoebe, Harper and Alinta, blared into the otherwise silent room. She glanced at the caller ID. Phoebe.

Smiling, she clicked onto speakerphone so she could chat and work at the same time. 'Hey, Phoebs, how's things?'

'Great.' A pause. 'Ivy Hurst, do I hear keyboard tapping? Please tell me you're not still at work. I left hours ago.'

Busted.

Ivy froze, her fingers hovering in mid-air as she glanced at the clock on the wall of her messy hospital office. Almost eight-thirty. 'Wow, it's late. How did that happen? I'm just catching up on paperwork. What's up?'

'Thought I'd share Harper's good news: Yarran's finally been discharged.'

Thank goodness.

Ivy breathed out slowly. They'd all been hoping and praying their friend Yarran—Alinta's twin brother—would pull through after a terrible firefighting accident. And here he was, healing and moving on with Harper.

'That is good news. So, they're actually living together now? All going well?' Ivy tried typing quietly so Phoebe wouldn't hear, but then gave up and focused on the conversation. 'I really need to check in with them, but I'm snowed under right now.'

'It's okay, we all understand what it's like to be a doctor, hon. And yes, they're very happy. Talk about loved up, the air almost crackles around them.' Phoebe chuckled, although Ivy imagined her friend also jokingly rolling her eyes. Out of the four of them Harper appeared to be the only one lucky in love, and that had happened only recently.

Ivy sighed. 'I'm so pleased for them. It's taken them a long time to get to this point.'

Harper and Yarran's relationship had been all on years ago, before Harper had gone to London for a job opportunity she just couldn't miss…breaking Yarran's heart in the process. But now she was back in Sydney and the sparks between Harper and Yarran had been rekindled. Ivy was delighted, but also aware of a pang of envy in her chest, because once upon a time she'd also believed in happily ever after.

'Yes. About twelve years, give or take,' her friend confirmed.

A lot longer than Ivy's last and failed relationship. 'Don't know if I could adjust to living with someone again these days. I don't think I'd be good at sharing my space.'

'You had Harper living with you,' Phoebe quipped back.

'Only until her apartment was ready. We both knew it was only temporary. I mean, sure I loved having her stay with me, she's so easy to have around. She does girl things, she's funny and kind, we're on the same wavelength. A guy…' Ivy shuddered, remembering how she'd had to tiptoe around her ex when he'd had a bad day. And, towards the end when he didn't come home the odd night and was cryptic about his plans, how she had her suspicions about where he was and with who. 'It's complicated navigating all that, right?'

Phoebe tsked. 'That's because you're too nice. You need to put yourself and your needs on an equal footing with everyone else.'

'Ha. I did that with my parents, and it didn't go down at all well. It's taken them years to forgive me. I'm not really sure they have.'

'If you'd gone into the army like they wanted you'd never have met us at medical school. Imagine a life without me, Alinta and Harper.'

'No, thanks. I don't want to think about that ever happening.' When Harper had left, Alinta had been almost as devastated as her brother and things between Harper and Alinta had become very strained. But now everything was settling down again and the four friends were back living in the same city. 'It's even better now we're all working at the Central too.'

'And Yarran just down the road at the fire station.'

'It's perfect. Well, almost. Unfortunately, Grant's still here.' Ivy shuddered again.

Phoebe's tone became all businesslike. 'With a bit of luck your no-good ex will find a job somewhere else. I'll keep an eye out on the job listings and forward him the ones the furthest away. I'm sure they need more urologists in Outer Mongolia. Anyway, Yarran is nothing like Grant.'

'True.' Ivy laughed. 'Harper wouldn't take any nonsense anyway. At least, not twice, like I did.'

'You're too forgiving, Ivy.'

'I did not forgive his cheating.'

'You gave him a second chance.'

I gave him a lot more than that. My heart. My trust. Which he stomped all over.

'He said it was a blip and the affair meant nothing to him.

That he loved me, and I was his life.' She put her head in her hands and laughed wryly. 'Until the next pretty woman came along. Men, huh? I'm way too old for all that game-playing.'

Phoebe snorted. 'You're not even forty. Unlike the rest of us.'

'Not far off. I'm staring it down. And, you know, I thought I'd be…well, *not single* at this ripe old age.'

'Hey, steady on with the old. It's not so bad. Honestly. Actually, it's fun.'

'If you keep men out of the equation.' Ivy knew Phoebe was also determinedly single.

But to her surprise Phoebe laughed. 'There are some good ones out there. Case in point: Yarran.'

'True. He's a keeper. But, to be honest, it's so much easier being single. No navigating emotional minefields, no second-guessing myself, and definitely no gaslighting. Men are strictly off limits from now on. Especially charming, good-looking ones.'

'Ahem.'

Oops.

The very masculine sound had Ivy whirling round in her swivel chair to find Lucas Matthews, Head of Reconstructive Surgery, leaning casually against her door frame. With his expensive-looking navy-blue suit, crisp white shirt and perfectly tousled dark hair, he wore the arrogant air of someone who knew he was good-looking and had a reputation almost as bad as her ex's. Apparently, he'd left a trail of broken hearts across the previous hospital he'd worked in and was making inroads into the single female staff population here at Sydney Central.

Good-looking: yes. Charming: big fat no.

At least she wouldn't be tempted by the likes of him.

She blinked as she regarded him. He had a sort of amused smile, which gave her the distinct impression he'd heard—or had been listening to—her conversation. Heat hit her cheeks.

Which, at the ripe age of thirty-nine, was something she really wished she had a handle on by now.

'Listen, Phoebs, got to go.' She grabbed her phone, jabbing at the buttons to cut the call before her friend could say anything more incriminating. Worse, Lucas Matthews now knew about her sad love life, which she generally chose to keep private given her ex was still employed at the Central too.

He straightened up. 'Sorry to interrupt your obviously *very important* conversation, Dr Hurst.' His tone was as sharp as his fancy jacket lapel points and, while their paths had crossed on more than a few occasions, they were very definitely not on first-name terms. 'But we need to talk.'

'We do?' What could they possibly need to talk about at this time of night?

And how dare he listen in on a private conversation and then judge it?

He stepped into the room, filling her space with his overbearing presence. 'About Emma Wilson. I've just been reviewing her up on the ward and hear you've been called in to assess her.'

Ah. Their shared patient: a twenty-six-year-old woman with bad burns to her lower legs following a house fire. Ivy wasn't sure what hackles were, but she felt hers immediately jump to attention. This wasn't the first time they'd discussed appropriate treatment plans and timelines for shared patients, and it probably wasn't going to be the last. He wanted to dive in early, Ivy wanted to make sure Emma was physically able to deal with any further intervention.

'And...?' she invited him to elucidate.

'I want to operate. Tomorrow.'

'Whoa. No way. Not so fast. I've only just been to see her.' Ivy held up her palm. 'I need to get to the bottom of her spiking temperatures and abdo pain before she has any more interventions.'

'And I need to operate.'

'I may need to, too.' She huffed. 'But I'm trying to avoid it if I can. She's twenty-eight weeks pregnant with twins and only recently been brought out of an induced coma. She has a lot going on and it's all a big draw on what little resources she has left. Surely plastic surgery can wait just a little bit longer until she's stable.'

His eyes widened in what she took as irritation. Possibly anger. 'It's not as if this is a vanity project, Dr Hurst. Firstly, I need to debride some of her grafts because the infection risk is real. And secondly, post-burn hypertrophic scars are thick, and painful. This poor woman, who, as you say, has been through a lot already, is at risk of developing contractions that could lead to limited movement, even deformity. If we're going to minimise long-term pain and scarring, time is of the essence.'

He had a point and, more, he seemed highly invested in Emma's care. Clearly, she wasn't the only doctor protective of her patients. She breathed out slowly in an effort to control her irritation. Why did she feel so combative around this man? There was something about him that rubbed her up the wrong way.

'If we can get on top of this current crisis then you can start the reconstruction surgery but I'm in no position to give you a timeline. The abdominal pain doesn't appear to be related to her pregnancy or accident, as far as we can tell. We're waiting on scans, swabs and white cell count. As soon as we get those we can target with the right treatment and appropriate antibiotics.'

'Thanks. I am aware of how to treat an infection, Dr Hurst.' His intense brown eyes bored into her. There was a thick, almost tangible, energy in the air.

But she refused to back down or look away. 'Good. Then you'll understand my reluctance to allow any further infection risk. My registrar is looking after Emma tonight and will keep me informed of any changes. So, I'll let you know as soon as I know.'

She turned back to face her monitor. Hopefully he'd get the hint and leave.

But his voice deepened. 'Make it quick.'

'Excuse me?' As she whirled back to look at him Ivy Hurst's dark eyes glittered with ill-concealed anger, her body tight and stiff. She jumped up, pushing back her office chair so brusquely she sent it barrelling towards him. '*What* did you say?'

Lucas cringed. As soon as the words had escaped his mouth he regretted them, but he'd been unable to stop them. There was something about her that brought out a niggly irritation in him. Who did she think she was to dictate when he should do his job?

Her caller had said she was too nice? Too forgiving? Ha! Not something he'd witnessed so far.

'I said…it needs to be quick.' He caught the chair as it slowed in front of him.

Her gaze drifted from him to the chair and back in mild interest. Then anything mild deserted her gaze the second she refocused on his face. 'Dr Matthews, I appreciate the concern for your patient, but this is not the army…' Her nostrils flared at that, then she added, 'I do not take orders from anyone. And particularly not when it comes to the welfare of my patient.'

Great.

He huffed out a breath. Today had been hard enough without this spat. He'd lost a patient in the operating theatre and had another run-in with his parents over the guest list for their charity fundraiser. Was he bringing a plus one? Another veiled attempt at finding out whether he was settling down, and no doubt another opportunity to parade what they believed to be suitable eligible women in front of him, hoping he'd pick one and settle down.

No, thanks.

Plus, he'd missed a call from his younger sister, Flora. As always, the familiar guilt yawned inside him. He worked too many hours, stayed away from the family home too much for him to give her the attention she so deserved.

Now this. He closed his eyes and dredged up some calm. When he opened them again Dr Hurst was still staring at him as if he were the devil incarnate. He raised his hand to try to mollify her. 'It wasn't an order. Just a request. Look, we both want what's best for Emma. We're on the same page.'

'Oh, trust me, we're not even in the same book.' She shoved a hand through her caramel-coloured bobbed hair and glared at him, her brown eyes glittering and sparking. This close he could see flashes of green and gold in her irises. An angry mouth. One triangle of her white cotton blouse hem had untucked from her short khaki linen skirt, which looked as if it had never seen an iron. She was ruffled in more ways than one.

She was petite and had to tilt her head to look up at him, but she had a distinct aura of authority. Given her seniority, she was probably around his age, and he knew how hard it was to work your way up the medical career ladder—she'd probably had to fight to get to the top. She wouldn't take fools gladly and right now she was standing her ground.

Too forgiving, my arse.

Talking of… He glanced down…yes, he hadn't noticed before—in truth, he'd never looked—but she had curves in all the right places. A formidable woman, passionate and fiery.

He stepped back. Because those kinds of thoughts about a colleague were inappropriate. 'I'd like to think we could at least have a civil conversation.'

An eyebrow rose. 'Why?'

'So we can work together on the best outcomes for Emma.

Surely it doesn't have to be this difficult. I'm not averse to compromise, as long as it doesn't negatively impact my patients.'

She looked away. Swallowed. Then turned back to him. 'I am working with you. Trying to get her well enough for your surgery. This is *all* about Emma.' She glanced down at the chair again. 'You don't need to barricade yourself in. I don't bite.'

Oh, but she wanted to.

He held in a laugh. 'I was trying to stop it from taking out both my legs.'

'Hey!' A frail man in a billowing hospital gown and wheeling an IV stand appeared at the door, one hand on the stand, the other a tight fist, which he thrust towards Dr Hurst. 'Get out. Get out of here.'

Her eyes grew wide. 'Mr Templeton? What on earth are you doing here…?'

The old man frowned, clearly confused and scared. His voice was wobbly and weak but laced with a thinly veiled threat. 'Why are you in my house? You'd better get the hell off my property before I call the police.'

'Mervyn, you're in hospital. You're recovering from an operation to your gallbladder. Look, we need to get you back to the ward. You need to rest and heal.' Clearly snapping straight into assessment mode, Dr Hurst started to walk towards the man with both her palms up in a gesture of conciliation, but not before she threw a quick look towards Lucas that said, *Join the hell in, why don't you?*

But he hadn't liked the man's deathly pallor, the shaking hands, and disorientation, so was already jabbing his phone. 'Can we have a porter to the third-floor admin suite? Now, please? Wheelchair if that's all you've got, but preferably a trolley. Now.'

'And who the hell left all the lights on in the middle of the nigh…? Ugh…' The man crumpled against the IV stand, gripping it, then tipping it as he fell to the floor. His IV line ripped from his arm, the stand crashing as it landed.

Lucas ran to him, joining Dr Hurst on the floor at Mervyn's side. She pressed her fingers against his carotid feeling for a pulse. 'Well, he's still alive. But damn. What the hell…? I only operated on him yesterday—he shouldn't be down here.'

'He's obviously confused, he must have wandered off the ward.' Lucas pressed his fingers against the man's IV site to stop the bleeding. 'Don't suppose there's any sterile packs in your office? I'll get this set up again in the other arm.'

'No packs. But hit the crash button. Behind my desk.'

He dashed back into her office, hit the button and returned with her stethoscope and a digital blood-pressure machine he'd found on her desk. He wrapped the cuff around Mervyn's thin arm.

'Mervyn! Oh, Merv. Please help him.' A frail voice came from behind them, followed by the sound of uncertain, halting steps.

'Mrs Templeton, it's not a good idea for you to be here seeing this.' Dr Hurst looked over at the elderly lady walking towards them. 'He's had a fall; we're just sorting him out.'

But the woman bent down and shook her husband's shoulder. 'Merv. Come on, get up.' She glared at Dr Hurst. 'What's wrong with him? You said you'd fixed his tummy.'

Dr Hurst glanced at the lady and gave her a half-smile that exuded professionalism and compassion and not the slightest bit of irritation, which she must have been feeling because, by unwittingly interrupting, this old lady was well and truly preventing her husband from getting the best possible attention.

But Dr Hurst's voice was soft and concerned…a million miles away from the way she'd spoken to Lucas. 'Please, Mrs Templeton, take a step back. I'm trying to find out what's going on.'

'Hypotensive and tachycardic.' Lucas chose to speak in medical jargon so as not to alert Mrs Templeton to the urgency of the situation. There was more going on here than a post-op faint.

A porter arrived with a stretcher then the crash team appeared, running down the corridor with the crash trolley. Mrs Templeton looked at them all and started to cry. 'What's going on?'

Dr Hurst stood and wrapped an arm around the older lady's shoulder. 'Mervyn's had a faint and we're trying to work out why. Is there anyone we can call to come and sit with you?'

Mrs Templeton worried the hem of her blouse. 'No. Just me and Merv. What can I do?'

'Let us do our job.' Lucas helped attach ECG sticky pads to Mervyn's chest and read the heart trace while Dr Hurst attached another bag of fluids to an IV she'd inserted in his inner elbow, saying, 'I need to take him to Theatre and see what's going on. It's got to be something to do with the surgery.'

'Don't let him die.' Mrs Templeton grabbed Dr Hurst's arm. 'You can't let him die.'

'Mrs Templeton, please let go of the doctor. We need to get him back to Theatre. That's the only way we can save him right now. Come with me. Let's go somewhere you can sit down. Maybe a cup of tea?' Lucas gently peeled the woman's fingers from the trolley, then caught Dr Hurst's eye. As she mouthed the words *thank you* he saw gratitude soften her features. The faintest glimmer of a smile.

Or he might have been imagining it.

Either way he felt an easing of the tension between them.

For now, anyway. Because he was going to operate on Emma at the earliest opportunity whether Dr Hurst wanted him to or not.

He put his palm on Mrs Templeton's shoulder and coaxed her away so the team could rush their patient towards the lift, but the old lady took a couple of faltering steps forward. 'Mervyn. Please—'

Lucas walked slowly away from the stretcher gently bringing Mrs Wilson with him. 'Dr Hurst will do everything she can to save him. I know she's an excellent doctor.'

If the way she protected Emma was anything to go by she was thorough, dedicated, determined. Stubborn almost. And damned pretty when she smiled. Very pretty actually. Which shouldn't have registered at all, but his skin prickled with something a lot like attraction.

Oh, no.

No way.

He closed his eyes briefly and the image of the corners of her mouth turning up because of something he'd said floated in front of his vision. The light in her eyes. The glint of grit and compassion. A heady mix. An alluring mix.

Just no. He was not going to be attracted to a firecracker like Ivy Hurst. Not when he was going to have to work with her.

That would only make his life a whole lot more difficult.

CHAPTER TWO

IVY STEPPED OUT of the theatre suite, exhaustion nipping at her
bones. Thankfully, the unexpected surgery had gone well, and
Mr Templeton was safe in Recovery. Now she could go home
and get some much-needed sleep.

But she stopped short as she caught sight of Lucas Matthews sitting on a white plastic chair, looking at his phone,
only metres from her.

Was he here for her? *No.* No, why would he be waiting for
her?

But that thought slid into her belly and made it jitter with
something she was annoyed to realise was excitement.

No.

She could not be excited at seeing this man. He was an annoyance. Even if he was a good-looking charmer of an annoyance.

He looked up, stood and put his phone away. She couldn't
quite read his expression but if she were to guess it would be
concerned. 'Dr Hurst? Hey.'

He *was* waiting for her. Wow. She didn't like the way her
skin prickled with excitement and her heart did a little dance
at that thought, so she ignored her treacherous body. What was
wrong with her today? Why was her body reacting to him like
this? 'Dr Matthews?'

And was that her voice? All scratchy and hoarse and come-
on sexy?

'Lucas, please.'

Lucas would make him human, and she didn't want that. It was far better to haul emotional barriers up around her. She changed her tone to one of indifference. 'Dr Matthews, what are you doing here?'

His mouth twitched at the corners as he registered her formality. 'I was concerned.'

'About me?'

His throat made a funny—possibly sarcastic—sound. 'About Mr Templeton. I told his wife I'd let her know how he's doing as soon as you came out of Theatre.'

Ah. Stupid treacherous body. 'Informing relatives about the status of *my* patients is my job.'

'I know. But she made me promise and I'm a man of my word.' He gave her a *what can you do?* kind of shrug.

'Oh, yes. Dr Dependable, I'm sure.' That was what Grant's patients had called him too, but she'd known differently. The only thing she could depend on her ex to do was cheat. Some people were very good at presenting a perfect image of themselves when underneath they were very different indeed. That said...she'd seen Lucas in action and noted the tender way he'd coaxed Mrs Templeton away. 'Where is she?'

'In the visitors' room on the ward. She's had tea, phoned her sister and is settled in watching reruns of *The Chase*.'

'Great. Thanks. I can take it from here.' Ivy started to make her way along the corridor towards the lift but was frustrated to feel Lucas Matthews's presence at her side. Worse, his scent wound round her, a mixture of something earthy and something decidedly masculine filling the air and making her belly contract with—she was horrified to realise—longing.

His jaw tightened. 'I said I'd see her, so I will.'

It was late, she was tired, and her defences were clearly wearing thin. She was struggling to ignore all her bodily reactions to this man, but if she didn't play ball, she had a feeling he'd nip at her heels anyway. 'I'm not going to get rid of you, am I?'

He pulled a face of pretend hurt. 'I'm afraid not.'

He was infuriating, but his expression made her smile. She shook her head in exasperation. 'Okay. Okay. You can come with me, but I do the talking.'

'Whatever.' He rolled his eyes but not before they glittered with amusement.

So, much against her better judgement, they both attended with Mrs Templeton, explained that Ivy had found a leaking artery from the previous surgery, that it was now cauterised, and Mr Templeton would be back home in no time.

They were rewarded with hugs and tears and the kind of gratitude that reminded Ivy why she'd chosen this career and not followed the rest of the family into the army...despite the conflict it had created between her and her parents. This job, helping people, was everything to her. Good-looking, charming colleagues notwithstanding.

Still, he made for good eye candy.

As they walked towards the hospital exit Ivy's stomach growled so loudly she put her hand to her belly, then glanced up at Lucas to see if he'd heard it.

Of course he had. The man had heard enough about her this evening to make her blush with embarrassment as she pressed her hand against her abdomen to try stop the sounds erupting from there again.

He grinned. 'Hungry?'

Another pained growl. Denying it was pointless. 'Starving. I can't remember when I last ate. Breakfast, maybe? But it's nothing a packet of noodles and a jug of boiling water won't sort out.'

He frowned. 'Two-minute noodles are not enough nourishment after a full day's work and then an unexpected surgery. You need proper food.'

They stepped out into a cool June night. Ivy pulled her coat tight around her. 'I like noodles.'

'I know a great place that serves the best noodles in Sydney. Proper thick noodles with a decent sauce and real meat. Even vegetables and real spices, not rehydrated ones. You want to come with?'

Did she? She looked up at him and felt her belly jitter with excitement again. Er…no. That way lay only danger. She patted her laptop bag. 'I… I've still got a ton of work to do.'

'Hey. No strings. Just two colleagues eating some much-needed food after a day from hell.' He brushed his fingers through his messy hair and gave a shrug she thought he might have intended to look nonchalant, but instead made him look as if he carried the weight of the world on those broad shoulders.

'You too, huh?' She knew how it went; medicine was hard mentally and emotionally. But she'd been so hell-bent on defending her territory she hadn't stopped to think about how Lucas's day had gone or what he'd been doing before he'd found her in her office. 'Care to share?'

He shrugged. 'I lost a patient this morning. Her apartment burnt down because she'd lit a candle too close to a curtain. She evacuated safely but then went back in to try to save her cat—which, it transpires, and very tragically for my patient, was already outside. Within minutes she'd succumbed to the smoke and had burns covering ninety per cent of her body. Yesterday, she had the rest of her life to look forward to and now she's just a victim of making the wrong call at the wrong time. Makes you re-evaluate a lot, right?' After the longest sentence she'd ever heard him say he blew out a slow breath, his shoulders slumping slightly. For someone who regularly dealt with these kinds of tragedies he looked genuinely affected.

Her heart contracted. 'I hate those kinds of days.'

'Don't we all?' His eyebrows rose. 'I also had some tough news to break to another patient this afternoon. And then a run-in with this particularly fiery doctor who wants to call all the shots on a shared patient and won't even try to negotiate terms.'

'Me? Fiery? And you make it sound like a hostile business takeover.' But then, she had been reluctant to listen to his point of view.

He shrugged again, but a smile played on his lips. 'Plus, an evening trying to soothe a very concerned relative while her husband was in the operating theatre. I sat with her for ages and then the aforementioned fiery doctor didn't even want me to help out with the post-op update.'

'Way to make a girl guilt-trip.'

He was still smiling. 'Just explaining how it was from my point of view.'

Okay, she'd assumed a whole lot of things about Lucas without actually considering what was happening in his world. With a shock she noticed the shift in her perspective and a desire to know more about what made this man so infuriating on a professional level and yet so attractive on a personal one. 'I'm kind of protective about my patients.'

'I can see that, and I get it. I just hope, now we know each other a little better, we can compromise.'

'Maybe.'

He looked as if he was heading towards the staff car park, so she took this as her opportunity to leave. This emotive conversation was making her soften towards him when she should keep those hackles up.

She stopped and looked up at him. Hot damn, he was actually gorgeous. And tall. And smelt just great. Her hackles wilted as his gaze snagged hers. Had she already noticed his eyes? She'd been too blindsided by frustration and irritation to look closely. But now she took notice. Dark and soulful and beautiful.

She'd noticed his eyes. This was most definitely her cue

to leave. 'Right, well, I live just round the corner, so I'll head on home. Thanks again for your help with the Templetons.'

'Last chance on the best Vietnamese food in Sydney. They do an amazing beef pho, and the lemongrass chicken noodle salad has to be eaten to be believed. I'm going regardless, makes little difference to me if you tag along.' He shrugged, his eyes glittering. 'But…you will regret for ever that you haven't tried the best pho in town.'

She wavered and clearly he saw that because he jumped in with, 'Come on, what's the harm?'

The harm was the softening towards him. The catch in her belly when he smiled. His eyes…oh, those eyes. It would be too easy to like the man. Which would go against everything she'd promised herself post-Grant, the charismatic charmer. No men. No risk of heartache. No tangle of commitment that would take months of pain to sift through and untangle.

But then her belly growled again and when Lucas bugged his eyes at her temptation got the better of her. She huffed out a breath. 'Okay. Okay. If the food is that good, I'll take a risk.'

'Good. But now you must call me Lucas, no more Dr Matthews. And I'm more than happy to give you a lift if you don't have your car here.'

'I don't, so thank you. But don't think for a minute that once I've eaten, I'll be less hangry or willing to change my mind about Emma's treatment schedule. *Lucas,*' she added with enough emphasis that said she was not going to take any nonsense from him.

'You think I'm bribing you with food? No way. How could you even think that?'

'Because you've clearly identified my weak point. I can never turn down the offer of food someone else has cooked.'

'Good to know.' He playfully wiggled his eyebrows then zapped his keys towards a flash silver e-sports car.

'Oh, you are such a stereotype.' She laughed as she climbed

into the plush passenger seat, hoping that if she could keep telling herself she wasn't attracted to him, and that this was purely to fill her empty belly, then she might start believing it.

The restaurant was not at all what she'd expected. Tucked away down an alley off Dixon Street in Chinatown, it was more street food than high-end, with plastic chairs and rickety Formica-topped tables, and plumes of steam and flames billowing from the open kitchen every few minutes. The delicious aromas of star anise, ginger and garlic filled the air as a waitress showed them to their table saying, 'Hi, Dr Lucas. Good to see you again. Three nights in a row. I'm impressed.'

Ivy turned to Lucas and laughed. 'Three nights in a row? Please don't tell me you've brought a different woman here every night too?'

The waitress chuckled. 'Dr Lucas brings all his friends here.'

Which wasn't exactly the answer Ivy had been looking for.

Grinning, Lucas took both menus and handed one to Ivy as the waitress went to attend another table. 'Um… Dr Hurst? Drink?'

'Just water, please. And it's Ivy. Please, call me Ivy.' Okay, so she was softening and she just couldn't help it. She peered up at the red lanterns hanging from the ceiling casting a vibrant glow over the wood and bamboo fixtures. 'This place is amazing. How did you find it?'

'I treated Binh, the head chef, when he had a bad burn from some hot oil. Anh, our waitress and the co-owner, is his wife.'

'A family affair. Nice.'

He grimaced. 'It works well for them, but I wouldn't say that working with my family is high on my to-do list.'

'Nor mine.' When he looked at her quizzically she changed the subject, not wanting to bring the conversation down by talking about the difficulties she had with her family. 'So you recommend the pho?'

'Definitely.' He beckoned Anh back and ordered two beef pho and water then frowned as his phone began to ring.

He took it out of his pocket, frowned some more, then put it on the table face down.

Ivy watched with interest. Girlfriend? Wife? God, she didn't know anything about him. The gossip grapevine informed her he was a playboy type, but what if it was wrong? What if he was in a relationship no one knew about? Worse, what if he was no better than her ex and didn't think cheating was a crime?

She glanced at the phone then back at him. 'You can answer it, you know. I promise I won't listen. *I* don't listen in on other people's phone calls.' She hoped she'd said it with enough playful barb for him to get the message.

He grinned. 'Aw, come on. It was a small room, you had it on speaker phone, what could I do?'

'Walk away? Put your fingers in your ears?' She found herself laughing as she watched him do exactly that. 'Ugh. What did you hear?'

'That your ex is a douchebag.'

'His reputation is almost as bad as yours.' Maybe this would eke out some personal details and make her feel better about being here with him.

He spluttered. 'I have a reputation?'

'Totally. Commitment-phobe, heartbreaker.'

His dark eyes lit up. 'Excellent. Because the last thing I need is for anyone to fall in love with me.'

'Because you're already married? Engaged? In a relationship?'

'None of the above.'

'Then how big-headed can you get thinking women are bound to fall in love with you? Oh, I know all about guys like you. Grant was exactly the same, so sure of himself. Now he's free and single and let loose on the hospital staff.' She shuddered. 'Poor women. He should come with a relationship health warning.'

'Grant? He works at the Central? Do I know him?'

'Grant Nelson.'

'The urologist?' His eyebrows hiked.

'The very same.'

'How long were you together?'

'Close on five years.'

'Whoa.' He looked impressed. 'And he walked away from *you*? The mighty Ivy Hurst?'

She laughed. Sure, she was confident and knew how to call the shots in her job, but her personal life was an entirely different matter. For a while, Grant had destroyed any self-esteem she had, although she was working hard to rebuild that now. She knew her worth. Knew what she was prepared to accept in a relationship, or from a date.

'Mighty? Me? No way. He thought I was a pushover and that he could treat me like something he scraped off his shoe. But I got the last word, dumping him by text after one of my friends caught him cheating on me. Then I threw his belongings onto the front yard for him to collect. In the rain.'

'Ouch.' His phone rang again. He blinked at the sound. Ignored it.

She glanced at it. 'Please answer it, it might be important.'

'It's my mother, I highly doubt that.'

He was ignoring a call from the famous and indubitable Dr Estelle Matthews, who, alongside her husband and other sons, had built up a stellar career as a plastic surgeon to Australia's rich and famous?

Interesting. Why wouldn't he answer her call?

Ivy thought about her difficult relationship with her own parents. 'At least she's phoning you.'

The ringing stopped then the sound of an incoming text had him reaching for his phone again. He read it and frowned. 'As I thought. She wants to know who I'm bringing to her charity fundraiser.'

'And who are you bringing?' Weird that her gut did a little jolt of interest mingled with surprising disappointment at the thought of him with another woman.

He shrugged nonchalantly as if he had a long list he had to consult before making his decision. He probably had. 'I haven't decided yet.'

'So many women to choose from?'

'Far from it. Trust me, I wouldn't want to inflict anyone I actually like to an evening with my parents. They'll be asking when we're getting married, how many kids we're planning. My mother does not know the meaning of discretion.'

'She wants you married off?' This was interesting.

'Only so she can organise some big fancy wedding to show off to her society friends. She mixes in very high Sydney circles.' He rolled his eyes again. 'And is very keen on dragging me into them too.'

'I was dragged from army base to army base growing up. I know a lot about family expectations and not living up to them, but little about high society. You have a very different life from me.'

'*They* do.' He leaned back in his chair, hands clenched around the back of his head, long legs stretching under the table. As he raised his arms his shirt tugged loose from his trouser waistband giving her an enticing glimpse of bare skin. Her body rippled with a sudden need to put her fingers there.

What the hell?

She dragged her eyes up and his gaze snagged hers. A long lazy smile formed on his lips, as if he could read her thoughts. 'Me? I'm just a regular guy.'

She took in his flash suit, the smart mouth. The infuriatingly beautiful eyes that too frequently glittered with amusement at something she inadvertently said or did. The reputation. The sports car. 'Sure you are.'

'And Grant Nelson is an idiot for letting you go.'

So Lucas was a flirt too. Interesting. But despite her misgivings she was transfixed by the deep, dark brown and the flashes of gold playing across his gaze. There was something about him that was powerful and engaging. His unwavering confidence of how damned gorgeous he was, accompanied by that undercurrent of compassion, was unbelievably, mind-blowingly sexy.

Regular? You really are not.

Ivy thought about a film she'd watched when Harper had stayed with her and they'd blobbed on the sofa and eaten a bucket of ice cream. 'So, it looks like you have two options.'

'Oh?' His eyes widened and he leaned forward. 'Tell me more.'

'You either tell your mum to back off from your private life, or tell her you're involved with someone just to get her off your case.'

'Ah.' He leaned back, looking slightly deflated. What had he thought she was going to say? He'd looked very interested. *Sexually* interested. 'I can't count the number of times I've told her to stay out of my business but she's my mother, she thinks it's her duty to be *in* my personal life.'

'So, take option b. Pretend you're involved with someone.'

His eyebrows knitted together. 'That sounds a lot like a cheesy romcom movie.'

'They're the best ones. The cheesier the better. As long as the pretend partner is fully aware of the plot it'll be fine. Get someone to play along. Pay someone?'

'Might work.' He drummed his fingers on the table as he considered her suggestion. Then his eyes met hers. 'Will you do it?'

'Me? Ha, ha. No.' She faked a laugh but her belly danced at the prospect of being with Lucas at some fancy ball. All the more reason to turn him down. 'Definitely not.'

'It's one fundraiser event. Where's the harm—?' He was interrupted by Anh carrying two huge bowls of pho and their water, which she put down in front of them.

Ivy sipped a spoonful of piping-hot pho, hoping to distract him from their previous conversation. There was no way she could go to an event with him even if he paid her. 'Oh, wow. This is delicious. I love the flavours.'

He gave her a self-satisfied smile. 'Told you. But you still haven't answered my question. Will you be my pretend partner?'

CHAPTER THREE

UGH. HE HADN'T been distracted. He really did want her to be his fake girlfriend. If she'd thought she'd be in this predicament she wouldn't have suggested it at all. 'No, Lucas. I won't. But I'm sure there are tons of women at work who'd take you up on the offer.'

'I'm not so sure. Besides, I'm not asking them, I'm asking you. Come with me to the ball to get my mother off my back. In return you get to show Grant Nelson that your heart is well and truly healed and he is missing so, so much.'

Interesting...

Tempting, even. 'How would Grant even find out? I doubt he'd be invited, it's not his kind of thing. And no way would anyone else ever find out about this.'

'The ball is reported in all the major newspapers. Mother makes sure of it. So, unless you wore a mask, your cover would be blown very quickly. Plus, how better for him to know how much you've moved on by seeing your picture in the media, a good-looking guy on your arm—'

'You really do have a high opinion of yourself.' Even so, she could feel herself wavering at the prospect of Grant getting a hit of jealousy.

'Okay...' A wry smile and a nod of assent. 'With a relatively passable-looking guy on your arm, dancing the night away at a glitzy charity do in a beautiful dress.'

Oh, so tempting.

How long since she'd been out dancing? She couldn't remember. Could barely remember the last time she'd been out at all. There'd been no men since Grant. The only dates she'd been on recently were ones involving just her, a bottle of wine and romcoms on her streaming service. So the prospect of a night out dancing was tempting. Hell, she only had a few months before she hit forty. She needed to increase her fun quotient before she was too old. 'When is this ball?'

'Three weeks from Saturday.'

'Okay...' Nowhere near enough time to get entangled emotionally. She would go to the ball, she would be in the papers. Grant would see it. She'd have some fun and play dress-ups in a pretty gown for a change instead of her usual green scrubs. She bit her bottom lip as she considered that the pros considerably outweighed the cons.

Lucas leaned forward and caught her gaze again, held her captured as he teased, 'Ivy Hurst, I do believe you're tempted.'

She blinked up at him. Even though he was exactly the kind of man she'd sworn off, there was something intensely attractive about him. She had to be careful. 'And afterwards? What about...us?'

Because in the movies the pretend *us* always became a real us in the end and she had to remind herself this was not the movies.

Us.

The word slipped into her chest and filled her with heat. She imagined those hands circling her waist and him pulling her closer. Those lips on hers.

A hum tingled low in her belly. Her mouth was suddenly dry and...the thought of hot sex with Lucas made her tingle with anticipation.

Geez, she was actually living in a cheesy romcom dream world. They were talking about a fake relationship. There would be an end…especially when there was no real begin-ning. No meet cute. No best-friends-to-lovers thing.

'Us?' His eyebrows rose as he considered her question. 'I would quietly announce to my family that we've decided it's not going to work. Job commitments…the usual.'

'Your usual, maybe. Not mine. And after that, we're done, that's it?'

'Absolutely. No strings.'

'No strings.' Drumming her fingers on the table, she took a chance on upping the negotiating game and playing to her advantage. 'And I get to call the shots on Emma's operation schedule.'

'Whoa. We did not agree to that.' Laughing, he leaned back and raised his hand. 'Ivy Hurst, you do not play fair.'

'I play to win.' She leaned towards him and grinned.

Gotcha.

She realised she was enjoying this sparring. There was a delicious danger in the subtext of their words. 'I like winning.'

'Luckily, I like playing. A lot.' His eyes sparked hot flashes of tease as he mused for a few moments, pursing his lips as he thought.

She imagined playing with him. And found herself shocked that she wanted to. Heat rushed through her, mixed with an-ticipation and excitement.

He raised his eyebrows. 'Hmm. Okay.'

'Okay as in yes? Really?' Who was being the pushover now?

He nodded assertively. 'Really.'

'Okay, then I'm in too.' Why the hell not? She was a grown woman of thirty-nine. 'It's about time I had a little fun.'

And took what she wanted for a change.

'Then we've got ourselves a deal. Shake on it?' He held out his hand and she slipped hers into it. The sparks firing across her skin from his touch almost whipped her breath away. Her gaze shot up to his and his eyes glittered with blatant wickedness. He'd felt that shiver of desire too. And, surprising herself more than anything, she didn't shy away, she leaned into it.

Was she playing with fire? Playing to her desires, more like. She'd never felt more alive or...was it just turned on?

He let go of her hand. 'I guess we're going to need to spend some time together to get our stories straight.'

'Fine with me.' She shrugged with a smile. 'The prospect of spending a little more time with you isn't entirely onerous.'

He guffawed, then raised his glass of water. 'Glad to hear it.'

'If it means payback to my ex,' she clarified, although she was not unaware of the shiver of excitement low in her belly.

'Right. Yes. Of course.' He looked momentarily shaken then beamed a generous smile. 'I'm looking forward to getting to know you better, Ivy.'

'And you, Lucas.' Her body tingled with that kind of promise. She clinked her glass against his. The deal, she realised, involved getting to know each other in many different ways.

Whoa. What was she actually doing? Why was she feeling like this?

But she had to admit she liked it.

Heat shimmied through her as her gaze meandered over his face, then his shoulders, chest. It had been a long time since she'd felt this attracted to anyone and she grasped the feeling and held on tight.

Then as he smiled a lazy smile full of promise, she imagined dancing in his arms, pressed against that chest. The tilt of his head as he lowered his mouth to hers.

Hell. Now she was *thinking* like a cheesy romcom. This was make-believe. Her life was far from a romcom. What had she agreed to? Her defences had been battered down by a disarming smile and a chance for some revenge on her ex and to be a woman instead of just a doctor married to her career.

She put her glass down and drew her eyes away from his. Picked up her pho bowl.

Looked back at the glass rather than look up at him and let him see the excitement and confusion she knew was in her gaze.

I've only had a glass of water. This man is dangerous. What the hell would I have agreed to with a couple of wines under my belt?

'This is so good.' Ivy tipped back the bowl of pho and drank the delicious liquid.

Lucas sat back and watched. Her pure enjoyment from the food was a jolt to his equilibrium. Since when did he get a kick out of watching someone enjoy eating?

But he knew it was a lot more than that. Ivy Hurst was... surprising. Her mouth was...it sounded crazy, but her mouth was the thing of dreams. Full soft lips, a hesitancy to curve into a smile but when they did it whisked his breath away, doing weird things to his gut and firing his imagination. That mouth against his. On him. Over him.

Well, hell. This deal wasn't exactly what he'd planned. Which had, honestly, only been about getting some food with a colleague.

It was far better than that. The woman in front of him was beautiful, intelligent and very, very sexy.

His mother would love her. His father might even raise an impressed eyebrow, if he could drag himself away from his golfing cronies.

His brothers would die of envy.

His sister...oh, lovely Flora...would she like Ivy and then be distraught when the *us* became just dull old single Lucas again?

He almost wavered at that thought; he had no desire to upset his sister. But truth was, she was probably utterly uninterested in his love life.

Now he'd peeled away some of the more authoritarian layers of Ivy he wanted to get to know her a whole lot better. And not just so he could fool his parents into thinking he was settling down with a good woman. There was something about her that got to him, that had slid beneath his skin. It wasn't just her fiery protectionism for her patients or the hard work ethic, it was something else. She had a professional calm veneer that belied the warm woman she really was.

'You were right. This is an epic restaurant.' Ivy wiped that gorgeous mouth with the back of her hand. 'I can't remember when I had food that tasted so delicious.'

'So next time I suggest something, go with it, okay?'

'That sounds dangerous.' Her eyes widened with something he could only describe as delight. 'Do women always do what you say?'

'Not enough.' He shrugged. A drip of pho trickled down her chin. He couldn't help but pick up his napkin, lean over and dab it away...wishing he could do it with his tongue instead.

She blinked up at him and pulled back with a frown, her mouth forming an angry 'o' shape. Had he misread the flirting? Was this purely a platonic plan?

Are we having sex as part of this deal?

It was way too early for that. He glanced at his watch. And far too late to still be here. He called Anh over and paid the bill then scraped his chair back. 'Okay, Dr Hurst. Come on.'

She frowned again. 'Where?'

'It's late, we both need to get some sleep. I'll drop you at home.'

'Thanks.' Her shoulders sagged a little and he could see the bruising exhaustion around her eyes. She'd worked a long day and done unexpected surgery, which had made it a long evening too. 'I'm too tired to argue and you're cheaper than a taxi.'

'Me? Cheap?'

Her smile returned as she laughed. 'Not even a little bit?'

'Never. And especially not when it comes to my...um, partners.'

Her cheeks bloomed with patches of pink and her pupils grew huge. 'And why would I need to know that?'

'In case you were wondering.'

'Ha. I wasn't.'

'But you are now.'

'I am not.' She rolled her eyes, but not before he saw the flare of desire. Was she imagining them in bed together? Just how good he was?

He leaned closer to her ear. 'Oh, but you are.'

And despite her previous frowns she *was* imagining it, he was sure of it, because he saw the shiver and the slightest tilt of her body towards him. The smile playing on her lips. Felt the graze of her fingertips across his chest before she abruptly turned and walked away.

Something tugged hard and deep in his gut. He wanted her. And even though she was trying damned hard not to, she wanted him too. The chemistry was off the scale.

He followed her outside to his car, watching the cute sway of her backside, then opened her door and watched as she slid in, her soft linen skirt riding up her bare legs, showing a glimpse of thigh and perfect creamy skin. Man, she was achingly beautiful. He closed his eyes, battling back a strong urge to pick her up and carry her up to his apartment. Lay her on his bed and strip her naked.

Instead, he climbed into the driver's seat and started the engine. They drove in silence save for her giving him directions to her apartment. The night was cool, but the atmosphere in the car was thick and heavy and loaded, filled with her perfume of something flowery, maybe some citrus. And the echoes of things said and unsaid.

I like to play.

I like to win.

They could do both, right?

He pulled up outside her apartment building, a smart new block around the corner from the hospital, and went to unbuckle his seat belt, but she stopped him. 'I can manage from here. Thanks.'

'Never in my life have I let a woman walk herself to her door and I'm not going to start now.'

She shrugged. 'Oh? And a gentleman too?'

'Not all the time.' But right now, he was going to be exactly that. Even so, he followed her up the steps aching to slide his hand across the small of her back. To just touch her.

She stopped on the top step, and he waited while she dug in her bag for her key. The light from an automatic night light illuminated her features in a soft glow. She was deep in concentration as she fumbled in her large bag, a little frown hovering over those dark eyes. He wondered what was running through her mind.

Was she going to invite him in? Did she feel this connection or was he imagining it?

'Here.' Grinning, she held up her key like a prize.

'Good. Right.' He nodded. 'I'll get going, then.'

'Okay.' She nodded too. But there was something in her eyes that gave him pause. He waited.

They looked at each other far longer than appropriate for two colleagues. He wanted to ask…but didn't. Hell, how many times had he seamlessly moved from front door to bedroom? But there was something about Ivy that made him want to do the right thing…which was whatever she wanted to do. Their agreement, after all, was about a pretend relationship. Sex had never been mentioned.

She nodded again. 'Goodnight. Thanks for dinner.'

'Night, Ivy.' He turned and left her standing there under

the light with the image of her soft alluring smile burnt into his brain.

He hadn't known what he'd been expecting, but it certainly wasn't to feel this…deflated. He hadn't realised just how much he'd wanted to spend more time with her. How much the prospect of getting to know her better had resonated with his mind and his libido.

He took a couple of steps down then heard, 'Lucas. Wait.'

He turned, his heart hammering. 'Yes?'

She held her key up again. 'Do you want to come in?'

She'd bantered with him, flirted with him and met him match for match, but when he'd dabbed her chin with his napkin she'd leaned away. He sure as heck wasn't going to assume anything. 'Why?'

'Hmm.' She bit her bottom lip. 'The thing is, I don't do this. I don't take impromptu dates. I don't make rash deals with dangerous men.'

'If anything is dangerous it's your damned smile.' He laughed. 'You have so got the wrong impression of me.'

'Oh, I think I've worked you out.' She drummed her fingers over her pretty lips. 'But tonight has been very out of my comfort zone and I've agreed to some ridiculous plan with an almost stranger.'

'Hey. You know where I work. We've had dinner. We've saved a guy's life and comforted his wife together. We've even had a stand-up row. I never usually get to that part of a relationship.'

'Why am I not surprised?' She giggled. 'I'm trying to work out if you're a good influence or a bad one.'

'I can be whichever one you want. But let it be noted that *you* convinced *me* to lie to my parents. *You* are the one seeking revenge on your ex. I'm just an innocent bystander.'

'Innocent?' She closed her eyes and put her palms together. 'Please, God, don't let him be innocent.'

Then she looked up at him, and her expression became…
curious. Playful. So damned sexy. He saw her eyes darken, the
soft dart of her tongue to wet her lips. Something passed between them. That connection again. An implicit understanding.

I see you. I want you.

He stepped closer. He couldn't not.

Without breaking eye contact and with blatant desire in
her gaze she rose up on tiptoe and put her hand to his cheek.

Then her mouth was on his.

CHAPTER FOUR

HE INHALED SHARPLY at the shock of her move but cupped her face and pulled her closer. Because it was the only possible response. And if he'd thought she might be cautious or coy he'd been wrong. Very wrong. She was as assured as he was, if not more so. She tasted salty from the pho and achingly sweet. She was hot and soft and yielding and he wanted to sink right in.

She bunched his shirt in her fist, moaning as he took the kiss deeper. And that sound was almost the undoing of him. He snaked an arm around her waist and pulled her closer, feeling the crush of her breasts against his chest, the press of her hip against his thigh.

This was not part of their deal. But it was the very best part of it all. Even though it was also a little crazy. This wasn't a one-night-stand arrangement. They would have to get to know each other if they were going to fool his family, and that meant getting his head in the game too, not just his body. He didn't do that. Not ever.

But separate his brain from this kind of action? No, thank you.

Her key clattered to the floor, making her jump away from him. 'Damn.'

Damn indeed. A sign from the gods that this wasn't meant to be?

Her breathing came faster, her eyes almost greedy with need

as she bent and patted the ground trying to find her key. She straightened, brandishing it. 'Come in, Lucas.'

He remembered her earlier retort and gave it back to her as he rested his forehead against hers, breathing in her delicate scent and wanting to be covered in it. 'Do men always do what you ask?'

'Not enough.' She shrugged in a bad imitation of himself.

He laughed. 'Well, I don't need asking twice.'

He grasped her hand and let her lead him inside, through a too-bright communal hallway, up the stairs to the first floor and into her kitchen.

He imagined her apartment was neat and tidy, and that there were no dishes draining on the sink. That any spilt crumbs had been efficiently wiped away the moment they'd been made. That it was decorated in feminine shades. He imagined her home to be like her; efficiently contained with soft edges.

But there was no opportunity to confirm his suspicions. His eyes were only on her. On the back of her neck. On the soft fabric of her blouse, the outline of her bra strap. Was this happening? Was this for real?

He thought she might stall and offer him the obligatory drink. But, instead, she threw her key onto a white painted table in the centre of the room, then turned and kissed him hard again.

There was that throaty sound again, making him hard and hot. He walked her backwards and pinned her against the kitchen wall, the kiss deepening into something feral and wild. He slid his hand up her blouse, laughing softly as she shuddered at his touch. He cupped her breast, first over then under her bra and she curled against him, whimpering into his mouth.

He shoved off her coat, removed her blouse, unclipped her bra and then bent to suck a perfect nipple into his mouth. She writhed against him, fingers in his hair. 'That is so good.'

'We haven't even started.' He slicked a trail of kisses up her throat and back to capture her mouth in another mind-melting wet kiss. Her hands skimmed his body, tugging his shirt from his waistband and unbuttoning. She threw the shirt onto the floor then her hands explored his chest, arms, shoulders.

'Nice. You work out, Dr Matthews?'

'Kite surfing mostly, when I get the chance.'

She slid her palms over his biceps, her eyes glittering with tease. 'I've always fancied doing that and even signed up for a lesson once, but chickened out at the last minute.'

'You should do it. It's the best thing ever. Like you're flying and harnessing the wind. It's a real buzz.' He loved that she was so casual and not self-conscious. That they could learn about each other in all these different ways.

Just to fool his family, he reminded himself. Then this deal was finished. Done. But until then…

She cupped his face and laughed. 'I can see the excitement in your eyes.'

'Trust me, any excitement you see right now has nothing to do with kite surfing.' He stole another kiss as he slid his hands down past her waist and unzipped her skirt. It fell in a pool at her feet.

She stepped out of it, leaving her naked but for a pair of white lace panties. 'A surf bum, huh? Not a reader of the classics or a social justice warrior. There are no hidden depths here.'

She reached up and tousled his hair then ran her fingers down over his cheek, to his throat. She traced a line down his chest, which she then followed with her tongue. Lower. Lower.

He thought he was going to go insane with need. He was going to lose it.

He put his hand to her cheek and brought her back to look at him. She thought she had the measure of him, which clearly gave her a rush of power, which he liked. And true, he liked to surf. Liked a beer. Liked women. No harm done. He grinned before he caught her mouth again.

And kept the fact that he actually set himself a book-reading target each year, which included at least two classics. That he'd spent the last few years trying to convince his parents to offer pro bono work at their swanky clinic. But he let her run with the all-brawn fantasy because it suited him too. 'You got me. I'm such an Aussie cliche. For my sins. Of which there are many.'

She kissed his neck. 'Good.'

'Good that I have many sins? Or good that I'm a surf bum?'

'All of the above. The last thing I need is a complicated, deep-thinking man who takes life too seriously. Let's keep it simple.'

'Simply sex. At your service.' He did a mock doff of his cap.

She caught his hand and slid one of his fingers into her mouth, which had him wishing it were other body parts there in that silky soft cocoon.

Then he couldn't bear it any longer, he had to taste her again in a long, hot kiss that seared his brain and made him so damned hard he wanted to sink deep inside her. He lifted one of her legs and she wrapped it around his backside. He fitted in between her legs as if he was meant to be there.

But she pulled back, her mouth slightly open, her lips swollen and pink. Looking impossibly sexy and mussed-up. Her hair, normally a perfect straight bob, was unruly and dishevelled. She was as undone as he was.

She put her hand on his hip, slid her fingers along his waistband. 'I am way too old for up-against-the-wall sex. The bedroom's through here.'

He laughed but again let her take him by the hand and lead him into the bedroom, where she pushed him onto the bed, slid his trousers off and climbed on top of him, straddling his thighs.

He lay there, his hands stroking her thighs, looking up into beautiful eyes that were commanding and dark but with a hint of...vulnerability? Caution? As if she wasn't quite as convinced by her act as she wanted to be. And some of it was an act, he was sure. Because he'd seen her at work. He'd seen the compassion and caring. He'd seen her answer an emergency with authority yet humanity. There were depths in her professional life, so there would surely be some in her personal one too.

Whatever. If she just wanted uncomplicated sex, he was her man. He stepped his fingertips up her thighs. 'Ivy Hurst. You like to be on top?'

'I like... Oh.' She shuddered as he slid his finger inside her. She was so hot and wet and ready for him. 'I like that. Very much.'

'I want to be inside you. Right now.' He couldn't get over the way they'd just clicked after all that antagonism. Couldn't get his head around the deal they'd made. And now this. It was like a dream. A fantasy. He'd gone from calling her 'Dr Hurst' in clipped tones to purring 'Ivy' against her neck in a matter of hours and she was about to ride him.

'Oh, no. Not yet.' She slid her palm over his trousers against the rock of erection, her eyes misted with desire, a sexed-up smile on her lips.

He slid his finger inside her again. Then another.

Leaning in and kissing him, she freed him. Took him in her hand and stroked long delicious pulls that made him moan in pleasure.

The faster she stroked, the faster he slid his fingers until she was pulsing against him. 'Lucas...that is...' She closed her eyes.

'Look at me. Ivy, *look* at me. I want to watch you.'

Her eyes flickered open and she looked directly at him as she rocked hard against his fingers. Then he felt her tighten and suck in fast shuddering breaths before she threw her head back and moaned, 'Oh. My. God. Lucas.'

The way she said his name was like a prayer and the punch of it slid under his ribcage and arrowed directly to his groin. He pushed her hand away from his erection before it was all over, before it properly began. 'Geez, Ivy. You are so freaking hot.'

'Thank you.' She fell forward, looking almost drunk on the orgasm, and kissed him. 'And you are excellent.'

'Condom?'

She shook her head, her features softened. 'Hot damn. No. I threw them all out.'

'Into the yard with the rest of his stuff?'

'Yes.' She shrugged ruefully. 'But I very much regret my rashness now.'

'Lucky I have one, then.' He stretched to the edge of the bed, reached down to his trouser pocket and fished out his wallet. Grabbed the foil and tore it open. Laughed as she helped him wiggle out of his boxers.

She grinned too, pursing her lips. 'You always carry condoms? You get that much sex?'

He guffawed. 'I'd like to get that much sex.'

'Me too.' She smiled, rubbing her cheek against his. 'Lots and lots of sex.'

'So when you said you were off men…'

'Whoa, whoa, whoa.' She bit her bottom lip and grinned. 'I didn't mean I was off sex. Or orgasms. The more of them, the merrier. Please.'

Man, she was funny, beautiful, hard core. He laughed. 'Then we'd better make a start.'

The mood got serious as he sheathed and slid her forward on his thighs, positioning his erection at her entrance. She bent and kissed him, and he cupped her breasts, soft and beautiful in his hands. Her mouth hot and wet. He didn't think he'd ever been so hard. It was taking all his strength not to explode right then and there.

This was Ivy freaking Hurst. Some kind of crazy dream.

And he didn't want to wake up.

Ivy inhaled as she lowered onto him, every nerve ending tingling with the last vestiges of her orgasm, but she was hungry for more.

Lucas's hands skimmed her waist and tugged her forward a little, raising her up on her shins. She sank down on him again, watching his beautiful face crease into ecstasy. She was doing this to him. She was making him wild with need.

But, *whoa*. This wasn't who she was.

She didn't have sex with someone she barely knew. She didn't take what she wanted. She didn't play. But here she was, doing just that. And she was loving this new version of herself.

He raised his hips and thrust inside her and her thoughts blurred. She clung onto now, to this. Sensation after sensation…an intense physical pleasure and something more…a catch in her heart as she looked at his face. A knowing as their eyes locked.

Look at me.

She couldn't look away.

She slid up his length and then sank slowly over him again. He groaned, deep and hoarse, then moved his hips in time with her slow rhythm.

She leaned forward and pressed her palms into his shoulders as his pace quickened into long, greedy thrusts. She tried to hold onto the sensations, to grasp each one as it rippled through her…the taste of him, the feel of him. The stirring in her belly, the ache for more of this. The blush of her skin under his gaze.

There were so many sensations coming so fast she let herself fall into them, into the long, fast strokes. Into the bright light in his eyes, then the clouding with pure pleasure. The rub of his palm, the wet of his mouth. The scruff of his hair against her chest bone. She fell and she fell and she fell. Faster. Harder. Until she felt his grip on her arms tighten and, as he called her name into the darkness, she shattered into a million pieces.

She closed her eyes, finally releasing herself from his hold.

Whatever demons she'd been exorcising were well and truly erased.

More, she'd probably made a deal with the devil and was likely going to hell for encouraging him to lie to his family. But she didn't regret a moment.

Not a single one.

Lucas lay back, cradling her against his chest and waiting for the buzz to fade. When he could finally manage to form words he admitted, 'Ivy, I lied to you.'

Her body stiffened and she looked up at him, frowning. 'You did what? Please tell me you're not in a relationship. I hate cheaters.'

'Hey, no way. I'm not. I told you that kite surfing was the best thing ever, but I think Ivy sex tops it.' He pressed a kiss on her cheek. 'You're my new favourite hobby.'

Geez. Cheesy? He didn't know. Didn't know much right now, his brain had been drained of anything sensible and all he wanted to do was wait five minutes then sink into her again.

She giggled. 'I think I prefer knitting, but you'll do as a second option. You know, when I get bored of knit one purl one.'

He looked around the pristine bedroom. Nothing out of place. A walk-in closet, door closed. An old-fashioned chair with a blue-cushioned window seat. No evidence of any kind of hobbies…of anything, other than sleeping. Not even a book on the nightstand. But there were some cool black and white photograph prints of twisty trees on the walls. 'You knit? I just can't imagine that. Nana.'

She laughed. 'Hey, it's actually a very cool thing to do. But,

in reality, I don't have time. I used to have lots of hobbies…
horse riding, yoga, thrift shopping…but now all I do is work.
So you don't need to find out much more about me to tell your
parents. Just say I'm a workaholic.'

'You really do need to spend your time more wisely.'

'Probably. I just sank all my energy into my career when
Grant left. Which I know was a mistake, but it was a really
good distraction. You got any ideas?'

'Lots.' He stroked a fingertip over her hip and pulled her
close, spooning round her, already planning which position
he'd like to try next. 'Well, at least I know what your apartment looks like. You have good taste in art—Mother would
like that.'

She twisted round to face him, elbow bent, propping her
head up in her hand. 'You're going to mention my photographs
of eucalypts?'

'Well, I can't exactly tell her how good you are in bed or
what your kisses are like, can I? For the record, they are mind-
blowing. But wait, actually, are they? I need to double-check.'
He took her face in both hands and slid his mouth over hers,
losing himself in her taste and the feel of her in his arms. When
he finally came up for air his chest felt as if it had been bathed
in warm honey. 'No. I cannot tell her about your kisses. But I
can mention that you have a jungle of houseplants.'

'Don't forget the ones outside too.' Her eyes darted to the
floor-to-ceiling blinds behind which, he assumed, was a ranch
slider door and her balcony.

'Out there?'

She nodded. 'My deck stretches all the way round to my
lounge too, so I get afternoon and evening sun. I wouldn't
want to live anywhere I couldn't sit outside. My potted plants
are my pride and joy. Does that make me sound old? I mean,
my days of clubbing until dawn are well and truly over.' She
shuddered and laughed. 'Thirty-nine is ancient, right?'

'Not as old as me. You're just wise now and want different things. Wise people know that plants make the world a better place. Green-fingered.' He sucked in air as she ran her fingers up his thigh and cupped his burgeoning erection. He kissed the crook of her neck. 'Oh, you have multi-talented fingers.'

'And your talents are what, Dr Matthews?'

'Other than spectacular kisses and amazing lovemaking?'

Her eyebrows rose as if she was calling him out. 'Anything I can actually mention in front of your mum?'

He pursed his lips as he thought about the deal again. About having to make a pretence in front of his family. That didn't make him feel good, despite how necessary. It had seemed an easy plan when they'd discussed it in the restaurant, but now he wasn't so sure.

He liked Ivy and had a bad feeling he might regret this whole agreement if things didn't turn out how they'd planned.

He liked her and was having sex with her and had committed to being in a pretend relationship with her for the next few weeks.

What could possibly go wrong?

Everything.

He turned his attention back to her and kept his tone light. 'I make damned fine coffee.'

'That's your job for tomorrow morning, then.' Then she winced. 'I mean…you don't have to stay, obviously. Only, work is just round the corner and…' She grimaced. 'Ugh. I'm not sure on our boundaries here. My last relationship was five years. He stayed. Until he didn't.'

Lucas didn't know how to answer this. Did he want to stay the night? Go to sleep here, with her? Wake up with her in the morning? Make her coffee? Play happy couples? Pretend on top of pretend?

It wasn't something he ever did. All the women he'd dated knew the score: he wasn't going to stick around. It was always,

always only temporary. He could not give himself, he could not love someone. He would never be responsible for anyone else's life, happiness or trust.

And yet…his chest contracted at the thought of leaving Ivy.

Geez, if that wasn't the biggest reason to hotfoot it out of here, he didn't know what was. He needed to get a grip.

He kissed the tip of her nose, avoiding any statement that sounded like either a commitment or a brush-off. 'I do need to go home and get a change of clothes and some other stuff for work.'

She blinked and nodded. 'Okay. Yes.'

And was he mistaken or did she look almost relieved at that? He wasn't sure he liked that either. Which meant he should probably leave right now.

Five more minutes.

The thought of getting out of this bed was very depressing. 'Hey, why did you pull away when I wiped the pho from your chin earlier?'

She grimaced. 'Sorry. But that's exactly the kind of thing Grant used to do. Treat me like I was a child, or a pet. I'm a grown woman.'

'You're hard core.' He cupped her backside and pulled her closer. 'But I get it. My little sister would hate it if I did that to her too. She'd also hate it if I called her little. She thinks I treat her like a baby. And she's probably right, but she's my kid sister. It's my job to protect her.'

And he'd failed. So badly.

Ivy smiled. 'How old is she?'

'Twenty-eight.'

'Oh? So not a baby at all. How old are you?'

'Forty-one.'

Her eyes narrowed and he guessed she was doing the maths. 'That's a big age difference.'

'Mum and Dad had three boys in quick succession. I'm the

youngest son. Then there was a long gap...probably while she got her head around having three boys to run around after. Flora was my mum's last-chance baby. I think she was hoping for maybe Flora and one more so they could grow up together, but the one more never happened. So, Flora was our pet.'

Until he'd ruined it all. Ruined her. Ruined everything. A startling reminder that he was no good being responsible for people.

His chest constricted and familiar self-loathing rushed through him. He shifted away from Ivy. 'Anyway. I won't stay tonight, thank you. We both need a decent sleep before work tomorrow.'

'And then what?'

The six-billion-dollar question. Normally he'd leave with no plans for another date but things were different here. Not only were they going to see each other at work, but they had a deal. 'We probably should catch up some time to discuss strategy going forward.'

She pressed her lips together as if holding in a laugh. And if she noted his rapid change of subject, she didn't show it. 'Strategy. Yes. Okay.'

'Saturday? Unless you're on call?'

She nodded. 'Saturday works. I'll make sure to message you about Emma's timeline too.'

'Great.' Back to work conversations. Good. He knew how to navigate those.

Where he was struggling was that he did not know how to navigate the warm and excited feelings in his chest at the thought of spending more time with Ivy Hurst.

CHAPTER FIVE

WHAT THE HELL had they done?

What the hell was she doing?

Ivy played with the handle on her Americano coffee cup and thought about last night.

Trouble was, she couldn't stop thinking about last night. Because this was what she did: second-guessed herself. And she was currently second-guessing the one good thing that had happened to her in years.

They were two consenting adults. It shouldn't matter to anyone else what they were doing in private together. If it felt right, and hurt no one else, then, hell, she should immerse herself in it and enjoy every second.

She sighed. It had been very good sex. Lucas had been surprisingly good.

'Morning, Ivy. Sorry I'm late.' Phoebe wrapped her in a warm hug then sat down across from her in one of the huge chesterfield sofas in Perc Up, the little cafe bar across the road from the hospital. Then she put her takeaway coffee cup on the table and grinned. 'Wow, you look…happy.'

'I am.' Ivy grinned back.

'Okay. Spill. What—or rather who—has put that smile on your face?'

Ivy lowered her voice so any nearby hospital staff couldn't overhear, although that was unlikely given the way the seating was arranged in cosy huddles with tables separated from other customers by palms and potted vines. It was like an indoor garden and the perfect place for sharing secrets. 'I had sex with Lucas Matthews last night.'

Phoebe almost choked on her coffee. 'Sorry, I think I'm going deaf. I thought you said you had *sex*. With Lucas Matthews. Reconstructive surgeon.'

A delicious wave of pride and lust prickled through Ivy. 'I did.'

Phoebe tapped the table. 'I knew it! I knew there was a man in your office. What the heck, Ivy? What's going on? I thought you didn't like him.'

'I didn't know him. I did that jumping-to-conclusions thing, assuming stuff about him when I didn't know him. He's actually…well, he's kind of hot.'

'There are plenty of hot men at work, but you don't have sex with them. What happened?'

'Um…well. We had an argument. Then an emergency. Then a debrief. Then dinner. Then I was…debriefed. Literally.' Ivy giggled. Oh, hell. She was giggling about a man. Since when did she do that?

Phoebe just gaped at her, blinking. 'Slowly. Tell me slowly.'

'Okay.' Ivy tried to control her dancing heartbeat. 'He came to my office to talk about Emma, and we got into a bit of a fight about her theatre schedule. Then one of my post-op patients turned up. Collapsed. Leaking artery. Theatre…et cetera… Then I had dinner with Lucas because he knows a great place and two-minute noodles aren't enough.' She sighed. This was far too much detail and yet she couldn't stop talking about it. And it made no sense and yet made complete sense. 'Then I agreed to be his fake girlfriend for a charity ball. And we went back to my place.'

Even now, saying it out loud sounded like something from a movie. This wasn't her life.

Phoebe shook her head, blinking rapidly. 'You did...what? I can't keep up.'

'It was awesome. All of it. And we've got another date planned for Saturday.'

'Whoa. So, for real? You slept with Lucas Matthews?' Phoebe's eyes widened and she looked suitably chastised when Ivy glared at her to quieten the heck down. 'And you're going to do it again?'

'Only until the ball, then we're done.' To be fair, they hadn't discussed whether sex would be part of it, but, after last night, she hoped so.

Phoebe shook her head. 'I have no words.'

Ivy chuckled, her post-sex glow keeping her mood buoyant, despite the fleeting second-guessing. 'Phoebe, you always have words.'

'I'm in shock. After Grant I thought...you said only last night...'

'I have well and truly exorcised Grant from my body and my mind.'

Phoebe's eyes grew huge, and she shifted uncomfortably in her seat. 'Talking of...incoming, on your left. Um...'

'What? Have you developed aphasia?' Then her friend's words sank in. 'Is he behind me? Is he...?' Lucas was here? Well, why not? This was the cafe closest to the hospital and many of her colleagues mainlined the fabulous coffee. She whirled round, excited and anxious and perturbed and turned on all at the same time, to come face to face with... 'Grant. Oh.'

Typical that her ex frequented this place too. Her excitement fizzled into frank irritation.

'Ivy.' Grant pressed a kiss to her cheek. 'What a coincidence. You look...well, you look amazing.'

'Please don't do that, Grant.' Ivy stood, not tall enough to make a physical impression but hopefully with enough gravitas to send him away.

But, as always, Grant couldn't read her. How had she wasted half a decade of her life on him? He stepped back, his gaze sweeping her from head to toe. 'What? I'm only saying what I see. You look...ethereal.'

'Don't kiss me again, Grant. Ever. I'm not your pet, or your child, and I'm certainly not your girlfriend.'

'Oh. I...' he spluttered. 'I just wanted—'

'What?' He'd cheated on her, humiliated her, broken her. And now he wanted to pass the time of day?

'I just came in to grab a coffee and there you are, looking amazing. And I thought...' He grimaced. 'Maybe we should have a catch-up. Maybe dinner?'

The gall of him. It was bad enough having to work in the same hospital and risk running into him every day, but catch up with dinner? No way.

She thought about last night and how much fun she'd had... how unburdened she'd felt. How free, for the first time in ages, just to be herself. The way Lucas had been interested in her and made her laugh and made her feel wanted and interesting.

And the sex...

'Grant, unless you have some work thing to discuss I'd prefer it if you didn't speak to me at all. We're done.' She grabbed her bag and made a play of hauling the strap up to her shoulder as if she were about to leave.

He watched her, his shoulders slumping, eyes shifting between Ivy and Phoebe. Finally, he took the hint. 'Don't go on my account. I'll head off. Bye, Phoebe.'

Phoebe pressed her lips together as if holding in a laugh then just about managed, 'Bye, Grant.'

He turned to go then whirled back to Ivy. 'You really do look amazing.'

Her patience ran right out. 'Grant—'

'I know,' he interrupted her, looking sheepish for the first time in his life. 'I'm sorry. For everything.'

'Good.' She turned away from him, sat down and counted to ten, then sagged and whispered to Phoebe, 'Has he gone yet?'

'The door is just closing behind him. He's walking up the street.' She whistled. 'I don't think he'll be bothering you again and definitely not kissing you. Way to go, girl. You were epic. And he's right, you do look…different. Ethereal, yes. Your eyes are shining, your skin is glowing. Sex suits you.'

'Good sex suits me. Lucas sex. Not Grant sex.'

Phoebe laughed. 'Who are you and what have you done with Ivy?'

'She's having fun for the first time in for ever.'

'I'm pleased for you. Honestly. But seriously…' Phoebe patted Ivy's hand. 'Be careful.'

'We're using contraception, if that's what you mean.' She made a mental note to pop by the pharmacy on the way home and get more supplies in case this became a regular thing.

Her tummy tightened at the thought. Saturday couldn't come soon enough.

'We both know that no contraception is one hundred per cent safe.' Phoebe rolled her eyes. 'But what I meant was be careful with your heart.'

'My heart will not be involved here. It's a temporary thing to get his mum off his back. We both know the score. It's a deal where we both win, and I've already got the one benefit I was hoping for.'

'Great sex?'

'Well, that and the fact Grant now knows exactly what he's missing.'

'He really does. But you trust too easily, Ivy. You give yourself. I don't want you hurt again. Grant did a real number on you, and it's taken you a long time to get over him. I don't want you opening yourself to that again.'

'I am walking into this with my eyes wide open.' *Look at me...* Her skin was suffused with heat at the memory. It felt as if she'd dreamt it, if not for the delicious aches in places she'd almost forgotten existed. 'This is something I'm doing for me. A self-esteem boost. No regrets.'

But Phoebe's smile was filled with concern. 'Okay. But I'm here for you. Always.'

'I know. Thank you. I'll be fine. Just fine.' Ivy's beeper began to vibrate. She looked at it and grimaced. 'Shoot. My reg needs to talk to me and it's not even starting-work time yet.'

'Yes, I need to get going too.' Phoebe stood. 'I almost managed to drink a whole cup of coffee this time. I'd call that a win.'

But Ivy's head was already back at the hospital, with her work and the chances of running into a particular surgeon who kissed like a god and made her feel better than she had in years.

Up on the ward Ivy caught up with her junior doctor, Samreen, who filled her in on the latest developments with Emma before they went to see her. 'The abdominal pain's getting worse and we can't seem to get on top of it.'

'Did we get the scan done last night?'

Samreen pressed her lips together and sighed. 'No. The on-call were busy with emergency work and they haven't had a chance. They've promised to do it first thing this morning.'

'It needs to be urgent. Give them another call and chase them up, please.' Ivy shook her head. Things weren't adding up with Emma. 'Babies are okay?'

Samreen tapped on the desk computer and searched for reports. 'Obstetric ultrasound yesterday reports nothing unusual. Both babies are doing fine despite the trauma poor Mum's endured.'

'Okay. Good. It's difficult dealing with a twin pregnancy

and such bad injuries from the fire, we have to make sure we keep an eye on everything. Any other symptoms?'

'No diarrhoea. Vomited three times this morning.'

'Okay. As far as I'm aware she hasn't had any other episodes of vomiting prior to this. The pain's getting worse, you say?'

'Yes.' Samreen looked at the charts she was holding. 'But she's on high-dose analgesics for her burns so the pain only shows up when her meds are wearing off.'

Ivy was coming to a conclusion she didn't want to have to draw, but it was like putting pieces of a difficult jigsaw together. 'I'll examine her again and see if we can work out what's happening. This poor woman has had multiple injuries and surgeries and is heavily pregnant, so there are lots of potential causes of abdominal pain. But the vomiting is new, so that's my biggest concern at this stage.'

Samreen nodded and scanned Emma's chart again. 'Blood results have just come in and her white cell count is creeping up. But that could be infection of a wound site, IV access or anything really. Even a UTI.'

Ivy always liked to use these kinds of conundrums as a teaching moment. 'Indeed. And the nausea and vomiting could be a side effect of her meds. But, if a normally healthy woman came in with temperature, right-radiating lower abdominal pain and vomiting, what would be your first thought?'

Samreen tapped her fingers on the desk as she thought. 'Possibly appendicitis.'

'Yes.' The unwanted conclusion Ivy was coming to. 'What do we think the chances of appendicitis are here?'

Her junior shrugged. 'About as much chance as any other person, I guess.'

'Exactly. And if it looks like a duck and talks like a duck, it's probably a duck, right?'

'Yes.'

'But it doesn't pay to jump to conclusions. If you could

chase that scan, I'll check to see if there are any theatres free this afternoon, just in case. I know she's been enjoying trying to eat and drink small amounts but let's keep her nil by mouth.'

'Oh? Is that Emma's chart?' Lucas's deep voice had her whirling round while her heart did a strange little jig.

He smiled. 'Hey, Ivy.'

'Hi, Lucas.' Ivy's belly contracted at the sight of him. That smiling mouth that had given her so much pleasure. Those hands. That man. She'd straddled him and now here she was trying to act normal. Her cheeks heated and she wondered exactly how much her body was giving away to her patients and colleagues.

That would not do. She was far too old to be thinking like this and swooning over a guy. And it was bad enough she had to dodge Grant, she didn't need to add Lucas to the avoid-at-work list.

Samreen handed him the chart. 'She's not doing so well today. We think she might have appendicitis.'

'Ah. I see.' He frowned and looked back to Ivy. 'On top of everything else?'

Ivy slid her hands into her pockets, more to stop herself from reaching out and touching him than anything else. 'Her symptoms point to it, but it could be one of a few things. We're going through a process of elimination until the abdo scan results come through.'

His expression flattened. 'Any problems with the babies?'

'As far as we know there are two happy little bunnies in there. It's like doing a game of pin the symptoms to the illness, but appendicitis would explain the shooting temps, high blood cell count and vomiting.'

'Geez. As if she hasn't had enough to deal with. Is nothing going to go right for her?' Once again, he looked genuinely concerned. Every time she saw Lucas deal with a patient she was impressed by his compassionate approach, but the way he treated Emma, fought for her…well, that was personal. Why? 'If it is appendicitis then at least I know I can fix that.'

'And then I can fix the grafts.' He bugged his eyes at her and laughed.

She rolled her eyes back at him. 'Give me time to get things under control.'

'Of course.' His voice was sing-song. 'Look at us negotiating like adults. Okay if I have a word with her?'

'Absolutely. I haven't seen her yet today either, so I'll come over too.' She smiled to herself. Yes, they were negotiating. Miracles did happen. The sex had definitely helped, but it was essential she kept that completely private and away from her professional life.

If only she could stop thinking about the way he'd kissed her up against her kitchen wall.

'Hi, Emma, how are you doing today?' His tone was completely different from the way he spoke to Ivy. When he talked to patients, he was calm and concerned and yet authoritative. She thought about the way he'd groaned against her throat and called her name when he'd come. Her cheeks heated again.

Saturday.

Would it be a rerun of last night, or would it be awkward?

Emma's face crumpled as she slowly ran her hand over her swollen belly. She was ashen, with dark circles under her eyes and exhaustion from fighting for herself and her babies written deep over her face. 'Not so good, Doc. I've got sore guts today.'

'Those babies kicking too hard?'

'I don't mind that.' Emma smiled and despite the pain Ivy could see so much mother's love there. 'I just wish they'd kick a different part. It makes me feel really sick.'

'Well, I've never been pregnant so I can't say I speak from experience…' Lucas flashed a very handsome smile at Emma '…but that doesn't sound great to me. But don't worry, Dr Hurst here is on the job and I know she'll get you sorted out.

Then we can get your grafts sorted and you back home, where you belong. No one wants to be in hospital if they can help it. Not even me.'

'I'll bet.' Emma gave a slightly pathetic-sounding laugh. 'You got family waiting for you at home?'

He blinked quickly. 'Just an empty flat. Though I do have siblings, parents...'

Emma nodded, understanding the context. No wife. No kids.

Ivy thought about the way he'd spoken about his family last night with barely any emotion, certainly lacking in affection, apart from the brief softening at the mention of his sister. And how he'd chosen not to speak to his mother when she'd called. She understood how family dynamics could be difficult. Hell, communication with her parents and siblings was minimal... but, even so, her mother was the lynchpin and everyone's news was passed on by her to each of them.

But Lucas had been almost disparaging, and he'd clammed up about his sister, steering the conversation into a different direction. He wasn't exactly the clamming-up type, which meant Lucas had hidden depths.

That wasn't exactly something she wanted to know.

She'd noted the softness in his tone when he'd spoken of Flora, then the quick diversion and an altogether different tone, kind of matter of fact. But whatever he'd been trying to do hadn't worked on her because she saw something in his eyes that he couldn't wipe away with just a change of subject. Something about his sister that made him wary, or sad or...she couldn't put her finger on it. Uncomfortable? No. He clearly loved his sister. But something had happened between them.

Had he been jealous of her sudden appearance when he was what...? Thirteen? Had his parents turned all their attention away from the boys?

She couldn't work out what was affecting him, but she was good at jigsaw puzzles. She'd get there in the end.

But why? Why did it matter anyway? Working him out would only mean she knew him better. And that way lay danger. It was easier not to get involved if she thought of him as purely physical.

'Excuse me, can I get through, please?' The sonographer pushed her way past Ivy, making her jump. She'd been in a dream world.

Her heart thumped hard against her chest. She could not let him derail her work. Ever. There was a definite line between her job and her private life. Between keeping things simple and getting deeply involved with a totally unsuitable man. With any man. Hadn't she promised herself she'd never run that risk again? So why was she trying to work him out?

She moved back to allow the sonographer some room. 'I'll be over by the nurses' station when you're done. Thanks.' Ivy nodded a smile towards Emma. 'Once we've got the results of the scan we can make a plan. In the meantime, just try and rest up. If you need anything use the call bell and we'll try to make you as comfortable as possible.'

Ivy turned to Lucas. 'I'll be in touch about the scan.'

Then she walked to the nurses' station and took some deep breaths to help her refocus on her job.

'So, Saturday.' His voice was close to her ear and the little hairs on her neck prickled to attention.

So much for the deep breaths because her whole body inclined towards him as if there were some kind of super-magnetic field around him and she were a battered old nickel unable to resist the attraction.

She turned and was barely an inch away from his mouth. It would have taken the tiniest of stretches to slide her lips over his. Heat rushed through her, pooling low in her belly. 'Yes? The deal. Yes. Right. The plan.'

She emphasised the last word to remind them both that this was about having a good cover story for his mum, and some very simple, albeit mind-blowing, sex.

Nothing else.

'The plan. Yes. I'll pick you up early. Say, eight?'

'In the morning? On my day off? You're joking, right?'

He leaned closer and whispered, 'You won't regret it. I promise.'

Almost shaking with need, Ivy glanced around, but for once all the staff were busy in cubicles and with patients, no one to notice their proximity. She stared up into those mesmerising eyes. 'I won't?'

'Not at all.' His smile was deliciously teasing. 'Wear long trousers. A jacket. It might get cold.'

'Why?'

'That would spoil the surprise.' He winked and turned away, then added loudly, 'Let me know asap about Emma.'

'Oh, I will.' And hot damn, with just one conversation all her promises had dissolved. She wanted him.

Saturday definitely could not come soon enough.

CHAPTER SIX

WAITING FOR SATURDAY morning had Lucas feeling like a kid on Christmas Eve with the promise of a present if he went to sleep.

But sleep had been elusive these past few nights because he'd relived that one evening with Ivy over and over. He still couldn't get over how it had gone from antagonism to bed so quickly.

He wanted to do it again. Even the antagonism and arguing. That had been weirdly, sexily fun too.

And here was the thing: he didn't do this. He didn't think about a woman to the point of sleeplessness. Didn't plan future dates. Certainly didn't call on favours from old mates he hadn't seen for months just so he could make a woman smile.

But here she was, grinning wildly as they parked up at his friends' acreage property on the edge of Kung Gai National park, as he pointed out the two horses all saddled up and waiting by the timber stable block. That giddy smile gave him the best gut punch of pride he'd ever had.

Her eyes sparkled as the reality of their next few hours dawned. 'Horse riding?'

'No. Airplane wing walking,' he quipped. The effect on his body just seeing her excitement was surreal. His arms ached to wrap around her. His mouth itched to kiss her. His...

'Of course it's horse riding. Idiot.' She threw him an eager yet faux-frustrated look, unclipped her seat belt and was out of the car before he'd turned the engine off. 'Thank you so much. I can't wait.'

He followed her across the gravel path to the stables. 'You said you used to do it so I hope it's a good idea.'

'The best.' She turned and looked a little discombobulated. 'I said I used to do a lot of things.'

'To be fair, yoga and knitting were a bit of a reach for me,' he admitted, finally giving in to temptation and slipping his hand into hers. And slightly regretting that he'd brought her here, and not suggested just cooking her breakfast at his place. Then eating it in bed. Eating her in bed.

'Hey, girl. Hey.' She cooed towards one of the horses. 'Oh, it's been such a long time since I rode a horse. I've been promising myself to book in some sessions but never get round to it. I've never thought about it for a…date.' She looked up at him and her easy smile wavered.

He saw the hesitation and he wondered, too, exactly what this was. Other than hopefully a prelude to more great sex, it was about getting to know each other, right? For their little charade. Not a date. They weren't dating. Even though this felt a lot like a date. 'I thought it would be good to get out and do something rather than just be in a restaurant again. I'm not good at sitting and chatting. I prefer to be active.'

'Me too.' The smile was reminiscent of her post-sex grin the other night and his body prickled in response.

'Lucas!' His old friend George and George's husband, Ivan, wandered out from the stables, arms outstretched in greeting. 'You made it.'

'Hey, guys. How's things?' Lucas shook hands with Ivan, while mentally forcing the tingling sensation to dissipate. 'Ivan, George, this is Ivy.'

'So pleased to meet you.' George shook Ivy's hand then wrapped Lucas in a hug, whispering, 'You sly old dog. This is very unlike you.'

'I know. But don't read anything into it.' He glanced over to Ivy, who was now wandering back to the horses with Ivan.

But George was not going to let him off the hook. 'Oh? That makes me very suspicious. I want all the details while she's being distracted.'

Lucas sighed, not knowing what to say. 'It's a long story.'

George looked at Ivy then back at Lucas. 'You have about two minutes. Be quick.'

'Seriously, have you been talking to my mother?' Lucas laughed. Their friendship had been initiated at a baby swim class both their mothers had attended at the local private gym, then cemented at school. He'd been honoured when George had asked him to be best man around four years ago. That wedding had been a huge surprise because George had always insisted he wasn't the settling-down type, like Lucas. But it was amazing to see how happy he was with Ivan. How one person could make such a difference. At least, for George. Lucas almost envied them...the way they finished each other's sentences, the knowledge that they were loved, cared for. That there was someone to share both adventures and the mundane. Just having each other.

Almost envied him because, for Lucas, it was better for all concerned if he remained uncommitted for the rest of his days. That way, no one got hurt.

'No mothers have been involved, I promise.' George grimaced, because their parents not only shared the same postcode, they also had similar values and expectations. 'I just hate to think of you sad and old and alone.'

'Geez, mate.' Lucas snorted. 'Cheers for the brutal precis of my life.'

'Brutal but true.' George shrugged but slapped him on the back. After forty-plus years' friendship, smack talk was their MO. 'But she seems nice, so I'm not sure what she's doing with you.'

He followed George's line of vision towards Ivy. She had her back to them and was laughing at something Ivan was saying and simultaneously stroking the horse. Her head was tipped back, her slender throat moving as she laughed. Her hair was shimmering different shades of bronze and gold in the sunlight. Her backside was like a peach in black skinny jeans. She was the total package. Beautiful. Funny. Caring. Sexy. His chest suddenly filled with warmth, as if the sun was shining right on him and not on her hair.

He wanted to strip those jeans from her. Lay her down… yes, even on some hay if that was where they were at, and slide inside her.

Ah. That was it.

That was what this weird feeling was. This attraction was entirely physical. He just hadn't had enough sex with her.

Well, that was an easy remedy.

He realised he was probably drooling so drew his gaze back to his old friend. 'Thanks for the loan of the horses. I owe you, big time.'

'Yes, you do. Maybe dinner some time? We can get better acquainted with Ivy.'

'Yeah, well…maybe.' Lucas didn't want to explain, but the thought of lying to his friends as well as his family didn't sit well with him. 'We're really just friends. It's nothing…permanent.'

'Sure it isn't. I've never known you have a girlfriend for longer than two minutes.' George's eyebrows rose as he grilled Lucas. 'You do know you're allowed to trust other people? Not everyone's out to get you.'

Oh, yeah. How had he known George would push him to this? Because it was what he did: dug deep for Lucas's truth. And Lucas knew he wouldn't be fobbed off. 'Trusting Ivy isn't the problem. It's trusting myself.'

His friend frowned. 'For what?'

'You know what.' Lucas knew his voice was almost a mumble now as the memory of what happened all those years ago shot through him like a knife. 'Keeping her safe. Keeping anyone safe.'

'Man, Lucas. If you're talking about what happened with Flora, then you have to forgive yourself.'

'I can't and I won't.' Lucas kept his voice low. 'Seriously. This is just a bit of a laugh. Nothing deep.' But the knife twisted a little more.

'And yet you want to borrow my horses to impress her.'

'I'm not trying to impress her. I just…' he was all out of words with how to describe why he'd suddenly decided to bring her horse riding just because he knew she liked doing it '…thought it would be a fun thing to do.'

George's eyebrows rose and he clearly didn't believe a word. 'I hope she can ride.'

Yes, she can, mate. Very well indeed.

He thought about her catching his rhythm. Or had he caught hers? They'd both been so in tune with each other, had known instinctively what the other wanted and needed. It had been wild and intense and he'd lost himself in her. He couldn't remember semantics. Just how she'd tasted. How she'd felt wrapped around him.

And how doing it again was top of his to-do list, despite all his talk about not committing. But, hell, this was sex, not marriage.

Ivy called over, 'Oh, it's been a while but I'm sure it'll come back to me. I'm itching to get going.'

Lucas wondered exactly how much of the conversation she'd heard but she laughed and looked over at him. 'I hope you can ride too, Lucas.'

'Oh, yes.' He caught her eye, making sure she understood the full innuendo, and she pressed her lips together, bugging her eyes at him to shut up. But he didn't miss the glitter and the heat there too.

She held her hand up to one of the horses, who gave it a good sniff. She stroked its muzzle.

'Aren't you beautiful?' She turned to Lucas and shook her head, her eyes full of tease. 'Just so you don't misunderstand, I was talking to the horse.'

'I wouldn't assume anything else.' But he had to admit he kind of liked the fact that she associated beautiful with him in any kind of way.

He handed her a helmet and then helped fasten it under her chin. The way she looked up at him as he clipped the straps in place, so close, so excited and trusting him to make her helmet safe. That mouth inches away.

It felt natural to press his lips against hers and kiss her.

But he didn't. He held back. Pulled back. Not wanting George to witness any of this and have him doubling down on his questions.

Grinning at them both, George handed him a small backpack. 'Here's a few snacks. There's a great picnic spot down by the marina. You can let the horses rest there a while too. Have fun.'

Lucas's gaze fixed on Ivy again as she put one foot in the stirrup and hoisted herself on top of her horse. She looked majestic up there, powerful like a warrior queen. Once again he thought about stripping her naked and harnessing that power for some serious lovemaking. 'Oh, don't worry. I intend to have fun. Lots.'

Ivy's heart thrilled as they trotted along an undulating path, first through George and Ivan's beautiful farmland, then deep into the native bush park. The air was alive with birdsong, such different sounds from the traffic and bustling street ones she heard from her apartment.

She stroked her horse Patty's neck. 'It's so good to be in the saddle again and breathing in this amazing fresh air after being in the city for so long.'

'Yes.' The path was just wide enough for them to trot side by side. Lucas turned to her and smiled. 'Stuck in the hospital with the air con and disinfectant smell. I'm glad you're enjoying it.'

'Switching off devices and just being in nature is very good for the soul.' She breathed in the cool crisp wintry air. 'I really should do this more often.'

Lucas was very good for the soul too. He looked great there on his horse, relaxed and yet strong. Confident in his physicality and his control of the animal. Lit by the dappled morning light, he looked beautiful and commanding and yet somehow relieved that she was enjoying herself. Just how much thought and effort had he put into this? Had he been anxious it would be a success?

Her heart did a lot more thrilling at this thought. He'd organised this all. For her. Because she said she used to enjoy it. But truth was she wasn't sure what to make of it all. Oh, she knew this was just a bit of fun for them to get to know each other better, but they could have done that in any cafe anywhere in the city. To bring her out here into the countryside, meeting his friends...meant something more. Something deeply personal.

Which made her want to simultaneously wish this perfect morning could last for ever, and also run far away to where the connections they were forming wouldn't get any stronger. Because it was getting harder to ignore the way her body felt when he was around. Not just turned on, but the way her heart smiled.

But if she was going to fulfil her part of the deal, she needed to know more about him so horse riding or coffees or sex...it was all just research. Right?

The path took them to a shallow, narrow, slow-moving creek. The horses stopped and drank the cool, clear water.

'So how do you know George?' Ivy asked him. Watching the way he'd chatted to his friend had intrigued her. They'd been in cahoots about something, heads close together, clearly trying not to be overheard.

Lucas patted his horse's shoulder. 'We go way back. His parents and my parents are friends. We grew up in the same neighbourhood and went to the same schools. He's like another brother to me, really. One who actually tolerates me.' He gave a wry laugh. 'He'll be at the ball too, with Ivan.'

'Great. Someone I'll actually know.' She hadn't missed the brother comment.

'I think you'll know plenty. Lots of the hospital bigwigs go. The Sydney medical scene is quite incestuous.'

'Tell me about it.' Her thoughts swung to Grant. He'd never have organised a horse-riding trip for her.

But she knew better than to compare. The two relationships were entirely different.

This one was bogus, for a start.

She focused back on Lucas, who was looking at her with a funny expression she couldn't read, reminding her that she didn't know enough about him to know his moods. And, bogus or not, there was something about him that made her want to know more. To understand him more deeply, in a way that probably wasn't going to be good for her in the end.

'Everything okay?' she asked him.

He blinked and snagged her gaze. 'Just thinking about the other night.'

'Oh?' Her body heated in immediate response. He'd been so close a few minutes ago and she'd ached to kiss him, but hadn't because George had been watching and also because they hadn't overtly stated that making out would be on the menu every time they met. 'What about it?'

'I didn't want to lie to George about our deal. I didn't mention it, but I did say we weren't serious. Now I'm wondering if I should have made more of a thing about it in case he mentions anything to his mum. Or mine.'

It was interesting to her that he cared so deeply about people: his friends and his patients. But was so offhand about his family. What was going on there? What had happened? Or was *undemonstrative* just the family dynamic?

He seemed to keep them at arm's length, but was still attending their ball. Was that out of duty? Hell, she knew all about that. Duty had been the Hursts' catch cry growing up. Yet she'd gone against that, against her parents' plans for her. And now her family kept her at arm's length.

Go figure.

'Do we really need to be so analytical about our relationship? We can say things got serious enough for more dates, hence the ball. Then we just…you know…lost interest.' She wondered how quickly she'd lose interest in Lucas and stop trying to work him out. After this 'date'? The next? After their next lovemaking? The time after that?

He nodded. 'You're probably right. Things can get intense and then wither, right? It's not always a straight path from dating to engagement and beyond.'

'Wither?' She laughed as her eyes darted to his trousers.

He sat up straighter in the saddle, chest puffed out. 'No chance of that happening here.'

'Yeah, right.' Giggling, she threw down the verbal gauntlet.

His eyes glittered and his smile was loaded with promise. 'If I wasn't on this horse, Ivy Hurst, I'd show you exactly what I mean.'

'You'd have to catch me first.' She tugged on the reins then squeezed her legs softly into Patty's flank and encouraged her to start off again, leaving Lucas in her dust. Putting space between them while she tried to deal with the way her heart danced at his words and the way her name on his lips made her chest heat and stole the breath from her lungs.

He caught her up quickly and reached out to touch her arm. Sparks of electricity fired across her skin. She inhaled in surprise. This wasn't good for her, all this *feeling*. Her skin, her heart, her chest. She didn't know what to do with it all.

She drew her arm away. Then immediately regretted it because every nerve, every cell in her body craved his touch.

They rode across to the other side of the creek and up a slight incline, past some interesting rock formations and overhangs revealing dark caves, offering what Ivy imagined would be a welcome shade in the height of summer. Then on to a path in a clearing that took them down to Cowan Creek, the main tributary that led eventually to the sea. A few hundred metres further down to the right was a marina and picnic tables, a couple of motorboats, some kayakers and tourists enjoying the winter sunshine. But here it was secluded and private.

Lucas slowed up and looked around. 'Hungry?'

'Starving.'

'Here's good, then. We can sit down on the riverbank in the sunshine.' He slid off his horse and secured the reins around a thick tree trunk with some rope in the backpack George had given them. Then he helped Ivy slip down from Patty, holding her close as she slid down, her body connecting with his at hip, belly, breasts. She clung onto his shoulders, her mouth a hair's breadth from his.

Delicious anticipation made her belly tighten.

He grinned. 'Seems I managed to catch you. In the end.'

'Seems you did.' Her body prickled at the greedy look in his eyes as his gaze roamed down her body as her feet touched the ground.

'You're very good at this.'

She smiled. 'Bit rusty, to be honest. But Patty's very tolerant.'

'I wasn't talking about horse riding.' He clicked his tongue and grabbed Patty's reins. Took a couple of seconds to secure her next to his horse, Hatty.

The heat of his body lingered on her skin. She was acutely aware of his every movement, every action. The way his hands worked to tie the reins up, how he fussed gently over the horses. His purposeful stride back to her. It was as if they were the only people in the world. As if everything else were less in focus. Less bright. Dimmed.

I'd show you exactly what I mean.

The anticipation tingled through her.

This feeling, these feelings…surely she could cope with them, wrangle them into a box in her heart and close the lid. She wasn't overwhelmed by them. She wouldn't allow herself to be. She wasn't a lustful teenager any more, or even a confused thirty-something trying to make sense of everything. Hell, she was a very experienced nearly forty-year-old; she wasn't about to start losing control over a man.

But for now…why the hell not?

CHAPTER SEVEN

SHE HELD HER breath as he reached out and cupped her cheek. Surprised by the serious way he looked at her, as if searching for an anchor, a lifeline. Then the softening of his gaze as his eyes met hers. As if he'd found it.

His lips touched hers and feverish need swelled through her.

This kiss was filled with all the bundled-up aching of the last few days, the secret smiles, the fleeting eye contact on the ward, in the hospital corridors. The promise.

She wove her arms around his neck as he backed her up against a tree, slipping his leg in between hers. She closed her eyes and pressed against the thick hard line of his erection. Wanting him deep inside her.

She moaned as his tongue slipped into her mouth and the kiss deepened, changing rhythm from slow and intense to heightened and wild. Flashing from a spark to a flame.

He played with the buttons on her denim jacket. Slipped his hands up under her sweater and cupped her breast over her bra. 'God, Ivy. I've been dreaming about doing this for five days. Every time I see you at work, I want to steal you away and explore your body.'

You too?

Thoughts of him doing this to her had driven her almost crazy over the last few days. He'd infiltrated her dreams and walked through her waking moments like a tantalising treat just out of reach. Every thought had stoked the need to touch him, taste him again.

Her head braced against the tree as she leaned back to look at his face. Her voice was raspy, her breath coming in short gasps as he stroked her tightening nipple through the lace. 'One sure way to get the sack.'

'Worth it, though.' He chuckled against her throat as he tugged her sweater neck down and kissed a trail across her collarbone. 'For this.'

'Really?' Her hands slid between their thighs and down his length and he groaned.

'Well, no, probably not. But almost.' He captured her mouth again. 'Actually. Yes. For more of this.'

The sound of children's laughter getting closer had him peeling himself away from her. 'Damn. Probably need to save the rest for later.'

'Yes.' She tugged her clothes back into position, her brain a fog that had barely registered they were in a public place. 'Later sounds good.'

He kissed her neck. 'Promise?'

'Try and stop me.' She shivered with desire and if it hadn't been for the precious horse riding that he'd arranged for her, she'd have suggested they go straight back to the city now, or that they find a hotel en route. But this had at least answered one question: this was where things stood between them. Desire. Lust. Need. And it made her feel the most alive she'd felt for years. 'Now, about the food…?'

'Sure, thing. Woman cannot live on sex alone, right? Let's see what pleasures Georgie boy has prepared for us.' He opened the rucksack and pulled out a picnic rug, which he flipped onto the grass, then emptied the rest of the contents of the bag onto it. A bottle of sparkling wine, cheese and crackers. Dates, grapes, apples. Cherry tomatoes. Melamine plates, picnic glasses and cutlery.

A small family group sauntered past along the path a few metres from their picnic spot. Lucas waved. Ivy followed suit, then settled back in the warm sunshine, immensely grateful that the children's excited laughter had put a stop to the making out. It seemed that whenever she was around Lucas she was too easily led into temptation.

He dug deeper into the bag. 'Seems George has catered for everything. What's this at the bottom?' He pulled out a small box and grimaced. 'Condoms.'

Ivy chuckled. 'Be prepared, right?'

'George was never a Boy Scout, trust me. He was never that well behaved.' He stuffed them back into the bag. 'I'll have a word. He shouldn't have. I'm sorry.'

'No. Don't. Unless it's to thank him for the laughs. It's funny. And he's right. Got to be safe.'

He shook his head but managed a rueful smile. 'I'll kill him.'

They ate and chatted some more about George and friendships in general. Ivy told him about some of the scrapes she, Harper, Phoebe and Ali had got into over the years and the tight friendship they all had again now that Ali and Harper's rift was healed. 'Honestly, I don't know how I'd have got through my split from Grant without them. You know who your true friends are when you hit hard times, right?'

He nodded. 'I don't know them well, only as colleagues. But they seem like good people.'

'They really are. And now we're all back at the same hospital. Such fun.'

'Not the same kind of fun that I imagine when I see you across a crowded ER.' His pupils flared with heat. But then he said, 'Hey, actually, I know we probably shouldn't be talking about work but...'

'Well, why not? It's what connects us, after all.'

'Is it? Not the amazing sex? Out-of-this-world kisses? Our

dodgy, daring deal?' He bugged his eyes at her and handed her some earthy Camembert on a cracker.

'You know what I mean.' She threw him a shady frown. 'Work is pretty much ninety per cent of my life so I'm happy to have a quick conversational diversion there if you want.'

'Okay. So, how's Emma doing post-surgery? I mean, I've seen the charts and chatted to her so I know physically she's doing well, but emotionally?'

'Emotionally?'

Interesting.

'She's good, actually. I think that as long as the babies are growing and developing, she's fine. She's obviously still very sore after yet another surgery, but happy to have one less thing to worry about. And an appendix removal was an easy fix, even though I'm worried about the amount of anaesthetic she and the babies are having.'

'I know. But I need to clean up some of those grafts. I want to get her healed and home and dealing with the scar management asap. If you think she's up to it all.'

'I do. She's been through a lot but she's a very strong woman. I'm happy for you to start on Monday. That way we can have her used to the protocol before her brain is filled up with baby delivery, feeding and everything else a new mum has to deal with.'

'Okay.' He blew out a deep breath. 'That's great. Brilliant.'

Something about his questioning over the last few weeks, though, had been niggling her. 'Okay, so what's going on with her?'

'What do you mean?' He blinked. Clearly confused. Rattled almost. And she immediately regretted steering the conversation into this territory. But she'd started now and she wanted to fill in some of the gaps of her understanding of how he ticked.

'I don't know. I see the way you deal with her, like treating her burns is…personal somehow.'

'I just want to do my best for her. Like all my patients.' He leaned away and frowned. The light in his eyes had dimmed and his posture was tight. He'd backed off emotionally and she wondered if she'd pressed too hard.

'Sorry, I don't want to make things sound weird. We all came into medicine to help people. Why did you choose to be a reconstructive surgeon? Was it the family thing?'

'What do you mean? Family…?' For the slightest moment he looked panic-stricken. His mouth formed a thin line, his shoulders rose and his eyes darted away. His reaction was oddly guarded.

'Their plastic surgery clinic,' she emphasised.

When he looked back at her there was a sort of forced jollity to his tone. 'Yes, of course. The clinic. I never wanted to work there, to be honest. Not that there's anything wrong with appearance medicine, it's just not my bag. I can do more good working for the public sector, helping those who can't afford it but really need it. And I like to see the treatment through from emergency admission to discharge.'

'All your family work there except you. Brothers and sister?'

'Yes. All happy to join the family firm. Flora's not a doctor, though. She was…' His eyes darkened. 'Well, she works in the administration department.'

What a strange reaction to her inane question. There was more to this family thing, she knew. He just wasn't going to elaborate.

Which intrigued her and niggled too, because, after everything they'd already done and his promise and clear desire to share more, he still couldn't trust her with his innermost thoughts.

It's just fun, she reminded herself.

They weren't soulmates. She didn't need to know everything about him. But she wanted to. And that was probably the biggest warning that she needed to stay away from him.

It was starting to dawn on her that her heart was at risk here. Because even though alarm bells were chiming, she just couldn't get enough of him.

Ivy had steered the conversation a little too close for Lucas's comfort. He wasn't ready to talk about Flora or why he stayed away from his family. It wasn't just because of his meddling mother, but because he simply didn't fit there. Every moment with them reminded him of that terrible day. Every look they gave him, he was sure, was imbued with blame.

He didn't know if he'd ever be ready to admit to Ivy what he'd done. That was something he never shared and only his closest friends from that time knew what had happened. Why bring it all up and ruin a good day?

The smell of grilled meat wafted towards them and he looked over to the picnic area down the shoreline to see four young guys—mid to late teens—standing at one of the barbecues.

After he'd skirted the conversation Ivy had seemingly taken it as ended so she picked up the plates and cutlery and was rinsing them in the river to clean them until they could wash them properly back at George's place. She looked over at the young men and raised her eyebrows. 'They look like they're having a good time.'

He watched the guys now chasing each other, play-fighting with kayak paddles, whooping and messing round.

'God, remember those carefree days?' He wandered over to the horses and gave them an apple each. 'In my head I'm still twenty-three.'

She laughed. 'Gosh, no, thanks. I don't want to live through that time again. All that angst and trying to impress people, working out who you are. I like knowing exactly who I am and what I want.'

After dealing with the horses, making sure they were

happy and comfortable, he wandered back to stand next to her. 'Which is what? Who are you, Ivy?'

She turned to him, eyes bright and focused. He had no doubt she knew exactly who she was and what she wanted. 'I'm a good doctor advancing well in my career. I'm a great mentor and grab teaching moments whenever appropriate. I'm a good friend, but I'd like to be a better one. I miss things every now and then because I work late.'

'Miss what kind of things?'

The young men's laughter wafted towards them. They'd finished eating and were now climbing into kayaks. None of them wore a life vest. She turned back to watch them. 'I missed that Harper and Yarran have moved in together and goodness knows what else. I'd like to be more a part of their lives.'

'I'm sure they understand. Doctors have a hard job, we work late and long hours.'

She shook her head. 'That's not a good enough excuse. We're all doctors. I'm trying to be better.'

'I get it. With George out here in the Woop Woops and me living in the city I don't get to see him nearly often enough.' He watched as she smiled in agreement, the way the dappled light made her skin all shadows and light.

He knew all about the light, he'd breathed it in when he'd slid inside her and had seen the shadows in her eyes as she'd talked about her break-up, but he didn't know much else about her. Hungry for more insight into her life, he asked, 'What about your family? You don't talk about them much.'

'Not a lot to say.' She looked out at the water, wrapped her arms around her chest.

He gently pushed to find out more. 'How many siblings?'

'One brother, one sister. I'm in the middle. Which probably explains a lot.' She rolled her eyes. 'The trouble-causing, rabble-rousing middle child.'

'Bring on the rabble-rousing. It sounds interesting.' When

she didn't elucidate on any previous rabbles, he said, 'You said you grew up in an army family.'

She turned to him, looking surprised. 'I'm impressed you remembered. Yes. We moved around a lot from one army base to another.'

'Must have been difficult to make friends if you were always on the go.'

She sighed. 'We had each other, I guess. But I was very happy when I came here to med school and met Phoebe, Ali and Harper. They became my surrogate family.'

'You weren't close to your real one any more?'

Her mouth formed a straight line. 'We had a falling-out.'

'You too?' But he couldn't imagine she'd done anything as bad as he had to cause the fall-out.

She sighed deeply and raised her eyebrows. 'The Hursts have a strong military tradition and they expected each of us to follow in their footsteps.'

'And you didn't want to?'

She shook her head. 'Not likely. I wanted to be a doctor from the moment I knew what one was. Earlier, probably.'

'You could have been a doctor in the army—' He glanced up as the sound of a boat engine roared through the congenial bush sounds. A motorboat was traveling at speed. Lucas gulped. 'Whoa. He's going fast.'

Ivy nodded, pale now and watching intensely. 'And heading straight towards the kayakers.'

'Oh, God.' Lucas ran to the shoreline and saw the trajectory the boat was on. The kayakers were playing some sort of game that involved hitting the water hard with their paddles and showering each other in plumes of spray. One was standing in his kayak, arms wide, singing at the top of his voice. The others were whooping and laughing and had music playing from a boom box so loud Lucas could hear it from the shoreline. None of them were paying any attention to anything else on the river. None of them had noticed the boat careening towards them.

Lucas shouted at the boat. 'Hey! Slow down. Kayakers!' He turned to Ivy, hoping she wasn't going to witness something tragic… He could see the inevitable unfolding of events and could barely look himself. 'He shouldn't be going that fast. Is he even looking where he's going?'

'Stop! Slow down!' Ivy shouted, waving her arms frantically in the air. 'Stop!'

But it happened before anyone could have stopped it. Three of the kayakers had somehow noticed and managed to get out of the way, but the one that had been standing up was still in direct line of the boat, now frantically paddling and making no significant headway away. The boat skipper appeared to see him just in time, steered the boat sharply right, but caught the side of the kayak.

It was difficult to see through the wash of the water but, when the boat had cleared and the swell calmed, the kayak was empty.

'Hell. Where is he?' Lucas scanned the water.

One of the kayakers had dived into the water. One was pointing into the river. One was hurling abuse at the boat skipper, who had quieted the engine.

'Phone for an ambulance. And the police. And stay here.' Lucas stripped off his top and jeans and waded waist deep into the freezing water, then dived under. When he surfaced he tried to catch his breath. It was so cold. Too cold. And none of them had life jackets.

He thrashed across the water towards the huddle of kayakers. Just as he reached them one of them surfaced, dragging the dunked kayaker with him. Blood was streaming from the injured man's nose and his cheek looked misshapen and lumpy.

'Get him up here.' Lucas helped lift the injured kayaker out and up onto the front of one of the kayaks. 'What's his name?'

'Sione,' his friend said.

'Sione, hi. My name is Lucas and I'm a doctor. Can you tell me where it hurts?'

'Here,' the guy croaked, holding his right hand up to his face, 'and here.' He pointed to his left biceps, where more blood streamed from a deep, thick gash.

Thank goodness he was breathing and moving all limbs. It could have been a whole lot worse. Lucas steadied himself on the rocking kayak. 'Okay. Let's take a look at the damage.'

He was just finishing assessing Sione's facial injuries when Ivy popped up out of the water. Her lips were blue, her face a ghostly white. He shook his head. She shouldn't be here in icy swirling water. What if something happened to her too? 'What the hell are you doing here? It's freezing.'

'Yes, it is.' She hauled herself up onto one of the other kayaks in just her bra and panties and stared at him. 'Thought you might need an extra pair of medical hands. Ambulance is on its way. ETA about five minutes. Luckily, there was one in the neighbourhood.'

Lucas grimaced at the clumsy way he'd spoken to her. He'd underestimated her. Or rather, had wanted to protect her from seeing this, being involved in this, getting wet. Getting cold. But he'd ignored the fact that she was a doctor and would want to help as much as he would. 'Looks like a broken nose and possibly fractured cheek. And a nasty gash on his biceps.'

The water was deceptively choppy and made it difficult to tend to the guy's injuries. They had nothing to stem the bleeding other than what little clothing they wore. Ivy crooked her finger at the boat skipper, who'd at least had the good grace to come back and help. 'Throw us a towel. Something, anything to stem the bleeding.'

Red-faced, the man threw a white fluffy towel. 'I'm sorry. I really am. Can I take him back to shore?'

'No way am I getting on that boat.' Sione shook his head sharply.

'Sione, honestly, it's the best way to get you warm and administer proper care.' Ivy held onto the one-person kayak as it rocked. She was cramped up, sitting on the deck with one of the other kayakers—some scrawny youth, with a smattering of facial hair that was pretending to be a beard, in the seat—and at risk of capsizing.

'No way. I should sue him.' Sione's lips were dark and his face pale with shock.

'Okay. We're wasting time here arguing and we're all going to get hypothermia on top of everything else.' Lucas nodded. 'I'll kayak you over. I think this is just about seaworthy.' He examined the side of the damaged kayak. There was a good deal of scraped and scratched fibreglass but it was not letting in water. 'Won't take long.'

The kid with the beard looked at Ivy, appraising her in her underwear. His lascivious smile said it all. 'You can definitely come with me.'

'Thanks. I appreciate that.' Ivy shuffled back a little and held on.

Lucas started to paddle, his annoyance fuelling his strokes. He did not like the way beard guy—beard *kid*—was looking at Ivy, even if she did look amazing, all perfect curves and slim legs. She was not for general consumption.

He did not like that she'd got wet and cold.

He did not like the twist in his chest at the thought of her being in any kind of danger. At all. Not when she was with him.

And he definitely didn't like all these emotions welling up in him. Over a...friend.

'Here we go.' Lucas helped Sione onto the jetty, secured

the kayak on the shore then looked around for something to warm his patient up.

The other two kayaks hit the shoreline and Ivy jumped off, shouting to the other kayakers, 'Go grab your clothes and towels and come straight back. We've got to warm Sione up.'

She was clearly on exactly the same wavelength.

'You want me to grab your stuff too?' beard guy asked as his eyes hungrily skimmed down Ivy's body.

She didn't seem to notice. 'Great. Thanks. It's over there in the clearing. Just bring our clothes, please, and make sure the horses are okay.'

'Gotcha.'

'Be quick. She's…' Lucas corrected himself even though his intention was getting Ivy warm. She was shivering so force-fully her legs were literally shaking. And then there was Sione to look after. '*We're* freezing.'

He threw beard kid an icy look. Stifling the urge to say something more was almost killing him, but he knew Ivy would be furious if he went all macho and protective on her. Theirs was not that kind of relationship.

But it didn't stop him wanting to throw the kid in the river just for looking at her.

The sound of an engine being cut had Lucas looking up. The motorboat skipper was running over to them. 'Mate. Se-riously, are you okay?'

Lucas had held back while he assessed Sione but irritation now flowed out of him, probably fuelled by beard guy too, if he was honest. 'You could have killed him. What the hell were you doing?'

'I was sorting out the water-ski rope.' The man shook his head and looked at his feet. 'I didn't see them.'

'That was obvious.'

He knelt next to Sione and handed him another towel. 'I'm sorry, mate.'

'I'm not your mate.' Sione held the towel to his nose, the white towelling slowly taking on a pink tinge. 'Like I said before, I should sue you.'

'Hey, who was the one messing around on the water?' the skipper threw back.

Lucas stood. 'We have enough witnesses who saw your carelessness. You were going too fast, not looking where you were going. It could have been a lot more serious. The police are on their way.' He ignored the man's huffing and turned to Sione. 'Give me that towel and I'll press it on your arm wound to try to stop the bleeding. You're making a mess of the jetty.' He threw him a smile just to soften the mood.

'Give it here, I'll do that. You hold the other towel to his face.' Ivy knelt down next to them. 'I wish I had my doctor's bag with me. I've got painkillers in there that would definitely help.'

Lucas nodded, trying to focus on Sione's injuries and not on the swell of Ivy's breasts in that white lacy bra. The frill of skimpy panties that caressed her backside. Her soft, smooth skin. She'd scraped her wet hair back off her face and she looked radiant, athletic. He remembered the press of her thighs as she rocked in rhythm with him. She was so damned hot.

And shivering with cold.

Beard kid turned up with their stuff at the same time the ambulance arrived. Within minutes everyone was warmed up either from their dry clothes, silver foil-blankets or hot chocolate from the nearby cafe. The cafe owner had come out to see what all the fuss had been about and returned with a tray of steaming drinks and biscuits.

By now the police had arrived too and were taking statements from everyone.

'Will I get into trouble?' Sione whispered to Lucas.

'For what? Having fun? As far as I'm aware there's no law against that.'

'I wasn't…concentrating. We were just having a laugh. My mum always tells me I'm too much of a clown and that I have to be more responsible.' Sione hung his head. 'And now there's the ambulance call-out fee to pay too. I'm so lame.'

Lucas's heart went out to him. How many times had he called himself worse names than that? How many nights had he lain awake wishing he could rewind time and make better decisions? And he'd been a lot younger than Sione here. 'You are not lame, Sione. That boat skipper should have been paying more attention. He was going far too fast and not watching where he was headed.'

'Yeah, but we should have been watching too.'

'True. But you weren't going to cause any real harm by messing about. Not like him. I doubt the police will have any cause to charge you. But for the record: wear a life jacket next time and pay attention.'

'Yes. Will do.' Sione stepped up into the ambulance. 'Thanks.'

'Oh, and give me a call if you have any trouble with that wound. It's nasty.' He gave Sione his number. 'I'm a burns and plastics surgeon, so I can help down the track if you need me to.'

'Yeah, man. Thanks again.'

A gentle nudge in his ribs had Lucas turning to see Ivy at his side. She winked at him. 'That was really nice of you.'

'Yeah. I'm like that.' He shrugged, feigning nonchalance but feeling a heat of pride under her gaze.

'Seriously, you didn't have to offer to help him. You've done enough already.'

'If I can help him, I will. He's just a kid.'

But the tumble in his chest as he watched the paramedics lead Sione to the ambulance wasn't nice at all. He remembered those feelings of shame and regret all too well. Stupid choices made by an immature kid. The physical hurt had meant little to him, but the emotional pain lingered to this day, like a brand on his heart that would be there for ever.

Ivy slipped her arm into his. 'We'd better get Patty and Hatty. They'll be missing us.'

'Sure.' Her presence was reassuring and anchoring. He wanted to wrap his arms around her, feel her heart beating against his. Breathe in her scent and hold her close. Not just because she was soft and warm and so damned sexy, but because he knew he'd feel better there. With her.

Which was crazy.

She turned to look up at him, her gaze soft and light. Her smile genuine. 'Are you okay, Lucas?'

He nodded, unable to answer in words. Because if he thought that someone else could erase his pain, he was a fool. No one ever had before. And more, he didn't deserve to have it erased anyway.

And yet, there was something about Ivy…her smile, her belief in him, her trust…that gave him hope for the first time in many years.

So, he wasn't sure he was okay at all.

CHAPTER EIGHT

LUCAS WAS QUIET all the way back to the city and Ivy wasn't sure why. Something had bothered him earlier and she couldn't put her finger on what. He'd been in superhero mode when he'd dived into the river to save Sione, but then later he'd shut down.

Oh, he still made conversation, and made sure she was warm and comfortable, and had been almost jolly with George and Ivan as if he'd made a real effort to seem cheerful, but it was as if his fire had gone out. She didn't think she'd said or done anything wrong, so she knew it wasn't about her. But he just seemed…troubled.

So when he invited her up to his apartment for a takeaway dinner she accepted. Just so she could dig a little deeper and unlock some of the things he wasn't telling her. Because she needed to know enough about him in case his parents referred to some shared family memory or joke from the past that was significant. Or in case he was just a moody old boot and they mentioned that too. So she could agree and laugh it off or defend him or…whatever. And to be able to describe his apartment if his mother asked.

And she wanted to see where he lived, and…if she was being totally honest with herself…to be with him a little longer, quiet or loud or anything in between.

'I think I'm going to get vertigo if this takes us up any higher.' She looked out of the elevator window as the build-

ings and trees grew smaller and smaller, and then there was
nothing but a concrete wall to look at as they shot skywards.

'You get used to it. Hold onto me if you want.' He grinned,
offering his arm, and for a few moments she had her old Lucas
back. But he didn't make any kind of move on her as she'd
thought he might. Hadn't pressed her against the elevator wall
as he had against the tree.

The lift jolted to a halt and the doors opened. He stepped
out and beckoned her forward. 'Here we go.'

'Wow! Just wow.' She stepped into his place and her breath
was sucked out of her lungs. From this vantage point she could
see the Sydney harbour bridge and endless ocean beyond,
but she was distracted by the alabaster decor and black and
white marble kitchen bench on the right of the open-plan living space. Truffle-coloured sofas by the window softened the
sleek lines of the white lacquered window frames.

It looked homely and comfortable but very, *very* expensive.

She had no idea how much a place like this would cost but
she'd bet it was more than she could ever afford. Which high-
lighted to her even more his wealthy background.

The thought of his parents grounded her to the reality of
their situation. The Matthewses were powerful movers in
the Sydney medical scene. They probably had influence and
friends who ran the Sydney Central hospital. One word from
them and her career progression could be suddenly limited,
or terminated altogether. So she needed to be careful exactly
how much she lied, how dressed up their stories were. Who
knew what could be at risk if she messed this up? Or upset
them in some way?

He walked her across white floorboards to a floor-to-ceiling window. Outside, the sun was starting to dip, bathing the
cirrocumulus clouds and harbour in a rich pinky orange glow.
Tiny lights flickered to life in numerous buildings across the
bay, like myriad new fireflies twinkling.

Kind of how she felt too when she was with Lucas. As if she'd been cocooned for years and now everything was fresh and bright and new. And, like fireflies' short life span, with a use-by date. A deadline.

She looked out and sighed. 'What an amazing view. I feel like I can see for miles.'

'That's because you can. As soon as I saw this place was being built, I jumped on it. It's the best view in Sydney. I could look at it for hours.' His smile was genuine and his shoulders relaxed. Finally. As if his home gave him sanctuary.

She liked that idea. That he was a homebody too and had his own personal place to unwind as she had. 'Well, I can definitely chat with your mum about this place. There aren't enough words to describe how amazing it is.'

'Sure.' He was still staring out of the window and she had a feeling she'd lost him to his thoughts again.

'Sure?' She drew her gaze away from the window and looked directly at him. 'You've been mightily distracted since Sione. Is something bothering you?'

He blinked and frowned. Then shook his head as if clearing away a thought. 'Ah, really? I'm fine. Just decompressing.'

'Oh, yes. I know that feeling. Sometimes I have so much pent-up adrenalin at the end of a hard day I don't know what to do. Running helps. A long soak. Quiet times.'

'Sorry.' He pulled her close and nuzzled against her head. 'I'm not always good company.'

She leaned her head against his chest and inhaled his scent. It grounded her, the way his embrace did. 'You are excellent company. You arranged for me to go horse riding and I had a fantastic time…apart from watching an almost disaster unfold.' Had that caused this shift in his demeanour? Something to do with the accident? 'I was a bit spooked, to be honest. I really thought that boat was going to do more damage.'

'The water was so cold and choppy. I didn't want you to

have to come in. I couldn't deal with you getting into trouble as well.' His eyes narrowed and it occurred to her that this was the same expression she'd seen on his face when she'd popped up out of the water by the kayaks. Fired up. Possessive, almost.

And the fact he'd cared so much about her well-being made her heart squeeze. 'But I was fine. I can swim probably as well as you.'

'Yeah, well. I know that now. I also didn't know you were so damned determined to be part of the rescue team.' His throat made a soft noise, like a chuckle. 'I needn't have worried. You are one capable woman.'

'Seriously, Lucas, you don't have to worry about me at all. You certainly don't have to protect me.' She stroked his cheek, relieved that his reserve had just been worry about keeping her—and no doubt everyone else—safe. 'I can handle myself perfectly well.'

'I can see that. I should have remembered about the time you tried to kneecap me with a chair on wheels.'

'That's me.' She giggled. 'Rabble-rousing again. But I can be nice too. Light and dark, right?'

Little wisdom lines fanned out at the corners of his eyes as he laughed. 'I was thinking exactly that earlier.'

'What? About me?'

'About the way you're so breezy and helpful…some might call it possessive…' He grinned pointedly at the accusation she'd once thrown at him. 'With your patients. So mindful of your friends and what you want out of life. And it makes me want to do something particularly nasty to Grant for treating you the way he did and dulling your light.'

'Oh, I never told you.' How could she have not mentioned she'd already sealed her part of the deal? 'I bumped into Grant the other day in Perc Up.'

Lucas stepped back, his smile folding. 'And?'

'I don't know. I'm not sure. He was a bit gushy…you can

never tell with Grant because he's the world's biggest flirt. But he said I looked great.'

'There you go. Result.' But he tilted his head and looked at her, eyes narrowing. His smile flatlined. 'Does he want you back?'

'Actually, I think he might.' She tried to hide the smile she knew would be just a tad smug. 'We were right about him being jealous when he sees what he's missing.'

Another step back. 'And you? Do you want him back?'

She shuddered at the thought. 'Come on. We're talking about Grant here. There is not a single part of me that wants anything to do with him. Besides, I am not in the habit of kissing one guy when I want to be with someone else.'

He froze, eyes growing wide. 'You want to *be* with me?'

Her heart seemed to stop beating. That wasn't the direction their relationship was going in.

Us. There would be no us.

She remembered their deal. Believed in it too. But the words had shot out before she'd had time to register them. Her brain scrambled to smooth things over.

'I mean… I wouldn't kiss one person then…' She closed her eyes and breathed out deeply. *Rewind.* 'It was just a turn of phrase. I meant I wouldn't be hanging out with two guys at the same time.' She laughed but knew it sounded forced. 'Fine for others to do it if they want, but I barely have the energy for one guy, let alone two.'

'Okay…' He breathed out, but looked as if he was still holding onto some air.

'I don't want to be with Grant. Or anyone… I'm just enjoying this time. Getting to play a little. I really, really like that.'

'It's just that I don't *be* with anyone.' He grimaced and laughed and the shadows in his face faded away. The atmosphere became lighter again. 'I have no idea what that even means.'

'It's okay. We're definitely on the same page. I'm surprised at myself, but I like you. I like getting to know a bit more about how the other half live. This really is something else.' She drew an arc pointing out the expensive apartment and the ten-million-dollar view. 'And I like the sex.'

Heat flared in his eyes at that. 'Me too.'

'But don't go getting all hung up thinking I'm going to hang around after the ball. I'm not the clingy type.' She thought about her little flat, her own unwinding place. Her sanctuary. She'd spent a long time making it all hers after Grant had moved out. She liked her own space. Not having someone else to clear up after or to take into account. Not having to make conversation when she didn't feel like it. And now she even felt guilty about pushing Lucas to talk when he'd clearly just needed some peace and quiet. 'I don't want to start sharing lives or anything.'

'Right. Good.' He nodded.

'Good.' She didn't know what else to say.

The silence between them stretched but she held his gaze, thinking about how they'd already shared so much just today. She'd learnt so much more about him: that he could ride a horse as well as she did. The fact he'd arranged that for her. She'd met his kind and loving friends who clearly held him in high esteem, had seen him stridently working in an emergency despite taking a risk of his own in freezing water and trying to make Sione feel better and offering further help. Learnt he had quiet times, that he did not hold himself in the same esteem his friends did.

Then sharing his personal place here.

They had a history now. Shared jokes. Whether or not she liked it, or wanted it, their lives were tangling. Not just out of necessity, but because there was this inescapable pull to spend time with him. And she had an inkling he felt it too. There was something more than physical.

Although the physical was *great*.

Her mind flipped to earlier when they'd almost been caught making out. She wanted to rewind them both to that playful moment against the tree rather than this more intense moment neither of them needed.

She let her eyes roam his face.

He watched her too, close enough to play with a lock of her hair, letting it run through his fingers. Every cell in her body ached for the touch of those fingers. Her nipples beaded at the thought.

His gaze was locked on hers. 'Ivy?'

She swallowed, wondering if he was thinking the same thing she was. 'Yes?'

'What exactly are you thinking right now?'

She giggled. 'Why?'

'Because your smile is…blowing my mind.'

'How so?'

'You look like you've just had the best sex of your life.'

'Wishful thinking.' Pressing her lips together, she reached out and touched his hand, curling her fingers around his. Just that moment of skin-on-skin contact sent shock waves of need through her. This was crazy. She touched people all the time—it was her job to touch people when she examined them, when she shook hands, when she comforted—but she never had this tingling, aching need the way she did with Lucas. 'Do you want to revisit that moment back at the tree?'

The growing bulge in his jeans told her he did but he shrugged nonchalantly, as if it would be no big deal. Even though they both knew it was. 'I guess I could be convinced.'

The smile he gave her said he already was.

His mouth was on hers before she took her next breath.

He didn't need asking twice. He pressed his mouth to hers, relishing her taste and tenderness. Yes, tender and soft. Kissing her was intoxicating. Each time was different. Good different. Mind-blowingly different. Tender. Soft. Wild. Undone. He was never sure which kiss he was going to get, which was the best, which kiss he wanted.

But she always gave him exactly what he needed. It was like mainlining an addictive drug. Dangerous and possibly life-altering, yet there was no way he wanted to—or could—give it up. And he wanted to see her reaction, didn't want to take his eyes away from hers. 'Look at me.'

Her pupils dilated, and a moan escaped her throat. That simple sound arrowed deep in his belly, stoking the desire, making him hot and hard. Hotter and harder.

He cupped her face, fingertips scraping her temples as the kiss deepened. Tongues dancing, exploring. Messy. Wet.

Somehow, he helped her off with her sweater and T-shirt. Wiggled her out of her jeans. She divulged him of his top and jeans too. He kissed her again, not wanting to ever be too far from her mouth, his hands sliding to her bra. It was still damp from the river. Her body prickled with goosebumps and she shivered. She was cold and he'd been too busy freaking out over how connected and intimate they were becoming he hadn't even noticed.

'Right.' He slid his arms under her knees and picked her up.

'What the actual hell are you doing?' She laughed. 'We're far too old for this. You'll hurt yourself.'

'Not a chance.' He strode through to the bathroom and put her down. 'Time to get you warm.'

He flicked on the shower tap in the large walk-in shower, then stripped her panties and bra off. When the water was the perfect temperature he threw off his boxers, took her hand and led her in.

He positioned her under the flow of water. Laughing, she tipped her head back and let the warm water stream down her slender throat, over her breasts and lower. He stood there, watching her, unable to move.

This was like something from a dream. He felt fifteen again, trying to get a grip on his libido.

And failing.

'You are the most beautiful woman I have ever seen.' He pumped shampoo from a tub and lathered it into bubbles, then massaged it into her hair.

'That feels so good.' Her head lolled back and she looked like something from a painting. Ecstasy on her face, perfection, vulnerability. Soaked. Perfect.

He rinsed the bubbles off then applied conditioner, followed by shower gel. Starting at her neck, he washed her back, then her breasts, flicking her nipples into tight buds that he sucked into his mouth one at a time.

She grasped his hair. 'Oh, Lucas.'

The sensuous slide of the liquid over skin was mesmerising, her body silky soft and smooth.

She pumped liquid soap into her palm and did the same to him. Her fingers slipping and sliding and rubbing over his shoulders, chest, belly. Then she slid her hands over his erection.

'God.' He groaned as she squeezed gently. 'I need to be inside you.'

She kissed her assent, sliding one leg up his thigh, pressing her intimate, soft part against his hardness.

'Here.' He reached over to the cabinet and pulled out a packet of condoms, grabbed a foil, tore it open and was sheathed in less than a minute.

'You have them stashed around the apartment?' She laughed. 'Lucas Matthews. You are a freaking stud.'

He growled. He was only a stud because she was a goddess. 'Bathroom and bedroom. Easy to reach.'

'Good.' She ran her fingertips down his chest and looked up at him. The playful replaced with serious. 'I want you, Lucas. Now.'

He grabbed her leg, hauling it up to his waist, and slid deep inside her, gasping at the feel of heat and wet. She inhaled on a cry.

He froze. He'd hurt her? Typical bloody Lucas. 'Hey, baby. You okay?'

'Better than okay. I just… God, that feels so good.' She rocked with him. 'I'm so hot for you I don't think I can hang on.'

'Then don't.' He gripped her waist and sank deeper into her. Over and over. He wanted to watch her lose control, wanted to take her over the edge. He thrust again and took her mouth with his, kissing her deeply. She moved her hips, angling so he could go deeper and harder.

Then he felt her tighten. And he was lost to the feeling of her orgasm pulsing around him, the soft wetness of her skin, the damp hair that fell over her face as she rocked, the melting hot kisses.

He'd worried he might lose her today in that swirling river. That he wouldn't be able to save her if she'd got into danger. But it had been her who'd saved him. By soft words and understanding. By believing in him. With the gift of her smile and her kisses.

And here she was now in his arms, crying out his name on scraggy breaths as she collapsed against him.

His heart tightened, his chest contracted. He thrust one more time, so deep, so hard and he followed her over that edge.

CHAPTER NINE

SPENT, SATISFIED AND BREATHLESS, he wrapped her in a towel, picked her up again and carried her through to his bed. He lay next to her and stroked her hip, allowing his mind to settle the way his body now had. At least for the moment.

It had been worth every second of the wait since he'd kissed her this morning. But he really, really hoped it wouldn't be that long…almost a whole week…before he was inside her again.

Give him five minutes…

Her eyes flickered open and she glanced over his shoulder to the other side of the room. She gripped his arm. 'Oh, my God, Lucas.'

'What? What is it?' He jumped and twisted and followed her gaze, putting his arm out to protect her. His heart stalled. What the hell?

'Your bookshelves span the entire wall.' She pointed to his huge white bookcase overflowing with books.

His heart started to beat again and he laughed. It seemed his need to protect her overrode everything, including common sense. 'Geez, woman, I thought there was an intruder. Or a spider. Yes? I have books.'

Her eyes twinkled with excitement. 'You said you were a beach bum.'

He laughed. '*You* said I was a beach bum.'

'You let me believe it.'

'You seemed to like the idea of me being all beefcake and a

bear of little brain.' He pulled her closer and whispered, 'You just want me for my body.'

'Well…it's not a bad body… I suppose. But your brain…and books? Delicious.' Giggling, she slid out of bed, wrapped the top sheet around her…as if he hadn't just soaped and kissed every inch of her…and wandered over to look at his book collection.

From this vantage point he could see the soft curve of her breast. The little upturned nose. The strident gaze as she perused his collection. His heart contracted. A book lover too. Was there no end to this attraction?

She ran her fingers across the book spines of classics mingled with the latest thrillers. 'You've read all these?'

'Most of them.'

She grinned and put her hand to her heart. 'You might just be the perfect man.'

'I doubt that very much.'

He did not allow his head to swerve back to that night all those years ago. He refused to allow those memories to intrude on this. He hadn't felt so contented and connected in a long time and he wanted to prolong the moment where someone actually liked him. Where she didn't believe he was the cause of all that hurt…because she didn't know.

And she wouldn't know because he wouldn't tell her. He didn't want to see that sharp intake of breath, the fake smile that she'd have to make to show she wasn't shocked, the insistence that it wasn't his fault. That everything was okay when it wasn't. How could it be okay when his sister still bore the scars?

But, right now, right here, just for once he wanted to forget all that. Because he wanted to make Ivy smile. Keep her smiling. Let her believe he was as good as she thought he was.

She came back to bed with a copy of the latest Amor Towles

book and put it on the bedside table. 'I've been wanting to read this for ages. Could I borrow it?'

'Have it. It's excellent. Better, I think, than his last one.'

'No way. I loved *A Gentleman in Moscow*.' She tucked her still-damp hair behind her ear. 'I'll read it and get back to you with a review.'

He chuckled. 'You do that. I'll be interested to hear what you think.' And he really would be. He'd never got this deep and close to a woman where they shared interests like this. Although, that was probably because he'd never given any relationship time to develop.

His fault, he knew. But this was…illuminating.

She poked him in the ribs, making him squirm. 'You're such a dark horse. How many more secrets do you have that I need to find out?'

Too many.

'What you see is what you get. Bear and brawn and…yeah, I guess, a small amount of brain.' He wrapped his arms around her and pulled her to lie down next to him. Because secrets didn't always need to be bad. 'Except…maybe you'll like this… No one except me knows this is even here.'

'What?' She leaned her head against his shoulder, and he inhaled her scent, which, like her touch and her taste, had imprinted on his memory banks.

'If I press this button…see what happens.' The crank of a machine broke through the silence and the shutters above his bed slid apart, bringing a blast of cold air into the room.

Her eyes grew wider as she stared upwards into the darkness. 'Wow. A skylight. The whole ceiling is a skylight?'

'Not all, but…well, most.'

'Oh, my God. This is amazing. I am literally seeing stars.'

He pressed a kiss to her head, enchanted by her excitement. Then he scrambled for his phone on the floor and found the

night sky app. 'Apparently there's a whole load of zodiac con-
stellations up there. What's your star sign?'

'You first.' She tilted her head to look at the sky from a
different angle.

'Capricorn. There.' He showed her the app and then found
it in the night sky. 'It looks like an arrowhead.'

'Oh, yes. I see it. Is that December? January?'

He nodded. 'December the twenty-eighth.'

'Sucks to have your birthday so close to Christmas.' She
turned to look at him and pouted.

He copied her expression. 'Indeed it does. Your celebration
gets lost in the post-Christmas flop and the pre-New Year excitement.'

'Poor baby.' She slicked a kiss onto his mouth. 'Does that
make you feel better?'

'Kind of. Maybe a bit more might help.'

She obliged with a long, silky, wet kiss that had his body
tingling with need.

Eventually, she pulled away and sighed. 'My brother's birthday is on January the second and he hates all the shared presents he gets. And he always complains that everyone's still
too hungover from New Year's Eve for his birthday party.'
Her eyes glittered as she smiled. 'Thank goodness we're talking about birthdays. I'd completely forgotten to even ask you
about it. It would seem weird to your mum if I didn't know
something that basic about you.'

His mum. The deal. There he'd been, almost convinced this
was real. He reminded himself that she was in this to make
Grant jealous. That was all...apart from the sex, of course. A
little bit of fun. She didn't want serious.

Neither did he.

Neither *had* he. 'What's your sign?'

'Libra.' She smiled at him and his heart blew wide open.

'Okay.' He peered at the shapes on his phone then found

them in the sky and pointed. 'There. You see the upside-down triangle shape?'

She looked up, scrutinising the sky with a frown. 'That looks nothing like weighing scales.'

'Clearly our ancestors weren't that great at drawing shapes.' He shrugged as she laughed. 'Libra. That's September-October, right? Birthday coming up fairly soon. Noted.'

'Don't worry, we'll be well and truly ancient history by then.'

'Ah. Yes. Of course.' It was as if a knife had speared his heart. The end was hurtling towards them and he had a sick feeling in the pit of his stomach at the thought of not having this.

Make the most of it.

That was what he needed to do. Have her. Then let her go. As agreed.

That was what she wanted, right? Hell, he'd had to talk her into this in the first place. She was probably counting down the days until it was all over.

And yet…he really liked the way she looked at him with such a soft gaze, laughing at his lame jokes, the press of her body against his telling him she wanted him. That wasn't all pretence, was it?

He squeezed her closer. 'If you had a completely free day, what would you do?'

'I'd…' She inhaled deeply then let out the breath slowly as she thought. 'Oh…so much. Depending on the weather. If it was raining, I'd sit in your window seat and read your library's worth of books. Sunshine? I'd spend the day in the mountains, hiking. Riding again. Or I'd do nothing and also do everything I could.'

He laughed into her hair. 'All in one day?'

'Yes. All of it. What would you do?'

Stare at your face. Watch the emotions scud by. Joy. Ex-

citement. Happiness. Satisfaction. Each one with its own special flavour.

A particular shine in her eyes, a certain tug on her lips. The way she almost shook with delight. Hell, happiness looked good on her.

Orgasms did too.

Kissing looked even better, all misty eyes and swollen lips and the secret, sexy smile. His chest filled with that now familiar Ivy warmth and a peculiar kind of pride that he'd made that smile happen just with his mouth. She was intoxicating. Breathtaking.

Whoa.

His mind whirred with a warning alarm.

Given a clear timetable he'd choose to do nothing but *watch her face*? He was starting to think like those romcoms she'd been talking about, and was clearly getting in deeper than he'd expected. And far, far quicker.

He needed to protect himself. Protect them both. Because this stupid deal had brought him closer to Ivy than he'd thought possible. They needed to stop with this soul searching and all this time together. Maybe communicate by text. Or something. Write a list of facts about himself and email it to her to memorise and get her to do the same. Then he wouldn't have to see her beautiful face. Taste her. Touch her. Talk to her. Hold her.

Yes.

No.

That wouldn't work. He'd still see her at work. He had a bad feeling he'd still want her too.

Scratch that. He *would* still want her. He knew that now.

'Lucas?'

'Huh?' He would still want her. Even after all this was over. His belly tightened. His heart started to race.

She poked him again. 'I said, it's your turn. Where is your head at?'

'Here.' He nuzzled her hair, trying to restore some sort of equilibrium in his mind and body. He could create space without hurting her. He was the king of letting women down kindly and with as little fuss as possible. 'I'm right here.'

'So, what would you do if you had a completely free day?'

'I don't know…kite surf. Catch up with mates.'

Her smile fell a little and she sat back. 'Yeah. Actually, I'd catch up with my friends too. Yes.'

He knew she was deflated by his answer, but he couldn't allow her to keep creeping under his skin like this.

A little frown hovered over her forehead as she looked at him. 'Are you okay?'

'Sure.'

She blinked and smiled. 'I just asked if you want to show me how to kite surf.'

'Oh. Sorry.' He'd completely missed that, worrying about how to let her go. 'I don't know.'

'Why not?'

'Because…' He couldn't say what he should say: that teaching her to kite surf was an epically bad idea, because he shouldn't spend any more time with her before the ball. But the words wouldn't come. Instead he said, his tone like that of a little kid greedy for more sugar, 'You'd really want to give it a go?'

She closed one eye and pursed those cute as hell lips as she pondered. 'You took me horse riding so we should do something you like to do. I think we'd get to know each other better in our natural environments.'

'I guess.' So, despite his better judgement, he found himself nodding. It was an outside activity. They couldn't get naked. They couldn't do this…all this intimacy and tenderness, all this kissing and lovemaking, not in crashing waves and cold. Where was the harm in one last outing? At least they'd be able to talk about another shared experience with his parents.

Her eyes narrowed. 'That is, if you think I'll be okay.'

'You'll be fine. Trust me.'

'Hmm…why do I feel nervous when you say that?' She laughed warily, completely oblivious to the turmoil swirling in his head.

He shrugged. 'I'm a pro. I've got your back.'

But he figured she was right. Trusting him was a very unwise thing to do.

It was becoming a habit now, walking onto the ward and hoping he was here, her tummy all excited with anticipation. Then riding the wave of disappointment when he wasn't. Four days since their wonderful day and she hadn't run into him, even though they shared the same patient. Seemed like either he was avoiding her or their schedules just hadn't coincided. She supposed she could call him or text him, but that wasn't their way. Yet.

But her belly danced as she spied the top of his head sticking out over the nurses' station desk in the centre of the ward. Suddenly her day got a whole lot brighter. 'Hey, Lucas.'

He looked up and grinned. 'Ivy. Looking great.'

She felt the blush creep up her cheeks. Not that anyone was listening, but she wasn't used to compliments at work. Or this endless ache to kiss him again. Just be with him. She shook herself. 'How's things?'

He pointed to the computer monitor. 'Just writing Emma's notes up.'

'Oh, how's she doing post-surgery?'

'It's early days, but she's in good spirits. The partial thickness grafts are healing well and the donor sites are looking great too. The full thickness grafts aren't causing her much more pain but make movement limited.'

'That will improve though?'

'Absolutely, with time and physiotherapy. I'd be really happy to get her to a stage where she can hold those twins on her lap when they're born. We haven't looked under the pressure dressings yet. I'm hopeful they're doing their job and I'm just glad we didn't have to wait any longer.'

Then he would discharge Emma and there'd be no more need for them to bump into each other here. Ivy's heart jittered. 'Quick question.'

His eyebrows peaked. 'Sure?'

'What's the actual dress code for the ball?'

'Man, you looked so serious for a minute I was starting to panic.' He laughed. 'Sorry, I haven't shown you the invitation. It's black tie. Ball gowns.'

'Okay. So the last time I went to a ball was probably after my graduation. Looks like I'm going to have to go shopping.'

'If you need any help, let me know.'

'Lucas, you are not coming shopping with me. I have girlfriends to do that with. It'll make a fun afternoon. I haven't seen them all for ages.'

'Okay.' He tugged her hand and pulled her down level with his face, lowering his voice to a tantalising teasing whisper. 'Too bad, I wanted to be in that fitting room with you. Now I'll just have to imagine you naked.'

'Lucas!' She lowered her voice too. 'I will have underwear on. No one tries on clothes without it. Ugh.'

'That is a big shame.' He mock-pouted.

'Not for me.' She straightened, all the better to keep the professional guise on. 'You still okay for kite surfing?'

'Certainly am. The weather forecast looks perfect but you'll need a wetsuit.'

She grinned and did a ticking motion with her hand. 'Check.'

'Excellent.' He tugged her down again, making her laugh. 'I will imagine you naked under that instead.'

'Ugh. All that rubber on my tender bits? Talk about chafing. No, thank you.'

'Aww, not into rubber?' He eyed her suspiciously, making her chuckle.

She put her palm on his cheek. 'Is it all just about sex with you?'

'Sure is.' His grin was good enough to kiss.

But she withdrew her hand in case she was drawn into temptation. Not here. Not at work. 'Good.'

'I'll pick you up at eight again.'

An idea occurred to her. 'You could…no. Sorry. Forget it.'

He frowned. 'What?'

'Nothing.'

'Come on, spit it out.' He glanced around. It was the patients' lunchtime and the staff were busy. 'No one can hear you. Is it about rubber? Getting naked?'

She couldn't help laughing and bugging her eyes at him. 'No. Well…maybe… I was just thinking you could come over for pizza on Friday night. Then we could head out to the beach together Saturday morning.' This was not what they did. The physical intimacy had been spontaneous so far. If he brought spare clothes and a toothbrush, if they planned cosy nights in, what would that mean?

He hesitated, as if thinking the same thing.

Ugh. She'd said the wrong thing. Thought the wrong thing. It was just about the sex and not about staying the night. Even after the horse riding and going back to his amazing apartment she'd eventually headed home to sleep. 'Like I said, forget it.'

He looked blindsided. Shook his head. 'No. It's just—'

'Ivy?' It was Alinta. Strolling towards her and grinning an *'Ivy and Lucas sitting in a tree'* kind of teasing smile.

Bad timing, girlfriend.

But she was still pleased to see her. If for nothing more than moral support to bolster her against Lucas's brief hesitant grimace. Had it been a grimace?

'Hey, Ali, it's been ages. How's things?' Ivy glanced at Lucas and she still couldn't read his expression. Was he working out how to let her down gently? 'Do you know Lucas Matthews?'

'From a distance.' Ali nodded in greeting. 'Hi. Alinta Edwards. Head of Obstetrics and Gynaecology.'

Was it her imagination or did Lucas looked relieved to have someone else here? It was probably her imagination, right? But maybe he really didn't want to spend the night. It seemed as if second-guessing had become her superpower.

He nodded back and smiled. 'Good to meet you, Ali.'

'I'm here to see Emma for her antenatal check,' Ali said. 'Any chance of a quick update?'

'All looking good from my end. The actual appendectomy shouldn't have caused any labour risk, but the new incision scars are still healing. Lucas has just been filling me in on her grafts too,' Ivy encouraged him to add any more information.

'They're healing well. If she continues improving like this, she'll be discharged from in-patient care with us. We'll just keep going with the dressings in the community with outpatient follow-up. And physiotherapy, of course.' He smiled his winning smile. 'She's come a long way.'

Ali blew out a slow breath. 'And has been through so many hospital specialties. Poor woman.'

'Here's hoping things keep heading in the right direction after her few hiccups.' Lucas looked at his watch. 'Sorry, but I've got a surgery starting soon. I need to dash. If you need any more info from me let me know. I'm happy to chat any time.'

'Nice to meet you properly.' Ali smiled, then as Lucas walked away she side-mouthed, 'Hubba-hubba. What's this I've been hearing about you and the delectable Dr Matthews?'

'What?' Ivy's heart drummed against her ribcage.

'Phoebe may have mentioned a certain deal you have going with that particular reconstructive surgeon.' Oh, her bestie was grinning now. 'Was it okay for her to tell me?'

'Of course. I can't have secrets from you guys, right? I would have told you myself, but I've been busy.'

'With the aforementioned reconstructive surgeon.' Ali bugged her eyes and laughed.

'Maybe. But also work.' To prove her point, Ivy shuffled the papers on the desk. Although it was really more for something to do with her hands, and to stop her looking at Ali and getting the expected knowing looks. And then having to admit she was in just a little bit deeper with Lucas than she'd planned to be.

Ali waved her hand dismissively. 'Work schmirk. You can admit he's hot, you know. Because he is. Seems nice too.'

Ivy decided not to encourage that conversation any further. 'Actually, I have an…issue I need to discuss with you.'

'Oh, my God, what? You need an obstetrician. You're pregnant? With him?' Ali looked shocked. Even though she was an obstetrician she'd never expressed a desire to have children of her own. None of her friends here had them. They'd all been too consumed with work and life and…the lack of suitable men and never the right timing. 'Honestly. No. I need a ball gown for a gala ball.'

'Phew.' Ali sighed and grinned. 'You had me concerned for a minute. Okay. Yes. Leave it with me. I'll rally the troops. We'll come and help you choose one. Saturday?'

'I can't. I'm going kite surfing.' Ivy picked up the papers now and refused to look Alinta in the eye at this admission. Her friends knew she was more of a land lubber than a fish.

'Say what?' Ali's eyes almost popped out of her head.

'Kite surfing. You know. Ocean. Sail. Board.'

'Why?'

'Apparently it's fun.'

'It's also cold and wet and winter. Oh… I get it. It's a date.

A wet date. Then you can warm up together.' Ali pulled a cheesy face, unwittingly getting to the heart of it all. 'Cute.'

Ivy bristled. She was so busted. 'Not a date. We're just getting to know each other so we can fool his family into believing we're together.'

'You can do that in a cafe. Or over the phone. By email. I know you, Ivy Hurst. There is no way you'd do anything as extreme as kite surfing if it wasn't a date.'

Alinta had a point. But Ivy had just wanted to do something Lucas was interested in so she could see him in his comfort zone. 'It's research.'

'Okay. Dress it up however you want. Lie to me. Just don't lie to yourself.'

'How is everyone into my business so much? I'm a grown woman completely in control. And I'm not lying.'

'Hmm.' Ali shot her a disbelieving look. 'Well, I can't do Sunday so...'

'How about next week Saturday? That'll still give me a week before the ball.'

'Okay. It's a date. Have fun in the ocean and...' Ali's eyes narrowed and she gave her a pointed look. 'Be. Careful.'

'I can swim just fine.'

'I wasn't talking about swimming.'

Ivy sighed. *Here we go again.* 'Oh, honestly. Why does everyone keep telling me to be careful?'

Ali wrapped an arm over Ivy's shoulder and hugged her close. 'Because we love you and don't want you to get hurt. We saw what Grant did to you and don't ever want to see you that upset again.'

'You sound just like Phoebe. It's kite surfing, Ali. There is nothing intimate about that. The only thing that might get hurt is my pride when I'm rubbish at it and get dumped in the water. Definitely not my heart. I'm immune to him, okay?' Even as she said the words she knew they weren't true. She was far from immune. She liked him, for goodness' sake. She liked him a lot.

Too much.

'Immune to a hunk of a man, all wet and pumping muscles? A rub-down with a towel? Or…a spa to warm you both up? Not to mention the way you watched him leave as if you wanted to go with him. Or eat him…whichever you got a chance to do first.' Alinta stepped away and frowned as she spoke. 'Come on, Ivy.'

'What?' Ivy put her palms up in submission and dug deep for a laugh. Because she knew Ali was right and that her friends cared deeply for her. And she loved them for it. 'We're not dating, okay?'

No matter how much she wanted to. Because, yes…okay, she wanted to date him. She didn't want this to end and she was fairly sure he couldn't wait until the ball and be done with her. She'd seen that hesitation. He didn't want to stay the night. He was more than happy for a booty call and she had been too. But…but something had changed. For her at least.

But there was no point wanting what she couldn't have. She'd done that too many times with Grant in the past. With her family too. She wasn't going to willingly walk into a situation where she could be rejected all over again.

Alinta's eyebrows gathered in. 'Hey, I'm sorry. I was just joking around. Are you okay?'

Ivy inhaled deeply then blew out slowly. There was no point in getting upset about things going exactly to plan. Although she was having a hard time convincing her pining heart of that. 'I'm fine. I'm absolutely fine.'

If she said it enough, she might just believe it.

CHAPTER TEN

LUCAS KNOCKED AT the door of Ivy's apartment, his heart giddy, waiting for her to answer.

She opened it a smidgeon as if assessing who might be calling round on a Friday evening. When she saw him, her eyes widened but there wasn't much of a smile as she said, 'Oh, hi, Lucas. I was just about to text you. I wasn't sure what we'd agreed.'

To be honest, he hadn't been sure either. When she'd asked him to stay over, he'd hesitated because he'd immediately wanted to scream *hell, yes*. A whole night with her? Holding her? Kissing her? Waking up with her? Morning sex?

But the sensible part of his brain had suggested he calm right down. It had been the same when she'd said, *'I am not in the habit of kissing one guy when I want to be with some-one else.'*

God help him, but he'd slid into that proclamation with so many emotions and all of them at odds with each other. Excitement. Panic. Want. Fear. Desire.

And even now he was grappling with the aftershocks. Ivy was compelling and alluring and…it almost felt too easy. Too comfortable. And yet wildly exhilarating at the same time. And that made him want to do things he'd always refused to do, like stay the night.

In the end, he'd decided to just ignore his brain and do what she'd suggested, but he wasn't sure she was overly excited at seeing him. Had he messed up by not being more definite? Should he have phoned first? Committed?

Ugh. Such a loaded word. Committed to having fun, yes. He held up his overnight bag and the pizza box. 'Dinner and a sleepover, right? Like teenage girls.'

She grimaced but the corners of her mouth did turn up a little. 'I sincerely hope not.'

'Aw, no pillow fights and painting our toenails?'

A hesitant smile. 'If you really want to.'

Yes, he should have phoned. 'Can I come in?'

She peered at the holdall hooked in his fingers. 'What's in the bag?'

'Toothbrush. Toiletries. PJs. Couple of bottles of wine. Red and white because I wasn't sure which you'd prefer.'

Her eyes widened. 'You wear pyjamas?'

'Not if I can help it. But you know...just in case it was cold.'

'Oh, don't worry, Lucas. It won't be cold.' Finally grinning, she opened the door wider. She was dressed casually in a T-shirt and shorts, her shapely legs attracting his attention as he followed her into her kitchen and put the pizza on the table, his bag on the floor. Then he turned to her.

She stared up at him. Gone was her hesitation. Yeah...there was an irony in the fact she was now the hesitant one. But she was looking at him with something akin to affection. Desire. As if he were a gift on her birthday.

He stroked her cheek. 'I should have phoned. I'm sorry.'

She nodded. 'I might have made other plans, so yes, a quick call would have been better. Wouldn't want that pizza to have gone to waste.'

'Other plans?' He didn't like the sound of that.

A shrug. 'Yes, Lucas. You are not the only person I want to spend time with.'

'Aw, heck, Ivy.' He tugged her closer and kissed that tender spot behind her ear. Then slicked a trail of kisses across her lips, making her moan against his mouth. 'But I'm the only person who does this to you.'

'Maybe...' She laughed and tapped the side of her nose. 'Maybe not.'

He tried to ignore the cleave in his chest at the thought of her with anyone else. Of another man touching her, kissing her. He was pretty damn sure there wasn't anyone else—hadn't she all but said she was a one-man woman? She was just teasing. 'Come on. Tell me who else makes you feel this hot.'

He claimed her mouth again, long and slow until she was writhing against him. 'Okay, okay. I'm glad you're here, Lucas.'

'Me too.'

There was some slow and sweet R & B music playing softly through her kitchen speakers. Her hair was rumpled as if she'd been sleeping or lying down, maybe reading a book? The book he'd given her? There was something wholesome and just damned good about that image. Her eyes were clear and bright. Her smile was sexy as hell. Wordlessly, she reached for his hand and interlaced her fingers between his. It was such a simple gesture, but deeply intimate. He didn't hold hands.

But his heart caught. His skin tightened. He relaxed and yet grew excited all at the same time. She stroked her fingers against his then lifted his hand to her lips and kissed them. Such a simple action but it felt pure, reverential. He brought their hands to his mouth and kissed them too, then kissed her palm, the inside of her wrist, the dip in her elbow. Everything felt slowed down, each second elongated. Pure. It was one of those moments he knew he'd tuck tight into his memory banks and keep revisiting.

Her eyes flickered closed as he reached her collarbone and pressed a trail of kisses there too. He noted the dancing pulse in her throat as he kissed her jawline. Then, because he simply couldn't wait any longer, he slid his mouth over hers again.

His heart swelled as he tasted her, as she responded with the tight, firm press of her body, the trail of her fingertips down his cheek. He'd been struggling with coming here tonight with the promise of increased intimacy, but he'd omitted that she would feel so good, taste so good.

'Lucas.' It was a throaty gasp that touched every part of him. *Sound so good.*

How could he have thought about denying himself this? 'Bedroom.'

'Yes.' Her voice was shaky and desperate, and she grasped at his jacket lapels. 'I need you inside me. It's been too long.'

'Five days, twenty-two hours and too many minutes.' It shocked him that he knew that, that he'd been subconsciously counting down the time until he could do this again. He'd hesitated when she'd asked him to stay. His brain had silenced him. What a damned fool.

'Too long.' She grabbed his hand and rushed him to her bedroom. Threw off her clothes and dragged his off too. Within moments he was sheathed and nudging into her.

The only place he wanted to be.

After, he kissed her long and slow, sated and satisfied but eager for more. She looked dazed and sleepy as he nestled her into the crook of his arm. He rested his cheek on the top of her head. 'That's better. So very much better.'

She chuckled against his chest. 'Bad day?'

'No, actually. A good day.' And getting better by the second. 'You?'

'Awful.' She pulled a face, wrinkling her nose. 'I had to tell a twenty-two-year-old they had bowel cancer today. It sucks.'

'Wow. That's so young.'

'It happens, sadly. He's an apprentice electrician. Just an ordinary guy. Kid really. He reminded me of Sione. All barely there facial hair, too long limbs that he was still growing into, an innocence I was crushing with the worst kind of news. And then he was all over the place. At first, he tried to make jokes about it. Then, as it sank in, he was incredulous. Then, when he heard about the treatment and his survival chances, he got angry. Trying so hard not to cry. So, so hard not to be seen as anything other than strong and brave.' Her mouth turned down. 'Which made me kind of wobble—'

'Hey, I know. I know exactly what you're saying. I've been there too many times. You have such compassion and a tender heart.' He stroked her cheek, tilted her chin and kissed her nose, her eyelids, her mouth.

Tears swam in her eyes and his own heart twisted. 'You want to tell me all about it?'

'It's fine. Grant always said we should leave work at work.' She swallowed and, with a wonky smile, shook her head. He knew it was an act of bravado.

'I'm not Grant.' He tried not to growl but the mention of that idiot who had treated her with such disrespect threatened to bring down his mood. 'Talk.'

So, she did. She lay in his arms and told him about her patient's hopes of being in a rock band and that his parents had told him he needed a proper job, so he'd started his electrician training. And how he was regretting that now and wished he'd followed his dreams instead of toeing his parents' line.

'I hear that a lot,' Lucas agreed. 'People doing things… spending lifetimes doing things…because it's expected, or they think it's the right thing to do. But for who? It's one thing to take other people's wants and needs into consideration, but you have to live your life for yourself. Makes me so glad that I struck out against the family dictate.'

'Me too.' Her fingertips ran across his chest. 'And yet, I also hear people wishing they'd mended the family feuds and been closer to their people. I wish things didn't have to be so complicated.'

'What exactly happened with you and your parents?'

Her shoulders slumped a little. 'They said I could be an army medic if I was so invested in being a doctor. That our life was about duty and service. That army life was all I'd known and I'd struggle with anything different. That they understood sacrifice but also that it was an honour to serve. But I was going through a rocky, possibly rebellious, phase.' She shot him a rueful smile. 'Definitely rebellious. You know me, light and dark. And I told them where to stick their service. That I wanted to be free from rules and orders.'

'Which explains a little of why you barked at me when you thought I'd given you an order that night in your office.' He chuckled at the memory. She'd been so fierce and vivid and vibrant that his interest—and libido—had been off the scale. Seemed that now he knew her better, she was all those things and so much more too, that his interest and libido hadn't waned at all. In fact, they'd both hit new heights.

She laughed. 'Yeah. I don't like being told what to do and not be allowed to discuss options. Living that army life didn't feel like an honour to me, it felt as though they had no control over their lives. I guess, looking back, I was blinded by my own subjectivity, because it's not really like that. They have a lot of autonomy while doing a very important job that needs boundaries and rules. But I didn't see it like that back then, I just wanted to be free. We had a huge argument, and they threw me out, saying I was ungrateful and spiteful and thought I was better than them.'

'That's hard.'

'It is.' Her eyes misted. 'Things have never been right ever since. Oh, we talk a couple of times a year to catch up on everyone's news but there's a distance between us that I'm not sure we'll ever overcome. We have different values and beliefs and desires. Different perspectives. I love them, but I don't necessarily like them for barking orders at me and expecting me to follow through.'

'I don't blame you. Well done for having the courage to walk away. That was brave.'

'Not brave. Desperate. I couldn't stay. I refused to do what they told me to do. I had no choice.'

'You became a doctor and you save lives, you make people better, you make their lives better. Your friends' lives too. And mine.' He swallowed. Hell, what was he saying? He couldn't encourage any further intimacy on this kind of level, but the sentiments kept tripping out of his mouth.

'Lucas?' She stared up at him and smiled, fingers grazing his jaw. 'Thank you.'

'For what?'

'Being you.'

Whoa. No one had ever said anything so heartfelt like that to him either. And it seemed to come as easy to her as it did to him. They had a tight connection on so many levels. Respect, fun, attraction, shared interests.

A man could fall into this, he thought. Maybe too deep and too hard and lose himself in the dream. And then she'd realise he wasn't all she thought he was. That he couldn't keep her safe. That he couldn't be trusted.

A dark shadow scudded across his chest. He needed to distract himself, so he sat up and dragged a pillow from behind. Took aim and whacked her gently on her arm.

'What the actual…? Lucas!' But she was still laughing and reaching for her pillow now.

'Sleepover pillow fight. Bring it on.'

'Oh, I'm going to bring it.' She knelt up and thwacked him with her pillow across the side of his face.

He took it and laughed. 'Right. This is war.' Then hit her legs, making her squeal.

'Lucas Matthews. You are so dead.' She hit him in the belly, but must have lost her balance because all of a sudden she was tilting towards him, screaming with laughter.

He tickled her just under her ribs until she was rolling on the bed, tears streaming down her face. 'I surrender! Surrender!'

'Aha.' He guffawed and pulled her closer so she couldn't wriggle away. 'Captured.'

'Help,' she whispered, grinning and looking the least scared anyone had looked ever. More, the expression on her face...of fun, affection and promises...hell, she was getting involved here. He couldn't let that happen. He couldn't have her hoping for more once this deal was done.

But it was he who hadn't been able to resist the pull of a sleepover. He who had ached to slide inside her. Be with her. He who yearned for this comfortable ease between them, and the wild sex too. So, in truth, it was he who was captured and captivated.

It was getting too much for his heart and his hopes. Man, hopes he'd never allowed himself to have before. Hopes he most certainly didn't deserve. He needed to slow it all down. But he didn't know how.

He slicked a kiss on the tip of her nose as her belly growled loudly. 'Hungry?'

She covered her stomach with her hand and giggled. 'Starving. I don't think I've eaten anything since breakfast.'

'Then stay here and I'll bring up a picnic.'

And in the meantime, try to wrestle these emotions into some kind of order.

He'd actually turned up. She hadn't known how to feel when she'd opened the door. Relief that he was here? Frustration that he hadn't confirmed beforehand?

Excitement. Yes, definitely that.

Then he'd showed her how much he'd missed her. And her heart was full again. Because the feeling had been entirely mutual. A craving to have him close, to be connected again instead of snatched conversations at work, watching him walk away from her. This time together was special.

Lucas returned with a tray of reheated pizza, two wine glasses and a bottle of chardonnay, which he placed onto the middle of her bed then bowed low, a tea towel over his arm. A bath towel, slung low around his slim waist, showcased his flat abs and that delicious arrow of hair that pointed lower and promised so much. He most certainly looked more appetising than the food.

He made a *ta-dah* motion with his hands. 'Dinner is served, ma'am. I wasn't sure what pizza you'd like so I took a punt on margherita.'

'Anything, as long as it's not got pine—'

'Pineapple?' he said at the same time she did.

'Great minds.' She reached for a piece of pizza, constantly amazed at just how in sync they were. 'Pineapple on pizza is the devil's food.'

'Never, ever put fruit on pizza.' He snatched a piece and chinked it with hers. 'Deal?'

'Deal.'

He grinned and nodded, playful and just so gorgeous her limbs felt weak just from her looking at him. 'And never anchovies.'

She shuddered at the thought. 'Absolutely not. I promise never anchovies.'

It felt as if they were planning ahead here. Beyond what they'd agreed.

Her phone rang. She leaned over and grabbed her shorts from the floor where she'd left them in her eagerness to have Lucas in her bed. Dug her phone out of the pocket and looked at the screen, unsure whether to take the call. 'It's Harper.'

He nodded. 'Take it.'

'Are you sure?'

'You said you don't catch up often enough. Take it. I can wait.' He caught her dubious expression and nodded. 'Honestly. Please, talk to her. I'll just fill my belly here.'

'Save me another piece. I promise I won't be long.' She slid to the edge of the bed and turned away to talk to her friend, aware of his gaze on her and wanting to hurry up to get back to their evening together. Which made her feel like a bad friend. But she didn't have much longer for this whatever it was with Lucas. Her mood took a little nosedive so she forced jollity into her tone. 'Hey, Harper. How's you?'

'Good. Great. Fantastic! I have news.' Her friend sounded breathless.

'What kind of news?' It was so good to hear her sound so cheerful after everything she'd been through caring for Yarran and his burns, finding her way back to him.

'I...well, I asked Yarran to marry me.'

'Oh, my God! No! You didn't? He said yes?'

'He said yes.' Harper's voice was filled with happiness.

'Wow! I'm so happy for you. I can't believe it, after all this time.' Ivy held the phone between her chin and shoulder and turned to Lucas, pointing to her left-hand ring finger.

His dark eyes flared with surprise, but he didn't look as excited as she was. But then, he didn't know Harper and Yarran or their history, hadn't lived through the break-up, supported them both.

Or was he just against relationships? And why?

Why?

And why did it matter so much?

She turned back to talk to Harper. 'Have you got a date planned?'

'No. We're going shopping for the rings tomorrow. But we're not rushing into getting married just yet. We need to wait until Yarran's fully healed and, well, just wallow in being an engaged couple.'

'I am so happy for you.' Yet her heart felt heavy and she couldn't quite put her finger on why.

But she had a niggling idea that it had something to do with Lucas's expression. She finished the conversation then turned back to him. 'So Harper asked Yarran to marry her.'

He was leaning back against the headboard, arms crossed. 'I guessed as much. She asked him?'

'Yes. I imagine it was the best way to show him she loves him and how committed she is.'

'But that's a bit quick, right? They haven't been together very long.'

'Well, yes and no. Yes, because they've only recently got together. No, because they were almost engaged twelve years ago, before Harper upped and left to go to London. They're going to go shopping for rings, but apparently waiting for a while before they actually get married.' She noticed a frown forming deep over his eyes. 'What is it?'

He shook his head. 'What's what?'

'Why are you frowning?'

'I'm not.' His features rearranged into a smile that lit his mouth but not his eyes. 'You seem very excited over the prospect of a wedding.'

'Their wedding, yes. She's one of my best friends and I'm thrilled she's so happy, at last. I'm sure you were happy about George and Ivan?'

'Knowing about George's inability to commit, it was a surprise but...' His eyebrows rose and he gave an empty laugh. 'A happy one, I guess.'

I guess?

A pause she didn't know how to fill yawned between them. Something didn't feel quite right here. The vibe had changed. He was too quiet. Was he against marriage full stop or just against *him* getting married?

Then he sat forward. 'Why didn't you and Grant get married? Oh, *were* you married?'

She laughed at the thought. 'It just never happened, thank goodness. That would have made everything even more messy. We talked about it, of course. But we were so busy with our jobs and building our careers we never got to the engagement stage.' In hindsight she realised she probably didn't want it enough for her to make it happen. 'I've learnt from that, though. If you want to be with someone you need to make them know it. You have to make that commitment and act on it.'

He nodded but the light in his eyes had definitely dimmed. 'I guess so.'

'You never wanted to get married?'

He gave a sharp shake of his head. Flat mouth. 'No.'

'That's it? Just no?'

'Just no, Ivy.'

She scrambled backwards up the bed and sat next to him, her head against the headboard too. But despite their proximity and the warm air coming from the heat pump she felt suddenly alone and cold.

Which didn't make sense. They were in this for another couple of weeks. She'd known that going in. They were doing exactly what they'd agreed. Whether Lucas wanted to get married or not, wanted to commit to someone or not, was none of her business. She was just fine. She had never given marriage to him a thought. She had exactly what she wanted here with a no-strings affair.

So why was her heart hurting?

CHAPTER ELEVEN

'IT'S FREEZING.' Ivy was sitting next to him on the beach, tugging a long wetsuit up her gorgeous legs. Goosebumps mushroomed across her beautiful skin. 'Why did I agree to this?'

He laughed, reaching back behind his shoulder to pull up his wetsuit zip. 'I did warn you. You could have stayed at home in that nice warm bed. We could have been doing something very different from this.'

She turned, face red with the effort of wrestling the neoprene, and grinned. Clearly very aware of what he was referring to. 'And miss the chance to see you in your happy place? Surely, you've brought a regular girlfriend here before? Not just this fake one?'

His heart tightened. This wasn't fake. Being here, doing this. Enjoying her company. Last night. Sleeping over. Not fake at all. Very real, in fact.

He shook his head, hoping the panic wasn't obvious in his expression. 'Nope. Not one.'

'Why not?'

He shrugged, choosing not to spell it out to her again: he didn't have girlfriends. Just dates. Just…sex really. 'It just never happened.'

Truth was, he'd almost not brought her here today. Had scrambled around for excuses but come up with nothing convincing. Plus, the temptation to be around her was as compelling as ever, despite the strange feeling in his chest when she'd talked about marriage.

Hell, she hadn't even been talking about their marriage. But it was balled up with the commitment thing, right? Long term. For ever stuff. Depending on someone, trusting them to hold your heart, and your dreams, wishes and hopes safe.

Geez, he couldn't even keep his sister physically safe, never mind anything else. And if he couldn't do it for her—someone he adored—how on earth could he do it for someone else?

Yet, here he was, doing this anyway because he wanted to make Ivy smile and the chances of spending more time with her were getting fewer and fewer as time zipped on, hurtling towards the ball. The end.

She knelt and wriggled the wetsuit over her hips and breasts then slid her arms in, shuffled back towards him. 'Zip me up?'

'Sure.' But it was too easy to slowly tug the zip down and slide his hands across her belly, to rake his fingers across her skin, delighting in the way she shivered against him.

'Lucas,' she whispered, his name whipping into the breeze, her gaze intent on the horizon, her expression serious.

He leaned his chin on her shoulder, heart thumping as he wondered what she was going to say. 'Ivy?'

'Take your freezing hands out of my wetsuit or there'll be no more sex for you. Not even a little bit.'

'You wouldn't dare.'

'Don't push me.' She laughed and twisted round so he had to quickly slide his hands out from her waist or risk two broken wrists.

'Wow, you really meant it.' He laughed too, because there'd really been no danger.

'I just hate being cold.' She bugged her eyes at him.

'Then you've come to the wrong place.' He jumped up before he stripped her naked and made love to her right here on this beach, which, given it was nine o'clock in the morning and already pretty busy, was not a good idea. 'Come on, let's get in the water. We'll start in the shallows first, so you get the hang of it.'

After he pumped up the leading edge and ran through the basics with her he took her knee-deep into the water. Showed her how to check that the lines were all separated, secured her safety harness and launched the kite. He then ran through how to relaunch once more.

Her hands literally shook with what he discovered was impatience. 'Yes. Yes. I understand all that. When do I get to board?'

'Patience, young Padawan. I need you to be safe and know how to get back to the beach. We don't want you ending up in New Zealand with a sharp gust of wind you can't control.'

'How do I get good enough to try the board?'

'You need to make your turns into the wind window a little sharper. More aggressive. Then you can get yourself from body dragging to body surfing.'

She grinned and grabbed hold of the leading edge again. 'Bring it. Let's go.'

Once she'd mastered control of the kite, he let her try with her feet on a board.

She was bent forward, water gushing into her face as the kite rushed her forward a few feet. 'Oh, my God! This is epic.'

'Lean back so you don't swallow half the ocean. Now you feel comfortable on the edge of the wind window, scoop your wings a little deeper. You'll fly in no time.'

He towed her out deeper. Kissed her cheek and let her go. 'Careful. Careful. Hold on.'

There was too much for her to remember all in one go. The wings dipped and scooped, but not enough. She didn't lean enough into the wind.

Then she did. 'Ivy! Go! You got it! You did it!'

'Yay!' Her happy screeches floated across the bay. She let

go with one hand and pumped her fist triumphantly in the air. His heart jolted with pride as if it fist-bumped right back. He watched her skim across the tops of the waves and his chest contracted with respect and admiration. Maybe more. He liked this woman. Really liked her. And he knew she liked him.

For a moment he metaphorically rode that excitement with her. Letting his imagination run wild with long nights and early mornings. With togetherness and sharing things, memories, life. Love.

His heart tangled itself around the vision of her fist-pumping the blue sky, harnessing an invisible power that was bigger than both of them. How hard would it be to let himself fall into something like that? With someone like her? How hard would it be to start trusting himself?

She met him back on the sand as they'd agreed, letting the breeze push her into the wash. He ran to her and she jumped up and down. 'I did it! I did it!'

'Way to go! I am so proud of you.' He picked her up and whirled her round in a circle.

She put her hands on his shoulders and kissed him quickly. But he wasn't going to let her go that soon. 'Come here,' he growled and pulled her flat against him, capturing her mouth. She tasted of salt and fresh air, elemental and happy. Yes, she tasted happy.

He pulled away, desperate to know if she felt the way she tasted. 'And?'

'It was amazing. I was flying. I was actually flying.' She put her hand to her heart. 'I think I've just had a religious experience.'

Well, she'd only barely lifted off the water, but he wasn't going to burst her bubble. 'You were awesome. You're a natural.'

'I love it.' Eyes shining brightly, she kissed him again. 'Thank you, Lucas. It is the best thing ever.'

Thank you.

She kept saying that. As if the things he did for her really mattered. He tucked it away into the Ivy corner of his heart.

'The pleasure was one hundred per cent mine.' He glanced at his watch, thinking that some cold water might help douse these tussling emotions. 'One more go before we head back? Tide's going to turn soon, and it'll make things more difficult for you.'

'Only if you come in too and I can watch you do some tricks.'

Oh, no. He was staying where he could see her. 'I won't be able to watch out for you properly if I'm not here. It's best if I stay on the beach, then, when you come in, I'll go out.'

She frowned and jabbed him in the ribs. 'Oh, come on. It'll be fine. The wind's practically shoving us towards the beach anyway.'

'No, Ivy.'

'Come on. You told me you love doing it. I want to see you excited by something.'

He stroked his fingers down her breasts. 'Here. These.'

She captured his fingers in hers. 'Something *else*. I can't talk to your mum about your breast obsession, can I? Come on. Just for five minutes. I want to see you fly too.'

'No.'

'Scared? Have you been lying to me all along? You can't really do this stuff, can you?' She was teasing, but it hit a nerve.

'Sure, I can.'

'Then prove it.'

She wanted to watch him. Wanted him to teach her. And hell, that was such a powerful punch to his chest he couldn't resist basking in the glory of her gaze. 'Okay. Just one trick. As long as you stay in the shallows where you'll be safe.'

She jumped up and down and clapped her hands. 'Yay! Now I get to see the professional in action.'

So, he launched her kite, then his. Made sure she was up and steady then blew her a kiss as he harnessed the full power of the wind, shouting, 'Don't try this at home!'

He flew across the tops of the waves, heading sharp east, jumped and turned, making a quick grab of his board because it always looked harder and more impressive than it was, and then aimed to head back to her, sharp west. As he turned he tried to spot her in the shallows. But she wasn't there.

Damn.

Where was she?

He scanned the water. She wasn't there. He steered towards the spot where he'd left her and caught sight of her crawling on her hands and knees along the shallows dragging the kite behind her.

She was hurt.

His stomach lurched up into his throat.

No.

No.

Too-familiar feelings of panic roiled in his gut and swelled through his chest.

He steered onto the beach and ran across the sand, his heart firing like rapid rifle shot against his ribcage. 'Ivy. Ivy, are you okay?'

'I'm…' She put her palm on her forehead and winced. 'I hope I don't have a bruise for the ball.'

'Hot damn, Ivy. I don't care about the ball.'

I care about you.

Yeah, he'd probably known that for a long time. But this was the first time he was admitting it.

He knelt in front of her and checked her over. Why had he been showing off?

Why had he let her talk him into going on the water when she was there? Why had he been so distracted to the point of not looking out for her?

Why…why…why? The same question that had run through his head so many times over the years like a song playing on repeat, the ear worm was always there. He'd thought he'd learnt about making stupid decisions, but obviously not.

Bile rose in his throat and he turned away from the bump he might as well have caused.

And there it was. Exactly why he shouldn't be allowed around people he cared about. Because when he stuffed up, he did it big time. He shouldn't have been fooling around to impress her, he should have been focused on making sure she was okay. Hadn't he already learnt that lesson?

He pushed her wet hair away from her forehead and gently examined the lump on her head. 'What happened?'

'I don't know. I think I caught too much wind. I panicked. The lines got tangled and I lifted off, somehow lost the board, which went flying and hit me on the head on its way back down.'

He started to untangle the lines and removed the safety harness from her waist in an effort to stop his hands shaking limply by his sides. 'Damn, Ivy.'

She flinched as if she'd been hit a second time. 'What?'

He changed the tone, lowering his voice, not wanting to make her feel any worse. 'Just damn and hell.'

'Lucas?'

Stupid. Careless. This is all your fault.

'Lucas. Look at me.'

His jaw stiffened and he ground his teeth together.

'Lucas. I'm fine. What's wrong?'

He shook his head until he had enough control over his emotions that he could look at her again. 'I shouldn't have been showing off like that. I should have been on the beach watching your every move. Out there I can't keep you safe.'

'It was just a gust of wind. An accident. You are not responsible for me, Lucas.'

'I am. You're…'

'Go on.' Her eyes bugged at him. 'What am I exactly?'

Everything.

These thoughts kept pelting him from all angles. He cared for her. She meant so much to him. Too much. Which was stupid and dangerous, but he couldn't keep away. Ached for her approval, her respect and admiration. And now look what had happened. She'd got hurt. 'This is my gig, Ivy. I'm supposed to look after you.'

'No, you're not. I can look after myself quite well, thanks. You were just teaching me how to kite surf. And it's only a small bump.' But she looked at him as if she were trying to solve a math equation or something. Trying to work him out.

Good luck with that.

'You're not going back in again.'

She frowned, putting the skin on her forehead under more pressure. Then winced. 'I beg your pardon?'

'We're going home.'

'Lucas, no. Stop.' She held up her palm, body taut and expression as fierce as that first evening together when she'd pushed her office chair at him. 'I don't know what you're thinking or who you think you are, but you're not the boss of me, and you certainly don't get to tell me what I can or can't do. If I want to go back in the water, I will. If I don't want to, then I won't. You're overreacting here.'

'I'm not.' Great, and now they were having an argument and that was his fault too. 'You know we can stop this any time, Ivy. You've already got your prize.' The words tumbled out of him. Self-preservation probably. But it was rude and unthinking. A gut reaction.

'What? I have one stupid, minor accident while learning to do a thing I've never done before and you want to call the whole thing off? You don't want to keep going until the ball because I hit my head?' Her eyes shimmered with hurt and he hated himself for causing that. 'I don't understand.'

'I'm just saying I won't hold you to it.'

'Wow, Lucas. Are you trying to get rid of me all of a sudden?'

'Just giving you options.'

'Options?' Her mouth dropped open as her eyebrows peaked. 'To stick to my word or cry off. Is that what you want? You want me to leave? Where is this coming from?'

'I just want to let you off the hook with this stupid deal. Grant thinks you're awesome again. I can manage my mother if needs be.'

'Whoa. I'm not a quitter, Lucas. I made you a promise.' She ran her fingertips over the red lump on her forehead. 'This isn't just about the accident, is it? It's about something else. Something you don't want to talk about. Or some emotion you've got going that you don't like. Maybe you do feel responsible for what happened just now but it wasn't your fault.' Her dark eyes bit deep into him. 'Or something that happened in the past? God knows what because every time we stray anywhere close to deep you back off. You won't talk about your family or why you don't spend time with them, so I'm guessing it's something about that. But hey, who knows? Because I certainly don't.'

She was dangerously close to the mark and she was right too, he didn't want to talk about it.

'It's too…' He chugged out a deep breath that felt as if all his stress and anger and self-loathing filled it. How could he explain what had happened? How could he tell her the magnitude of his mistake? *Neglect.* Not mistake. 'It's history I don't want to talk about. Ground that doesn't need raking over. Stuff you don't need to know for the ball.'

'I might not need to know, but I want to know. That's what friends are for, right? We share stuff. The good, the bad and the messy.' She glared at him. A few moments ago her eyes had been shining with pride and excitement and light and he'd snuffed it out. 'Because we are friends, Lucas. Above all else. When this deal's finished, that's what we'll be.'

He didn't even want to think about what they'd mean to each other...after.

He looked at his knees. His feet. The sand. But none of them had any answers. He raised his head to look at her, struggling for words to describe what had happened. 'I don't know what to tell you, Ivy. I can't... I don't... I mean, I want to. I just... don't know how.'

She held his gaze, long and steady as if assessing him...no, *scrutinising* him. As if she had X-ray vision deep into his soul and wasn't overly impressed by what she saw there.

She had no idea.

'You want to. That's a start. I guess.' She sat for a moment, legs pulled up, arms wrapped around her knees as she stared out to sea, as if the endless ocean had the answer.

He waited. Words he couldn't say tripped through his head. *Third-degree burns. Intensive care. Poor prognosis.*

Then images of his little sister, screaming in pain. Hooked up to tubes. Drugged and still, so still he'd thought she'd died. Thought he'd killed her.

Felt the shame fill every cell of his body.

How could he convey all that to Ivy and hope she wouldn't think less of him?

Eventually she said, 'So, you're not going to say you want to stop, but you're asking me to say it. Unlucky, Lucas. Because if you're leaving the decision to me then I opt to carry on. I promised I'd be your date to the ball to get your mother off your back and I will.'

Relief shimmered through him and his heart recovered. 'I don't deserve that. But thank you.'

She turned to look at him, her features softening with a small smile. 'Did we just have our first argument?'

'I think so.'

'You *think* so because I did a lot of growling and pushing, but you didn't say much at all. That's not how arguments work.' She shivered and pulled the towel round her shoulders.

'I haven't had much experience with relationship disagreements, to be fair. But I can't say I enjoyed that one.'

'I was in a five-year thing with Grant and let's just say we perfected the art of fighting. But just a heads up, Lucas, next time it will work better if you join in and say a few things. Extrapolate a little. Tell me what's going on in your head. There's nothing worse than arguing all on your own.'

He was pretty sure she wouldn't want to know what was going on in his head. Confusion. Remorse. Attraction. Need. 'I'll try to be a better sparring partner, then.'

'Excellent.' She leaned forward and touched her lips to his, so close he could see the little rivulets of sea water dripping down her face, taste the salt. 'It's a good job I'm just in it for the sex, because you really need to work on your interpersonal skills.'

'Yeah. Thank God for that. And noted. I've got some homework to do.'

'Or your mother's going to see that we're off kilter on the communication front.'

'Practice makes perfect, then.' He grinned and kissed her again.

'Come here.' She opened her arms. 'Let's start practising our non-verbal skills too.'

He held her tight against him, pretending it was to keep her warm, or for reconciliation, but it was more than that. This hug was for him. To hold onto something good when his head was swimming with memories of that day, all those years ago when he'd been unable to protect his sister. To hold onto Ivy just a little bit longer.

Truth was, he was wildly relieved she'd said she wanted to continue their charade, deeply ashamed he didn't have words to explain to her what had happened in the past and what held him back from being the person she wanted him to be.

And scared as hell about what it all might mean.

CHAPTER TWELVE

'WE'RE KIND OF falling into a routine, I suppose. What is it they call it when you're scared of spiders, so they stick you in a room full of them? Flooding therapy? We're learning as much about each other as we can.' Ivy stepped out from the changing room in the champagne-coloured dress that Ali had picked out for her. 'Too short?'

'It's more belt than dress. You've got great legs, but I don't think it's suitable for a charity ball or meeting parents. Put it this way, they'd get to meet a lot more of you than you might want.' Harper grinned over at Ivy from her seat between Phoebe and Ali, on the velvet couch in the ball-gown shop. The third ball-gown shop they'd visited, and so far Ivy had managed to dodge the Lucas questions, but now she just couldn't as Harper pinned her with a laser look and asked, 'So this flooding therapy involves sleepovers?'

'Maybe.' Ivy feigned lack of interest. But couldn't help herself. Because if she didn't tell someone she'd likely explode with all the excitement. 'Oh, okay. He's been over four out of seven nights.'

'Wow.' Ali's eyes grew wide. 'Intense.'

Intense indeed. And wildly sexy. 'And I may have stayed over two out of seven nights at his.'

'So you're practically living together.' Phoebe looked at the other two girls and bugged her eyes. 'Are you sure that's wise?'

Ivy turned away from her friends to, ostensibly, look in the mirror at the dress…but more, to not have to look them in the eye, or for them not to see the emotions she knew would be showing on her face. Because she was so confused now about how she felt. 'It's only for another week. Then we're done.'

We can stop this any time. I won't hold you to it.

She didn't want to stop. And even though the sex was great and the connection was still tight, she felt him retreating already. Oh, he hadn't been as outspoken about it as he had at the beach, and hadn't suggested again that they stop before the ball, but he still veered away from any deep conversations about the past or relationships and shuddered every time she mentioned Harper and Yarran's engagement.

He had her back, of course. She knew he did. Unlike with Grant, she knew Lucas was as good as his word. He did what he said he was going to do. He turned up on time. He made no grand gestures or rash promises. This was fun. This was sex. This was a ruse for his parents. This was simple.

Only, somewhere along the line it had become serious too. Serious for her at least. She'd started to think that she might not be able to let him go quite so easily after the ball and she knew now, without a shadow of a doubt, that she was in far deeper than she'd planned. She liked him. Too much. Wanted him. Too much. And knew her heart was at risk again. But she couldn't put a stop to it no matter how much at risk she was.

'How about the burgundy one there?' Phoebe pointed to another rack in the corner of the room. 'Third one along with the beads on the bodice.'

'This one?' Ivy refocused on the matter in hand: a suitable dress for parent-meeting. She pulled out a slinky red number and held it up, grimacing. 'Too tight. I won't be able to eat anything.'

'No. Not the red one. The burgundy one.' Phoebe pointed to the rack then sighed and stood up. 'Let me show…oh.' She blinked. Wobbled. Put her hand out.

Ivy dashed over and put her arm out for Phoebe to steady herself. 'You okay, Phoebs?'

Her friend nodded, all the colour leeching from her face. 'I think I stood up too quickly.'

'Too much champagne at lunch? Wait...you didn't have any.' Ivy frowned. This was very unlike Phoebe, who was normally healthier than all of them. 'Not enough champagne, clearly.'

Phoebe's cheeks gained some colour. And a little bit more. 'Like I said, I'm just getting over some stupid stomach bug. I can't even think about drinking at the moment.'

Ali eyed her suspiciously. 'Are you sure you're okay? Should we take your blood pressure?'

'Honestly, that's the problem with doctor friends. Always too eager to intervene.' Phoebe laughed ruefully and slotted herself back onto the sofa. 'I'm fine. I feel much better already.'

'Did you have breakfast?'

'Are you pregnant?' A scuttle of laughter and a chorus of giggles. *As if!*

'I'd need a man for that, right?' Phoebe joked, but Ivy couldn't help noting that the joke seemed forced.

As Ivy tried on the burgundy dress she could hear Ali and Harper giving Phoebe the full interrogation on her diet and exercise regime and a lecture on the causes of a sudden drop in blood pressure, as if Phoebe wouldn't know that. But Ivy was glad someone else was in the spotlight for a change.

She tugged up the zip at the back and remembered how Lucas had slid his hands underneath her wetsuit when she'd asked him for zip help. Her body prickled at the memory. The way he made her feel with his touch and his kisses was beyond wonderful.

She smoothed down the skirt, looked in the mirror and sighed. *Oh, yes.* Phoebe had been right. This was the one. The off-the-shoulder lace bodice was studded with pearl beads and layers of organza cascaded in gentle waves from her waist to the floor. It was grown up and sophisticated with the perfect twirl factor for when she danced. It was demure yet sexy. She felt like a princess.

An older than usual princess, but one nevertheless.

She stepped back into the shop and all three of her friends stopped talking and stared at her.

Her heart hammered. 'What do you think?'

Phoebe, looking almost back to normal but still a little peaky, clapped. 'Oh, Ivy. It's absolutely perfect!'

Harper and Ali nodded in agreement and high-fived each other. 'Yay. You look fabulous.'

Ivy twirled in front of the large gilt-edged mirror. 'I hope Lucas likes it.'

'He'll love it.' Harper smiled. 'How can he not? You look amazing.'

'I feel amazing,' she had to admit. It *was* absolutely perfect.

But, with the ball and, inevitably, *the end* hurtling towards her, she didn't think she'd feel this great for long.

'We don't often get lip injuries this severe, so I'm glad you had the chance to see it first hand,' Lucas said to Chao, his new registrar. Their Thursday lunchtime ward round had been derailed with the arrival of a patient in ER requiring emergency surgery, which meant he'd have to catch up on Emma's progress later. She was on the road to recovery now and he just wanted to make sure she got over the line before those babies arrived. 'It's imperative we try to keep the cupid arch symmetry and also be very careful to rebuild the mucocutaneous junction so we don't have shifting between red and white lip.'

'Tricky.' Chao nodded, his keen interest visible only from his eyes. The rest of his face was covered by a surgical mask and cap. 'It was a nasty dog bite.'

'Indeed. Here's a life lesson: some people like to kiss their dogs. But some dogs don't like people's faces so close. I've just about finished the nasolabial flap, how about you close up the skin layer now?' Lucas stepped aside to allow Chao better access, and glanced over towards the theatre door.

His heart danced before his brain even registered that there was someone outside.

Was that Ivy he could see through the glass?

Or was it wishful thinking?

He could only see the back of her, but he'd know her anywhere. Know that hair, that stance. Yes, it was Ivy talking to her anaesthetist. She was probably scheduled for this theatre after him.

As if she could sense him, she turned round. Their eyes met. She smiled briefly then turned away to continue her conversation.

Somehow it felt as if it wasn't enough. Hell, they'd spent the last few nights together. Having the best sex of his life. How could one glance, one smile not be enough?

'Lucas?' The male voice at his side brought him back to the now.

He shifted his focus back to the very capable Chao. Lucas assessed the wound closure. 'Done? Excellent work. Really excellent. Thanks, everyone, patient is now ready to go through to Recovery, whenever our anaesthetist is ready. Chao, make sure we keep a very close eye on infection control. IV antibiotics, please. I'll go out and let Mrs Jameson's husband know that everything went well.' Via a very quick detour.

He found Ivy in Theatre Reception, chatting to someone who looked a lot like a concerned relative. He waited until she'd finished then caught her arm. 'Got a minute?'

She glanced around them. 'Just the one, I've got surgery.'

'It occurred to me we haven't made any arrangements about the ball. Getting there et cetera.'

'We could talk tonight?'

'I'm on call, remember? And I already have patients waiting in ER. It's going to be busy.'

She pulled a sad face. 'Oh, yes. And I'm on call tomorrow. Judging how it was last time with us being so short-staffed, I don't think I'll get much chance to sleep, let alone chat.'

No getting together, then. Their last time could already have been and gone. His gut tightened like a vice. 'Sometimes schedules suck.'

'I know. But we're doctors, it's just how it is.' She laid her palm on his arm. 'I'm so sorry, but I have to work for most of this weekend too. I've been trying to get out of it, but one of the general surgeons has had to dash back to Melbourne because his father's just died, and the other is away on holiday. I've at least got Samreen covering Saturday night and Sunday morning, so I'll get a chance to recover from the ball before coming back to work.'

He understood, of course he did, but his chest felt hollow. Time was running out. 'Sure. No worries. I'll come and collect you on Saturday whenever you need me to.'

'That's sweet, but I'm guessing you need to be there to support the family. Won't they need you for the set-up?'

'Probably. But they can do without me for an hour. They certainly do without me for a lot longer than that usually.'

'Not looking forward to it?'

'Now it's actually staring me in the face? No. I hate getting dressed up in a suit, might as well be a straitjacket.' He was beyond grateful he'd have her on his arm as a distraction from all his many failings that he would no doubt be reminded of. 'I can bring you straight to the hotel after work. I'll take your stuff over earlier and we can get ready together in our suite.'

Her eyes twinkled. 'Our suite? Not our room?'

'I booked one at the hotel where the ball is going to be held. That way we don't have to panic about getting home afterwards. All we need to do is walk upstairs.'

Her eyes narrowed and she looked uncertain. 'You want me to stay that night? After the ball?'

He hadn't even thought about that when he'd booked. 'I… well…'

But she laughed. 'Hey, you booked a suite. I am so going to take advantage of that. A suite! So fancy. But then, I keep forgetting that you are a Matthews.'

'I get the feeling you won't forget after Saturday.'

She stroked his arm. 'It will be fine.'

He doubted that it would be fine at all.

And this time he wasn't thinking about spending the evening with his family, but about trying to move on from Ivy the day after.

CHAPTER THIRTEEN

SO THIS WAS IT.

The end.

Although it was still only the beginning of the evening.

Ivy's heart crumpled a little as she walked across the ornately decorated five-star-hotel foyer on the arm of the most handsome man there. All dressed up in black tie, he looked like something from a movie red-carpet affair.

She felt his steadiness as they walked, the comfort of his arm. The rightness of them being together. The way it felt so natural and in step. They'd come a long way in just over three weeks from frosty beginnings to an understanding and connection deeper than anything she'd known before.

Her heart crumpled a little more, although the prospect of trying to convince everyone she and Lucas were an item kept it buoyant and agitated.

The foyer was filled with guests dressed in finery, chatting and laughing. There was a string quartet playing classical music, something she recognised—Albinoni's Adagio in G— so soulful and stirring it always made her cry. Great choice of music to sink her mood lower.

Pull on your big panties, girlfriend.

She was supposed to be happy and in love.

Love?

She looked up at the man next to her and her heart twinged. Her body automatically leaned towards him as if pulled there by an invisible thread. She liked him, yes. But love? That was a stretch. Surely?

A lump bloomed in her throat. She swallowed it away. This was supposed to be a fun evening. She didn't want to bring the vibe down. He was showing her off. They were happy. Besotted. Excited to meet his family.

Across the room she eyed some of the Sydney Central hospital bigwigs, the CEO and CFO, a couple of senior doctors and their partners. Grant standing alone in a corner, an empty glass in his hand. Looking a little lost. His eyes lit up when he glanced in her direction.

What the…? She stared at him, and he stared back, mouth agape as his gaze roamed over her.

Lucas squeezed her arm, leaning closer and whispering, 'I see him. I see the effect you're having on him in that dress, and I don't blame him, to be honest. I can't wait to strip it off you later and kiss every inch of your body. You're the most beautiful woman in this whole room. Milk it, Ivy.'

But she didn't feel like milking it. She only wanted to bask in Lucas's gaze. To have this dress stripped from her. To have him make love to her, slowly, quickly. She'd almost forgotten that her prize in this was to make Grant jealous.

Before she could say anything, she felt herself being propelled towards Grant.

Her ex's mouth went slack. 'Ivy. Wow. Hello.'

'Grant.' She nodded at him, wondering how she'd ever found him attractive. He was shorter and thinner than Lucas. His eyes not nearly so beautiful. He was just…unimpressive. 'I wasn't expecting to see you here.'

'I'm a plus one with Miriam over there.' He pointed to a tall blonde woman at the coat desk.

Ivy followed his gaze. 'Oh? Doesn't she work in the hospital pharmacy?'

'She does. But we're not together, together. Ivy, I…' He nodded and glanced up at Lucas, who was standing stock-still by her side, saying nothing. Grant swallowed. Closed his mouth against whatever it was he'd been going to say.

'Are you going to introduce us, darling?' Lucas's arm slid around her waist and suddenly she felt the sting of tears. He was playing the devoted boyfriend role so well, she almost believed it herself. But she wasn't as good at acting or pretending, she'd discovered.

She recovered herself and knew full well that Grant and Lucas must already know each other but this was a game, a power play that Lucas was determined to win. 'Oh, Lucas. This is Grant. Grant this is my…um…boyfriend. Lucas Matthews.'

There was an awkward silence while the men nodded and glared at each other like two male lions prowling and protecting their pride, ready to attack. Then Lucas pressed a kiss to her cheek. 'We'd better get going, darling. Places to be. People to see.'

As they walked away Lucas grinned like the cat who'd got the cream. 'How did I do?'

Darling.

So much of her wished that he meant it. 'What do you mean?'

'Was I possessive enough? Do you think he got the message?'

She glanced back at Grant, who was still watching her. 'I'm sure he did. It's not important now anyway.'

Lucas looked confused. 'But I thought you wanted to show him what he's missing.'

She sighed. 'I don't care about that any more. Or about him. I most certainly didn't want to encourage a conversation, or jealousy or anything.'

'Hey, wait.' He tilted her chin so she could see his eyes. 'This was the whole point of the deal for you. Are you okay?'

'I'm fine.' She shook her jaw out of his hold. This public

display of affection or possession, or whatever it was, was just a little over the top even for a supposedly loved-up new couple who were apparently besotted. And then somewhere down the track but very soon...not besotted and broken up. She decided to change tack. 'Are your parents here?'

'Ah. You're nervous about meeting them. I get it. It's okay.' He wrapped her in a hug and kissed the top of her head. 'I guess the sooner we get it over with, the better.' He raised his eyebrows and nodded, took a deep breath then gestured to a group of people in the middle of the room. 'My mother is the one in the long blue gown. Dad is on the left of her. Bald.'

Even though she was at the very pinnacle of her career and reputation, Estelle Matthews seemed softer than Ivy had imagined her. Less severe than Lucas had painted her. She looked over warmly at her son and smiled. His father, Bob, was shaking the hand of another older man, laughing. But friendly, not garrulous or obnoxious or loud. 'Oh, Lucas, they look nice.'

'Looks can be deceiving,' Lucas side-mouthed.

'Don't we know it.' She squeezed his arm as his mother waved to them, beckoning them over. 'I hope we can pull this off.'

'If you don't know the answer to anything, just be vague. Ready?'

'To lie to your parents' faces? No. But let's do it anyway.' She grabbed his hand, hoping it would make them look more like a couple. Knowing that holding onto him would make her feel better about all of this.

Her heart was drumming like a percussionist on steroids. What if she messed this up? What if Mrs Matthews saw right through them?

She held her breath as the introductions were made, smiled politely at Lucas's parents, then his brothers. Each of them smiled and nodded and shook her hand. Lucas's mother even kissed her cheek. More air-kissed, to be honest.

And they were just about to embark on what Ivy knew was going to be an excruciating conversation when they were all ushered into the ballroom and taken to their seats.

'Saved by the bell,' she whispered to Lucas as he held her chair out for her.

'Only a temporary reprieve, I'm afraid.' He smiled grimly. 'You're doing great. Just be you.'

Oh, sure. Question was, who the hell was Ivy Hurst now?

A lying unscrupulous woman? A dedicated doctor? A perfect partner for their son?

She closed her eyes briefly as she realised she was all of them. At least…when they were together, she felt things could be absolutely perfect if both she and Lucas could be truly honest and open with each other. If they allowed themselves to open their hearts just a little bit more.

But he didn't want to.

She was seated between Lucas and his father…boy, girl, boy, girl style. It felt surreal, as if she were an animal in the zoo being watched, and careful not to make a false move. But she needn't have worried, Bob was a total gentleman. Their light conversation was interrupted at times by the delivery of food and speeches, but they stuck mostly to her work history and career.

Estelle was listening in from Bob's other side and interjected often. 'You have plans to stay in Sydney? Not thinking of setting up a clinic across the country anywhere?'

Ivy interpreted this as *Will you either break my son's heart by leaving, or break our hearts by taking him with you?*

She smiled, hopefully reassuringly. 'I love Sydney and my job here. I have no plans to leave.'

'Oh, good. That's very good. Nice to have family close.' Estelle blew out a deep breath, as if she'd been holding it waiting for Ivy's answer. She clearly cared deeply for her son regardless of what he said.

Ivy chose not to elucidate that she chose not to have her own family close.

'You enjoy the public system?' Bob looked startled at such an admission.

'Absolutely. It's busy, of course, and the paperwork is challenging and taking over...' she grinned at his nod of understanding '...but I do get a kick out of helping people, especially those who don't have the ability to pay. I find that side of it very rewarding. The waiting lists are long, of course, and we're constantly running to keep up, but the satisfaction that you've helped someone is pretty amazing.'

'Indeed.' He nodded, tilting his head slightly the way Lucas did.

'Do you offer pro bono work at your clinic, Dr Matthews?'

'Bob, please.' He shook his head. 'We've talked about it—'

'Oh, good. It's such a fabulous and generous thing to do. You won't regret it,' she interrupted, before he could say something like, *But I decided against it.* 'The world needs more decent people like you offering to give a helping hand. When will you start? If you don't mind me asking.' She knew it was difficult to deny the ask for help. Everyone wanted to help, didn't they? 'There are so many people on the public waiting list, the system isn't serving them as well as it could. I'm sure Lucas has told you all about it...'

'It's...' Bob looked at his wife questioningly, then smiled, his arched shoulders relaxing. 'We'll add it to the agenda first thing Monday.'

'I can't wait to hear your plans. That's fantastic.' The smile she gave him wasn't fake at all.

Lucas nudged his foot against hers. She turned to him and saw his shocked expression. He gave her a sly thumbs up and mouthed, *Well done.* He'd mentioned he'd been badgering them to offer some pro bono slots at their private clinic for a while and never got past Go.

Bingo. Score another point in her favour.

They were interrupted again, this time by George, who wrapped Ivy in a huge warm embrace. 'Ivy! So good to see you again. I hope you weren't too sore after the horse riding.' He winked and beamed at her, his eyes twinkling with mischief.

Oh, she liked this cheeky friend so much and instantly relaxed. 'Well, it's been a while, so I did ache a bit the next day.'

'The horses are there for you any time.' George looked first at Ivy then Lucas. 'We don't see enough of you. Come and stay for the weekend and we'll take the boat out on the river.'

Lucas stared blankly back as if trying to think of some kind of answer that wasn't a lie. Ivy jumped straight in to cover for him, knowing how badly he felt about not being honest with his friends and family. 'We'd love to. It's so peaceful out there. We just need to get our calendars synced. Our on-calls have been clashing a bit recently and we haven't seen anywhere near enough of each other.'

'Oh, you've met darling George?' Estelle sighed, her features shining with happiness.

Ivy felt another jolt of shame that she was stringing all these lovely people along. 'Yes. He very kindly lent us his horses for the day.' At least that wasn't a lie.

Estelle stared at her son. 'Wow. This is something.'

Lucas gave his mother a warning stare and grumbled, 'Mother.'

'Oops.' George clearly understood all the subtext of the family dynamics and winked at Ivy. 'Light the touchpaper and retreat, that's me. See you soon, Ivy. Lucas, *call me*.' He made the universal phone gesture with his hand, then he was gone.

Estelle leaned across her husband and grasped Ivy's hand. 'I know, I know. I'm sorry, I shouldn't pry, but Lucas has never talked about his girlfriends before, never mind brought one to the ball. Which makes you very special.'

'Oh, I don't think so.'

'I do.' Estelle's mouth curved upwards as her eyes roamed Ivy's face. 'I can see you are. I see the way you look at each other.'

Ivy glanced at Lucas, panic rising in her gut. Was it obvious to everyone that this had gone far deeper for her than for him? Did he see her emotions on her face?

Estelle was still talking. 'And meeting George too? He and Lucas have been tight friends for so long, George is practically family.'

'He's lovely.' Another not-lie. Unfortunately the not-lies were far outweighed by the lies. She hated herself for agreeing to this. Estelle and Bob only wanted Lucas to be happy and they would be heartbroken when he told them it was over.

They wouldn't be the only ones.

'The things they used to get up to, and the stories George tells…oh, he's so funny. He'd make a fantastic best man. Although Lucas has his brothers too. It would be a difficult choice—'

'Ivy. Let's dance.' Lucas glared again at his mother and grasped Ivy's hand. She had no choice but to stand and walk with him to the dance floor. The band was playing something fast and it was difficult to talk, but Lucas made his displeasure with his mother pretty obvious. He twirled Ivy round. 'See what I mean about prying? About the heavy pressure? George will make a great best man…what the hell?'

'She loves you.' She twirled under his arm.

'She meddles.'

'Because she wants to see you settled and happy.' Ivy put her arms around his neck and wiggled in time to the music. Letting her hands stroke his shoulders, caress his back. It felt so good to be in his arms, even if this was the last time. Even though she felt so bad about the lies, she would not regret having had these last few weeks getting to know him. It had been magical, wonderful. 'How did we do? Do you think they believed us?'

'Definitely. You were perfect. Just perfect.' The music tempo changed to something slow and he grasped her waist, pulling her close, nuzzling his nose in her hair. 'They love you. I...'

She gripped him too. Her senses on full alert. What was he about to say? 'Yes? You...you what?'

'I...' He shook his head, his expression flatlining. 'Wanted to tell you again that you look amazing. This dress is beautiful. You are beautiful, Ivy. Thank you, for everything.'

I wish it weren't a lie. I wish it weren't the end.

Her throat filled with what felt like the pressure of unshed tears.

'Ivy...'

Her heart hammered hard as hope filled her chest. 'Yes?'

He looked down, tilted his mouth to hers and it felt as if the whole world started to ebb away. How she ached for his kisses. Even if this kept going for one night, one week, one year, she'd never have enough.

But then he stopped moving. Just stared down at her.

'What's the matter?' Her gut tightened like a vice. This wasn't a face filled with faux adoration, it was filled with panic.

This was it. This was the end. Right here. On the dance floor. And she'd still have to keep up the pretence of being happy because she would not be humiliated in front of all these people. His family. People she worked with. She would just have to keep smiling until she could break down somewhere private.

'Nothing. I mean...' He stepped away, his face pale. Eyes haunted and dark. 'I have to... I'll just be a minute.'

'But...'

He turned and stalked across the dance floor.

She frowned, watching his taut back disappear through the crowds. What was going on?

She watched him go. Probably not for the last time. They had to say a proper goodbye, at least. Surely?

But her heart followed him out of the door.

Lucas couldn't breathe.

He felt as if his chest was constricting. God, how stupid was he?

He'd almost said...done...

He'd been on the verge of kissing her, looked down and saw the expression on her face...something serene and beautiful, and the way she was looking at him, the way his mother had described, as if Ivy truly, honestly cared for him. Which he...couldn't compute. She was in this to get back at Grant.

But maybe, what if...what if she'd become embroiled in this as he had?

His heart tied itself in knots. Because, despite everything, he was glad she looked that way. He *wanted* her to look that way at him. And he'd almost...almost blurted out his feelings for her. Which, he now knew, were deep and tangled and too much.

This was *fake*. For God's sake. It wasn't real.

But the kisses were real. The lovemaking was. The heart song when he was with her was very real. The ache to be with her was too. So, yeah, his feelings for her were tangible and irrefutable, that much was clear, and he could not let them get any deeper.

With shaking hands, he untied his bow tie and tugged his shirt collar open, let the cool night air sluice the stress from his skin. Out here on the balcony he could see the city lights, heard the loud cawing of birds settling down for the night. He imagined he could see his apartment block, wished he were there with her in his arms, wound back a few weeks so he could live it all again. Wishing he could rewind his whole damned life back to that day when everything changed. So that he could pay attention, be present, be the caring brother. And then maybe he could have had a different life with Ivy. One with a future. One that he deserved.

Not like the one he was currently living where he reminded himself every single day that he deserved nothing.

At what point had things between him and Ivy become serious and entangled? At what point had this turned from fake to real for him? He didn't know. After that first night? The horse riding? Working together? Sharing the hours of tenderness and passion?

Hell, he'd lost track of the time they'd spent together, exploring each other's bodies and minds. Somehow she'd become a part of him—the corner of his heart that was Ivy shaped had grown and now filled the space.

He sucked in more air. This was not good. He needed to minimise that space and clear his heart. He needed to play the game for a few more hours then leave. As they'd planned. Put an end to everything, before either of them got hurt. Lock away the memories of the caring, the lovemaking. The laughter. Her wide-open heart. The way she'd blown his open too. The love.

He closed his eyes as his gut snarled up.

Love?

He'd almost said it. It had come from nowhere, just an overwhelming feeling with her in his arms, the smile on her face, the music. Everything. The not wanting it to stop. The ache to whisk her upstairs.

He… Did he…?

No.

No.

He'd vowed he'd never get involved with anyone.

He forced himself to look out at the city and beyond. Westwards to the Blue Mountains. Reminded himself of the pain he'd caused before.

And that reinserted the rod of steel into his spine. He could not be responsible for anyone else. He could not love anyone while Flora was so…damaged. And, dammit, he was a reconstructive surgeon, he knew she would live with those scars for life. His life was hers. Not anyone else's.

He swallowed. He was not in love with Ivy, it was just an overreaction to the encroaching end. An overreaction to spending so much time with someone and opening his heart—as far as he was able, or allowed himself to do—to someone he knew would hold it.

But he was okay. He could do this. Yes.

He could do this.

Having regained his composure, he turned to go back and spend the last few hours with her. Then he stopped in his tracks. He could see through the glass door that she was making her way over to a table, towards Flora.

Flora? His chest tightened again. What was she doing here? Why had his sister come to this event? She never came, refused to socialise past her small, tight group of trusted friends.

Oh, hell.

He closed his eyes.

It was too late now anyway.

There was no need for him to call anything off or worry about Ivy becoming too involved here now. After talking to Flora, she'd hate him.

Almost as much as he hated himself.

Ivy wandered over and sat down at a table across the room from the Matthews family, trying to regain her composure. Should she stay and wait for him to come back? Should she go up to their suite and wait? Or just go home?

She didn't know what to do.

'Hi.' A young woman was sitting across from her. Ivy had been so consumed with confusion and dismay she hadn't noticed her.

'Oh, hi. Is it okay if I sit here for a minute? My feet are killing me. I'm so not used to wearing stilettos. Clogs are more my comfort footwear of choice.'

'Sure.' The woman gestured for Ivy to move closer. As she reached out Ivy saw her arms were covered in scars. The kind of scarring you got from serious burns.

'Thanks.' Ivy tried not to stare as she hobbled over to sit next to the woman. 'I'm Ivy. Oh, and I'm a doctor and wear rubber clogs for surgery, just in case you were wondering about my questionable fashion sense.'

'Hey, I loved clogs back in the day with all those little charms you could attach to them.' The woman laughed. As Ivy looked closer she noticed burn contracture scarring on the left-hand side of the woman's face and neck too. 'And I know who you are, Dr Ivy Hurst.'

'Oh?' Had the gossip machine whirled into action already? Was this someone else she was going to have to lie to? 'You do?'

'Lucas is my brother and I have to admit I've been snooping around, watching you two dance together. I'm Flora.' Smiling shyly, she stuck out her hand. Her other hand fluttered over her neck as if she was trying to cover up her scars.

Ivy desperately wanted to ask what had happened but didn't. It wasn't her business. She shook Flora's hand. 'Nice to meet you. I didn't see you at the dinner. All of your family were on my table. Or rather, I was on theirs.'

'God, I never usually come to these things. Boring as hell and my parents like to parade us around a bit too much for my liking. And…well… I've had enough of the gawking benefactors staring at the poor burnt girl. I'm so over that.'

'I can imagine.' Ivy was fully aware of just how many eyes

had been on her and Lucas this evening. Imagine how much worse that would be if you were self-conscious of your appearance too.

'But as soon as Mum told me Lucas was bringing a girlfriend I had to come and spy. Sorry. I sneaked in after the speeches and sat where I could watch but not be seen.' Flora winced in apology. 'Lucas has never brought a date to any of these things before...not one he's willingly chosen to bring anyway. The burning questions...pardon the pun...in the family were, what's she like? Who is this mystery woman he likes enough to bring to meet us all?'

Lucas had never mentioned his sister had been injured or burnt but he had hesitated when he'd spoken about her. What had he said...? *'Flora's not a doctor, though. She was...'* His whole demeanour had changed.

Had he had something to do with the injuries?

Oh, God. Maybe he had.

Things started to fall into place. Things Lucas hadn't said about his motivation to treat burns patients. Things he hadn't told her about why his work seemed so personal to him. Because it *was* personal. Ivy's insides were roiling at the omissions. She clearly didn't know Lucas as well as she'd thought she did. Or did he not trust her? They were, after all, playing a game, right?

He hadn't shared his deepest secrets. He hadn't told her fundamental truths about his family, his life. Having a sister so badly injured must have impacted hugely and heavily on them all. 'Ah. I hope I didn't disappoint.'

'Disappoint us?' Flora's expression was one of confusion. 'Far from it. I can see how much you mean to him. And if someone can make Lucas happy after everything, then I want to thank them.'

How much you mean to him?

Not enough for him to talk about the things that mattered

to him. Like his sister's burnt body. 'After…everything?' Ivy asked gently.

'Everything… The accident. Hasn't he told you?'

'No. Nothing about an accident.'

Flora looked at her arms. Ran her palm across the scrunched-up skin all along her left arm. 'It was a long time ago, but he's never really got over it.'

'I… I didn't realise. I didn't know.'

'That's my brother for you. Always keeps himself to himself. But ask him, Ivy. It'll be good for him to talk about it.' Flora's gaze wandered towards a smartly dressed, very good-looking guy walking towards them with two drinks in his hands. She smiled up at him. 'Well, I'm very glad I came, actually. This evening is shaping up to be a lot more fun than I thought it would be. First time I've enjoyed going out for a very long time. And finally meeting someone who can see past the scars makes a nice change. Very nice indeed.'

Ivy smiled to herself and didn't want to rake up the past when Flora was clearly very much living in the now. Any more questions would be intrusive, but she sure as heck needed to talk to Lucas about it all.

What accident?

They'd shared so much, why had he never talked about it and how much it affected him—if Flora was to be believed? And why not believe her? She was his little sister, she probably knew him better than most.

Her skin prickled, the way it did whenever he was around. Which meant… She looked up and there he was, back from wherever it was he'd dashed to. Standing in the corner of the room, looking frozen to the spot as he stared at her sitting next to Flora.

None of this made sense.

Unless he thought Ivy might be telling his sister the truth about their deal.

Oh, Ivy. What the hell have you done? Getting involved in all of this.

It was such a mess. Everything.

Worst of all, she didn't want to lie to his family any more than she already had. They were good people. Especially when she knew she was lying to herself too. Because despite everything she'd promised, everything she'd made him agree to, she'd fallen for him. Deeply. Irrevocably.

Panic crept through her body, making her limbs tremble. This was all too much, too far. Too deep.

She had to get out of here.

CHAPTER FOURTEEN

'WHAT ARE YOU DOING?' His voice, echoing through the hotel suite, made her freeze. Hell, she'd heard him calling her name as she'd fled the banqueting hall, registered the sound of the key-card buzz, and his sharp intake of breath. She'd expected him to speak but wasn't prepared for the tremble in his tone.

She swallowed away all the emotions tumbling through her. 'I'm packing my things.'

'You're leaving? Now?' He stood in front of her, shaking his head. His tie hung loosely round his neck, the top button of his shirt had been undone. He looked, if possible, even more handsome than before.

Not that it mattered. This was done.

She looked up into those dark eyes that made her weak with desire. More, made her weak to his charm and to the effect he had on her promises. On her heart. 'That was the deal, right? After the ball, we're done? Well, it's finished. At least, for me anyway.'

Ask me to stay. Tell me your secrets.

He nodded and shoved his hands deep into his pockets. 'You met Flora.'

'I did.'

'And you talked?'

Did he think she'd been discussing this fake dating charade?

She reached for her toiletry bag on the bed, put it in the overnight bag and slammed the rigid lid closed.

'You're angry.' He seemed surprised.

Was there any point in explaining? Probably not, but she'd feel a whole lot better. And after the brutal arguments with her parents she'd learnt to always bite back her anger, particularly with Grant, and been the capitulating girlfriend. She'd hidden the dark side of herself because she'd wanted him to only see the light in her. And look where that had got her.

But a) Lucas wasn't her boyfriend, so she could say what she damned well wanted. They were breaking this up now anyway. And b) the dark was as much a part of her as anything else, he'd said so himself. What did she have to lose?

She put her hands on the suitcase lid but didn't look at him. 'Yes, I am angry, Lucas. I'm angry that you left me alone on the dance floor looking like an idiot. I'm angry that you didn't tell me about Flora's injuries and accident. I was blindsided when I met her, to be honest.'

His eyebrows rose. 'I didn't want to make a big thing of it. I didn't think you'd get to meet her.'

She whirled to face him. 'Because this is our last day and she never comes to the ball so you thought you might get away with me not meeting her? Conveniently not telling me that she had an accident that massively impacted her life. Or that apparently you blame yourself for it.'

His jaw tightened. 'Because it was my fault.'

'How would I know?' She raised her palm and waved him away. 'I know nothing about it.'

'She…didn't tell you?' His eyes grew wider. Darker.

'No, and you look somehow relieved that she didn't share your secret.'

His jaw worked as if he were grinding his teeth or subconsciously keeping his mouth clamped closed so he didn't have to talk. But then he said, 'I'm relieved she didn't have to talk about it and therefore live through it all again.'

'Well, your sister told me to ask you about it. She wants

me to know what happened. So tell me, Lucas. Tell me what happened.'

His eyes blazed anger and pain. 'Why? So I can add you to the list of people who will never forgive me? So you can see what kind of person I really am?'

Despite her own anger and frustration, she put her palm on his chest, felt his raging heart under her fingertips. 'I know what kind of person you are, Lucas. You're good and kind and sexy and funny. You're an amazing man who has a lot to give. But something inside you is stopping you from giving all of you. And I think it's to do with this accident. Whatever happened to Flora is holding you back.'

He turned away and stalked to the window. Stared out into the blackness. 'She's not the person she was. Or the person she could have been. She lost so much that day and that was my fault.'

Ivy thought of the intelligent, funny, bright woman she'd just met. 'She's not as damaged as you think, and I reckon she'd hate to hear you describe her like that. She's recovering. She's healing. She's a lot better than you allow yourself to believe her to be. Tell me.'

His back tensed. 'No.'

'Tell me, or I walk out of here right now.'

He turned slowly and glared at her. 'You should probably do that anyway.'

'For God's sake, Lucas. I am so tired of you hedging. Be honest with me. Please.' She knew her voice was getting louder and more desperate, but she couldn't help it. 'One last time. Let. Me. In.'

He looked at her for a long time and so many emotions scudded across his face. Fear. Panic. Hurt. Then he sighed and turned back to the window, his shoulders sloped forward in defeat. 'She was so little. Just turned three. I was sixteen and old enough to know better. Do better.'

'You were also just a kid, really,' she whispered, afraid that saying too much might make him clam up again.

'We were doing this stupid wilderness glamping thing in the outback in the Blue Mountains…back before glamping was a real thing. The whole family getting back to nature and all that, swag tents, bush walks, campfires. Not something we'd ever done before and it was a real adventure.

'The first morning we were due to go off on a nature walk, but Mum had to stay at the camp because Flora was too little and still asleep, and she'd had a difficult night so we didn't know when she'd wake up.'

His hands fisted into balls at his side. 'But I could see that Mum really wanted to go. So, I told her I'd stay behind and look after Flora. Truth was, I didn't feel too great because of some virus I'd caught, but I hadn't wanted to mention it in case they called the trip off. We were all so excited to be going, I didn't want to ruin everyone's holiday.'

He inhaled and then let out the breath slowly. 'So…off they went. It was early morning. The guide had cooked breakfast on a roaring campfire… I was still feeling off and hadn't had a great sleep myself, plagued by stomach pains and nausea. I was sitting in a sunny spot, reading a book and waiting for Flora to wake up.' He shook his head and turned to look at her, his beautiful face filled with anguish. 'I must have fallen asleep again. Because next thing, I was jolted awake by my little sister screaming.'

'Oh, Lucas.' Ivy could guess what had happened.

'She'd fallen into the campfire embers.'

Her hand hit her mouth as horrible images filled her head. 'It wasn't put out? Surely it's basic campfire rules?'

'The guide swore he'd put it out, but…whatever. By the time I got to her she'd got burns on her arms and legs and face. Her beautiful unblemished skin was…' He turned away. He didn't need to say anything more, Ivy had seen it. She was a doctor. She knew.

She also knew about guilt and shame and the pain when the people you love see you as less, as other, as separate. Ivy walked to him and put her palm gently on his shoulder. 'That's a lot to carry, Lucas. Too much.'

She could see his reflection in the darkened window, the pain etched on his face, held in every inch of his taut body. He shook his head. 'I should have stayed awake. It was my job. It was my duty.'

She sucked in a deep breath to try to shift the lump in her throat and the heaviness in her heart. He'd been barely a man and an ill one at that. She knew how hard the pull of sleep was when you were sick and exhausted. 'I know a lot about duty, Lucas. And I know how deep that goes. I understand why you feel like it was your fault.'

'Because it was,' he said through gritted teeth.

'No. The guide should have made sure the fire was out. Your parents should have too. They should have seen you weren't well. Flora doesn't blame you, I'm sure of it.'

'She just doesn't say it out loud. Not like the rest of the family.'

'I didn't hear them say a single thing.'

'Not any more. But they don't have to say the words for me to hear them. Feel them in here.' He tapped his chest, and turned back to look at her, his expression crestfallen. Bereft.

She closed her eyes to stop the tears. He'd carried this with him every day. No wonder he'd chosen to be a reconstructive specialist, because if he couldn't help his sister, he could relieve some of his burden by helping others like her. But the guilt had also stopped him from giving himself, from sharing his life with other people. He'd felt he'd been responsible for Flora's life and he'd failed.

Back that day when they were horse riding he'd said he

couldn't deal with Ivy getting into trouble too. She'd thought he'd meant that he didn't have enough physical capacity to save her as well as Sione. Not that he didn't have enough emotional space. Then again when kite surfing he'd said he was responsible for her little head knock. Even though he wasn't. He took safety very seriously and here was the reason. The desperately sad reason.

'You have to move on from this, Lucas. Flora has. It's clear she doesn't think you're to blame.'

'I don't need her forgiveness when I can't forgive myself.' He turned back to the window and stared out for a long time. So long she felt the moment had passed for them to continue the conversation. He was clearly taking time to gather himself. To grieve. To…what else she didn't know.

She didn't want to leave him here in this fug, but she also didn't know what to do. This deal was over. Their 'relationship' was over. That had been the plan. And he hadn't given her any indication of wanting otherwise.

So, quietly she zipped up her overnight bag and slipped her trainers on. Picked up her phone and started to search for the taxi number.

He turned to look at her. 'What are you doing?'

'Calling a taxi.'

'No.' He took two steps towards her, his face filled with sadness and pain and need. So much need. For company, she imagined. For affection, for a balm and distraction. He reached a hand out to her. 'Stay, Ivy. Stay, please.'

Stay. It was all she'd wanted to hear from him these last few days. The want in his voice had her dropping the phone onto the bed. She wouldn't ask what he meant by that. Whether he meant all night. All week or for ever.

But she took his face in her hands and kissed him. Tried to kiss away the pain and the guilt and the torture of having seen his little sister go through so much, and to feel responsible. Kissed away the shame. Kissed away the hurt.

And kissed into him everything she knew him to be now. A good man, a devoted surgeon, a compassionate doctor who must have repaid his debt over and over with his dedication and his skills. A wonderful, thoughtful, sexy man.

As she kissed him she felt his body respond. His kisses became urgent, his hardness pressed against her centre. She was lost in his taste once again. His gaze was tender and soft and there was something almost ethereal about his touch. Like an echo or a shadow tracing over her skin.

He wanted her, she knew, as much as she wanted him, but he couldn't allow himself to fall into more than what they had now...sex, fun times. Nothing serious. No commitment. He was too damaged. Too filled with shame and hurt to let other emotions in. Too locked up inside the memory and guilt to allow himself to break free.

But when he turned her around and slowly unzipped her beautiful dress she closed her eyes and let the need overwhelm her too.

When he kissed the nape of her neck she pressed against him, when he slid deep inside her she held him tight. Hoping it could last for ever, but knowing that some dreams were impossible.

After, he held her close and she watched him drift to sleep. Settled again. But for how long?

They could be a perfect match. But...he couldn't do it. She'd seen it in his eyes. Felt it in his kisses. As if he was letting her go, kiss by kiss. Touch by touch.

He was letting her go.

And she would leave, because that had been the plan. No amount of wanting could change that. No amount of loving him could make him love himself, and then allow himself to love her too.

Her throat felt raw and thick, her chest heavy with grief. She forced her eyes closed, would not allow herself to cry again over a man. She was done with that.

She'd come into this for a stupid deal around her own insecurities, trying to win some petty game against a man she didn't even care for, and hadn't counted on falling for Lucas. Hadn't contemplated losing her heart to someone who didn't have the capacity to fall for her.

I love you.

There it was.

She loved him.

No matter how much she'd tried not to. No matter how many lies she'd told herself: that this was fake, this was temporary, there was no time to learn to love him, faults and all. That she was in control.

Because she wasn't. She did love him. Wholly, totally. Irrevocably.

And now she would be forced to see him at work, bump into him in the corridors, on the wards. Hear his laughter, his voice. Watch his tenderness in action, with his patients and colleagues.

She would be forced to stand on the sidelines of his life with just the memories of this precious time when she'd been caught up in the magic of Lucas Matthews.

As quietly as possible she slipped from his arms, then the bed, careful not to wake him. She dressed and booked a taxi to take her home. Her body alive with the imprint of his touch, and her heart breaking.

She pressed a soft kiss to his forehead, careful again not to wake him up. After years of carrying guilt and shame he deserved some peace.

I love you.
Wishing this could last a lifetime.
But knowing it was their last goodbye.

CHAPTER FIFTEEN

I LOVE YOU. Had she said that? Had he imagined it? A dream, maybe?

Lucas lay in the comfort of the hotel bed, eyes still closed, in that foggy space between sleep and wakefulness and his heart…swelled. He'd told her everything. The world hadn't fallen in. In fact, the space in his heart that was Ivy-shaped had grown even bigger.

What would it be like to have this all the time? This connection and warmth in his chest? This feeling that he wasn't alone, that someone was looking out for him. Her…love.

His heart juddered. Had she said that? Her voice had been so quiet he wasn't sure.

She loved him?

Geez, he didn't know what to think or feel other than a good deal of panic, a smattering of hope. So many things. Did he love her?

Again. The same answer as last night. He cared for her, but love? That whole for ever thing?

Pointless analysing it. He didn't know if he could love anyone. But if he could, Ivy would be top of the list. The only one on the list.

After the heart-searching on the hotel balcony he'd come to tell her it was over, but when he'd seen her packing he'd panicked, realising his head and his heart were acutely at odds. Too much had been swirling round his mind. He'd wanted her so badly, and yet understood that making more of this would be a mistake.

But she'd stayed. That was something.

He reached to her side of the bed to pull her close. Her side, yes. Because they'd fallen into a delightful routine. A life. Together.

She wasn't here.

He jolted upright and peered at the empty bed and then scanned across the room.

No beautiful dress slung over the sofa where he'd thrown it last night after reverently removing it from her perfect body. No glittery sandals. Her bag was gone.

He jumped out of bed, his chest contracting like a vice around his heart. There was no sign of her in the bathroom. He ran back to the bedroom and ran his hands over the sheets. Her side of the bed was cold.

She'd been gone some time.

She'd left him.

Ivy. He slumped onto the mattress, holding his head in his hands. She'd gone. As he'd expected her to. As he'd wanted... before.

Where had she gone?

If she loved him, *why* had she gone? He needed to talk to her.

He grabbed his phone and quickly scrolled for her number. But as he stared at it he remembered that first night, making the deal. The idea of her getting revenge on her ex if she pretended to be his girlfriend.

And reality sank in. She'd gone because that had been the arrangement. The deal was over. Kind of like his life. Because what was his life now she wasn't in it?

Could he carry on as if this hadn't happened? As if she hadn't made a permanent mark on his heart? And where the hell did the idea of her saying *I love you* come from? Wishful thinking? Well, that was a one-eighty swerve from his no-commitment promises. He should be relieved she'd left him without any drama, without him having to make excuses or…

'Ivy!' he shouted her name. 'Ivy.' But there was no relief, just a sharp stabbing in his chest.

Eventually, after God knew how long he'd been sitting there staring at her number numb with indecision, he slunk into the shower and washed away the scent of their lovemaking, all trace of her. Gone.

He grabbed a towel and slung it round his hips. Dripped through to the lounge and sat on the sofa unsure what to do now. Unsure what was next. Because he'd expected this to end, but hadn't expected the weight in his chest to be this heavy or the grief to be this acute.

He'd told her everything and his world had, in fact, fallen in.

Because she'd gone.

Ivy threw her overnight bag onto the bed and closed her eyes tight to stop the tears from flowing. Tears that she'd been trying not to shed since she'd left that hotel suite.

But it was getting harder and harder, the further she was away from him.

Her phone rang.

Alinta.

Not ready to talk to anyone yet, she ignored it and started to unpack. She hung her dress on the bedroom door, and stroked it. It had been wonderful to walk into the ball on his arm. And yes, to see Grant's haunted face. To meet Lucas's family. Lovely Flora, who bore him absolutely no blame. If only he could see that.

Her phone rang again.

Phoebe.

Ivy refused to pick up. Because what could she say?

I was in control. I agreed not to get involved. I promised not to fall in love. I've made the biggest mistake of my life.

It wasn't as if they didn't warn her. And there she'd been, cocky and confident that she wouldn't lose her heart again.

A beep. A message to the four friends' chat group from Harper.

Well?? Ivy?? How did it go?

Ivy barely had any energy, and certainly little enthusiasm to go into details, but if she didn't answer the girls would be round in person and she couldn't face them. She typed out a reply.

It went.

A quick-fire response from Harper.

What do you mean?

Time for some honesty because, truly, Ivy was all out of lying to everyone.

We did what we agreed to do.

Alinta jumped straight back.

You broke up?

Ivy inhaled on a sob. Swallowed her sadness away. Tried to, at least. She would not cry. She was a fool who'd broken the deal by getting involved. She only had herself to blame.

She typed back.

How can we break something that was never something in the first place?

Harper:

Oh, hon. We'll be over ASAP.

No. Not least because she had to start her shift in a few hours.

Oh, she wanted a hug and some girl time, but not yet. She needed time and space to get her head around all this before she could face anyone else. How to refuse without sounding ungrateful or unfriendly?

But then her beeper pinged.

There was a surge of hope in her chest. Lucas? He hadn't called or messaged, or turned up here searching for her, wondering where she'd gone in the middle of the night. He clearly didn't care enough to find out, which she'd known all along.

And anyway, he'd phone or text, not use her work beeper. *Stupid woman.*

Her heart was getting ahead of itself. Actually, her heart needed resuscitation or life support or something drastic to ease this ache right in the centre of her chest, of her life.

She loved him.

She hit her forehead with the palm of her hand. 'Stupid woman. Stop, stop, stupid woman. You are way too old for all of this.'

After she read the message she breathed out a little. Then typed a message to the group chat.

Sorry. Samreen needs me at work. Urgent splenectomy.

It was a relief to have something else to think about. She was doing exactly what she'd done after Grant, throwing herself into work, and quite frankly she didn't care. She loved her job. Other than her friends it was her only constant. The one thing she could rely on and she'd put it in jeopardy with her silly deal. What if it had all unravelled in front of her bosses?

Work was the only way to deal with heartbreak. Okay, getting drunk with her friends could also help her forget the man she loved.

No. Nothing would erase Lucas from her heart.

But friends might make it bearable.

Hammering at the door drew Lucas from…where had he been? He wasn't sure. It was cold in the hotel suite now and he was still sitting here in his towel staring at Ivy's name on his phone.

Was she…here?

'Ivy!' He dashed to the door and threw it open, his heart snagging in surprise. 'Oh. Flora. Hello.'

'Morning.' After giving him a quick peck on the cheek she peered first down at the towel then round him into the room. 'Oh. I hope I'm not interrupting anything, but I wondered if you and Ivy fancied a quick coffee before I head off home.'

He stood back and let her in, knowing she'd walk right in anyway, and tried not to let his gaze settle on her scars. She was a constant reminder of his failures. 'Actually, I'm just heading back to my place.'

To, probably, stare endlessly at nothing for another few hours, wishing he'd done things very differently. Story of his life.

Flora walked round in a circle then put her palms out in question. 'Um. Where is she? Shower? Bed? Oh, don't tell me… I did interrupt something.' She winced. 'God, sorry, big brother.'

He blinked, not understanding. 'Who? Ivy?'

Flora flicked her hand at him. 'Yes, of course Ivy.'

Lucas breathed out heavily. 'She's…gone.'

'Gone as in needed to get back to her apartment to feed her cat or something? Or gone as in…' She peered closer at him, scrutinising him the way only a sibling could. Then she frowned and shook her head disappointedly. 'Oh, Lucas. Not again.'

'What do you mean *again*?' He couldn't remember ever feeling this kind of hopelessness over a woman before. And also, how could his sister read him so well?

Flora huffed. 'What is it with you and women? They never seem to hang around.'

'Out of design.'

'You like being lonely?'

'I'm not lonely.' He hadn't been until he'd woken up and found Ivy gone.

'Liar. I liked Ivy. She was nice and funny and far too good for you.' Flora gently punched him on his biceps. 'Joking. But she is lovely, Lucas. You seemed to like her last night. Couldn't take your eyes off her.'

Because it hadn't been fake.

Here it was. Time for the answer he and Ivy had been rehearsing for the last few weeks and the statement he knew Flora would relay back to his parents. 'Things just didn't work out. You know how it is. Timetables never quite in sync…we thought we'd call it a day.'

'I don't believe you. Not after the way you looked last night.' She slumped down on the brocade sofa, chin in her hands. 'Oh, Lucas. What did you do?'

'Why do you assume it's because of something I did?'

'Because it's always something you did. Ivy is lovely and she clearly adores you.' She sat back and shook her head, sighing. She was quiet for a moment and then jolted forward. 'Oh, God. Lucas. Was it because of me? I told her to ask you about the accident. You told her?'

'Yes. I did.'

'And you told her it wasn't your fault, right?'

'You know it was. Look at you, Flora.' He could barely look at her without remembering that day. The moment everything changed.

She ran her hand over the scarring on her left arm then glowered at him. 'Lucas. For goodness' sake, stop it. I am so over this. You feeling sorry for yourself, blaming yourself. Smothering me with your over-protection. Refusing to move on from it. It's been over twenty years. I've moved on, you need to move on too. I'm *fine*.'

How could she be? After all that pain and the operations and physiotherapy? 'You're not—'

'Whoa!' Her nostrils flared and her eyes sparked fury as she held her palm up to shut him up. 'Don't you dare say I'm not fine, Lucas. Don't you dare diminish me. Sure, I've got scars and they're not pretty. I've accepted I'm not going to win any beauty contests, and that's okay. But I like who I am, scars and all. I'm a good person. I've got a great life, a good job and after you left last night I even met someone who actually likes me for who I am inside as well as out. It's time you started liking who you are too.'

She was actually a little scary and he was starting to feel a little vulnerable here in just a towel rather than his work-suit armour. Any clothes, really. 'That's easy for you to say, Flora.'

'You lifted me out of the fire. You called for help. You *saved* me, Lucas.'

He sat down next to her. Had he saved her? No...well yes, he'd done those things too, but he hadn't stopped her falling into it in the first place. He'd spent all his years since the accident protecting her, trying to make amends. Or, in her words, smothering her. 'You should never have fallen into it in the first place.'

'So? Bad things happen, Lucas. I was three years old and

a bit of a tearaway like you used to be. Remember that? How carefree you were before the accident? Mum used to say you were the joker in the family and then you...weren't.'

He shrugged. 'People change.'

She reached over and put her palm over his hand. 'I don't blame you for what happened. I never have. So, instead, you blame yourself and refuse to be happy. Can you imagine how that makes me feel? Because of something I did all those years ago I get to watch you steep yourself in blame and hurt, and curtail your joy because you think you don't deserve to be happy again. Well, it's time to take your hair shirt off and stop punishing yourself, Lucas. Because the best way to feel better about what happened is to find happiness. *That* would make me happy. Seeing you in love and living your life would make me happy. Not this...' She waved her hand at him. 'Pushing people away, being too afraid to commit, feeling responsible. You're not responsible for anyone's life but your own. Or anyone else's happiness. So go out and damned well find some.'

She blinked rapidly then and looked almost as shocked as Lucas felt at her outburst. Flora, his timid little sister, had grown up. Not just that, she was incredible. How had he not seen that before?

Because he was too intent on whipping himself with a metaphorical stick. Seeing her as trapped as he was by the accident. But somewhere along the line she'd flown free, whereas he'd tightened the ropes around his life and kept everyone out.

Go figure. She was incredible and insightful too.

But he had a feeling there was only one thing that could make him happy and that was Ivy. 'It's too late. Ivy's gone.'

'Why? You clearly care about her. Doesn't she feel the same way about you?'

'I don't know.'

'How so?'

He couldn't confess about the deal now. Admit the whole relationship had been fake. Then messy and wonderful. And now ended. 'It's complicated.'

I love you.

Had he dreamt it?

'Okay, dial back a bit, bear of little brain.' Flora was smiling now, looking at him as if he were a small child she was very fond of. 'I'll start with easy questions. We can work up to difficult later. Firstly, do you love her?'

'Easy?' He closed his eyes as images of Ivy swam in his head. Ivy laughing. Ivy naked. Ivy… Her smile and her tenderness, her generosity of spirit. He ached for her. He missed her. So damned much. It was only and always her. He had never admitted anything like this to anyone before. Hell, he'd never felt like this before.

He raised his head and looked at his sister. Took a deep breath. 'Yes. I think I do. I love her.'

And he'd let her go. Forced her away with his intransigence.

'Whoop.' Flora clapped her hands. 'So what are you going to do?'

'What can I do? She's gone.'

'Oh. Lucas. Lucas.' A disdainful shake of her head. 'You're a brilliant surgeon and a wonderful man but hopeless at romance.'

'What can I say? I haven't had much practice.' Sex, yes. Love…not so much. Not at all in fact. Until now.

Flora's eyes lit up. 'Well, now's your chance. You have to tell her.'

'What if she doesn't want me?'

I love you.

Had it been a dream? He didn't think so. And he'd thrown it all away by not allowing himself to love her back. Bloody fool.

Flora squeezed his hand. 'Is she worth the risk?'

'Oh, yes.' He nodded. Resolute. Panicked. Kind of scared about how she'd react. But yes, resolute. 'More than anything.'

Flora laughed. 'Well, I suggest you put some clothes on and come up with a plan.'

CHAPTER SIXTEEN

'THANKS, EVERYONE. GOOD WORK,' Ivy said to the operating theatre team as she finished closing up their patient. 'You can take him through to Recovery now.'

Recovery.

That would be nice.

Work was great at distracting her from the ache in her chest, but it didn't stop it. Was there somewhere called Recovery where you could go to heal a broken heart, not just a broken body?

It's called time.

Too bad it had been less than a week. She missed Lucas. Found herself looking out for him down every corridor, in every ward, in the cafe. But somehow their paths hadn't crossed yet. Or he was avoiding her.

She'd heard on the grapevine he'd immersed himself in helping his parents set up their pro bono clinic and that gave her a huge sense of pride. But…she hadn't seen him.

They were bound to bump into each other eventually and she wasn't sure how she was going to react. He still hadn't messaged her, hadn't called. It was as if their affair hadn't even happened. He really was glad she'd gone. While she ached. So much. Walking away had taken every ounce of courage she'd had but it hadn't stopped her wanting him. Dreaming about him. Wishing things could have been so different. She loved him. That was all.

That was *everything*.

'You okay, boss?' Samreen asked her as they paused to write up the surgery notes.

Ivy glanced at her junior, who had become more friend now than colleague. 'I'm fine. Why?'

Samreen smiled softly. 'You've been very quiet these last few days. I mean… I know it's none of my business, but just checking you're okay.'

The same thing Alinta had said when they'd met up for a coffee and that Harper had mentioned over a glass of wine after work. It felt as if the world was tiptoeing around her. *Here's Ivy. Handle With Care.* That was what broken hearts did to you. They made you vulnerable and soft. Well, she wasn't going to be like that any more.

She snapped her gloves off decisively and threw them in the bin. 'Samreen, I'm fine. Thank you for noticing and asking. But I did a stupid thing and now I'm living with the consequences.'

Samreen's eyes grew bigger. 'You? Stupid? No way.'

'Unfortunately, yes. I met a guy and liked him more than he liked me. It ended. You know how it goes.' This was probably way too much information, but it was honest. She'd decided there had been too many lies recently and she was going to be honest from now on, or say nothing.

To be fair, she'd probably stick to the say nothing part a little more because it hurt too much to say the words *I love him and I miss him* out loud.

Samreen shrugged. 'I married my first love, so I'm afraid I don't know. But I can imagine. I'm sorry, Ivy.'

'Thanks. Well, I'm over it now.' If she said it enough it might sink in.

Samreen's eyebrows rose as if to say, *Really?* 'If you need a chat, I'm here.' Then her bleeper blared and she glanced down. 'Sorry, Ivy. Got to go.'

'See you.' Ivy inhaled deeply. Right. A quick shower and then Friday night drinks with the girls. She'd have to put on her game face. Or maybe tell them exactly how much she was still hurting. Stop pretending.

Half an hour later she stepped out of the theatre suite and stopped short, her heart hammering hard against her ribcage. Her belly did a little jig.

Déjà vu?

She closed her eyes. Opened them again. Yes, it was Lucas, looking devastating in a pale blue collared shirt and navy chinos. And his expression…so dark.

He was here for her? No. He hadn't been in contact, he wasn't here for her. He must be waiting for a patient. Just as she'd imagined, they'd bump into each other sometime.

Oh, well, here goes nothing. Big breath.

'Lucas?'

'Ivy.' He stood, so serious. He did not run to her, did not kiss her. Did not do any of the things she'd secretly hoped he would do. As they did in the romcoms.

Her heart-hammering turned into full-blown tachycardia. 'What is it? What's happened?'

He took one step towards her. 'Can we talk?'

'Here?' She gestured to the theatre block behind her. 'Really? You want to do this here?' Whatever *this* was.

'I don't care. Anywhere.' But he took her arm and walked her into the wintry sunshine and up to the hospital's lush rooftop garden. He gestured to her to sit on a bench, but she stood tall.

'What's this about, Lucas?'

'Us.'

She raised her palm. 'There is no us. You've made that abundantly clear since we started this thing.' Except, she noted, the sleepovers, the sex, the fun and games. The intense conversations. But he hadn't trusted her with his deepest secrets, or with his heart.

He shook his head. Took her hand. 'I know, and I'm sorry. I kept telling myself it was all some kind of dream…this feeling, every time I saw you. When you laughed and my chest heated. When I saw you hard at work and my gut tightened in pride. When I watched you come, all undone and satisfied. I kept trying to put a distance between us, a veil of pretence that this dream wasn't real. Couldn't be real. Because I don't deserve to have this, Ivy. I don't deserve to feel this way. To be happy.'

She made him happy and he was fighting it.

Oh, Lucas.

'Yes, you do. You just don't want to be happy. You've spent most of your life being ashamed and guilty for something that happened when you were a boy. You're scared.'

He looked at his feet, then back at her. 'I am. Yes. I'm scared about being responsible for you, protecting you. And failing.'

'I'm quite capable of being responsible for myself.' So this was just an apology. Too little too late. Her heart felt as if it were collapsing in on itself.

He gave her a hesitant smile. 'I know that now. I wouldn't dream of being responsible for you. Maybe alongside you, though? Flora pointed out that I've been an idiot for years, trying to cut myself off from everyone as some sort of punishment.'

'An idiot, eh? I do like your sister.'

He huffed out a breath. 'Well, she's right. I'm also scared of letting all that go and just…being part of something. I've never had a relationship that lasted longer than about ten minutes, never mind a lifetime.'

'It was a fling, Lucas. No, it wasn't even a fling, it was *pretend*. Fake.' Because she didn't dare hope where this was going, she gave him an out.

But he looked as if she'd just punched him in the stomach. 'Is that how you feel? Because if that's what you really believe then I'll walk away, right now. Just say it's over and I'll go.'

Stay.

Tears pricked her eyes. She would not cry. 'Oh, Lucas. This is not how I thought things would play out. I—'

'Wait.' He held up his index finger. 'We're tying ourselves in knots here. Can I ask you a question?'

She pressed her lips together, trying not blurt out, *I love you, you idiot,* and eventually managed, 'Sure.'

'That last night, in the suite. After we'd made love. Did you tell me that you loved me?'

'What?' Had she? Had she said those words out loud as she'd left him? 'I...don't think so.'

'It must have been wishful thinking, then.' He swallowed, panic rushing across his features. 'So, you don't love me?'

'I...' God, how much of a fool was she going to make of herself now?

He took her other hand and gazed into her eyes. 'Because I love you, Ivy Hurst. I love you so much. God knows, I tried not to, but I've fallen hard. I want you. I miss you. I want to grow old with you. I want *us*. For ever.'

'Us. Yes. Us.'

He loved her? A rogue tear escaped down her cheek.

He leaned in and kissed it away. 'I'm so sorry about not being honest with you about how I feel. I promise that, if you'll have me, I'll tell you every day how much I love you.'

'I'll hold you to that.' She couldn't stop the smile growing deep inside her heart reaching her face. He'd come a long way and he wanted to keep on trying. How could she not love him? Or trust and believe in him? 'I do love you, Lucas.'

'You do?'

She nodded and squeezed his hands. 'I do.'

'Words I hope you'll repeat to me some day. With a ring.'

What was he saying? Her heart swelled. 'Whoa. Wait. What? Are you...?'

He dropped her hands and then...suddenly, he was on one knee. Somehow, he'd magicked a small velvet box into his right hand and was opening it.

Was that...? She couldn't believe it. A beautiful, glittering diamond ring. *Oh. My.*

He cleared his throat. Her strong, perfectly confident man was nervous. 'Ivy Hurst. I love you. You make my world perfect. You are perfect in every way. Would you...will you... marry me?'

This was a surprise. A pinch-me, exciting surprise. She blinked back more tears. 'You've come a very long way from a no-strings fling.'

He grinned. 'I got swept off my feet by an amazing, wonderful, beautiful woman. What can I say? Other than, will you have me? After all this? Please. Don't keep me waiting. My knee's killing me.'

She giggled. 'Yes. Yes, of course. I'll have you *because* of all this, Lucas. You've shown me how to overcome the worst things imaginable. To learn how to listen to your heart. To trust in someone. And in love.'

'You taught me all those things too. And more.' He stood, slid his arms around her waist and drew her closer. 'Now, let's go celebrate.'

She winced. 'I'm supposed to be meeting the girls.'

'Do you think they'd mind, just this once, if I stole you away for a private celebration? It's not every day you decide to spend the rest of your life with someone.' He took her hand and walked her out of the garden and down to the car park. His little sports car was parked right there, the roof concertinaed back, the back seat filled with flowers. 'For you. Everyone knows the world is a better place with plants, right?'

'Oh, Lucas.' She gasped at this out-of-character romantic

gesture from a resolute commitment-phobe. And then remembered all the romantic things he'd done already: the horse riding, the picnic, the kite surfing. He hadn't been holding back, he'd just wooed her with stealth. And she'd fallen. Utterly.

'You remembered. That first night at my place.'

'I'll never forget one moment of being with you. I love you, Ivy.'

'I love you too, Lucas.'

'Never stop saying that.' He wrapped her into his arms and kissed her again, long and deep and hard.

'Hey! You two! Congratulations!' Harper and Ali were walking towards them and cheering, waving their arms in the air.

'Woot!' Phoebe cried out. 'Get a room!'

'That's the plan! But I'm going to have to take a rain check on drinks.'

'Go for it,' Harper called as Ivy climbed into the car and waved at them. 'Call us!'

'I will!'

'We want all the details.'

'Later.' She blew them a kiss.

Then Lucas charged the engine and they drove off towards their future, with the wind in their hair and a lifetime of love in their hearts.

* * * * *

COMING SOON!

We really hope you enjoyed reading this book. If you're looking for more romance be sure to head to the shops when new books are available on

Thursday 6th July

To see which titles are coming soon, please visit

millsandboon.co.uk/nextmonth

MILLS & BOON

MILLS & BOON®

Coming next month

BROUGHT TOGETHER BY HIS BABY
Kristine Lynn

"Why don't you stay here?"

He hoped the look he shot her—confusion mixed with something less inhibited—implied that it wasn't a good idea. And if he was an artist, he'd commission a whole piece in the shade of red her cheeks turned as she realized how her question had come across.

"I mean in the cabin I have on the property. It's not being used, and you can make it your home as long as you need."

"Why would you offer that to a stranger?"

"You aren't a stranger; you're Emma's dad. And you're trusting me to help raise her. For now," she added when he opened his mouth to reply. "And if I'm being honest, it serves my designs, too. I don't know how to be away from her for very long, and if you're here I won't have to. And if you ever need help with her, I'll be next door."

He considered that. It checked a lot of boxes. It would probably be cheaper than any of the dumps he'd find in town. He knew the landlady already—and trusted her. But the stone tipping the scales was that he'd never be far from Emma either.

"I'll insist on paying rent."

"Fine. If that's what you need. It's furnished, but you can make it your own."

"And, to be honest, I'm not sure I'll be comfortable taking her overnight—not until we find our rhythm, anyway."

"That's fine. Just let me know when you're ready."

Liam sipped at his water, looking out over the expansive deck to the ocean below. It was more than he deserved.

"Thank you. I've put the end of my marriage behind me, but I know I've still got work to do to build your trust—and Emma's, too. I don't take that lightly."

"Good. Me neither. Now, let's talk about getting you a job. Are you set on downtown?"

Liam smiled so hard he felt it in his cheeks. He hadn't been sure at all about coming out here, about meeting Emma and what would come of that first meeting, but now, deep in his soul—the one he'd built from scratch after the first one had been obliterated in combat—he rejoiced.

Things were shaping up for the better for the first time in his life, and he had a feeling he owed a lot of it to the beautiful woman holding his child.

But imagining her as more than that was as off-the-table as imagining how he was going tell his dad to find someone else to fill the Everson Health board seat. Because Liam wasn't going home anytime soon.

Continue reading
BROUGHT TOGETHER BY HIS BABY
Kristine Lynn

Available next month
www.millsandboon.co.uk

LET'S TALK

Romance

For exclusive extracts, competitions and special offers, find us online:

f MillsandBoon

𝕏 @MillsandBoon

◎ @MillsandBoonUK

♪ @MillsandBoonUK

Get in touch on 01413 063 232

MILLS & BOON

THE HEART OF ROMANCE

A ROMANCE FOR EVERY READER

MODERN

Prepare to be swept off your feet by sophisticated, sexy and seductive heroes, in some of the world's most glamourous and romantic locations, where power and passion collide.

HISTORICAL

Escape with historical heroes from time gone by. Whether your passion is for wicked Regency Rakes, muscled Vikings or rugged Highlanders, awaken the romance of the past.

MEDICAL

Set your pulse racing with dedicated, delectable doctors in the high-pressure world of medicine, where emotions run high and passion, comfort and love are the best medicine.

True Love

Celebrate true love with tender stories of heartfelt romance, from the rush of falling in love to the joy a new baby can bring, and a focus on the emotional heart of a relationship.

Desire

Indulge in secrets and scandal, intense drama and sizzling hot action with heroes who have it all: wealth, status, good looks…everything but the right woman.

HEROES

The excitement of a gripping thriller, with intense romance at its heart. Resourceful, true-to-life women and strong, fearless men face danger and desire - a killer combination!

To see which titles are coming soon, please visit

millsandboon.co.uk/nextmonth